# SOUL CAGE

## SOULBREAKER BOOK 1

L. R. SCHULZ

Soul Cage

Copyright ©2024 Luke Schulz

Luke Schulz asserts the moral rights to be identified as the author of this work.

All rights reserved. No part of this book may be reproduced or used in any manner, including stored in a retrieval system, or transmitted in any form or by any means, electronic, mechanical, photocopying, recording or otherwise, without the prior written consent of the copyright owner. The only exception is for the use of brief quotations or excerpts in a book review.

This novel is a work of fiction. Any names, characters, places or incidents are a work of the author's imagination. Any resemblances to actual persons, either living or dead, or locations, or events is purely coincidental and not intended by the author.

First paperback edition: 2024

Edited by Luke Marty - yourbetareader.com

Cover art by Nino Is- https://www.artstation.com/isnino

Map created by Lena – Instagram: @bluidu_streams

For more information, please visit:

or Instagram: @luke_schulz_author

EBOOK ISBN: 978-0-6454574-4-5

L. R. SCHULZ

# Prologue

"Master Myddrin, why do people kill each other?"

Myddrin stiffened. He tilted his head to meet the watery eyes of the child and found himself lost for words.

He was a scholar, a man of learning, his job was to study this very question. Why then did he find it so hard to answer? Why should a child not yet past his seventh summer be forced to ponder such a weighty question?

Myddrin made to answer in what ways he could when a horn suddenly blasted in the distance. Dust trickled from the ceiling as Athedale's grand library shook from the impact of men at war not a half-dozen streets to the east.

The children in his care buckled. One screamed. Another cried. Two called for parents that were no longer there, their souls already claimed by the invading Lord Doonaval and his legion of Skullsworn.

The boy who had asked the question tugged on his robe. He looked on the verge of tears, his face scrunched into a ball as he tried desperately to stay strong.

Myddrin clasped his tiny hand in his own, hoping that by the time his mouth opened the right words would come to him.

When his lips finally parted, he gasped only empty air. What words would comfort a child in a time like this? What lies would he have to spread to calm his nerves?

Warmth washed over his other hand then, a familiar warmth. Fingers intertwined with his own. A figure emerged to his left, accompanied by the rich and fruity scent of jasmine.

Myddrin turned to see his wife, Ismey. Her grip tightened in his hand, though otherwise she ignored him. Instead, she bent over, the metal plates of her gleaming white armour clinking as she smiled at the boy. It was the kind of bright smile that stole the heart of any who looked upon it, with deep dimples accentuated by rosy cheeks and vibrant, sapphire-blue eyes.

Myddrin took a steadying breath, reminding himself that they were safe in the library. While the Knights of Aen protected them, while his *wife* protected them, no soul-hungry savage from Mirimar would touch them.

With her free hand, Ismey wiped away a freshly fallen tear from the child's chin before lightly cupping it with her fingers. "What's your name?" she said. Her voice was soft and steady.

"W — Will," the boy said.

His wife's smile stretched even further. "You're Haylin and Alina's son, aren't you?"

The boy issued a weak nod, bottom lip still trembling.

Myddrin took a step back as his wife let go of his hand and bent down even further, now level with Will. "Well Will, there are some bad, horrible people in the world."

"Ismey…" Myddrin interjected. "He is still young…"

His wife disarmed him with a slight curve of her lips. She placed a calming hand on his waist, and Myddrin stood down. He trusted her.

Ismey returned her attention to the boy. "The bad people want only one thing, our souls," she said, pointing towards her chest.

Will's eyes narrowed, focusing first on Ismey, then lowering towards his own chest.

"Souls are powerful," Ismey continued. "Very powerful. And the only way to get them, is to take them," she finished by thrusting her fist forward in the air, then pulling it back in one quick jerk.

Will jumped, but did not cry.

"However, just as there are bad people in the world, there are also good people. Your parents are Knights of Aen, aren't they Will?"

He nodded. "Like you?" Will said, chin rising.

"Yes, like me. Knights of Aen live to protect. We try to stop the killing, so that when boys like you grow up, the world is safer."

"They fight the bad men?" Will asked, rubbing at his eye.

"Exactly. And when all the bad men are gone, only the good remain. It is my belief that one day, all the souls stolen by the bad men will be set free and be at peace. Until that day, I live to protect the good people, to help them and keep them safe. Would you like to help keep them safe with me?"

Will jumped, eyes alight with renewed energy. Other children followed, having listened in on the conversation. "I want to fight the bad men!" Will said.

"Me too!"

"Me too!"

Myddrin shook his head, not knowing whether to praise his wife for raising their spirits or chastise her for turning them all into future Knights just like her.

He moved to hold her, to show her how amazing he found her and how lucky he was to be her life partner, when another tremble rocked him off balance.

He steadied and caught himself before he fell, as around him the children began to panic once more. There were twelve under his care, and many more under the supervision of other educators spread out through the expansive library.

One child began to cough uncontrollably. Dribble frothed at her mouth as her cough turned into a moan. Myddrin placed a soothing hand on her back, quietly lulling her into a state of relative comfort by softly humming a familiar tune.

He bent to a crouch, gesturing for them all to gather by his feet. "Don't worry, children. Aen will protect us. Our Knights are strong, the strongest in all the lands!" He opened his posture, throwing his arms wide. "Nothing can get to us, not while my wife protects us. The Gracelands are a safe place. No bad men can reach us here."

Though he smiled outwardly, internally he shuddered. Children were impressionable. They believed what they heard, what their eyes told them. If someone they trusted said they would be safe, then that is what they would think.

He reached for his pack and pulled out a children's book. It was a magnificent work of both art and fiction. Titled 'Opie the Seven-Tentacled Octopus', it was a story of obscurity, of being different and finding companionship in the strangest of places. Myddrin read through the first page, his lips forming into a genuine smile as Will jumped from his seat and moved to touch the book. It was an interactive storybook; some of the pictures were drawn in with ink, others were made to stand out with real-world material. Will ran his hand over the texture of a tentacle, all sense of the outside danger seemingly non-existent in this moment. Other children grew agitated, calling for Will to move and trying to find another angle from which to see the story, but all were completely engrossed.

Myddrin continued, making sure to emphasise his speech at the appropriate moments and taking pleasure in his listeners' joy. As he finished, the door behind them burst open.

Myddrin turned as a Knight stumbled in, left hand holding his right shoulder. Blood flowed freely between the cracks in his fingers, trickling down his hand and staining his white plate a dark shade of red. "Ismey!" he said after a laboured breath. "The northern wall has been breached. The city is falling. Orders are to get the children out and take them through the keep. We make for

Spree with haste."

The mood in the library shifted as other educators overheard and began to panic. Ismey reached for her hip and with a resounding ring unsheathed her silver longsword. "How long do we have?"

The Knight shook his head vigorously. "Only moments. They are just behind—"

"SKULLSWORN!" The shout from an educator echoed from the other end of the library.

Myddrin snapped the picture book shut and rose to his feet.

"GET THE CHILDREN OUT!" came another cry.

A figure appeared atop a platform on the second story of the library. Highlighted by numerous lanterns, a black shape began to form in front of him. The very fabric of the world seemed to tear as a rift appeared, and with it, an instrument of destruction in the form of a giant sword, black as tar. The phantom shape shimmered and solidified. It must have been at least twenty times the size of Ismey's.

Ismey's mouth hung open, though she quickly shut it, turning to face the invader. "Carthon," she muttered under her breath.

Myddrin froze. Carthon, son of Lord Doonaval, Prince of the Skull Kingdom and Reaper of Mirimar, was here. The sword shifted, moving with its conjurer as Carthon stepped forward on the raised platform, the room still too dark for Myddrin to distinguish his features.

Carthon raised his fist, and the oversized black sword shot forward. Myddrin couldn't see the devastation the blade caused, but he could hear it. Dozens of people expended their final breaths with ragged screams that tore from their throats as their lives ended. The souls of the dead visibly flowed from their corpses in a multi-coloured wave of energy. They drifted into the air as glowing orbs, only instead of transferring to the peace offered by the *otherside*, they made their way into the chest of their murderer — trapped within his soul-cage.

More image-magic appeared as humans born from the shadowed plains of Mirimar barged into the now open library.

Ismey shifted and, with her free hand, clasped Myddrin on the wrist. "Get the children to safety. I'll hold them off. Whatever happens, know that my soul is yours, not even death can change that. Now go!"

Myddrin didn't even have time to savour the moment as the children in his care prepared to scatter. He caught one before she fled, forcing her to stay still with a calming hand. "Remember what we practised," he called. "Take the hand of the person next to you. Don't let go. Follow me in a line. Quickly now."

Despite the horror of their situation, the children listened, rushing to clasp the hand of their chosen partner. Once organised, Myddrin led them away from the invading Skullsworn. Constantly checking to see if they were all with him, he followed the appointed path down one of the narrow corridors. Other educators did the same, leading their students to one of the exit points and hopefully out towards the safety offered by Stonekeep.

The urge to turn back and help proved nearly overwhelming, but Myddrin had a job to do, a responsibility to keep these twelve children safe so they might live to see the light of a new day.

He turned, calculating a quick headcount before ushering his students towards the exit. Another educator and her students followed them, though they had broken from routine, their line a haphazard mess as their educator sprinted ahead.

Myddrin caught her by the arm as she made to pass. He looked her in the eye. "Glade, gather yourself! If we panic, the children will follow suit. Keep them in line. Do it now!"

The woman, Glade, seemed to compose herself. She sucked in a deep breath, red hair a tangled mess. Her hand visibly shook.

Myddrin grabbed it, squeezed it. "For the children," he said.

Together, they calmed the horrified students, moving them as quickly as possible through the narrowing tunnel and out into the dark of the night.

They moved at a faster pace now, focusing on their two groups as they followed the trail away from the library and back towards the towering structure of Stonekeep.

Around them, foot soldiers scurried about, either repositioning or attempting to safeguard the groups of children as they filtered out of the library.

A flash of red zipped through the air to their left. The projectile met its target, spearing through the chest of a defending soldier and leaving him dangling from the stone parapet above.

A moment later, the red projectile vanished into mist and the body dropped to the floor. A single measly soul flowed from the corpse and into the assailant, who bore the sigil of a skull and two crossed bones on his breast. *Skullsworn*.

"This shouldn't be happening," Myddrin said to Glade. "They shouldn't be this deep inside the capital!"

Before she could offer a response, one of her students broke from the line.

Myddrin ran to intercept. He had no weapons of his own, no means to defend himself, just the false confidence that overcame a man when all other options were exhausted. He spread his arms wide in defence of the child, placing his body between the invader and the youngling.

"Go back to where you belong, Reaper!" he shouted.

The Soul-Reaper refused to falter. Red eyes stared hungrily above a twisted grin. There would be no reasoning with this man. Rational thought had long since left his conscience. He was here for one reason, to harvest their souls.

The man of the Skull took a step forward. His chest burned

bright red as his already acquired souls attempted to pull forth an image from the *otherside*. The air around him parted, and in its place materialised a crimson shard the length of Myddrin's forearm.

"Take them and run!" Myddrin called over his shoulder to Glade.

The spiked tip of the shard shot forward, and Myddrin closed his eyes.

When pain and death did not come, he opened them. A bright blue wall hovered before him. It stretched the length of the small courtyard. The blurred vision of the invader grew agitated behind it, yelling something incoherent and conjuring another half-dozen crimson shards.

Myddrin looked up to see his wife standing on the stone parapet.

"Go! Take them to the keep! I'll hold them off," Ismey said.

As she spoke, Ismey thrust her arm forward and twisted her hands. The blue wall moved, morphing and engulfing the invader. She squeezed. Bones snapped as the Reaper perished, his souls leaving his body to join those already inside of his wife's cage.

"Come, children," Myddrin said, forcing them back into a line. "Hold hands. Let's go."

Two children refused to move, their prone forms frozen on hands and knees. Myddrin picked them up and tucked them under his arms. Snot mixed with tears, and Myddrin's sleeves soon became wet rags. The others followed, Glade trying her best to pursue.

Together, they ran as fast as the children's little feet would allow. Finally, Myddrin stopped before a pile of rubble. "Something's wrong!" he shouted over the commotion. "There should be an archway here leading to the keep."

"The path is blocked," Glade said, arm around a child. "We must find another."

Myddrin shifted, searching for an alternate route. The tip of Stonekeep stood out like a corkscrew beyond the rubble, but reaching it seemed impossible. "I don't understand," Myddrin said. "This path, it was caved in from the other side. It can't be true. Has the king abandoned us?"

He stood silent for a moment, his mind rattling as he tried to comprehend the ramifications of such an act of cowardice.

There was no time to waste, though. He looked to his left, where a massive mound of white stone stretched into the night sky like a finger. Behind them, Ismey stumbled into view, her blue wall now holding back at least a dozen Skullsworn.

"To White-Rock!" he shouted. He led the children over a dirt path and towards the distant stone. As they approached, they reached a massive clearing and stopped still. Beneath White-Rock's shadow, a battle raged.

Radiant colour lit the sky as the very fabric of the world was ripped open by mages attempting to draw forth power from the *otherside*. Magic flowed. Arrows rained. Swords clashed. People died.

The defenders of Athedale rallied. Pockets of soldiers formed behind several Knights of Aen, their white armour a symbol of protection.

The children huddled behind Myddrin and Glade. They had no place here. They also had no choice.

The invaders swarmed. The allure of power fuelled their movements, their lust insatiable. They charged the defending Knights with no regard for their own safety. Both Knight and Skullsworn drew from the dead, forcing their collection of souls to generate a magic that should never have existed.

Colour met colour. Image met image. Those without any

souls to draw from used regular weapons; sword, spear, anything sharp.

Panic flared inside Myddrin's chest. He had led the children onto a battlefield.

He moved to go back, but his wife still fought behind them. These children didn't belong here. He didn't belong here. This wasn't supposed to happen. They were supposed to be safe.

He searched for a way through the mess, a safe path. One stood out, a pocket of space beneath the giant white rock and behind the defending soldiers. If he could get the children there, they might be able to reach the keep.

Two figures appeared atop White-Rock, silhouetted in the light of the moon. The air above them ripped and rippled, distorting reality as each drew forth power only those hoarding an uncountable number of souls could produce.

The whole battlefield stilled. Fighting stopped as eyes turned to witness the scale of the clash above their heads.

A silver lion shimmered into existence, its features real and alive despite being a construct born of the conjurer's imagination, from the tasselled tail all the way to the pointed teeth. It must have been at least ten times the size of any other image down below.

Opposing the lion, a serpent of deep ebony rose up. It slithered forward, silver meeting black as the two titans of the *otherside* clashed.

There were only two men in existence Myddrin knew to be capable of generating such massive images. The first was the King's Mage, Halvair Silverhair. With at least a hundred-thousand souls in his cage, he was Athedale's last hope. The second was none other than Lord Doonaval himself. The most powerful mage to ever exist. Innumerable souls slept within his cage. Myddrin shuddered at the mere thought of so much raw power.

This clash of titans would decide the fate of the city, and all in view knew it. The ground below his feet shook. The fight spilled onto the battlefield below, their images inadvertently flattening a large swath of defenders and aggressors alike. Souls streamed upwards from corpses in a wave of orbs, flowing into one of Halvair or Doonaval as they fought at the edge of White-Rock.

Myddrin took advantage of the distraction. He gathered the children, drawing their attention by flapping his arms up and down like a bird. They looked to him, their one known in a situation full of unknowns.

Together, they hastened towards the stone, the battle between Halvair and Doonaval raging above their heads. A little girl tripped, rising to find a large gash on her knee. She screamed, arms to her sides as she experienced real pain for likely one of the first times in her young life.

Myddrin stalled. He ran back for her, only for another child to scatter. Glade was having the same trouble with her students.

The crying grew louder as another joined, then another. Myddrin's fingers itched with indecision.

Several horses neighed to his right. He spared a glance. Will walked towards them, his young eyes fixed on the four-legged beasts.

"Will, come back here!" Myddrin shouted.

The boy refused to listen, his mind in his own little world.

The horses were attached to a large, abandoned supply wagon, with a number of spears fixed to the wagon's rim.

An idea sparked. Myddrin turned to Glade. "I'll bring the wagon around! Ready the children!"

Myddrin sprinted. Around the wagon, friendly soldiers scampered past, oblivious to his plight as they ran to join the ensuing conflict.

He grabbed Will, practically throwing him into the wagon,

then climbed atop. He quickly cleared it of anything sharp, though the spears seemed immovable, so he left them alone for now.

He zipped into motion, leaping to the front and grabbing the reins. His legs wobbled as the horses responded. Slowly, they turned, and Myddrin urged them into a trot.

He returned to a worse scene than the one he had left. Half the children were unresponsive, unable to comprehend the scene playing out around them. Myddrin and Glade began lifting them and placing them into the wagon. Some worked with him, others kicked and screamed.

Beads of sweat ran down his brow. He bent, hands on knees, panting.

Myddrin turned. The pursuing Skullsworn from the library had broken through Ismey's wall. Ismey ran, at least two dozen of them behind her, ready to crash into the rear of the defending army.

Myddrin watched, helpless, as his wife pulled from the *otherside*. One hand gripped the hilt of her blade, the other crafted pointed shapes in the air. The ghostly images solidified, and she shot them forward.

One, two, three men of the skull fell, their bloody bodies tripping those behind.

A figure emerged from their ranks, pulling forth energy from the other plane of existence. The Skullsworn parted, making way. He was too far away to distinguish, but from the colour and size of his image Myddrin knew it to be Carthon, the illborn son of Lord Doonaval.

A shape formed, black as pitch, almost indistinguishable in the night sky.

"Myddrin, we have to go, now!" Glade called from over his shoulder.

Ismey's blue met with the black.

The children were loaded, all but one. This was his chance to get them to safety, yet his eyes would not part from the scene.

Ismey slashed at the black with a wave of her hand. She retreated a step, surrounding herself within a sphere of magic.

The Reaper of Mirimar curled his hands. The black compressed around Ismey and her sphere.

"Myddrin, now!" Glade shouted.

A tear ran down his cheek, but he turned to gather the last child.

Rock tumbled from above. Huge chunks of it crashed onto the ground next to them, splitting on impact. Part of the broken rock rolled, then caught the legs of the last child Myddrin had been about to load.

The child cried out in a shriek of pain as it pinned her to the ground. Myddrin ran to the child, a small girl with a face now caked in tears. He braced his legs and pushed against the fallen rock, but it proved too strong for him to move.

He grit his teeth and tried again, to no avail.

Through the motion of aiding the fallen child, he spared a glance towards his wife.

There was no more blue.

Only black.

*Where had the blue gone?*

Thousands of souls flowed from the impenetrable black. They rose and filtered into Carthon's chest. Into his cage.

"ISMEY!" Myddrin shouted, still pushing against the stone.

Glade handed him something, a spear. "Use it to pry the rock free! Quickly!"

Myddrin couldn't move, could barely function. What had he just witnessed?

The strangled cry of the wounded child pulled him back to

reality. He needed to act, to do something, to save her. It was his duty.

He thrust the butt end of the spear under the fallen rock, gripped the haft in a tight embrace, and pushed on it with all his might until it stood vertical.

He felt something come loose, saw Glade whisk the child away.

Before Myddrin could let go of the spear and the true nature of grief could overcome him, the rock above them once again split and fell. More stone rained down.

His world went black as a body fell from the sky, landing directly on top of him.

Myddrin gasped, desperate to regain his breath after the impact. Dust swirled, then cleared. A man lay sprawled in the dirt beside him, twisted around the spear he'd been holding. Blood coated the shaft from the spearhead to where it burst from the man's body.

Myddrin's chest convulsed. He stood, then fell. He crawled from the scene, closing the distance between him and his dead wife inch by slow inch.

A storm of intangible globes flowed from the corpse fixed to the spear and into him. He choked, fighting for air. His mind swirled, assaulted by an incomprehensible force. He felt power, raw, unimaginable power. It coursed through his veins, centred in his chest.

A power born only through death.

# Chapter 1
# - Myddrin -

Outside, waves lapped a sandy shoreline. Myddrin peered through the window with bleary eyes. White foam frothed over the splintered wood of dozens of abandoned ships before retreating into the wide sea.

He broadened his view. Not another strip of land in sight. That was how he liked it. Isolation was what he needed. People were dangerous. He was dangerous.

His head and body ached with a dull pain. Forcing his arm to move through it, he reached for the half-empty bottle of wine on the desk to his right and took a swig.

The voices of the dead swirled in his mind, their presence a constant reminder of the burden he carried. A burden he'd never wanted.

*Let me out*
*Set me free*
*Give up*

"Shut up," Myddrin said.

Other voices joined, congregating into a mass of inaudible whispers.

"Shut up, shut up, SHUT UP!"

Myddrin reached for his pocket and pulled out his long wooden pipe. He grabbed a finger full of moss from his pot and shoved it into the end. His fingers shook as he placed a strip of char cloth over flint and attempted to catch a flame.

Eventually a spark caught, and he lit the pipe before slowly inhaling the substance.

He slumped back into his chair in a daze. The voices receded and Myddrin took comfort in their temporary absence.

Taking a steady breath, he returned to his studies. Piles upon piles of open books were spread out to his left in a haphazard jumble of paper and leather. He ran a finger over the closest page, scanning its contents for anything useful.

Nothing. Always nothing. Ten years he had searched, looking for a way to correct the world, to rid himself and everyone else of this burden, with no results.

He giggled. There was something darkly humorous to it. Out of everyone in the world, he was the most powerful. People literally *killed* for but a fraction of what he possessed, yet Myddrin wanted nothing to do with it. He hadn't sought this power, and he definitely hadn't wanted the reputation that came with it.

He went for another swig of wine when a hand clasped around his shoulder.

His body jolted forwards, smoke catching in his throat. He doubled over in a fit of coughing and wheezing, inadvertently knocking the pot full of moss from his desk and sending a cloud of green flakes and smoke billowing into the air. Air came and went in shallow breaths as he found himself crawling on the ground, grasping at a piece of brown fabric covering the bony legs of his servant.

He righted himself, taking control of his breathing once more. "Knock next time will you, Mees. A man has work to do."

Mees, Myddrin's gangly-looking Hand, stood perfectly still. His arms were crossed, face expressionless, as usual. "Of course, Master."

Myddrin squinted as the voices inside made another mental assault. He coughed, reaching again for the wine.

Mees frowned. "It's getting worse, Master. Perhaps you

should stop mixing the wine and the moss. I worry the combination is bad for your health."

Myddrin clutched at the bottle and took a long pull before throwing it at the wall, where it shattered. What was left of the wine splashed to the floor, staining stray pieces of open parchment a deep red. Shards of broken glass littered the floorboards. "Sour.

"Both are necessary," Myddrin continued after a deep breath. "Alcohol dulls the pain. Moss calms the voices. You know this, Mees."

"I just worry, is all. If the souls should take you, I—"

"I'm fine! I just need more books. One of them will hold the answer. Pass me the map would you. There must be somewhere besides Val Taroth itself that we haven't searched."

Mees did as he was bid, handing Myddrin a lengthy piece of parchment that held the image of Otor with numerous 'X' symbols scratched onto it.

"You need to eat and rebuild your strength, Master," Mees said. "I have prepared dinner."

Myddrin smiled. If there was one thing he liked more than wine and moss, it was a well cooked meal. "What's on the menu today?"

Mees left the room. He returned shortly after, wheeling a wooden trencher. Myddrin inclined his head. He rubbed his hands together and pursed his lips. The earthy smell of his soon-to-be meal filtered into his nostrils.

Mees lifted the lid, revealing the tantalising meal within. "Poached cod cooked in a lemongrass broth. I had the spices imported all the way from En Belin."

Myddrin rubbed his hands faster, his body tingling with excitement. "You spoil me, Mees. Now, go fetch me some more wine will you."

Mees raised an unkempt brow, showing a hint of emotion for the first time in a long while. "You know, for the most powerful mage in all of Otor, you certainly have a lazy streak."

"Hah! Tell me something I don't know."

Myddrin reached again for his flint, ready to spark up another light for his pipe when the sharp sound of glass shattering filled the room. Too quick for him to follow, an object flew through the window, slicing straight through his dinner plate before embedding itself into the door frame a mere two inches from where Mees still stood. Stray pieces of paper, shattered glass, and spilt broth surrounded him.

Mees stood motionless. If anything, the slight twitch in his lip showed a hint of boredom. Myddrin let out an exasperated groan as he bent over and grieved for his lost dinner. He made for the object embedded into the doorframe. It looked like a spear. Only it wasn't a spear. It was an image-spear. It was hued a deep shade of red, though it was completely transparent. He ran a hand over the shaft, feeling as the magically conjured spear turned from a solid as hard as steel into a faint mist, and then into nothing. It disappeared as though it had never existed, the broken glass and the hole in the doorframe the only evidence left behind.

Myddrin sighed. "Not again, Mees. These troublesome soul-hunters. Why must they bother me so? The result is always the same."

"DOONSLAYER!" came a cry from beyond the window.

Myddrin spared a glance out the broken pane, watching as a shadowed figure emerged from a rowboat onto the sand.

Myddrin rolled his eyes. "Must they call me that every time?"

"DOONSLAYER!" came the call again. "YOU WILL ANSWER ME."

Myddrin rubbed at his beard, then brushed a strand of his shoulder-length hair behind his ear. "I suppose I have to handle this now, don't I? The last thing I want is for dessert to be ruined as well."

"I could tackle this one for you if you like, Master?"

"No, no. You've already labelled me lazy once today. Can't have you thinking me some layabout who can't handle his own mess."

"Yes, can't have that at all," Mees said, no small hint of sarcasm in his tone.

"DOONSLA—"

"Yes, yes. I'm here," Myddrin said, opening the front door and shuffling out into the sands below the setting sun. "What do you want?"

A burly man with broad shoulders stepped forward. He wore little armour over his loose cotton breeches, only a leather cuirass, cut at the shoulder to reveal two thickly muscled arms that inched towards an iron axe dangling from his hip-buckle. His hardy face was scarred with a thousand blemishes. "I am Salvar Bloodheir. I come here to claim your life, Doonslayer. Your souls will be mine by night's end."

Myddrin stepped forward and issued an unamused groan. "And what makes you so special, Salvar, was it? What makes you think yourself better than all the others who have tried to take my magic?" He gestured towards the boats scattered about the coast.

Salvar grunted. "I have over one hundred kills to my name. Over five thousand souls sleep within me. Once I've killed you, I'll rule all of the Harrows. Prepare yourself."

Myddrin exuded another of his characteristic sighs, wishing more than anything to be back in his chair enjoying a tender bite of fish.

With their talking at an end, the soul-hunter raised his hands high into the air. His chest glowed a deep red as the souls within his body began their work. Fragments of the air around him began to turn solid with, at first a couple, and then at least two-dozen image-spears, swords, and any kind of weapon imaginable hovering above his head. Salvar thrust both hands forward, and the weapon constructs flew through the air towards Myddrin at the speed of a freshly loosed arrow.

Without hesitation, Myddrin conjured a giant wall of transparent image-stone. The weapons splintered against its green-glowing surface, breaking apart before disappearing as though they had never been made.

Salvar grit his teeth but did not relent, continuing his magical barrage. Myddrin's magic was the stronger, though, and his wall held. Myddrin yawned, covering his mouth with his hand, all the while wondering if Mees was done making dessert.

Salvar continued his barrage, exhausting his cage and throwing everything he had all at once.

"I'll have your souls, Doonslayer!"

With a tired hand, Myddrin reached out into the air. He closed his eyes, picturing an image in his head. His chest flared green as his trapped souls began to feed him their strength, their magic. His nose twitched as the voices inside began to assert themselves.

Myddrin opened his eyes, solidifying his image. The giant, crystalline talons of a dragon stretched into the cloudless sky. The beast glowed a deep emerald, a ghostly shimmer coating its entire length. It flapped its great wings, hovering over the ground, its barbed tail dragging beneath it. The image-dragon made no sound, its existence dependant entirely on Myddrin's magic.

Salvar looked up. The dragon towered above him, at least ten times his size.

Myddrin commanded the dragon forward. Salvar ceased his assault, staring with wide eyes as the beast swooped down upon him. He cowed backwards and tripped over a pointed stone. As he fell, the dragon bit down with razor sharp teeth. It jerked, and the motion ripped Salvar's arm clean off.

Salvar screamed. It was the kind of scream only someone who had been sure of their abilities could make; the primal sound of false confidence being shattered.

Myddrin dismissed his wall and calmly walked in the direction of the shivering soul-hunter. He waved his hands, calling the dragon back to his side. Salvar crawled on one arm back towards his rowboat.

"You shouldn't have come here," Myddrin said. "Go. Be gone from this place. I've no desire to carry your burden. And you don't want to carry mine."

Salvar's face went pale. "Y-you're a monster."

Myddrin shrugged. "I've been called worse. Now go! Get out of here and you may live." He turned to leave, showing his back to the dishevelled soul-hunter. He had almost reached the bank of his home when he felt a shift in the air. It was a shift he knew well, one that only happened when someone drew from the *otherside*.

Myddrin snapped his fingers and his image-dragon leapt behind him, a spear splintering against its hard scales.

"They never learn," Myddrin whispered to himself, before his dragon turned and devoured the soul-hunter from head to toe.

Myddrin winced. His arms flung backwards. His mouth swung open, and his chest expanded. Thousands of tiny, intangible globes of light flowed forth from Salvar's corpse, forcing their way into Myddrin's already plentiful soul-cage.

Myddrin doubled over. His head felt light. He licked his lips, opening the door of his home to see Mees standing there, a tray of sweet cakes and strawberry tarts held before him. "How many this time, Master?" Mees asked.

Myddrin bowed his head in exhaustion. "Too many, Mees."

# Chapter 2
# - Will -

Will's wrist glided across the page. He gripped the black of the charcoal marker so hard it stained his fingers, but he didn't care.

He swept his hand in a broad arc, taking delight as the thickness of his stroke portrayed the shape of the Knight's cloak to perfection. Changing his grip, he applied less pressure, beginning to fix the cloak with finer details and shading. He added some cross-hatching, then used his thumb to blend and smudge the thicker parts to better show the lighting.

He sat cross-legged in the comfort of his bed in his room. His safe place. The place where he could most easily find order in the patterns of the world.

To Will, everything was a pattern. Patterns were how he made sense of the world, how he processed things. From the petals on a flower to the wings on a butterfly, from the waves of the ocean to the webs of a spider, from the veins on a leaf to formation of a cloud.

Everything had a pattern, and every pattern was different, unique.

He looked at his drawing, searching for a way to improve it, for a missing link in the chain of his pattern, or for a new one to create. With his free hand he rapped a beat on his knee.

*One, two, three, four, five, stop.*
*One, two, three, four, five, stop.*
*One, two, three, four, five, stop.*

*One, two, three, four, five, stop.*
*One, two, three, four, five, stop.*

Five was his number. He knew that to others it didn't make any sense, but to him it did. He had five fingers on each hand, five toes on each foot. Five was a central number. It brought balance to a world he sometimes struggled to make sense of.

Satisfied with his drawing, he lifted it above his head and grinned. He held it to the light shining through his bedroom window, revelling in his own artwork.

Myddrin, the Doonslayer, Hero of White-Rock, stood tall on a small hill within the confines of the page. Spear in hand, he stood triumphant above the body of Lord Doonaval.

Will turned and ran to the opposite wall, holding up his artwork again, although this time he had something to compare it to. At least fifty charcoal sketches were pinned to the length of the wall, all portraying a famous Knight of Aen in their glory. All his favourites were here – Calder Whiteclaw, Silas Battledrum, Ophelia Redwolf, Thane Stoneheart, and of course Myddrin Doonslayer, placed in the centre of them all. Will held up his new picture to the older one he had drawn. Confident that his new drawing was better, he made a mental note to wrap it in varnish and swap it later in the day.

He turned, and in his excitement dropped his sketchbook. He bent over to pick it up and saw the crimson cape of his father brushing the floorboards clean as he came to stand before him.

Will rose, clutching his sketchbook close to his chest. Already dressed and ready for duty, his father stared down at him with his vibrant blue eyes. The light from the window reflected against his metal-plated breast, highlighting the emblem given to those who held the title of Knight of Aen – a spiralling pattern surrounding a single circle. The circle represented a human soul, and the spiral was meant to symbolize the cycle of life, though many people believed it was open to interpretation.

"You could be one of those heroes on your wall before long if you spent more time training and less time drawing," his father said. "Don't waste your life on petty hobbies, Will. Do you know how much I've sacrificed to secure you a place in this year's Passing?"

Will's brain itched. He began rapping his hand on his stomach in his beat of five. "Yes, Father, I know how hard you—"

"Do you really? Do you *really* understand just what it means to represent the Gracelands in such a manner? Being a Knight means to sacrifice everything. Our minds must be focused, our bodies honed. The Passing is in two days, you must prepare. Go get dressed, your grandfather is waiting for you in the field."

His father left. Will sauntered over to his bed and buried his face in his pillow. He rolled over, then flipped open his sketchbook. He knew exactly which page to turn to. The charcoal sketch of his mother stared back at him with a warm smile. Will missed her more than words could describe. After she'd passed, Father had changed. He'd grown cold, cruel. Will hated him, wanted to leave. At least when he finally became a Knight, Will could get away from his father.

After getting changed, Will walked into the living room and poured himself some water from the pitcher. The embers from the hearth still simmered in the background as he took a seat at the table. He craned his stiff neck and listened as it made a satisfying click.

The sound of heavy boots on wood echoed around the house, and the stocky figure of his father appeared. Fearing another scolding, Will turned to leave. A measure of relief came in the form of a knock on the door.

Will jumped to his feet, his chair scraping against the floor as he rushed to meet their guest. "I'll get it." He twisted the knob and pulled, eyes squinting as he adjusted to the light. A broad smile stretched the length of his cheeks as he saw a familiar face. "Kalle!"

Will had never been good at making friends, although he didn't really know why.

The other day, things had changed. He had made a real friend, someone he could talk to, train with. Kalle.

His friend stood before him, her long brown hair tied up into a knot and pinned by a silver brooch in the shape of a leaf. Avoiding her honeycomb-coloured eyes, he searched her face for a smile. Smiles were a sign of affection, a show of positive emotion towards another, or so his grandfather had told him. He was surprised then, to see her lips twist into a frown.

Her thread-like arms were crossed over her chest. Did crossed arms mean she was nervous? Perhaps worried? What could she be worried about?

"What's the matter—" Will went to say, when the dark shadow of a man loomed over her, shading her pale skin in a coat of blackness. An inky contour lined the stretch beneath Kalle's eyes as she stared at the ground.

"Haylin!" a voice boomed over her.

A shuffle of footsteps sounded behind Will as his father approached. He opened the door wide, father and daughter now face-to-face with father and son. "Edlian," Will's father said. "What can we do for you?"

Edlian towered over them all, his boulder-like shoulders blocking out the rising sun. His scowl made Will's father's seem like a child's in comparison. He brushed a hand through slick, jet-black hair before cracking stiff knuckles. "You can keep your son away from my daughter, is what you can do," he said.

Will shrank as his father's fingers tightened over his shoulder. "My boy is not the type to make unwelcome advances on young women. I'm sure there must be some misunderstanding."

Edlian huffed in displeasure. "It's not the boy's prick I'm worried about. It's his rotten mouth."

Will tensed, his father's warm breath itching at his neck as his own caught in his throat.

"You best be sure before you accuse my son of treachery," Haylin said.

Edlian stepped forward, brushing Kalle aside. "My daughter is to take this year's Passing two days hence. Never has a son or daughter of the Eldric household missed their Passing. What am I to think, when I return home to hear whispers of forsaking the Knights, of skipping Passing Day. Words better off as discarded thoughts. Words learned no doubt, from your rot of a son."

Will's father stepped forward menacingly. His eyes narrowed into slits as he peered up at the taller and more established Knight. Both men held over a thousand souls within their soul-cage. Either could conjure a storm of solidified images if the need arose.

Edlian's chest began to glow a dark green, the light seeping through his linen shirt. Haylin's own glowed an ocean blue, the signs of a pair of mages about to turn thoughts into reality. The two stood straight, teeth bared, each with one hand slowly moving for the hilt of their sword. Fighting was banned this deep inside the capital, punishable by flogging, and in some cases death, even in the order of the Knights of Aen.

Will ignored the two brutes, instead focusing on the cowering form of his friend. He felt his stomach drop. Why wasn't she looking at him? They were friends, weren't they?

"Be careful how you speak of my boy, Edlian," Will's father said. "Whatever delusions have clouded your daughter's mind, be sure my son is not involved."

Edlian grunted, his oversized shoulders relaxing, the green glow disappearing. "Come Kalle, we are leaving. You are not to come back here. This boy and his father are poison."

Will searched her eyes then for some sign of forgiveness, but received only the cold, blank look so many others had given him in his youth. He wanted to speak, to tell her it was all okay, that he was sorry. But the words wouldn't come, and his father's vice-like grip on his shoulder returned. He half raised his right hand, hoping Kalle would see his gesture of goodwill, but it was no use.

Then she was gone, whisked away by her father.

Once the two were out of sight, Will's father spun him around and shoved him hard in the back. Will surged through the doorframe, tripped over his own feet and tumbled to the floor with a loud thud. He rubbed at his forearm, where he was sure a bruise was already forming.

His father twisted, checking to see if anyone was within earshot before slamming the door behind him. "Is it true?" he asked.

Will just stared dumbly at him.

"Answer me, boy. Is it true? Have you been speaking to that girl about abandoning your duty?"

"No...Yes...Maybe," Will said, confused. "I want to be a Knight. You know I do. I've wanted it my whole life. All I said was that we shouldn't have to kill our own to become one of them."

"Oh Will, don't be so naive. I know people think you're different, but you're not. You understand what a Knight of Aen is, even more than others. The Passing is a necessity. It is our way of life, and the very reason we haven't been overrun by the savages beyond our borders."

"I just don't want Grandpa to die!" Will shouted. "He still has life left to live. Why should he sacrifice it so that someone like me can rise? It's wrong."

"It's the way of the world!" his father shouted back. "People die, others rise. It's better this way than the lawlessness of the Harrows. At least here we get to choose our fate. The outside world isn't so fortunate. Is that what you would have us be?"

Will offered no response. He shied his head, again rapping his beat of five, this time on his chest.

"You have two days to prepare. I will not have you fail this family. I will not have you fail me. And you will not see that girl anymore, am I clear?"

Will nodded, defeated, grudgingly accepting the fact that he was destined to live out his life without the comfort of a friend.

His grandfather stood atop a lone boulder amidst a meadow of long grass, his famous kite shield resting by his side. Will had fond memories of the shield and had sketched it many times in his book. It was the first weapon he'd been permitted to use. Will remembered spending hours just staring at the shiny piece of metal, studying the various patterns carved into its almond shaped face. A lion's head was fitted into the centre, looking out into the world through calm eyes.

Will stumbled over. "Sorry I'm late," he said, bowing low.

His grandfather offered a pleasing smile. "You worry too much. I can see the lines plain on your face. Haylin isn't giving you a hard time, is he?"

Will frowned, unable to mask his emotion. "I made a friend," he said. "Then I lost her. I don't understand Grandpa. Why couldn't she look at me? It makes no sense."

"Slow down, Will. Tell me what happened. We can walk through it together."

Will centred his breathing, tried to focus his thoughts as his grandfather had taught him, and then he explained what had happened.

"Ah, I see," his grandfather said after he had finished. "Come, sit with me."

The two moved towards a closely cropped patch of grass in the meadow and sat cross-legged adjacent to each other. His grandfather rubbed at the patch of grey stubble on his chin.

"You are worried about me. This is why you sought to express yourself to this girl, Kalle, correct?"

"I guess so," Will said. "I don't want you to die. I want to be a Knight, but not if it means someone like you has to trade places with me."

His grandfather took a long, steady breath. "Look into my eyes, Will. Tell me what you see."

Will squinted and leaned forward. "I don't understand. They're just grey."

"Exactly," his grandfather said. "My eyes used to be as blue as the sky itself. They are fading."

His grandfather pulled at the top of his own tunic and slowly exposed his chest.

Will gasped. The skin above his heart was frail and flaky. Cracks spread outward from a central point like a hammer had struck against stone. Below the surface he could see swirls of colour. They seemed to swim inside of him, mixing together and pressing hard against his skin.

"I am dying, Will. I have lived a long life, but harbouring the souls of the dead has its price, and it is my time to pay it. Better I pass on my power to another before it is lost forever."

"I don't understand," Will said. "Won't your burden then just become someone else's?"

"You are correct. The burden of my accumulated souls will

fall upon another. But my mind is old, Will, my body frail. The youth of the world is strong. Minds like yours are more capable of holding such a power in check. And when given proper training you will be able to use this power to keep our people safe.

"I have accepted my role in the future of Athedale. If that means I have to die so that my souls may live inside of someone else, then so be it. You must be ready. You must prepare yourself for the possibility that it might be you who is drawn to end my life."

Will closed his eyes. The thought of killing his own grandfather had already crossed his mind. It was all he seemed to think about of late.

"Magic is a part of us. We are all born with a single soul whether we like it or not. What if the soul-hunters venture in from the Harrows? What if you come face-to-face with the Skullsworn? Or even worse, a Reaper. They will show no mercy, be sure. They will kill and harvest men, women, and children alike. What will you do then? Dying is inevitable. At least this way I get to choose when and what I die for."

Will stood. His fists tightened and his body tensed. "I know what I need to do, but every time I think about it, about becoming a Knight, I just… I can't help thinking about Mother, and what happened to her."

His grandfather closed his shirt and slowly began to rise.

"I see," he said. "Your mother…" he trailed off, staring into the distance for a moment before continuing. "Your mother's death was hard on all of us. The day she was born was the day my life truly started. I can't imagine the pain it caused you, to witness her in such a state."

"But that's the problem," Will said. "I can't remember. I know I was there, but it's like there's a cloud over my mind. Why can't I remember?"

Will rapped his beat of five, counting in his mind as he did so.

"The mind works in mysterious ways, Will. Sometimes it blocks out memories as painful as this one, to protect you. Perhaps this is what happened. I encourage you to not dwell upon her death, but instead cherish the memories of her life. If I know my daughter, that is what she would want for you."

"But now you're going to die too. I can't... Too much is changing. I don't like it."

"I'm not dead yet," his grandfather said, bending over to pick up his practice sword. "Perhaps I still have a lesson or two to teach you."

He threw Will a sword and took a defensive stance.

Will rose and replicated his grandfather's pose. Long blades of grass swayed at their feet.

His bones may have been old, but his grandfather moved with a swiftness honed over years of combat. He shifted his feet, and with one powerful stride narrowed the distance between them, his sword flicking out gracefully.

Will blocked, sword raised, only for another cut to come from his left. Will moved his sword like a stick of charcoal, parrying in a circular motion before taking a backward step.

"That's it, Will!" his grandfather said through laboured breaths, still pressing his attack. "Use what you know. Predict my movements, maximize your advantage."

Will set his feet. His mind went into overdrive. His grandfather's hip moved an inch to the right. Will knew this pattern. His right arm would follow, then his left foot would move forward, exposing his chest for a blow.

Before any of this even happened, Will set his sword-arm into motion. His grandfather moved just as the pattern had predicted. Will's sword caught him in the chest, and his grandfather retreated, gasping from the impact.

His grandfather regained his breath and started laughing. His smile stretched wide, and his belly expanded as his laugh deepened.

"I don't understand," Will said. "You lost. Why are you laughing?"

The laughter settled, ending in a long sigh. "You, my boy. You make me laugh."

Confused, Will lowered his guard.

"Again!" his grandfather shouted, recovering and jumping into the air with a spinning slash.

Will predicted the pattern of the spin, shifted his feet, and deflected the blow, this time disarming him in the process.

Exposed, Will went in for another easy strike to his ribcage. He thrust his arm forward. It struck hard, too hard. He'd been expecting the spongy softness of flesh beneath his blunted sword, but instead it rebounded, shock vibrating through his wrist. He dropped his sword, the metal landing on the overturned grass with a thud.

Will turned, feeling the cool tip of a blade against his neck. "Yield?" asked his grandfather.

"I yield," Will said, slumping his shoulders. Only now did he notice the radiant blue shimmer of an image-shield floating in the air before his grandfather's ribcage. It was formed in the exact shape of his kite shield, the same lion melded to its core.

"There is no such thing as a fair fight in the Harrows, Will. Even less so in the dark pits of Mirimar. You will need to get used to fighting against mages of a high calibre. Once you have enough souls of your own, you will learn to combat magic with magic, but it is of equal importance you learn how to fight without it. Magic is a dangerous enemy, but even more dangerous is a mage who thinks he knows how to use it, and yet does not."

"So, will I be able to make this soon?" Will asked.

"Perhaps, yes."

The blue shimmer of his grandfather's conjured shield disappeared as he dismissed it, moving to where his actual shield lay at the foot of the boulder. "Take this, Will. It's yours," he said, handing it to him.

Will took it tentatively. "You're giving it to me? But you love this shield more than anything in the world!"

"That's why I'm giving it to you."

Will cradled the shield like he would a newborn child.

His grandfather offered another of his characteristic wide smiles.

"I don't understand, Grandpa. You're about to die. Why are you smiling so much?"

"Ha! Ah, my boy. I wish I had more time with you, to see you grow into the man I know you will become. Don't be saddened by my venture to the *otherside*. It's my time. As to why I smile, why, it's you, Will. You're the reason I smile."

# Chapter 3
## - Myddrin -

*She's dead, Myddrin*
*We can help you*
*Ease your pain*
*There is a better path*
*An easy path*
*Let us show you*
*Release us*

"Ismey!"

Myddrin woke with a start. His chest beat like a drum, air coming and going in short breaths. In his panic, his elbow smashed into an empty wine bottle, sending a tingle up his arm.

The pain thrust away the voices, and Myddrin took a steadying breath before the familiar throb in his head that accompanied the morning after a night of heavy drinking began to set in.

He sat up fully in his chair and his eyes shifted towards the picture frame below the windowsill. He reached a hand over at least three open books and grabbed hold of the frame. His head tilted and his eyes began to water as his mind wandered back to a time when he was happy.

When she was alive.

"I'm sorry, Ismey," he whispered. "But I can't be with you. Not yet. Not until I complete your vision. I can't let them win."

He placed the frame down and looked to his left where a plate of buttered bread slices sat. He grabbed one and stuffed it into his mouth.

*Still warm.*

Mees must have just brought them in.

He rubbed at his eyes, then made to shove another into his mouth when Mees called from down the hall.

"Master, you have a visitor."

Myddrin coughed, choking on the bread before spitting out a response. "Not another damn soul-hunter is it? My cage is plenty full already."

Mees said nothing, leaving Myddrin the task of moving from his chair and into the lounge.

"Damn Hand," Myddrin whispered. "He'll be the death of me one of these days."

His chair creaked as he rose. He brushed some crumbs off his robe, squared his shoulders, and cleared his throat before leaving the study and entering the dining hall.

The prominent flicker of a red cloak came into view. Myddrin's face went slack as a figure turned to face him. He had long, brown hair so light it was almost gold. He was fitted in full plate below the neck, the famous spiral crest of a Knight of Aen embossed upon his breast. A long steel sword was strapped to his back, its hilt poking out over his shoulder. He stared at Myddrin through light, brooding eyes. "You look like you've seen better days."

Myddrin grunted his acknowledgement, moving to the kitchen to take a lengthy swig of wine. "What is it this time, Estevan? Did the king fall off his chair? Does the royal palace need redecorating? Oh, oh! I've got it! Perhaps the princess has come of age and needs a husband? I can think of no better suitor than myself. Dashing good looks, the strength of an ox, and not a single wrinkle to show for my thirty-five summers."

Myddrin turned, expecting Estevan to at least share a laugh at his expense, but his expression was cold, with not even the quiver of a lip.

"I see," Myddrin said. "This is not a leisurely trip then?"

"We need to talk, Myddrin," Estevan said, taking another step forward.

Myddrin sighed. He grabbed two glasses and filled them both almost to the rim before offering the slightly emptier one to Estevan.

"Must we go straight into the gritty details?" Myddrin said. "Information is sparse out here in the Mirror Sea. Can we not start with a more pleasant conversation before I inevitably deny your request for me to return to the capital?"

"I did not come here to play games. Not this time," Estevan said, placing the glass of wine on the counter, untouched. "These are dark times. You are all alone out here. You do not see how the world changes."

"There is a reason I am out here alone!" Myddrin snapped.

"Maybe so, but we need you back. The king has requested your presence in Athedale."

"If the king wants an audience, he can come here himself."

"Damn it, Myddrin!" Estavan yelled, slamming a fist onto the bench. "Don't be so naive. There is nothing for you here. The Gracelands are in trouble. The Harrows are in a frenzy. Soul-hunters are running rampant, flocking to—"

"Soul-hunters have always ruled the Harrows. This means nothing to me. You're a Knight of Aen, do your job."

"You're a stubborn fool. Don't you care for the people of the Gracelands anymore? What would your former students think of you? What would *she* think of you?"

Myddrin's grip tightened, snapping the glass in his hand. Wine and glass fell to the floor. Around him, the air began to ripple. His chest glowed green. The floor of his home vibrated as his trapped souls began to work their magic.

Dust trickled from the ceiling and Estevan took a backward step.

"You go too far," Myddrin said.

The Knight's face went slack, eyes darting to every corner of the room as it shook.

"Don't you see?" Myddrin said. He calmed, whatever image his mind had prepared to form disappearing before he killed them both. "I can't return. I'm dangerous, and not just to myself. I don't belong around people. My path is set. This is my destiny, and likely where I die."

For a moment, Myddrin thought Estevan was intimidated, too scared to continue pressing. Perhaps he was, but with a shuffle of a foot, his resolve seemingly strengthened. He took a step forward, jaw tightening. "I did not come here to treat with a dying man. I came to find the Hero of White-Rock."

"You and I both know that story is false. I am no hero to be worshipped."

"False or not, you were a hero that day Myddrin. Those children that were in your care are alive now because of you. Because of your actions. I know what you lost that day, but this is not the time for self-loathing. A new power has risen from Mirimar. A figure has reclaimed the five Skull Thrones and united them as one. He's named himself emperor and declared war on the Gracelands.

"Worthy or no, you are the most powerful mage in Otor. We need you Myddrin. The Gracelands needs you."

"Who?" Myddrin queried. "Who is this proclaimed emperor?"

Estevan paused, taking a deep breath. "It's Carthon."

Myddrin's head began to spin, his eyes blurred as he was hit by a sudden pain behind his temples. "Mees," Myddrin said. "Pack our bags."

# Chapter 4
# - Tvora -

Tvora despised the fighting pits: the stench, the sweat, the humidity. The scent of dried blood was everywhere, flowing through the vast catacombs beneath the dead city of Brane. No matter her feelings toward the pits, she couldn't deny the benefits they brought her, the souls she could reap. The pits were rife with headstrong soul-hunters seeking to fill their cage.

Cecco's talons curled around her shoulder, the scarlet-hued hawk settling on his perch. *Are you sure about this?* he asked, his words audible only in her mind. *We haven't faced this many at a time before.*

Tvora smiled, stroking the image-hawk's feathery wings with a soft hand. "Don't doubt yourself, Cecco. This is the only path forward. Our soul-cage isn't full enough to sustain you indefinitely yet. We need their power."

*Don't be a coward*, another voice sounded.

Lucia prowled up behind them. The violet-coloured image-panther brushed against Tvora's leg, her six-foot-long frame sending her off-balance.

*Not everyone has spears for teeth and a neck as thick as a tree*, Cecco retorted.

"Hush, you two," Tvora said. "These men are weak. I can see it in their eyes."

The sound of men shouting, bones cracking, and coin exchanging boomed across the gloomy death pit. A ring of fire surrounded her, illuminating the makeshift battlefield and her assailants within.

Seven bearded men took tentative steps toward her, the closest coming to a halt as the silent form of Lucia stalked in front of her.

*I had always wanted to grow a beard*, Cecco said from his perch. *They say that some men in northern Ganta can grow their beards up to twenty feet long. Can you believe it, twenty feet!*

Lucia inclined her boulder-like head. *What is the bird yapping about this time?*

Tvora let out an exhausted breath. "Just let him have it. You know he always spouts useless facts when he's nervous."

*What is there to be nervous about?* Lucia said. *These men are weaklings, they have no magic.*

"You're wrong," Tvora said. "They have some magic of their own, I can sense it on them."

*Then let me feast, for I am hungry,* Lucia said.

One of the men squinted at her. His face twitched in confusion as he raised his axe in a non-aggressive action. "This bitch is crazy," he said. "She talks to herself."

His comments were met by a grumble of reverberating laughter across the ranks of men lining up to fight her.

Tvora tightened the hood around her face, concealing her eyes from view. They weren't ready to see her for who she was. Not just yet.

"She's mine," called another. A big brute of a man stepped forward. A dog's skull rested on his fur-covered shoulder pad. "It'll be me who strikes the killing blow."

The other six men growled and hissed in response. All drew their weapons, their chests and eyes glowing with the colour of their inner magic.

Tvora's smile widened as Cecco took flight.

*Should we not call upon Gowther?* the image-hawk said.

"Gowther won't be needed here," Tvora responded, drawing her twin blades, Naex and Naev, from their respective sheaths.

The seven bearded men rushed at her, each eager to win the bounty of Tvora's plentiful soul-cage. One brandished a series of image-weapons and hurled them at her. Another flicked his wrists and a transparent vine rose from the ground before her feet, wrapping around her legs and holding her in place. But their magic was weak, the strength of their constructs nothing compared to hers.

Lucia sprung off powerful legs, flying through the air and crashing into the nearest assailant. Her claws raked across his face, teeth sinking deep into the pink of his neck. Crimson blood gushed over his garment and pooled at the foot of his now dead body.

The weight of the vine around her legs disappeared, its master's souls flowing into Tvora in a rush of light.

She spun, whirling Naex and Naev around her in an overzealous show of skill. The twin blades bit into two image-weapons, deflecting their course. Her assailant conjured more and flung them towards her, again and again. Tvora pivoted, then launched into the air, twirling between the coloured arrows and landing with a wide sweep of her arm.

The amateur soul-hunter responsible for them began to panic. He tried to pull forth more power from the *otherside*. The air around him parted and a new image began to form. His chest pulsed with emerald light, but it faded almost as soon as it started. There were not enough souls inside of his cage to sustain it.

Tvora grinned, wasting no time. Drawing her blades behind her back, she cut at the man wearing the dog's skull.

Naev sliced a thin line through the skull, continuing forward to sink into the shoulder of the heavyset man. He bent over with a growl of pain, and Tvora left him behind to focus on her next victim.

The five men left standing were no longer so eager to rush her. One fumbled at his belt buckle in a dire attempt to remove his second axe, but was too late as Tvora embedded Naex into his once crystal-blue eye.

More souls flowed into her, and she felt her power growing. She turned to see the sharp point of a spear poised above, arcing downwards in a strike that would surely end her.

Cecco returned before the spear could gather momentum, however. The hawk swooped with unnatural speed, tearing apart flesh and bone as he cut himself a hole through the man's chest. He appeared again on the other side. The man with the spear stared dumbly at the gaping hole before dropping face first to the ground.

Tvora and Lucia took down the next two with little effort. Blood spattered, painting the dirt a familiar shade of red.

The final combatant charged her with a wild swing of his sword. Tvora retreated, though the tip of the sword cut into her garment, ripping a hole in the fabric from collar to chest. Her hood flung backward.

The final assailant stopped and stared.

"Y-y-your chest. It's hollow. Your eyes… they're white. You're broken!" he said. "I wasn't told of this. Spare me, I beg you. I didn't know… I didn't know!"

Tvora grimaced. She looked down at her exposed chest. Above her breast and over her heart stretched an open hole. Inside the hole swirled thousands of souls of varying colour. No blood lined its rim, no pain entered her mind. This was how it had been since she'd broken, since she had succumbed to the voices, her soul-cage held together by magic beyond her comprehension.

Tvora sheathed her twin blades while Lucia circled the pleading warrior, waiting for the opportunity to strike. The crowd were on their feet, toothless men and dishevelled women screaming at her from behind the fire to finish him.

Lucia obliged, moving in for the kill, but the man was quick, springing backwards and dodging Lucia before running as fast as his legs would take him through the fire and into the angry crowd.

He didn't get far, however, as the now raging crowd stopped him in his path, each taking pleasure as they tore him limb from limb. The dying man's cry echoed around the chamber. Tvora grit her teeth in an annoyed snarl.

One man celebrated, the combatant's souls flowing into him after striking the killing blow. He was met with an axe to his skull as a woman claimed the stolen souls for herself.

A frenzy ensued as all turned to chaos. Bodies were dragged and weapons drawn as they fought over tiny scraps of magic.

Tvora grimaced. They were stealing *her* magic. She had earned it, and one way or another would claim it.

"Gowther!" she called. "Come forth! Kill them all."

The entire cavern rumbled as the air around her parted. A blue shape began to shimmer into existence. Tvora pulled from the *otherside*. Her entire body tensed as she siphoned power from every soul in her cage. The image began to take shape.

*Tvora!* Lucia called.

Tvora looked to her right. Beside her, the violet form of the panther began to fade. She looked to her left, and the hawk faded too.

"Lucia! Cecco!" she yelled.

Veins popped from her forearm as she fought desperately to keep all three images solidified. All three *friends*.

She looked down to her open cage. The light of her souls was fading, each of them turning from bright as a shining sun to dull as a dying candle. Eventually, she could take the strain no more, and all three images faded from existence.

Frustrated, she turned and left the slaughter to play out as it may without her hand. Her friends would return, but her souls needed rest, sustenance. Tvora needed to replenish her strength, and that of her souls. She needed to become stronger, for her friends' sake. She needed more souls, and there was only one way to get them.

Tvora walked through the dank catacombs alone. Her head beat like a constant drum as her new souls met with the old, begging, pleading to be set free. She held strong. She had lost her hold on them once, and it had nearly destroyed her. If her friends hadn't rescued her, hadn't chased away the other voices, then who knows what would have happened to her. She shuddered at the thought of being trapped in her own body, a host for a thousand minds.

She owed them more than this. Her friends deserved their lives back, or at least whatever facsimile she could give them.

"It's not enough!" she cried, slamming a fist into the stone wall hard enough to draw blood.

A shadow curled at the mouth of the cavern. Tvora spun, drawing Naex.

The silhouette of a figure emerged, creeping closer. Heavy footsteps landed on damp rocks. A sliver of sunlight seeped through the cavern entrance, causing the contour of the figure's shadow to crawl its way up the stalactite mound which rose from the rocky surface.

Tvora grit her teeth and snarled. A series of slow, audible claps rang through the deep cavern. A man appeared. His features were shaded, but his shoulders were broad, his legs thick with muscle.

"Leave, or those steps will be your last," Tvora said,

brandishing Naev.

"But I want to congratulate you, Tvora Soul-Broken," the man said. His voice was deep and unwavering, and he projected an air of confidence. The clapping ceased, his hands relaxing as he clasped them together.

"I don't need your congratulations. Who are you?"

He took another slow step forward. "I am simply an admirer."

Tvora grasped at the handle of Naev. "Take one step closer and you can admire the sting of my blade."

The man just laughed, a deep cackle of sound through closed lips. "Such fire, such tenacity. And you are so..." he paused. "Complete."

Tvora just stared at him.

"Usually when the voices win, when the pressure on a person's cage becomes too much, they break. Their minds fade into the background, overridden by whichever voice shouts the loudest. But you, your eyes say you are broken, but your actions speak otherwise. I have never known someone to regain control after being broken. It is a feat worthy of recognition. And after watching you fight in the pits, it seems you brought friends with you. Another accolade worthy of praise."

Tvora shifted her feet. It bothered her that this man knew so much. There were few who knew of her origin, even fewer after she had gutted most of them.

"I ask again, who are you? And how did you come to know me?"

The man crossed his arms and sighed. "Very well. My name is Carthon. As to how I know you, I have been following your progress for some time."

Tvora tensed. It couldn't be. *The* Carthon, Emperor of Mirimar, Conqueror of the Skull Thrones. "Liar!" she spat. "Such a man wouldn't bother himself with the likes of me."

"Oh, but he would," the man — Carthon, said. "You can be more than this," he continued, gesturing to the distant cries of the frenzied crowd and taking another step forward. "Join me. Become one of my Reapers, and you will have all that you desire and more."

Tvora bared her teeth. She felt a pressure. Her chest began to flare, her souls drawn to those inside this man. The force of his magic commanded attention, like a powerful aura she was unable to look away from. Just how many souls slept inside of him?

"I fight alone," she insisted. "My journey is my own. I don't need you."

Carthon took another step forward. "I think you do. Even now your power fades, I can see it. You fight to save your friends, to keep them alive, give them the bodies that were taken from them. I can give you what you need to sustain them, to feed them for eternity and beyond. That is what you want, is it not?"

Tvora took a backward step and snarled. She hated that he knew her so, it made her uncomfortable.

Carthon unclasped his hands. "Join me, reap and harvest my enemies and add their magic to your own," he said, his mouth relaxing into a pleased smile. "I am building an army. Fight for me, and together we will re-shape the world."

# Chapter 5
# - Will -

Will still didn't understand. Was Kalle really not his friend anymore? She hadn't even spoken. One stray word and she cut him off? He hated not understanding things. Why couldn't people just speak plainly?

That's why he had followed her up here.

Sure-footed and quiet, Will skipped over a fallen tree branch and continued up the rock-face of the mountain. Kalle was a clumsy climber, easy to follow. A broken twig here, a patch of squashed vegetation there, not to mention the sounds. Her feet fell like hammers, and he could hear her grunting from all the way down at the bottom.

Why had she come here?

Eventually, the rock levelled out and Will rose to find a clearing. He took a breath and studied his surroundings. A miniature forest spread out before him, carved into the side of the mountain in a wash of green. Will smiled. He liked nature. Nature was simple. Colourful flowers, large sprawling trees, thousands of creatures both small and large, all acting on instinct, doing what life dictated. There were no confusing emotions, no moral dilemmas, just life and death.

Will turned back to take in the complete view of Athedale.

Built on a large incline, and set within the side of the mountain, the city housed thousands. The houses themselves were spread out haphazardly. There seemed to be no pattern to it. It irked him. The houses looked as if they were pebbles at the bottom of a stream, large winding pathways of yellow and brown flowing in-between them. He turned his head to peer at the western wall. If the houses were pebbles, then the wall was a boulder. It stood tall, the curtain of white dwarfing the entire city.

He liked being up high. He wasn't entirely sure why, though he reasoned maybe it had something to do with how he felt inside. This view brought his life into perspective. Down there, all Will could think about were his problems. He felt overwhelmed, as though the entire world was pressing in on him and his issues were all he could see. Up here, things felt different. There were thousands of people below, each with their own lives, their own problems. It was too much to think about at once, but if Will was to become a Knight, then he needed to start thinking beyond himself.

He forgot about Kalle for the moment, she would be easy to find later. Instead, he followed the call of a distant bird. It played a familiar tune, reminding him of a song his mother used to sing for him before bed each night.

He crept deeper into the thicket of woods, listening as the tune became louder and louder. He bent even lower and placed a hand on a nearby oak. His eyes widened as he found the source of the sound.

Resting on a small branch overlooking the ravine perched a Ruby-Crested Songbird. Slowly, he reached inside his jacket for his sketchbook and charcoal stick, careful not to make any sudden movements.

He simply had to draw it. This type of songbird was rare in these parts, and he couldn't forgo the opportunity to capture its essence on paper.

He began by lightly sketching its outline, starting with the small, round head, then moving to the compact body. He added a slight curve to the breast, attached a sharp, triangular beak and then finished by shaping two short wings and a long, elegant tail. He started dotting the pattern on the feathers and made a mental note of the colours to add later when he had his full palette with him.

Nearly finished, he reached inside his pack for a thicker stick of charcoal to add some darker shading. Suddenly, a rustle sounded from his right, and Will rose to see the shaft of an arrow shoot from the brush.

"No!" Will shouted.

The bird made one final, high-pitched note before falling from the branch.

"Shit," someone said from behind tree cover.

Will ignored it, running instead for the fallen bird. With panicked hands, he picked it up and cupped it in his palms. No arrow pierced its body, though blood seeped from its left wing. Will set it down. The bird tried to fly away, but couldn't manage to lift itself with its clipped wing.

"Step aside," a voice said from behind.

Will turned to see a face he knew well.

Rath.

Another arrow lined his bow. Muscled arms held the string taught behind his ear, which was covered with slick, jet black hair. His left eye was marked with a large, red scar in the shape of a leaf, though the skin crinkled as his eye narrowed in on the bird.

Will stood in front of it. "What are you doing, Rath? It's just a bird."

"Just a bird? Do you know how much these things fetch on the open market? I could sell it for a small fortune."

"Why would I know that?" Will responded, not moving an inch.

Rath shook his head in a gesture Will didn't understand, then pulled the string even tighter.

"What are you doing here?" Rath said.

"I was..." Will said as another figure emerged from behind Rath.

"Will? Why are you here? Did you follow me?"

"Kalle," Will said. "I... yes, I did."

He paused, confused. Softly, he rapped his beat of five on his ribs as he struggled to think of something to say. "I wanted to find out if we were still friends, after yesterday. You didn't say anything. I don't understand."

Kalle went silent. Rath lowered his bow and started laughing. Will scowled. He hated when people laughed at his expense, especially when he didn't know why.

"You're pathetic," Rath said. "You and Kalle were never 'friends'. What on Otor gave you that impression?"

Will ignored him, instead focussing on Kalle, who had the same look on her face as when she and her father had confronted him the other day.

"Will," she said, placing a calming hand over Rath's bow. "We had one conversation. It was nice, sure, and I appreciated your help. But that doesn't make us friends. My father... it doesn't matter. Go home, Will, it's for the best."

Will rapped his beat faster. His face twisted, but there was nothing he could do. He had asked, and she had told him. That was that.

Beside her, Rath shook his head. "I can't believe he's to take the Passing with us," he said to Kalle. "Look at him, he can't even think straight."

"That's impossible." Will said. "To think straight. That doesn't even make sense. How can someone think in a direction?"

He waited for a response but received only another bout of laughter. Rath ran a hand over his own face. "This is ridiculous," he said. "The Knight's standards are slipping to let a half-wit like him take the Passing."

"That's enough, Rath." Kalle said. "Just ignore him. Go home, Will, please."

"It's not enough," Rath continued, brushing past her. "It's a disgrace. The Knights of Aen need powerful warriors, not kids like him."

"Rath!"

"Think about it. Is he the type of person you want defending your children when you're older? Defending *our* children," he added, moving a hand around her waist.

"Rath," Kalle said again, this time in what Will interpreted as more of a playful tone. "Not here."

She took his hand and moved to plant a soft kiss on his lips. "Just let him go, then I'm all yours."

Will looked away. He felt anger stir in his chest, though he didn't know why. Why was Kalle with Rath? He was a bully. He picked on people because he could, because of his status. It didn't make sense. And why was his hand around her waist?

"Fine," Rath said. "But I'm taking the bird with me." In one fluid motion, Rath knocked an arrow and drew it behind his ear.

A chirp sounded to his right and Will looked down. He had lost concentration and the bird had crawled out of his reach.

He pushed off the ground, fully prepared to throw himself in front of the bird to keep it safe, but even as he did so he knew he was too late, the arrow too quick.

Will's chest burned. He felt power, his thoughts consumed with keeping the songbird safe.

He closed his eyes, willing something, anything to happen. A new power in his chest answered his call. Where had this come from?

Light materialised before the bird. He pulled on it and the light solidified. A blue image of his grandfather's lion-crested shield hovered over the bird, fixed in place. The arrow splintered against its surface.

"What the..." Rath said. His eyes went wide, then narrowed in on Will. "Murderer! You've killed before. You must have. That's an image from the *otherside*!"

Will stood, dumbfounded. He hadn't created that, had he? His eyes darted back and forth, looking to his hands, to the shield, then to Rath. He blinked, lost focus, and the image disappeared. He wasted no time, bending forward and cupping the wounded bird in his hands. Rath backed away.

The bird chirped, its tiny, taloned feet curling over his finger. It began innocently pecking at the pink flesh of his hand. Will stroked its coloured crest, taking care to avoid the injured wing, which was folded over its breast.

"Leave, Rath. Now!" Will said, his voice taking on a hard edge.

Rath took another backward step. "You're finished," he said. "Done. You'll never take the Passing. Father won't allow it."

He fled, taking a frightened Kalle by the hand and running towards the city.

Will exhaled slowly. What had he meant by that?

Will's head grew dizzy. He clutched at his chest. He leaned over, using a tree to steady his weight. He heard voices, whispers. They took over his thoughts, his mind. He shook his head, willing them to disappear.

What was happening to him?

As he stretched a weak hand out into the air his dizziness returned tenfold. The flash of a memory imprinted itself onto his mind, but its origin was impossible to discern. He saw his mother, a flash of lights, hollow eyes, his hands slick with blood.

He shook his head as the voices returned inside, assaulting him, pulling at his mind.

"Peck! Peck!" came a high-pitched, shaky voice from somewhere in the distance. Will fought through the mental intrusion as the bird chirped in his hand.

"Peck!" the cry came again, this time closer.

The bird continued chirping. He thought about letting it go, but that wouldn't do, the bird couldn't fly.

Through foggy eyes he thought he saw an elderly lady clothed in black limping towards him. She held a wooden walking stick, her back hunched over as she took one small step at a time. Her mangy grey hair was a matted mess, all tangled as though she hadn't had a bath in years. He had to peg his nose shut to avoid the thick stench of sweat and body odour.

Will noticed the old lady was staring at him. Or rather not at him, but at the bird.

"Hand her over, hand her over," she said. "Quickly now. Come to Mother Molde."

Will shook himself out of his stupor, handing the wounded bird over to the lady. She didn't seem dangerous. And, apparently, she knew the bird?

"Bah. What have they done to you? Meddling little brats. No concept of the world around them. Ignorant of anyone but themselves," the lady said, her dark eyes flickering towards Will as she growled under her breath.

"I wasn't trying to hurt it," Will said.

"Peck," the old lady said. "Her name is Peck."

"I wasn't trying to hurt Peck. I was trying to help her."

The old lady's eyes narrowed even further, her wrinkled neck turning to scan him. She stopped, pausing to observe the air around where Will had made the shield appear. She swiped an arm over the area. "You've touched the *otherside*," she said.

Will held his breath.

"Don't bother denying it. I can see the residual light still fading in the air."

Will gulped a heavy lump down his throat. "I — I couldn't have. I haven't taken the Passing yet. Peck was in danger. Rath was going to kill her. I — I just wanted to protect her."

The old lady pursed her lips, humming a sickly tune and studying him as if she were a teacher and he her pupil. "I see. Although, even if you are telling the truth, there is still the matter of how you acquired the ability. Only dark deeds gift you the power to wield it. What is your name?"

"My name is Will," he said. "Will Harte."

"Will? You mean Haylin's child?"

Will nodded.

The old lady mused, pulling at a lock of matted hair with one hand while stroking Peck with the other. "The Passing is tomorrow. What is Haylin up to? Hiding secrets no doubt. You say this is the first time you've touched the *otherside*?"

Will made to protest. "It's not… I haven't…"

"Only a fool would deny what is plainly obvious. There's no use lying to me."

"I don't even know what happened," Will said. "One minute Peck was in danger, the next a shield was before her. If it was me, I've never done anything like it before in my life. I swear it."

Molde furrowed her brow. "Curious. You seem genuinely oblivious to your magical powers. Either that, or you are a more accomplished liar than I would give you credit for. I've lived a long life. I would like to believe I know when a man is telling the truth and when he is not. My name is Molde. And you have already met Peck here."

Will nodded, barely aware of what was happening.

"You said it was Rath after my bird?" Molde said. "Estevan's boy?"

Will nodded.

"And he saw you touch the *otherside*?"

Will nodded again.

"Then you must prepare for what's to come. Whatever reason you have, self-defence or no, you best be ready to answer for your crimes. The Council won't be happy to hear of a would-be Knight using magic before taking the Passing."

Will stumbled. The voices inside of him returned. He rapped his beat of five. "The Council? I don't… I — I need to get out of here," he said. "To clear my head."

He ran. He was expecting Molde to protest, to call out and grab hold of him, but she didn't. He ran and refused to look back. Had he really just used magic? Magic only came to those who had killed. He hadn't killed, had he?

# Chapter 6
## - Myddrin -

Myddrin's legs buckled as Estevan's galley swayed along the coast. Estevan stood on the wooden foredeck with his back toward Myddrin, strong hands placed over hips as he stared at the high, arching cliffs.

Waves crashed into the boat with increasing vigour, causing Myddrin to stagger forward and backward. His stomach churned and his throat gagged. He had never liked the open ocean. The sea always made him sick, though the watered-down wine already in his stomach wasn't helping. The journey had taken about six days, and he had stayed sober for exactly zero of them.

He wobbled his way over toward the wooden railing, a canteen quarter-full of wine in one hand and his pipe in the other. Mees followed his every step, the competent Hand never complaining.

Myddrin sidled up beside Estevan, watching as the cliff-face loomed ever closer. Rocks protruded from its side like a line of spears raining from the sky.

Myddrin opened his mouth to speak, but his stomach had other plans. He quickly leaned over the railing and puked the contents of his guts into the Mirror Sea. Once recovered, he looked down to see colourful swirls of motion churning at sea level as mages worked to keep the ship moving fast. Several curved propellers were fixed to shafts on the ship's hull, the huge temporary machines born of magic from the *otherside*. They cut through waves like knives through butter.

"Is all this really necessary?" Myddrin said, wiping at his lip and then gesturing towards the massive propellers.

"Much has changed since you were last here," Estevan replied. "Innovation is the future. If the Gracelands are to stay strong, we must use what we have, to become more efficient."

"Yes, but I mean is it all necessary for me? The capital must have hundreds of Knights these days. Why am I so important that your king would spare so many just to find me?"

Estevan turned to face him. "You know why. You hold the—"

"I hold the most souls in the world. I know, I know. But I'm just one person."

"You said it yourself, you're dangerous. We need you, Myddrin, if not for your power, then for your reputation. The city loves you, and our enemies fear you. That counts for more than you know."

"And what if I snap, hm? What if I lose my mind in the middle of Stonekeep? What will you do then? I'm just as likely to kill everybody as I am to save them."

Estevan took a slow step towards him, Myddrin remembering for the first time in a long while that the Knight was actually an inch or so taller than him.

"You want the truth? The truth is that we have no choice. It was the king who pushed for your involvement, no one else. I agreed to help, but I went against the church on this one. They hate you, Myddrin, despise you simply for what you are; an abnormality, disconnected from Aen. They don't see what I see. They don't venture outside their stone walls. They don't see what has become of the Harrows, how Carthon has picked them clean. Most of all, they don't understand what's coming.

"I made the choice to come for you. So, if your soul is to break, that's on me. I take responsibility, and I won't hesitate to kill you on the spot."

"Trust me, you don't want this burden," Myddrin replied.

"Then I will gladly die with it."

Myddrin paused, expecting his friend's demeanour to waver, his posture to lapse. When it didn't, he issued a slow nod of respect.

"I'll do my best to keep it together, you have my word."

Estevan sighed, then moved and placed his elbows on the railing. "You know, there are better ways to calm the voices. New techniques, breathing exercises, meditation. I can teach you some if you—"

"Believe me, I've tried it all. If you want the Hero of White-Rock, then this is what he comes with," Myddrin finished by holding up his canteen of wine with one hand and brandishing his pipe with the other.

Estevan let out a small sound of resignation through thin lips before the ship rounded a bend.

Myddrin grimaced as the tip of White-Rock gleamed in the morning sunlight. He took a lengthy puff from his pipe and blew a ring of smoke into the air.

"Is Halvair still here?"

"He is."

"Is he still pissed?"

"He is."

Myddrin laughed, though it came out as more of a chortle.

Not long after, the galley pulled into the Calaster Gulf. The ship followed the coast, passing through the Kastar channel, then made port on the northern edge of Athedale.

The Azier Mountains stretched like a giant green hand to his left, marking the end of the Gracelander territory and the beginning of the Harrows. The Mirror Sea extended right to the base of the mountain. Nestled into its side lay the sprawling city of Athedale.

The gulf was sort of an in-between, a finger of water stretching into the rear of the mountain range and granting access to the back of the city.

The magic of the propellers vanished into nothing. Oars were recalled and ropes were flung as men bustled about the pier. A wooden ramp was lowered, and Estevan gestured for Myddrin to step off the ship.

He did so, holding one hand over his eyes as if the sun were fire, his mind still a foggy haze. Mees wasn't far behind, lifting his luggage with the ease of a man twice his size. They were escorted off the pier and onto the cobblestone tiling.

The city walls stretched like a curtain of stone as far as his eyes could see. Athedale must have been at least triple the size of the entire island Myddrin had called home for the past ten years.

"What am I doing here?" Myddrin muttered, almost inaudibly. A surge of memories flooded his mind the further he went, pressing against his temples in a relentless barrage of images. He stopped in the middle of the street. He thought he saw children, frightened and alone. They needed him, were depending on him. He knew they weren't there, that was the past, they were a figment of his imagination, but he waved an unsteady hand in the air anyway.

His chest tightened. He saw a blue sphere, the image fixed into his mind for all of eternity. The sphere vanished and his heart wrenched. *Ismey!*

*She's gone,* came a whisper in his mind.
*Let us out*
*We can help you forget*
*Let us OUT*

Myddrin doubled over, holding his head in his palms.

He looked up to see Mees standing above him. Mees raised

his arm and backhanded him hard across the face.

Pain lanced across his cheek, jolting his vision both out of and then back into focus. The voices vanished, as did the visions.

"Thank you, Mees," Myddrin said, straightening and pulling his cloak tight. As much as he chastised the handy servant, for the past ten years Mees had done more for Myddrin than he could ever repay. He struggled to show it, but Myddrin's care for the trusty Hand ran deep.

Estevan curled a bushy brow before gesturing for the gawking sailors to go about their business.

"I'll be okay," Myddrin said with false confidence.

Slowly, Estevan released his grip on the hilt of his sword and gestured for him to continue.

Thick iron gates creaked open, stretching wide and coming to a halt with an ominous thud. Myddrin followed Estevan's crimson cape as the Knight escorted him through winding streets. A sense of paranoia crept up his spine as onlookers leered at him. Their numbers swelled the deeper into Athedale they ventured. Soon, a large group followed at their heels, with more congregating atop houses and buildings as word of his arrival spread faster than he could walk.

He clawed at the shirt collar around his neck, hoping to release some of the tension from his throat. He hated the fame, the spotlight. It was one of the reasons he'd left in the first place.

Whispers of 'The Hero of White-Rock' and 'The Doonslayer returns' were everywhere, echoing like a constant drum and only growing louder.

The twin spires of Stonekeep shot out of the ground like massive corkscrews in the near distance. Black as the night itself, they stared down at the entire city as if through watchful eyes.

The keep was built directly into the mountain, it's defence a mixture of man-made and natural fortifications.

Estevan's guard escorted them up a winding staircase leading toward a courtyard. Myddrin wheezed at the effort. Behind him stretched an endless, interconnected string of bridges attached to one main one. They went all the way to the outer walls, connecting them and Stonekeep in one long path.

The Mage-Way.

He ran a hand over the stone. "This is new," he pointed out.

"Yes. Well, it was remade ten years ago, after its collapse," Estevan said.

Myddrin stopped in his tracks, assaulted by another memory. No voices accompanied it this time, just the frightening visual of nearly two-dozen children trapped and afraid.

The crown had claimed the bridge's collapse was a result of Skullsworn attacks, though Myddrin had a heavy suspicion the king had ordered it caved in as a defensive manoeuvre to protect his own court. A suspicion that, of course, he could never prove, but it left a sour taste in his mouth all the same.

On either side of the pathway rested dozens of statues atop plinths. They meandered around the courtyard and swept into another, narrower pathway which divided into a walkway to Stonekeep.

The likeness of famous mages stared down at him, their stone faces brought to life by what must have been the finest craftsmen Athedale had to offer.

Myddrin nearly choked at the thought of his own face on display like that. He had enough trouble showing his face in public, he couldn't imagine the thought of people staring at him for all of eternity.

"Welcome! Our long-lost hero returns to us at last," came a voice from further down the Mage-Way.

Myddrin turned to see none other than the King of Athedale, Remen Anders, walking towards him. His arms were open wide, and a brazen smile stretched the length of his face. His teeth glistened a radiant white. They were the kind of teeth only those who had lived a life of privilege could boast, and they were complimented by a crown of white gold atop his head, the ornament reminiscent of the enormous white rock that stood as a landmark in the centre of the city. The king's thin, spindly arms were draped in a cape of red velvet similar to Estevan's, though the king wore his longer, and it was less suited for combat and more for display.

"My king," Myddrin said, tucking his arm to his waist and bowing low. "It's been a long time."

"Too long. Must be nearly ten summers since I last saw the Doonslayer in the flesh."

Myddrin winced, hoping his fake smile would hold up.

"I trust Estevan has treated you well?" Remen continued.

"He has," Myddrin replied. "Your kingdom is in safe hands with him."

The king looked to Estevan and back to Myddrin. "Estevan is quite capable, yes. But these are troubling times, Myddrin, and troubling times call for a great hero!"

Myddrin said nothing, just grunted.

"But come," Remen continued. "Trouble can wait another hour or so. First, I must show you to your gift!"

Myddrin exhaled, hoping his gift was a cup of wine and a warm bath.

"Come, come. It is close!"

The king ushered him down the short end of the Mage-Way.

"So, what do you think of the capital so far? Is it all that you remembered? Better even, hm?" the king said, speaking as though he had personally rebuilt every block with his own hands.

"Uh, it's fine, sure."

Estevan gave him a subtle nudge on the shoulder.

"Magnificent! Yes," Myddrin corrected "You've done a marvellous job, I can see. Though I find the statues a little odd, personally. I can't imagine my face up there etched into the stone. Wouldn't that be a laugh."

He knew his nervous quip wasn't exactly funny, but he had expected a laugh, or even a feigned smile. Instead, he received only the slackened face of a man offended.

He followed the king's outstretched hand and turned to see a giant, chiselled-stone statue of himself. His jaw dropped as the mirror image of his youthful self stared back at him. The stone-Myddrin wore a fighting uniform. It held a stern expression, mouth wide and eyes focused. Its arm was pointed toward the sky, and upon closer inspection he could see that the stone-Myddrin held in its hand the exact spear Doonaval had fallen to.

Myddrin stifled a cough.

"Your 'gift'," the king said.

Myddrin broke from his reverie. He looked to Mees, and then to Estevan, who was trying his best to stifle a laugh.

"Surely I am not worthy of being among such company?" Myddrin said.

The king straightened his tunic, trying his best to recover from his embarrassment. "Nonsense," Remen said. "I can think of few more worthy than the Doonslayer himself. Who knows what would have happened to the Gracelands if not for you. Now come, I have been told you like to indulge in food and drink. Let's get you washed up, then I have prepared a spread I believe you will be most interested in."

Myddrin blushed, though to be honest he had stopped listening after food and drink. His stomach led the way as he walked into Stonekeep.

Myddrin felt refreshed. He had been given a room, some time to bathe, and fresh clothes. They fit surprisingly well, and were a welcome relief after the constant chafing that accompanied a long span at sea. Eventually a servant called, and he left Mees behind to go to dinner.

The Great Hall of Stonekeep was just as lavish as he remembered. Large tapestries draped from the high, vaulted ceiling, depicting ancient battles and past kings and queens in all their glory. Dozens of guests shared drink and laughter down below in a wide room as a minstrel played an up-beat tune, his voice loud enough to be a choir.

Myddrin's hand shook from anxiety. Ten years he had spent in isolation with no one but Mees and the odd soul-hunter for company. Now suddenly he was thrust into a room full of loud people.

He looked up from his seat at the high table to see two steely grey eyes staring back at him from the other end. Halvair, the King's Mage, leered at him the way Myddrin would if someone took the last cup of wine. Long silver hair, neatly combed into straight lines, ran down the side of his face. His bony hands were clasped together, his impressively straight posture never faltering as he seemingly took pleasure in making Myddrin uncomfortable.

King Remen sat by Halvair's side, chatting idly with the queen.

Myddrin gulped, hoping to avoid Halvair's spiteful glare by looking around the table. The King's Council was all here. Estevan was his one comfort. He sat next to him, his one known in this new world he had stumbled into. Estevan had briefed him on what to expect, however.

General Strupp issued a large belly laugh at something the king had said, jolting the table as his huge fists slammed onto its top. Myddrin remembered him as a promising soldier; the big brute had been on his way to becoming a captain when Myddrin left.

The person at the table who surprised him the most was Glade. He remembered her as the frightened but capable teacher he had fled the library with so long ago now. What was she doing here? Their eyes met briefly, though they were sat at opposite ends of the table and would have had to yell over everyone else to have a conversation.

He found her beauty breathtaking. Long, scarlet hair fell to her hips, curling at the end. Her face was all sharp lines and angles, her high-set cheekbones and full lips leaving Myddrin blushing.

He quickly righted himself. He didn't think himself an ugly man, he was tall and been told he had a kind face, but even the thought of being with another woman sent a pang of guilt twisting through his gut. There would only ever be one woman for him, and she was long passed from this world.

One other figure rounded out the table. Myddrin had never seen him before, though Estevan had named him Beyan. He wore the blood red robes of a monk. His head was fully shaven, and Myddrin thought he could see the intricate patterns of a tattoo climbing up under his sleeves.

Not much of a conversationalist, Myddrin instead focused on what he did know, and that was food. The king hadn't been lying when he said he had prepared a feast. To his left lay a ring of freshly baked white bread, a bowl of whipped butter in its centre. To his right were sugared almonds served in small bowls, and honey-mustard eggs cut in half for convenience. A roasted chicken was the centrepiece of the table, its breast already carved into neat lines of meat, half of it already inside of Myddrin.

He lowered his spoon toward his bowl of chilled strawberry

soup and grimaced as it came up empty. After indulging in a long pull of spiced wine instead, he licked his lips clean and finally felt full enough to survey his surroundings properly.

The more his vision wandered, the more he began to sense the strange mood of the event. There was a sombre undertone to the proceedings, not quite a sense of dread, but a perceived melancholy among the gathered guests.

They were all, old…

Not quite ready to drop dead, but an array of wrinkled faces and weathered skin stared back at him as he looked. He knew some of those faces. They were Knights of Aen all. Some were veterans, famous even when he was a young boy roaming the castle grounds. Others were lesser mages, though he supposed anything could have happened in his long absence. He searched their expressions, finding one common trait among them all. Their eyes were dull and grey, absent of colour.

Something within his mind clicked, and suddenly he knew why such a feast had been prepared. This was the final feast of the Passing. The last meal shared between the older Knights in the Great Hall before they passed their souls onto the younger generation.

He dropped his spoon, letting it clatter noisily on the oaken table.

"I was wondering how long it would take you," Estevan said.

Myddrin lowered his gaze. "How long do they have left?"

"The Passing is in two days."

"I never did like the Passing. You couldn't have delayed our arrival a few sleeps longer?" Myddrin said.

"I am head of the entire order, I don't think my absence would have gone down too well. Besides, my son is due to take the Passing this year. His feet have grown a little too big for his boots, and he still has much to learn on the way of the world, but he is my son, and I wouldn't miss it."

Myddrin grunted. He patted his belly, and as if his full stomach were a cue, the entire table fell deathly silent.

"I trust you are well satisfied?" King Remen said, gesturing to the empty plates before him.

Myddrin thumped a fist on his chest, burping as the last of his food digested. "I am, you are most generous."

"Perfect. I see you have noticed our guests," Remen said, gesturing to the old Knights down below.

Myddrin spared another glance, grimaced, and then nodded.

"Excellent," Remen continued. "Would you do us the honour of overseeing this year's Passing ritual? It would do well for the younger generation to see such an accomplished mage in the flesh."

Myddrin noticed that he hadn't used the title *Knight*. Technically, Myddrin wasn't one, he'd never been inducted into their order.

Beside the king, Halvair scoffed, covering it with a cough.

Myddrin blinked. He would rather not watch as the younger generation put the older to the knife, but it was a fair and expected request. "If it pleases you, Highness, it would be my honour," he said.

"Wonderful," Remen said. "Now that the matter is settled, let us move on to the purpose of your summoning."

Myddrin attempted to sit straight and listen.

Remen paused, and the whole table grew still. Myddrin stared, and for the first time he noticed the dark rings hanging like angry clouds beneath the king's eyes. Remen planted two hands wide on the table.

"The Gracelands are at war, Myddrin, and we are losing. Our influence over the Harrows diminishes by the day. Carthon has once again united the Skull Thrones of Mirimar and declared himself emperor. Already we have seen the ramifications of his ascendancy flowing into the Gracelands. His Reapers run rampant over the Harrows, gathering once independent soul-hunters to his cause, and those who will not join him flee into our sovereign lands unchecked."

Myddrin nodded along, Estevan had already explained this much.

"I want you to fight with us," Remon continued. "To join the order, become a Knight of Aen and defend the Gracelands against Carthon and his legion."

Myddrin shifted awkwardly in his chair.

The king leaned forward. "I know why you left us so many years ago. I know why you abandoned your duty and fled to the Mirror Sea. I know what you lost...

"But what you did was a crime. You took the souls of the most powerful man in the world and ran away with them. It is a crime I am willing to forgive, for to the public, and to us, you are a hero. Now I need you to be the Doonslayer again. I need Mirimar to fear you. I want Carthon to hesitate, to know the man who defeated his father sits comfortable behind these walls once more."

Beside the king, Halvair's clenched knuckles began to go white.

Myddrin paused. He withdrew into his thoughts, fingers itching for his pipe and some moss to dull his over-active mind.

Did the king truly know what he was asking? Did he know how he suffered? The danger he posed? Did he know how close he was to breaking? What would happen if he did? Remen wasn't just asking him to defend the Gracelands, he was asking him to die for it.

"I..." he began, but words failed him.

Everyone stared, waited.

Remen placed an open hand in the air. "I understand your hesitation. It is a lot to ask. Let me alleviate some weight from your decision. I know what it is you seek, what you have spent the past ten years searching for."

Myddrin looked to Estevan, mentally chastising him for passing along information which, in reality, he should have expected him to betray.

"You search for a way to connect the soul-road, to free your trapped souls and for an end to image-magic. A noble quest, certainly, no matter how futile. Regardless, I believe I am in a position to help you."

Myddrin stopped fiddling for his pipe and instead leaned forward with renewed intrigue. "Go on."

"Tell me, in all of your studies, did your research ever lead you towards the city of Drin?"

Myddrin perked up. Drin was indeed a city of note in many of his texts, said to be the place a number of scholars fled after the Sundering and the burning of books that followed. It lay deep in the mountain ranges of the Harrows, impossible to get to and heavily guarded.

Myddrin nodded, then took a small sip of his freshly refilled cup of wine.

"A battle has recently been fought there, and lost," Remen said, biting back those last two words as though they were a sting to his pride. "Carthon and his Reapers launched an assault on the city, burned it to the ground. They killed many of our agents there in the process, including Calder, a heavy loss indeed.

"One positive has come of the whole mess, though. A number of texts were recovered by our Knights during the commotion. Texts from before, and soon after, the Sundering. Texts that were supposed to have been burnt."

"What are you saying?" Myddrin pressed.

"I am saying I will grant you access to those texts, if you wish it. Alongside my own scholars, of course. You may continue your research here, while also defending our sovereign nation from Mirimar."

"So, you're bribing me with information?" Myddrin said.

The king leaned back in his chair and opened his posture. "You are the Doonslayer, the most powerful mage in the world. You did not have to come here with Estevan. He certainly couldn't have forced you. Yet here you are. You must have come for a reason. I merely seek to ensure that we both benefit from your presence."

Myddrin paused again, a mannerism sure to frustrate all listening. "Are you not scared? What if I break? What if I wake up tomorrow morning, the porridge goes down the wrong way, and I snap?"

"That's a risk we are willing to take," Remen said. "These are troubling times. Besides, we have procedures in place, plans to follow in the case of any Knight becoming soul-broken. I don't see why you would be any different."

Myddrin took a long, steady breath. He knew his decision had already been made. It had been made the moment he left his home, but to speak it, to verbally agree to give up his life in service of the crown, was a bitter pill to swallow. Slowly, he nodded. "Very well. I'll stay."

"Perfect," Remen said, clasping his hands together. "To the return of the Doonslayer," Remen said, clinking his cup with General Strupp's. Any tension in the air vanished, and shoulders relaxed as drinks were raised.

A Hand came to the table then, the attendant walking up to Estevan and whispering something in his ear. He made Myddrin think of Mees. He hoped he was ready to settle in for the long haul.

"What?" Estevan said. "My son is here? He should know better. Bring him here, I'll talk to him."

The Hand flitted away, returning shortly after with a boy. He seemed tall for his age, his youthful face resembling a young Estevan, though a nasty looking scar covered his right eye. His cheeks flushed red as he approached.

"Father," he said, bowing low before moving in to speak quietly in his ear.

"Rath, my boy. This is not the time," Estevan said, probably louder than he should have. "I have only just returned. There will be time to speak later this evening."

"Father," Rath pleaded, "this can't wait. There's a boy, Haylin's son. He can touch the *otherside* before taking the Passing. I've seen him do it. He's killed! And he must answer for it."

# Chapter 7
# - Will -

Hands over knees, Will rocked back and forth in his bed, struggling for breath. A thousand thoughts plagued his mind, rivalled only by the thousand voices whispering into his ear. Each one overlapped the other, all vying for control.

*You know what you did*
*You're not worthy*
*Set us free*

Will continued rocking, placing one hand on his temple as if that would subdue them. With his other he rapped his beat of five on his chest faster than ever before. Along with the beat he spoke the names of his favourite Knights.

"Calder, Silas, Ophelia, Thane, Myddrin.

"Calder, Silas, Ophelia, Thane, Myddrin.

"Calder, Silas, Ophelia, Thane, Myddrin.

"Calder, Silas, Ophelia, Thane, Myddrin.

"Calder, Silas, Ophelia, Thane, Myddrin."

Slowly, he began to calm down. The voices subsided, and his mind began to clear. With this clarity came a question.

What were these voices inside his head?

As much as he didn't want to admit it, he knew the answer. These voices were the burden all Knights carried. The price for the sins of a killer.

He had touched the *otherside*, brought forth an image to protect the bird from Rath. But how? He hadn't killed, had he?

A memory began to assault him, pressing against the edge of

his mind. He suppressed it, refusing to acknowledge it. He locked it away.

Again, he rapped his beat of five.

"Calder, Silas, Ophelia, Thane, Myddrin.

"Calder, Silas, Ophelia, Thane, Myddrin.

"Calder, Silas, Ophelia, Thane, Myddrin.

"Calder, Silas, Ophelia, Thane, Myddrin.

"Calder, Silas, Ophelia, Thane, Myddrin."

A thump sounded from the front door, causing Will to shrink deeper into the sheets.

It sounded again. This time it was louder, more aggressive.

"Alright, alright!" Will heard his father say through the thin walls of their home. "I'm coming."

Will rushed over to his bedroom door and pressed his ear against the wood.

"Haylin Harte, Knight of the Seventh Division," a muffled voice at the front door said.

"Clethar? What business does the king's herald have in my household?" Will heard his father respond.

"You and your son are summoned to the king's court this evening to face trial."

"On what grounds?"

"Your son has been accused of illegal use of magic. He will be questioned for murder, as well as trialled for disobeying the laws of the Passing."

Will's chest constricted. Air refused to come. He lost the ability to speak even the names of the five, as his entire world began to collapse around him.

Flanked by soldiers dressed in shining metal, Will stared at the ground the entire trek up the slope from his home to Stonekeep. Father walked beside him. Will spared a glance, trying to examine his expression as Grandfather had taught him, to find a measure of comfort, though his father's stone face looked devoid of emotion.

Will returned his gaze to the cobblestoned ground. He couldn't even look up to admire the keep as two wide doors of thick oak split down the middle and parted. He held his arms to his chest as hundreds of faceless people began to gawk at him.

*Look away!* he screamed internally, though he found himself unable to voice his thoughts.

Led under heavy guard, he walked through a set of winding corridors and finally into an open room already filled with people.

He gulped a heavy lump down his throat. Finding a small measure of courage, he began to assess his surroundings. Twin staircases circled the room, winding around and coming together to form a platform which seemed to almost hover slightly above the rest of the room.

Atop the platform rested a long table, visible from the entire right side of the room. Seated at the table were the most important people in Athedale, perhaps even the world. King Anders sat in the middle, dressed in red velvet. His hands were interlaced, elbows planted firmly on the high table. Will had only ever seen the king once or twice, and even then, not from this close. For a brief moment, their eyes met, and immediately Will shied away.

The guards came to a halt and ushered him into a seat beside his father at a small table in the middle of the room.

Those around him chatted, no doubt about him. The outskirts of the room consisted of at least eight rows of people, with each row elevated a head taller than the last.

Will cupped his ears. He wanted to seem brave, to hold it together, but this was all just too much. Too many sounds. Too many people.

As he began to rap his beat of five, his father gripped his wrist with a firm grasp. "Not here," he said. "Get yourself together. This is the king's court."

Will didn't like it, but he forced himself to compose, silently rapping his beat of five via a tap of the foot instead.

He risked another look above. The king's attention had been diverted, thankfully, and Will's eyes widened as he took stock of the other people present.

Thane Stoneheart sat among those at the high table. His chest spanned twice the width of a normal man's, set between two arms that were thick with muscle. A twisted scar ran down the length of his left cheek. He looked just like he did in Will's sketches.

It dawned on Will then that he was about to be judged in front of his heroes, perhaps even *by* them.

What had he done wrong?

Other prominent Knights lined the table. Halvair Silverhair sat idle beside the king, with arms crossed and lips pursed into an expression Will thought to be one of either boredom or complete concentration, he couldn't decide.

Will bit his tongue as he saw Rath poke his head over the railing. He sat beside his own father, Estevan, head of the Knights of Aen. Will's eyes met Rath's, though Will shied away, knowing Rath would only seek to put him down again somehow.

The doors to the back of the courtroom creaked open, and in stumbled a man dressed in all black. He carried a bowl of nuts in one hand and was using the other to pick his way through them. He stopped, taking a backward step as if caught off guard by the amount of people in the room. Then he continued, working his way down the corridor and placing himself next to an old lady.

Will's jaw dropped.

Molde?

What was the old lady from the woods doing here? Had she come to confirm Rath's story? To condemn him for the use of magic before taking the Passing?

Will stopped tapping his foot. He scanned the chamber. Everyone stared, not at Will, but rather the man eating the nuts.

Recognition dawned. For a moment Will was back in his room, staring at the piece of parchment on his wall.

Myddrin! The Doonslayer. He was here, in Athedale. At his trial.

His frame was slimmer than Will remembered, and he had grown a peppery beard too. His eyes looked sunken, as though he hadn't slept in days, but Will could never forget the face of the man who had saved him. The man who had saved all of the Gracelands.

He waved a non-threatening hand in the air in what Will interpreted as a shooing gesture. Everyone averted their gaze at once. Instead, they began muttering to the people next to them.

Atop the platform, the man named Estevan stood, and the room stilled. He clasped his hands together and spoke. "We gather here today, on the eve of the Passing, to discuss a serious crime." He paused to let his words sink in. "Our laws are clear, our way of life concrete. Murder is not permitted within the Gracelands. Unsanctioned use of magic is not permitted here in Athedale. Will Harte, son of Knights Haylin and Alina, grandson to the great Knight Gawain, stands accused of both of these crimes. Will is due to take the Passing this year by right of ascension, but as of now, I place this right on hold.

"As commander of the Knights of Aen, it is my duty to see that Will has a fair trial, and the chance to deny and defend himself against these accusations. I call upon my son Rath to speak, so that he might declare his accusation publicly."

Will's stomach churned. His nails bit a splinter from the armrest as Rath rose from his seat. "I accuse Will of using magic before his Passing Day. I saw it with my own eyes. A blue shield, born from the magic of the *otherside*. There's no doubt in my mind. It came from him."

Will flinched as Rath pointed an accusatory finger.

Beside him, Will's father bared his teeth. Will turned to him, begging, pleading for him to step in, to offer some kind of explanation. None came, he couldn't even look him in the eye, his own son.

Rath took a seat and Estevan replaced him on the railing. He looked directly toward Will. "How do you plead?"

Will froze. His chest tightened into what felt like a hundred knots. He looked to the left, then to the right. Air came and went in short breaths. What should he say? What *could* he say?

"We need an answer," Estevan prompted.

Will withdrew into his shell, blocking out the rest of the courtroom. He wanted to run, and he would have if not for the dozen guards barring the doorway. No options remained. He felt trapped.

"Calder, Silas, Ophelia, Thane, Myddrin.

"Calder, Silas, Ophelia, Thane, Myddrin.

"Calder, Silas, Ophelia, Thane, Myddrin.

"Calder, Silas, Ophelia, Thane, Myddrin."

"Calder, Silas, Ophelia, Thane, Myddrin."

He whispered his calming words, trying his best to ignore the hundred or so people staring.

"What was that?" he heard a voice say in the distance.

Beside him, his father shifted. His eyebrows twisted into an expression which usually followed with a tirade of insults.

"I — I don't know," Will managed to squeeze out.

"You don't know?" Estevan said. "I'll keep this simple. Did you, or did you not use magic? Keep in mind that lying here will cost you your life, and there is another witness to call upon should the need arise."

Will snapped into attention. Kalle? She was here?

He scanned the room but couldn't find her anywhere. He clenched his fists. Of course she would be here.

"I — I did it, yes," Will said, watching as his father shied beneath the cover of his hand.

"Very well," Estevan continued. "Now that you have admitted to the use of unsanctioned magic, we come to the matter of how you attained said magic. There is only one way to acquire the ability to touch the *otherside*, not to mention the number of souls it would take to generate an image as large as a shield. Who did you kill, Will? Whose souls did you steal to fill your cage?"

Will had known the question was coming, but it still took him off guard. "I didn't... I... I would never. I don't... I must have. I have no explanation, sir. I don't know why the shield appeared. I just wanted to protect the bird, to keep it safe."

"Not good enough," Estevan said with a raised voice. "Actions have consequences. There must be a victim, a powerful one. Who did you murder for your magic?"

Will tensed, and the voices inside chose this exact moment to assault him.

*You know what you did*
*You killed her*
*Remember*
*Surrender to us*
*Break*
*Let us out*

"Go away!" Will snapped and grasped his head, causing those in the first row of bystanders to take a backward step.

"Get a hold of yourself, boy! If you break here, your life is forfeit," Estevan called.

Will steadied, and with a mental strength he didn't know he possessed he pushed away the voices.

He looked up to Estevan, who had brandished a series of documents. "It says here your mother passed from this world one year ago. Alina's death was marked a suicide, as declared by your father."

Beside Will, his father's knuckles grew white.

"Your mother was a powerful mage. She served our order faithfully until the end. I understand this is a difficult question, so I will ask this only once. Did you take the life of your birth mother and claim her souls for your own?"

Will's world went black. Something inside shattered. Memories assaulted him; memories once locked away, now brought to the surface.

In his mind he saw white eyes, crazed eyes. Shaking. So much shaking. Her arms, they were not her own. He saw legs moving as if on threads. Images formed, broke and then re-formed, distortions of reality which seemed to serve no purpose. She came at him, came at Father.

Will rapped his beat of five so fast he barely even stopped to pause in-between.

He looked up to see hundreds of eyes staring, waiting. They were ready to pounce, to judge, to sentence him for his crime. A crime he may be guilty of committing.

Will fumbled for words, ready to accept their condemnation, to admit his guilt.

"It's my fault,"

Will lifted his head, thinking it had been him who spoke, though he hadn't yet found the courage to open his mouth.

He turned to his right. Tears streamed down his father's cheeks. "It's my fault," Will's father repeated. "I should have seen it coming. I should have done more."

Will watched as his father wiped his eyes clean, only for more tears to follow. "She broke," he continued. "Right in front of me.

Her eyes. They were filled with madness. They were not her own. Her cage burst. Her souls, they took her, became her.

"She came at me, came at Will. I tried to stop her, to save her."

Will's father ripped open the front of his shirt. Broken buttons bounced onto the tiled floor below. He pointed to a scar the size of a finger just below his right collarbone. "Whatever host which consumed her mind stabbed me with a fragment of magic. It would have killed me, would have killed us. Will tried…" he paused, and for the first time in a long while his father looked at him with something other than contempt. "Will tried to stop her, to separate us. He pulled, and together they fell from a ledge. The fall, it killed her. Will hit his head, lost consciousness. He… when he woke, he didn't remember. He didn't know what he had done, didn't understand the burden he now carried.

"I covered it up. I marked her death as a suicide and buried the evidence. I — I'm sorry, Will. I blamed you, hated you even. But in truth, the blame was mine alone."

A long silence stretched for what seemed like an eternity. No one spoke, the courtroom quiet but for the sound of a few broken sobs.

Eventually, Estevan cleared his throat and spoke. "That is indeed a sad story. The breaking of one's soul is a serious matter," he said. "If it were accounted for at the time of the crime, I'm sure we could have been more lenient. However, you have allowed a year to pass, and no confession has come forth. Not only have you deceived us, but you then had the audacity to enter Will into this year's Passing having already consumed your wife's souls. What were you thinking Haylin? What purpose did this serve?"

Beside him, Will's father clenched his fists. He bared his teeth and then lifted his chin before speaking. "I did what I thought necessary. Will already had souls inside of him. They had managed to stay quiet for a time, likely because of his amnesia, but eventually I knew they would speak to him. He needed to be a Knight. He needed the training to be able to control them, the position to claim them legitimately. If I had told the truth, his punishment would have been death or exile. It was my only choice."

"Your recklessness would have gotten him killed anyway," Estevan said. "It is not for you to make these decisions. You are a Knight of Aen!" He sighed heavily. "But no longer. The law is clear. For the crime of covering up the nature of the death of your wife, and for enrolling your son into our order with the knowledge of his active soul-cage, I hereby strip you, Haylin Harte, of your rank, and sentence you to death."

Will froze, as did his father beside him. Death?

"No," Will said. "You can't. It was my fault. I did it! I killed her, take my life inst—"

"Enough!" Pain lanced through Will's arm and he looked down to see his father's grip tight around his wrist. "Allow me this, Will, please."

Estevan spoke again, his voice ringing loud. "In honour of what you once were, I will allow your death to be part of the Passing. If you should choose it, you may die beside your father-in-law on Passing Day, so that the souls inside of you may continue to serve the Gracelands in their plight against the evils beyond our border."

Will's father stood tall. "I accept my punishment as just, though might I first plead for you to allow my son to become a Knight. Please, let him serve in your order as I have, as his mother and grandfather have for so many years. Let him know what it means to become a warrior, to fight for this kingdom."

Estevan paused to consider.

To everyone's surprise, Rath jumped out of his seat from above. "You can't be serious. This boy killed his own mother! He is weak, I've seen it. His mind is wrong. He won't serve us. He's nothing but a waste of souls."

"Quiet!" Estevan said. He followed his command with a backhand to the face, leaving Rath with a red cheek and an angry expression. "Learn your place."

Beside them both, the king watched on, his face unmoving. So too were Thane and Halvair, all resigned to allow Estevan to carry out their business.

"Forgive my son, for he is brash. But his words are not without merit. Accidental or not, you have committed a crime. You are old enough now to become your own man, but you are forbidden to take this year's Passing, and will never become a Knight of Aen. Your sentence is exile. If you are found to be using your magic again within our borders, the sentence will be death."

Will gulped.

Exile? Will panicked. What would he do? Where would he go? The Harrows would swallow him whole. If people found out who he was, what he could do, he would be hunted, killed.

"If I may, Your Majesty," came a voice from the crowd.

Will turned to see the man next to Molde on his feet.

Estevan relaxed, surprise crossing his face. "Myddrin? I did not expect you to be interested in the matters of our order."

Will's jaw opened wide. Why was the Doonslayer interjecting in his trial?

"I beg your forgiveness, but I have been conversing with my mother," he said. "She has met this boy, said he saved one of her birds from harm."

*His mother? Molde? Molde was Myddrin's mother!?*

"I too have a connection to the child," Myddrin continued. "He was one of my pupils during Doonaval's invasion. I believe it would be a waste of magical talent to let this boy slip through the Knight's grasp. I plead for you to let him join the order, so that he might learn to control his thoughts and harness his potential for the betterment of the Gracelands."

Estevan rocked back in his chair. "The boy cannot take the Passing. He already has enough souls of his own, I would not see him take on anymore."

"I agree," Myddrin said. "Let his mother's souls count as his Passing, and see that he is joined among the other students after the Passing is complete."

Estevan looked to Will. "Is this what you want, boy? To become a member of our order?"

Will shivered. All he had ever wanted was to become a Knight, to be like his mother and father. To become one the sketches on his wall. Why then was he now hesitating?

He planted his feet, tensed his arms, and hardened his resolve. He imagined himself atop the mountain, staring out at all the people down below, and tried to think beyond himself. "I want to protect people. I don't want my father to die, nor my grandfather, but these souls inside of me are my mother's. If I am to have them, if I am to carry her burden, then I would use them to protect others. So yes, I want to become a Knight, if you will have me."

Estevan paused, and for a moment Will thought he was going to throw him out of the room. Instead, he turned to Myddrin. "I accept your request. The boy will not take the Passing, but I will grant him the opportunity to prove his worth amongst our order."

# Chapter 8
## - Tvora -

Tvora stood alone on a sea of pebbles at the base of a mountain.

Alone.

She always ended up alone. Every day. She couldn't sustain them, her friends. Not for long. They deserved better.

She felt her souls begin to regenerate, to replenish as Tvora's own strength grew. She welcomed it. Soon she would be able to bring them back, though the cycle would only repeat until she had enough souls to keep them with her. She needed to hunt.

She ran a calloused hand over the rip in her shirt. The hole of her exposed chest would create a problem. Her hollow eyes presented enough of a complication when trying to blend in, though people usually just kept their distance. If she walked into a village with a visibly open soul-cage, then she was sure people would run outright.

She needed new clothes.

Carthon's proposition continued to pry at her mind. It couldn't be real. Her, a Reaper of Mirimar?

But it *was* real. She had felt his souls, his strength. That amount of power couldn't be faked. With him, she could be someone. She could take what she wanted, could attain the power to sustain her friends indefinitely.

She needed to decide. But first, she needed food and water. And a new shirt.

Her feet took her to a nearby village, which consisted of

nothing more than a few ramshackle buildings which looked ready to fall over. That's how it was with most of the Harrows. People lived here, sure, but most stuck to small-numbered communities. With the rise in power hungry soul-hunters, the larger communities just became targets, prey for them to feed upon.

Tvora would never prey on the weak. Not after what had happened to her village.

No. She much preferred to feed on the strong. The more souls in their cage, the better.

She covered up the rip in her shirt as best she could and strolled into the centre of the village. To her left, six children played happily in a small little pen with a half-splintered wooden fence, throwing a ball back and forth. One laughed as another dropped it, making a show about how unfair the throw had been.

Tvora couldn't help but stare. This had been her. Lucia, Cecco, even Gowther. This had been them, in a lost life. One of the children caught her stare and moved to the edge of the fence. "I like your eyes," she said, smiling at her as Tvora had once smiled at Gowther.

"Edith! Stay away from her!" came a shrill voice. A woman came running over and wrapped her arms around the small child. The woman looked to Tvora and began to shiver. Her hands trembled and her lip began to quiver. "Please, we have nothing. We are just a small town. These children, they have no other home. Please leave us be."

Tvora said nothing. She had no intention of harming anyone here, but this was how it had been ever since…

Since she had broken.

"Harlette!" came another voice. An older lady emerged from the building attached to the playpen. She held a wooden cane and used it to limp her way towards the three of them.

"Harlette," she said again, a little out of breath. "This is no way to treat a guest." She turned to Tvora and, to her surprise, didn't waver. Tvora studied her. Her eyes were a dying grey. They stared absently, unfocused. For a fleeting moment Tvora thought her broken too, but after a second glance she realised the woman was just blind.

"Please, would you join us for some tea?" the old lady said.

"Mother!" the younger woman said. "She's... she's... broken."

The old lady was silent for a time. Then she looked up, meeting Tvora's eyes with her own dead ones. "Do you mean this place harm?" she queried, her voice calm and collected.

Tvora hesitated, then spoke. "No. I simply wish to purchase some food and clothes. Then I'll be on my way."

The old lady smiled, then motioned for Harlette to move. "Go fetch us some tea, would you? There's hot water boiling above the hearth." She grabbed Tvora by the hand before feeling at her shirt. "Come, come. You must be tired, I can feel it in your clothes, all tattered and broken. Let me fix that shirt for you. Actually, Harlette should have a spare. You can have one of hers."

For a long moment Tvora just stood there, unmoving. This woman, she seemed familiar, too familiar. This place, it felt like home. Smaller perhaps, less populated, but as she walked into the makeshift home, she felt safe, like she had back in the orphanage.

*Is this woman not scared? Does she not fear me like everyone else? She should...*

Tvora took a seat and bit down on a dry piece of mutton.

"We don't have much here, but what's ours is yours. Feel free to stay the night if you need. There's a spare bed in the back. It's not very comfortable, but better than being out in the cold, that's for sure."

"Why are you doing this? You don't know me," Tvora said,

deciding to speak for the first time.

The old lady's smile deepened. "Because you are lost dear. I can sense it in you. This place," she continued, "we are all lost here, and we take care of our own."

As she spoke, three children ran in, still wrestling over the ball. One tripped and fell, landing atop Tvora's foot. She rose with a bloody nose.

A second child ran to her defence, pushing back against the younger child with one arm as if sheltering her beneath her wing. Given her frame, she was likely a year or two shy of entering her teenage years, but from her stance... the look in her eye... she would die to protect this child. Straight, black hair covered one side of her face, and she bit back a vicious snarl.

Tvora reached out a weak hand, her mind in a haze, as if she were living in the past. "L — Lucia, is that you?" she said.

The girl stepped back, nose scrunching in confusion.

"Gertrude, that's enough!" the old lady said. "Take Edith and go get her cleaned up. Now, please. Quick, quick!"

The child — Gertrude, slowly turned and ushered Edith into another room.

"I'm sorry about her," the old lady said. "We don't see many visitors here in these parts of the Harrows. And those we do, well, she's just a little protective of Edith."

Tvora blinked, as if waking from a dream. This scene, it was all too familiar. "Thank you," she said. "For your hospitality."

"Nonsense. My name is Emma, though 'old crone' works too, according to my daughter," she finished, inclining her head towards Harlette, who smothered a slight smile as she began emptying and refilling the water pot. "Do you have a name?"

"Tvora."

"Well, Tvora, please stay as long as you like."

"I need to keep moving."

"I understand. But the day is fading. Spend the night, and you can head out in the morning, when it's safe."

Tvora nodded. She didn't know why exactly she had decided to stay here, but her instincts told her these were good people, and good people were a rare sight this deep into the Harrows.

When her tea was finished, Tvora made her way to the bed, only now realising just how tired she was. Come morning, her souls would be fully recovered.

Tvora woke in a panic. Sweat drenched what remained of her clothes. Her breathing came harsh and ragged. She sat up, frantically patting at her exposed chest. Though the external pain had gone, the fractured memory of breaking remained.

She took in a slow breath, steadying her heart. She woke like this every morning, lost and afraid, alone in her torment.

Not for long.

Her friends were here. They were with her. She just needed more time, then they would be complete.

More memories assaulted her, memories she thought had been lost. It was this place. The familiarity. She couldn't remember much of her past. So much history was lost in that single moment where her mind broke, but she remembered enough. She remembered her friends and what they meant to her. For now, that would have to be enough.

She looked to her right to find a freshly washed linen shirt sitting on the table beside her. Tvora stripped herself bare and replaced her tattered shirt with the newer one. Naex and Naev still hung tight at her hips, though she still triple-checked their buckles before moving to leave.

Part of her didn't want to go, but these people, these children, they would be better without her. One way or another she would just wind up getting them killed.

She left without a goodbye, content to put that part of her life behind her. She couldn't go back. The pain was too much. She couldn't go through that again.

When she was a safe distance away from the village, she mentally reached for her soul-cage. The strength of her souls had returned, and she felt her friend's minds touch her own. She grinned, and with a wave of her hand she split the air, opening access to the *otherside*.

Within moments, the image in her mind began to appear. Bone, muscle, and sinew formed, changing from the ghost of a picture into a solidified image, and then into a living creature. Violet flashed into existence, the light temporarily blinding. Tvora closed and then opened her eyes to see Lucia standing there on four legs, staring at her in the form of her chosen spectre. The panther shimmered, and with a spark the connection to Lucia's mind re-established.

"It's good to have you back," she said, genuinely relieved to once again have her friend by her side, to no longer feel alone.

*I see we missed quite a lot*, Lucia said. While Lucia couldn't necessarily speak to her while her spectre was dormant, she could still see and hear everything Tvora could, and could press on her consciousness if she desired.

"That you did," Tvora said. "Hold on. I'll get Cecco and Gowther."

*Gowther won't be coming*, Lucia said, her smooth voice resonating in Tvora's mind.

"What do you mean?"

*He's decided to remain dormant for now, until you're strong enough to sustain us all.*

"Stubborn fool," Tvora spat. "Why does he always have to be so damn noble?"

Lucia made a kind of huffing noise in her mind. *For what it's worth, I stand with you. His selflessness will likely get us all killed one day soon.*

Tvora grimaced, but she had to respect Gowther's decision. She suspected he would answer her call if they had urgent need of him, but for now, she let him sleep.

She reached out with her hands once again and pulled on the power of her souls. Scarlet light flashed as the air rippled and vibrated. Cecco appeared a second later, his hawk spectre soaring into the blue sky as if he had been crafted already in motion.

He flapped radiant wings before turning his hooked beak toward her and landed on her shoulder. His sharp talons scratched at her collarbone, and even though it hurt, she always felt safer with Cecco by her side.

*Ah, this is the life,* the image-hawk said. *The wind in my feathers. No feet to drag me down. No Over-Mother telling me what to do every day. Just bliss.*

Tvora gave Cecco a little pet beneath his chin, which he always seemed to like. Out of all her friends who had become trapped in her mind after she broke, Cecco seemed the most comfortable in his new body.

Gowther mainly just grumbled, agreeing to it more out of necessity than anything else, but Lucia outright hated it. She wanted her old body back, even though she knew it to be impossible, her old form now a burnt-up pile of ashes. She did relish her new strength though. The swipe and jaw-strength of a panther was nothing to be trifled with, and Tvora new she enjoyed a little thrill every time she cut down an enemy with them.

Cecco, however, loved being a hawk.

He launched off her shoulder, zipping around in the morning air currents, taking joy in every moment of it.

*What are we going to do about Carthon?* Lucia said, steering the conversation down a more serious route.

"Do you think it was a real offer?" Tvora said.

*I think someone with as much influence as Carthon wouldn't bother coming all the way out here to play games. He wants us. Sees value in us. I think we need him too. We are nothing in the Harrows. We have nothing. Now we have the chance to be someone, to become a Reaper,* Lucia said.

"Do you understand what that means?" Tvora questioned. "What it truly means to become one of them?"

*I know they're powerful. I know they take what they want, when they want it. Think about it, Tvora. As a Reaper we would be respected, admired even. No longer would we have to hide in the shadows. No longer would we have to pick through the scraps left behind by the war between Mirimar and the Gracelands. We will be part of that war, can feed on their Knights. Do you know how many souls a single Knight of Aen hordes? We could sustain our forms indefinitely.*

Tvora took a deep breath. "I understand, but this man, Carthon... I felt his souls, his energy. It was black. As black as I've seen. I fear... I fear if we go with him, we will lose ourselves, our purpose. I'm not sure. What do you think, Cecco?"

*I agree with Lucia,* Cecco said, causing Tvora to shift back around. *We are lost. The Harrows is a graveyard. There is no meaning here, no life to live. At least with Carthon we will be somebody, somebody important, respected. A Reaper is not a mere servant. They're the most dangerous soul-hunters in Otor. Their reputation alone keeps them safe. We should at least travel to Val Taroth, see if his offer is true.*

Tvora sniffed the air. "Is that smoke?"

As one, Tvora and her friends turned to face where they had just come from. Smoke billowed into the air.

"That's no smoke from a cooking fire," Tvora said. "Cecco, fly over! Tell me what you see."

Without a word, Cecco flew down the mountain path towards

the smoke. Tvora and Lucia followed, running at a sprint.

Cecco flapped his wings to a halt on return. *Tvora... the village... I wouldn't go... It's...*

"What is it? Spit it out!"

*They're all dead.*

Tvora clenched a tight fist around Naex. She drew the forearm-length blade, bared her teeth, then ran for the village.

She charged through the smoke, ready to fight, to kill, to ruin the day of anyone who would dare do such a thing as harm these innocent villagers.

She stopped still, however, when she came across the crumpled form of Edith.

Her tiny arms were pulled tight to her chest, bloodied fingers still clutching the ball she had been playing with when Tvora last saw her.

Her back was a mess. Fresh blood trickled down her shirt from a gaping wound. The body of Gertrude lay just behind Edith, hand reaching for her, trying to protect her even as she took her last breath.

More forms littered the now open playpen. More children. All dead, their souls unable even to travel to the *otherside*, forced to spend eternity in the cage of another human.

Around her, the entire village burned.

Through the smoke, a form appeared. Distant, but visible, walking away. Not running, but walking.

Tvora ran toward it. Hand over her mouth, she charged through the smoke and called out. "Stay where you are, soul-hunter!"

The man slowly turned. He held a long, blood-stained sword with two hands. His face and shirt were also caked in blood. The blood of the innocent. "Well, who do we have here?" he said, eyeing Cecco and Lucia, who were now by her side. "Souls! Hah!

What a lucky day for me. What a lucky day indeed. Lucky, lucky, LUCKY."

"Why did you do this!" Tvora screamed. "These people were innocent! They didn't deserve to die."

The soul-hunter craned his head, and Tvora noticed what looked like a collar around his neck. It wasn't a collar though, it was a tattoo, a series of markings. She knew what they meant. Some hunters liked to mark their kills, to show-off their feats.

"No one *deserves* to die," the soul-hunter said, taking a confident step towards her. "Don't think of it as permanent. They yet live!" he tapped on his chest. "It is more than they could have hoped for, really. What lives could they have led out here? I saved them from their fate. Now they get to watch. More than that, they get to help, to be my fuel, to witness my ascension!"

The crazed man thrust a single arm into the air as if he were in a stage play.

Tvora had heard enough. She had seen this type of man before. They were all the same. All bled red.

Anger blossomed in her chest. Tvora's souls worked as the image of Lucia and Cecco grew, expanded. Together, they rushed the hunter. Tvora ducked as he swung his heavy sword in a horizontal arc. Naex bit into his hamstring as she slid past his non-existent defence.

She emerged on the other side, blade dripping with soul-hunter blood.

The hunter cried out in pain, his earlier confidence shattered. He scrambled to his feet, leaning heavily on his uninjured leg. He reached desperately for his souls, ripping a path to the *otherside* and bringing forth the ghost of an image.

He didn't even have time to solidify it into something usable as Lucia swiped a heavy paw. The markings on his neck turned red as his skin split open. Blood pulsed, gushing from the lethal strike.

Cecco followed up by landing on the hunter's shoulder and pecking at an eyeball. It wasn't needed, the hunter was already about to die, but this man deserved a gruesome death. He deserved to suffer, to feel the same kind of pain as all of his victims had.

Tvora revelled in his death, enjoyed it even. Hundreds of souls poured from his cage and into her own as the last of the life drained from his face. She welcomed them. In a way, she was just as bad as him. She enjoyed killing. Now Edith's soul flowed within her cage. Instead of fuel for this hunter, the innocence of her soul now fuelled Tvora.

Why was the world like this? What deity would allow this kind of torture? Encourage it even.

The world didn't make sense. It was just as fractured as she was. Only the strong survived, And Tvora needed to survive. For her friends. For herself. So, she needed to become stronger.

She saw only one way to obtain such strength, to survive. She needed position. She needed power. She needed someone like Carthon.

# Chapter 9
# - Will -

Will sat in his room. The next day and a half went by in a blur. He tried to accept it, to comprehend what had happened, but every time he thought about the passing, his chest felt like it was splitting in two.

Both his father and his grandfather were going to die.

There was nothing he could do about it, no solution other than to accept the inevitable. The revelation about his mother would forever stain his soul. He looked down at his hands. Hands that had killed her. Whether intentional or not, he had been the one to do it, and now he had to live with the consequences.

For the first time since the voices made themselves known, he listened, truly listened to them. Most were much the same. They wanted control, wanted to be set free, and wouldn't stop hounding him until they got their wish. It made him wonder, was his mother's soul in there somewhere? Could she speak to him? Find him?

He tried to concentrate, to search for her, but there were too many. Isolating a single one seemed an impossible task.

Beyond the thin walls of his lonely room, Will could hear his father pottering around the house. Will couldn't imagine what he must be feeling, to know this was his last day to live.

Will stood on his bed and peered through the window. Several Knights stood guard outside their home. Father wouldn't run away. He was many things, cruel and tough at times, but above it all he was a man ruled by pride.

Will wanted to be angry at him, to hate him for hiding what had really happened from him for the past year, and perhaps he should have been. But in truth, Will was glad for it. He wished he still didn't know. The knowledge tore him up inside, made him want to quit, to throw himself off a cliff just to avoid thinking about it.

The door of his room creaked open, and Will began mentally preparing to face his father, but he was greeted with a friendlier figure.

"Grandpa!"

He leapt down off his bed and ran to the door. He went to wrap his hands around his waist but his head grew light and he began to tilt sideways.

His grandfather's strong grip kept him in place.

"W — what was that?" Will said.

His grandfather pointed a firm finger towards his chest and poked him there. "Your souls are now active. They can sense my own, are drawn to them. Come, sit with me."

He led Will over to the bed and together, they took a seat. His grandfather took stock of the room before settling his attention back on Will. "You're quite the artist, aren't you, boy. Any pictures of me up there?" he said, gesturing to the wall full of Knights.

Will glanced away.

His grandfather simply laughed; a sound Will would miss dearly.

Will averted his gaze again. "Do you hate me?" he said. "For what I did?"

His grandfather went quiet, and Will peered up to see blank eyes that were devoid of more than just colour. He was hurting.

"Of course not, Will," he said after a time. "Your mother, her soul broke. There is no coming back from that. If anyone is to blame, it's myself and your father. We should have seen it coming, noticed the signs. Perhaps then we could have done something."

His hands clenched, and Will reached out a tentative hand of his own. "I don't want you to go. I'll be alone."

His grandfather took a long, steady breath. "I wish it weren't so, but there's nothing to be done. You are to be a Knight, Will. That's what you always wanted, isn't it?"

"I — yes. But, what if I'm not strong enough? What if Rath was right? To be a Knight you need to be a powerful warrior. What if I'm not enough?"

"Rath? Estevan's brat? What in Otor are you listening to him for? He wouldn't know power if I hit him in the face with it."

"I see the way people look at me. They think I'm different, weak, not worth it. A waste of breath."

Will frowned. His grandfather just looked at him and smiled. "So?"

"So? What do you mean 'so'?"

"So what if people think that. You *are* different. So what if you are? If people think you're weak, then prove them wrong. Show them your strength." His grandfather pressed a firm finger into his chest. "You see things others can't even dream of. Your mind is creative beyond my comprehension, your thoughts capable of feats I couldn't even imagine. The proof is in your swordplay. The proof is in your artwork. What do you think Knights do, Will? They create. You were made to become a Knight."

Will felt too stunned to move. Was he right? Was he all of these things?

"But your mind is clouded by fear," his grandfather continued. "By anxiety, and innocence. That doesn't make you weak, but rather leaves you room to grow, to improve.

"It's something I can't teach you. It can only be learned through experience. But you must try, Will. Allow yourself time to grieve, but promise me that you will place what is about to happen to me and your father aside, that you will grow into the man I know you can be."

Will gulped. His first reaction was to shy away, to curl into a ball and return into the depths of his mind, where it was safe. He forced himself to steady, to look his grandfather in the eye. "I'll try. I promise."

The door to his room creaked open, and the shadow of his father slowly began to appear. "Can I have a moment?" he said.

Will's grandfather nodded, squeezed his hand, and then left.

His father walked into the room and sat on his bed. "I'm… I'm sorry Will, for how I treated you. What happened to your mother, it was… It was a tragedy. It ruined me. I wanted to hide it, to pretend it never happened. There were certainly times I blamed you for it, but you weren't to blame. I just wanted you to know that, before my time is up."

Will said nothing. He just sat there and listened.

"You're on your own now," Father continued. "My fate is set. You have your own path to carve. Learn from my mistakes, Will."

Then he left.

Will wanted to speak, to comfort him before he was lost forever, but nothing came. He let him walk away, let him shut the door.

Then Will was alone again.

Moonlight shone bright over the semicircular amphitheatre, bathing the open field below in light. Surrounding the field towered a massive stone structure with high walls and two arched entrances. Rows of delicately carved stone seating rose from the ground all the way up to the tallest tier, upon which Will now sat.

Fixed into the centre of the open field was a raised platform in front of a wooden staircase. Colourful tapestries hung from its rim, blowing wildly in the night breeze.

Inside, Will's stomach churned. His chest expanded. Now that his souls were active, he understood what his grandfather had meant. His souls sensed power, sought it out even.

Gathered down below were the accumulated souls of dozens of Knights, all old and withered, past their prime, with eyes more than likely turning grey like his grandfather's. They sat in neat rows, stalwart even in the face of death.

Around him, people talked, watched, grieved. Beside him, a middle-aged man wearing a black scarf bit into a particularly crunchy apple. Will tried to part the sound from his mind, but the consistent squelching seemed never ending.

Crunch.

Will winced.

Crunch.

Will winced again.

He covered his ears with his hands, hoping that would dull the noise.

It didn't.

Crunch.

Will's arm reacted without rational thought. He turned to his left to see his thumb and index finger around the aggravator's chin, pressing lightly in an upward direction and closing the mouth.

The man's first reaction was to do nothing, but shortly after, his brow knitted and he grabbed Will by the wrist, pushing him off. "Excuse me! Do you mind?" he said, staring at Will in the manner most people did when he did something apparently wrong.

"You're crunching too loud. Please stop," Will said.

Will didn't bother to watch the man's next reaction, returning his focus toward the fields below, though he did notice the crunching stopped.

He wanted them all to go away, all the people. He wanted to say his final goodbyes in peace. But he knew that wouldn't happen.

Knights had travelled from all corners of the Gracelands to participate in the Passing. Accompanying them were dozens of youths just like him, chosen by the church and represented by their lords.

Will counted himself lucky, in a way. Both of his parents were Knights. He had been born into this role, his place in the Passing ensured by the reputation and service of his family, just like Rath and Kalle. Not that it mattered much now. But most of the people down there more than likely had to fight tooth and nail for their opportunity to represent the Gracelands as Knights of Aen.

Will's attention shifted as a chorus of loud chants sounded from his right. All eyes turned as two rows of soldiers marched through the archway. They walked and chanted in sync, arms and legs moving in stiff motions, while their heads refused to turn, focused forward with trained discipline. Flanking the marching soldiers, several bannermen waved flags bearing the sigil of Kastar, a black raven pitched against a sea of white. Once inside the amphitheatre, the two rows split and separated. One half took their place in the open space before the platform next to the elderly, where Will's grandfather and father currently sat. The other half took their place behind the youths chosen to take this year's Passing.

Will's mother had often spoken highly of the Knights in Kastar. Situated on the Gracelands' northern coast, Kastar was prone to raids from pirates and sea-faring soul-hunters. She once told him that this had given the soldiers there a hard edge and a sense of unrivalled discipline born through constant vigilance, for they never knew when and where the pirates would strike next.

Other banners fluttered around the theatre. Will spotted the sigil of the Crimson Wolf, the people of Spree spread beneath it. His eyes widened as they fell upon their commander, Ophelia Redwolf. She stood proud in her metal-studded armour. Strong hands rested upon wide hips as she cast her steely glare over her soldiers.

Will wondered just how many of his childhood heroes were here. Did they all now know who he was, like Thane and Myddrin? Did they all now know his shame?

More soldiers flooded the arena, and it soon reached capacity. Warriors from every corner of the Gracelands had flocked to the capital to either witness or partake in the sacred ritual. He spotted the Iron Lotus banner of Kildeen, the Jade Bear of Sunmire, and even the Golden Tiger of Emberwell.

A man sat next to him then, his head shrouded by a black hood. He stank heavily of smoke and ash. The man made a half-turn towards Will and exhaled a deep sigh. Will recoiled. His breath stank of liquor and fermenting fruit.

Will rapped his beat of five on his chest, unable to concentrate any further due to the irritation of the smoker and the apple eater, who had since resumed his crunching.

He couldn't take it anymore. He rose and made to move to another seat. He stopped still, however, when the smoker lowered his hood.

"D — Doonsla—"

"Don't. Please. Don't call me that. My name is Myddrin," he said, interrupting.

Will sat back down. "I'm sorry, I didn't mean to. It's what everyone calls you."

Myddrin waved a dismissive hand. "It's no matter."

Will stared at Myddrin's coat, still unable to part the smell from his mind. "You smell like fruit and ash. I don't like it," he said.

Will risked a glance towards Myddrin's eyeline and found him to be staring.

"You're a strange fellow, aren't you," Myddrin said.

Will made a kind of half-shrug. He knew sometimes what he said annoyed people, but he couldn't figure out how to stop himself.

"T — thank you," Will decided to say, still not quite believing Myddrin himself sat next to him. "For standing for me during my trial."

Myddrin drew a pipe from his waist pocket, made to spark a light, then stopped himself short. He sighed, then placed the pipe back in his pocket without lighting it.

"You should be thanking my mother," he said. "She told me what happened."

"You mean the old lady from the mountain? I didn't know she was your mother."

Myddrin issued a slow nod. "Molde. The one and only."

"Why are you here?" Will asked. "Next to me, I mean. It's good that you are! I mean, I'm glad to see you, but shouldn't you be down there or something?" Will pointed to the platform where just now a group of well-dressed, assumedly important people began to gather.

Myddrin shrugged. "I wanted to talk to you. You don't remember me, do you?"

"Of course I do. You're the most—"

"I don't mean remember who I am. I mean remember *me*."

The question struck Will as odd, though he thought he gathered his meaning. "I — Yes. You were my teacher when I was little. I remember. You saved us, saved me. I wouldn't forget."

Myddrin issued another of his slow nods, which was beginning to irritate Will more than the smell.

"Are you sure this is a life you want? To be a Knight?" Myddrin said.

Will frowned. "Of course. I want to protect people, like you and your wife did when I was little. Why do you ask?"

Myddrin grunted, then turned his head to the side. "I just want to make sure I made the right choice."

"You think I'm going to die, don't you. You think I'm weak." Will waited for Myddrin to respond, but when he didn't, Will spoke again. "It's okay, I'm used to it. But I'm strong, really strong. I know I don't seem it, but my grandfather says so, and he wouldn't lie to me."

Myddrin squeezed his lips together and scratched at his unkempt beard. Then he rocked backward and laughed. "Very well, I believe you. I trust you know what comes next, then? After... this," he finished, pointing towards the central platform.

Will followed his finger. "You mean after I watch my father and grandfather die?"

Myddrin gasped, then coughed and beat at his chest to try to stifle it. "I'm sorry, that was insensitive of me. You probably don't want to—"

"Why? Why is it insensitive? You aren't the one killing them. You didn't cause this."

"Yes, well... but—"

"I can feel them," Will interrupted, moving his hand to touch Myddrin's vest just above his chest.

"Ah, what?"

"Your souls. I can feel them."

He could. There were so many. His own souls flared inside of his chest. It's like they were banging, scratching, clawing at him from within, trying to escape but finding their attempts in vain.

Now Will understood why they called it a cage.

"They tend to have that effect," Myddrin said, lightly clasping

Will's hand and setting it aside.

"How do you stop them? The voices I mean?" Will asked.

"Didn't your family teach you?"

"They did, yes. I spend an hour every day in meditation. Grandfather taught me how to control my breathing and focus my thoughts. I haven't had much time to practice yet, and the voices are mostly just whispers right now. But you, you have so many. Surely it must be difficult."

"That's good, that you've had some practice already," Myddrin said. "The voices, they're the bane of every mage, and the downfall of many, if they're not careful."

"What do you do? To stop them I mean?"

Myddrin paused, then reached into his pocket and re-drew his pipe. "I smoke. And I drink," he said, fumbling into his other pocket and pulling out a small flask. He unstopped the lid and took a lengthy swig. A red liquid dripped down his chin. He wiped it clean with his sleeve and placed the flask away. "Pain works too, though that's more of a temporary solution, resets the mind in a way."

"And they all work?" Will asked.

"Yes, and also no," Myddrin said. "I don't recommend it."

"Why not? You're the most powerful person in the world. If it will help me to become stronger, then why shouldn't I?"

Will sniffed the air. His nose twisted. He still hated the smell, but if it would help him, then maybe it was worth considering.

"No!" Myddrin snapped. "I — I'm sorry. I shouldn't have told you that. Don't listen to me. Ah, you're a fool Myddrin." Below, torchlight flickered as the surrounding platform lit with radiant light.

"I must go," Myddrin said. "But please, don't listen to me. Follow your grandfather's advice, and you'll be fine. I'll see you around, Will. I'm sorry."

With that he left, leaving Will more confused than when he had come.

A lone figure made his way onto the platform. He raised a single straight arm into the air in a purposeful motion. The crowd stilled.

A black vestment covered the length of the figure's body, marking him as some sort of priest. Draped around his neck was a long strip of fabric. It flowed over his shoulders and down to almost knee-level. Will's eyes fixed onto the intricate patterns woven into the fabric. Twin golden spirals stood out like fire in the night. The symbol of Aen.

Their creator.

God.

The priest lowered his arm and spoke loudly to the now quiet crowd.

"Welcome, all who are loved by Aen, to the Passing. We are blessed this day, to welcome brave Knights both young and old from all corners of the Gracelands.

"We of the church understand that today is a day of pain. It is a day of sacrifice, and one of hardship. But I would ask for you to rejoice! For these brave Knights are what keep us safe, what keep us strong. They sacrifice more than just their lives, they sacrifice the purity of their souls so that we might fight back against those who would seek to destroy us." The priest paused. He seemed well spoken, placing emphasis on all the right words.

"We all know that magic is tainted," the priest continued. "It is foul, a seed born from a jealous god. To touch it is to forever stain one's soul. Aen created the Promised Lands so that we, his creations, might enjoy a peaceful afterlife. When we die, our souls live on in paradise. A world free of sin, free of pain, free of MURDER." The priest's voice changed on that last word. He spoke with slow purpose. "To kill another is to taint not just your own soul, but to condemn your victim's as well. To take another's life is to deny them entry to the *otherside*, to the Promised Lands.

"I say this not to dishearten, but to highlight what these Knights sacrifice. They deny *themselves* entry into the Promised Lands as well. They give up their freedom, all so they might become strong enough to protect what we have. To ensure that we, the citizens of the Gracelands, might one day find peace in the afterlife."

The priest clasped his hands together and lowered his gaze to the cluster of elderly Knights. "I speak now directly to you, brave Knights. The time has come to fulfil your oath. You have served our order faithfully, and have defended our lands with a vigour more than worthy of a place in the afterlife. Unfortunately, this is something I cannot grant you. Your strength is fading. All are eventually consumed by the pull of the dead. You are at an age where your mind and body can no longer sustain the power within. It is here we must say goodbye. We must hope that your spirit lives on through a new generation of Knights, that they may take your place in the defence of our Kingdom. For this, on behalf of all of us, we thank you."

The priest lingered a moment longer, then shuffled his way towards the edge of the platform. New figures emerged then. Some were Knights, clad head to toe in shining armour. They fanned out around the platform, drew their swords, and stood still as statues. Other people dressed in long robes scuttled around. Two rolled out a long mat. Another two brought a small table and placed what seemed like a bottle and two glasses on its top. The last one unsheathed a short sword the length of Will's forearm and placed it on the mat.

A man donning a red cape ascended the staircase and presented himself to the crowd. This man, Will knew. Estevan stood tall and proud. He was dressed in full plate this time, his cape fanning around his shoulders and clipping onto a buckle at his breast, which sat just above the spiral symbol of Aen.

"Kalle Eldric," Estevan's voice called, ringing across the amphitheatre.

Will stood as Kalle rose from the crowd and walked across the clearing. She climbed the staircase and took her place atop the raised platform.

"Sit down, boy!" a voice from behind him sounded, causing Will to jolt back into his seat. He couldn't believe it. Kalle was first?

"Raina Pentbridge."

An elderly lady from the other half of the theatre, a woman of Spree by the red of her garment, rose and took her place on the block beside Kalle. The two exchanged a nod of mutual respect. The lady named Raina placed a soft hand on Kalle's shoulder before she bent to her knees to welcome death.

Estevan stood over the pair. "We thank you, Raina Pentbridge, daughter of Kanan Pentbridge, for all you have done in servitude of our Kingdom.

"Kalle, before you enter our order, I ask that you first take your oath," Estevan said.

Will continued to watch. It was hard to hear, but they spoke loudly so that all might witness.

Kalle nodded and spoke. "I vow to honour this Knight by taking their burden as my own.

"I accept this curse with Aen's blessing, and carry it for the sole purpose of protecting what is good and pure in this world.

"I vow never to use my powers for evil, to uphold the laws of the holy church, and to defend the Gracelands from those who would seek to do wrong.

"When my mind and body become too weak to serve, I vow to pass on my souls to someone worthy, that they may continue the fight against sin."

Estevan moved to the table and poured two glasses of liquid. "If you would please share this holy drink, signifying the beginning of this connection. May Raina's soul protect you and may Aen's light guide you in this new journey together."

Together, Kalle and Raina downed the contents of their glasses, and then Estevan presented Kalle with the sword. Kalle grasped the handle and took in a long breath. Raina opened her chest, arms spread wide, accepting her fate with dignity. Kalle drew the sword back and thrust the point tip first into Raina's heart.

The elderly woman gasped. Her head flung backward. Blood trickled down her shirt. Kalle pulled and the sword came free. Raina dropped to the floor, her lifeless body going limp.

For a long moment, nothing happened. The entire amphitheatre grew still, waiting, expecting.

Then came the light. Thousands of intangible globes of light illuminated the sky. They flowed from Raina and into Kalle like a gust of wind. Kalle's entire body arched. Her head rocked back as the souls of the dead seeped into her cage, filling her with their strength.

The whole process finished in a few short breaths, but its impact was lasting. Will flinched, suddenly glad he didn't have to go through this. One of the robed men rushed over to Kalle, and forced her to drink a milky white substance from a bottle. After Kalle drank, she collapsed.

The gruesome ritual continued for much of the night, growing ever less pleasant to watch. After each Passing, the bodies were carried away and the floor cleaned. Souls transferred over and over. All seemed to blur into one and Will began to feel sick to his stomach, but he forced himself to watch.

His heart wrenched as Estevan called a name he had been

dreading.

"Haylin Harte."

Will's limbs refused to function. He tried to move his hand, to rap his beat of five, but it refused to listen. His mind hadn't even registered the name of the person his father had been paired with, some boy from Kastar.

He watched, numb, as his father rose to take his position. People around him began to mutter and murmur, whispering things Will would rather they had not. He looked at the stone below his feet, suddenly wishing he had replied when his father had spoken to him earlier. Why hadn't he said anything? He was going to die, and Will had said nothing.

The souls inside of his cage chose this moment to rise against him.

*This is your fault*
*You caused this*
*His death is on your hands*
*Let us out*
*We can ease the pain*
*Set us free*

"No!" Will said, louder than he had anticipated.

Those around him stopped and stared, though Will paid them no mind. He focused on his breathing, taking in deep breaths and holding them for five seconds each before releasing. He felt the voices begin to subside and his mind begin to clear.

Then the sword struck.

His whole body tensed as his father took his last breath. His death was swift, souls flowing immediately from his body and into the boy from Kastar.

Just like that, a life ended. Just like that, his father was dead, their family broken.

Will slumped down below the stone bench. Around him,

people continued to stare, but he didn't care. He wrapped both arms around his legs and began to weep.

Rage. Pain. Regret. All consumed him.

"Calder, Silas, Ophelia, Thane, Myddrin.

"Calder, Silas, Ophelia, Thane, Myddrin.

"Calder, Silas, Ophelia, Thane, Myddrin.

"Calder, Silas, Ophelia, Thane, Myddrin.

"Calder, Silas, Ophelia, Thane, Myddrin."

He breathed deeply between each beat of five, fighting his anxiety. He wanted to be strong, had promised he would be. He needed to be.

He rose, taking his place on the bench as the next name was called.

"Rath Torbane."

Will instinctively clenched his fists. His nails bit into the palms of his hands. Why him? Why did he get to be here? He had caused all of this. Will's father might still be alive if not for Rath.

"Gawain Darkmane."

All of Will's hatred collapsed in that instant. His vision faded, replaced by a foggy haze. His eyes clouded with tears as he watched his grandfather rise from his seat and take his place before Rath.

# Chapter 10
## - Myddrin -

"I must insist, sir, that you do not smoke in here," said Abbot Mikel, as he dropped a stack of heavy books on the table.

Myddrin inclined his head, puffed one last ring of smoke, rolled his eyes, and set about hiding his pipe within the confines of his cloak. He looked to Mikel, offered a sarcastic smile, then turned to Mees. "Remind me again why I agreed to stay here?"

"Fire and paper are ancient foes," Mees said. "I suggest you show respect."

"Hah! Now even you're against me. Will I ever be able to smoke in peace again?"

The abbot held back a retort through squeezed lips, then turned to leave.

Dozens of volumes surrounded Myddrin. Scattered on the desk in front of him were piles of age-weathered parchments and scrolls. He palmed his way through hardened and torn paper. Some were still intact, covered only by a thick layer of dust, others were barely serviceable.

The king hadn't been lying when he said Myddrin could have access. He had been fitted in a private room in the castle library, free to come and go as he pleased. The king's scholars worked feverishly to organise and categorise each of the accumulated texts, and they didn't hold back their scowls each time Myddrin interrupted their work by taking a book from their shelves.

Abbot Mikel returned to the room a moment later carrying a cup of tea. He placed it on the table before Myddrin.

Myddrin placed a hand on his brow. His body ached for wine. Without it, the pain and memories would return. His free hand shook as he picked up the cup of tea and downed the contents.

"Perhaps we could speed up this process if you would but tell us what you are looking for?" Mikel said, failing to hide the irritation in his tone.

Myddrin combed a hand through his hair, eyes blinking from exhaustion. "Very well. We are searching for any texts from before the Sundering. We want to know what life was like before the curse of magic tainted this land."

Mikel raised a single, curious brow. "All books from before the Sundering were burned on the decree of the First King. Those that were not, have been lost to the world."

"I am aware," Myddrin said. "But the king told me himself that some were recovered and brought to the capital. So, either you are lying to me, and you really did find some books from before the Sundering, or," Myddrin raised a single finger, "the king lied to me, and there are no such books here. Tell me, which am I more likely to believe?"

Mikel said nothing for a long moment.

"I would appreciate you notifying me if any are found," Myddrin said.

"Of course. We would be happy to comply. Might I suggest first searching what is here. These texts are worth—"

"I know what these texts are worth," Myddrin interrupted. "They are not what I came here for. Now, if you can't help me, I would be left in peace."

Mikel gave a curt half-bow and departed.

Myddrin snorted. "These priests are all the same," he said to Mees. "Their minds are fixed, unable to comprehend change, to accept that the world doesn't always have to be the way they see it."

"You forget that I was once a servant of Aen, Master," Mees said.

Myddrin scoffed. "Don't tell me you're of the same mind as them?"

Mees barely looked up from his book. "I am merely a servant, what does my opinion matter?"

Myddrin lowered his head. "Servant or no, I value your opinion."

"Then you should know that on this, we are of the same mind. Otor will be a better place when all of the dead can rest peacefully. The church may not have brought magic into this world, but they certainly horde enough of it. You need to tread carefully, Master. Especially here. The Knights of Aen may be the ones with the souls, but the church holds the real power, remember that. Our search for an end to magic directly opposes their control of the Gracelands."

Myddrin scratched at his chin. Mees was right. He'd been treading a dangerous line, one he'd only been allowed to walk because of his reputation as the Doonslayer. Did he really want to test how thin that line could become?

He rose, peeked surreptitiously around the frame of the door, then drew his pipe from his pocket. He made to spark a light, then stopped short, his hand shaking.

"What's wrong, Master?" Mees queried.

"I—"

His hands continued to tremble. The pipe fell from his grip, flakes of moss clouding up and staining a rolled up parchment.

"I want to quit. Smoking, I mean. And drinking. They — I want to stop."

Mees looked up from his text. "That's good, Master. What brought this on?"

"I — I was an educator, once. People used to look up to me. I taught children. It was my job to mould their minds, to help them become decent human beings. But last night, I told that boy, Will... I told him what I do to keep the voices at bay, showed him even, and he... he wanted to try it. Without hesitation. He hated the smell, couldn't stand it even, but he was willing to indulge, to do what it took, because I was his hero." Myddrin leaned against the door frame. "Is this who I've become? Is this who I want to be?"

Mees snapped his book shut with an audible thump. "It's not so simple, Master. If what you want is to quit, then of course I will help you, but there is also the matter of your sanity. Your souls will not rest because of a simple change of heart. We must think this through, take the steps required to—"

Mees' voice cut off as a woman slid into the room. A wave of scarlet whipped Myddrin in the face as the woman turned and closed the door with a quiet touch.

"Glade?" Myddrin said.

Glade pressed a finger to her lips and gestured for Myddrin to take a seat.

"Glade, what are you doing here?" Myddrin said as he sat. He averted his gaze, trying not to stare, but he couldn't deny her beauty.

He recoiled as her hand clasped his own. Soft fingers gripped his sweaty palm. He looked up to see big brown eyes searching his own. Even her scent, like lilacs, reminded him of—

"I must be quick, we don't have much time. Mikel will be back soon," she said.

"I — uh, Glade? It's been a long time. You, uh, you look well."

She blushed, red cheeks now complimenting her fiery hair, making her look even more alluring.

Her eyes re-settled on him. Myddrin brushed at his coat, and a couple of peanut crumbs fell to the floor. He straightened and fixed his face into something he hoped resembled his usual, unembarrassed self.

"I see you're on the King's Council now," he said. "Are congratulations in order?"

"A lot can change in ten years," Glade said. "I wish I had the time to reminisce, but for now there is something more pressing you must know."

Myddrin frowned. "What is it?"

Glade bit her lip. She edged closer, as if afraid someone would overhear her. "They are lying to you," she whispered.

"Who?"

"The king. The church. Everyone. These books, they contain nothing. They're just a bunch of old texts to waste your time, to keep you here."

Myddrin spared a glance at the dusty tomes Mikel had just placed on the desk. "So, they're not from Drin?" he asked.

"Oh, they are from Drin. They're just not what you've been searching for."

"And you know this how?"

Glade leaned back and crossed her arms. "It's as you said, I'm on the King's Council. I hear things."

"Okay…" Myddrin said. "But why are you telling us this?"

"Because," Glade responded. She stood, cracked the door open, peeked outside, then closed it again. "Because they're hiding something. Something big. I took this."

Myddrin rose from his seat as Glade withdrew a dusty book from beneath the confines of her cloak. She handed it to him, or rather shoved it into his chest and covered it with his coat.

"Read it," she said. "Alone. Or just the two of you," she finished, acknowledging Mees for the first time. "There might be some answers in there about the origin of magic. Nothing concrete, but I think you can make better use of the information than I can."

"You've read it?"

Glade nodded.

"Won't you get into trouble for taking it?"

"If they find out, sure."

"Right."

Glade made to leave, but Myddrin grabbed her by the arm. When she turned, he released her, afraid he had pressed too hard.

"I—" he stuttered. "Why are you helping me?"

She took a closing step. "Because I want to. I don't know what's happened to you in the past ten years, nor where you've been, but I know you're a good man. I, more than any, know the truth of what happened that day, of how you got your power. Others, like Halvair, may think you're a fraud, but I know that you're a true hero. Not because you took Doonaval's souls, but for what you did before that. You saved me, Myddrin. You saved all those children.

"If you really are searching for a way to end magic for good, then I will do what I can to help."

Myddrin went to speak, to thank her properly, but she had already turned around.

"I was never here," she said as she parted.

Immediately, Myddrin withdrew the book. It had no title, nor much of a cover. He flipped open the blank leather casing. Some of the writing had been blurred, likely due to water damage, but much of the rest seemed readable. The pages were stiff and fragile. Myddrin started to turn another when the door creaked open again.

"More books," Mikel said. The abbot walked into the room carrying eight of the thickest tombs Myddrin had ever seen. The abbot placed them on the table with a loud *thunk*, feigned a smile, and then left.

"We're never going to be able to read in peace here," Myddrin said, slumping back into his chair.

Myddrin waited what he thought was an appropriate amount of time before leaving the library. Hours had passed, yet Glade's book remained unread. He had to wait. He owed her that much.

His head throbbed. It ached for wine, for moss. Sensing his weakness, the voices came to him as he stumbled on tired legs towards his given quarters.

*There you are*
*We found you*
*Let us out*
*You can't do this alone*

As always, the voices started off few, then rose into an indecipherable crescendo of sounds that pounded against his mind like a thousand hammers.

Mees at his heels, he climbed a staircase and kicked open the door to his room. Without even thinking, he drew his pipe and began to light it.

The pipe made it half-way into his mouth before he stopped it. He held it in his hand for a moment, clenched it in his fist nearly tight enough to make it crack, then threw it against the back wall.

"Go away!" he yelled at the voices. "Leave me alone!"

He held his head in his hands before reverting to an old technique. He breathed in deeply, allowing the air to fill his lungs entirely, then released it in one slow exhale. He repeated the process several times, until the voices began to ease. They were still there, and his head still burned like fire, but at least it was something.

He withdrew the book and tried to read. The words jumbled together, his foggy mind unable to process the information on the page. He handed it to Mees. "Read it. I need to rest. When I wake, tell me what I need to know."

Mees took the book without complaint. Myddrin had every intention of reading it himself, but this way at least Mees could summarise its worth before he started.

His wobbly legs took him three steps towards the bed, then gave way. Mees caught him as he collapsed and helped him the rest of the way, his world going black as sleep welcomed him.

Myddrin woke to birds chirping. Sunlight seeped in through a ceiling-height window. He wiped at a sweat-laden face. His nose twitched. He rose to see a tray of warm bread and butter waiting for him. He didn't waste any time before scoffing it down, easing its passing with a cup of water.

He cleared his throat and moved over towards where Mees was still in his chair, sifting through the contents of the book Glade had given them.

The throbbing in his head persisted, and the voices returned, sensing his mind was once again conscious. Worse than the voices, though, were the memories that came. It was this place. Every time he closed his eyes, Ismey was there. He watched her die. Watched the blue sphere vanish into mist. Watched her soul transfer into that monster. Over and over and over.

Myddrin moved to where he had previously hidden a bottle of Kastarian wine, unstopped the lid, and prepared to chug.

"What are you doing, Master?" Mees said, peeking above the book. "I thought you were quitting?"

Myddrin grunted, then set the bottle down. "Get off my back, will you." He eyed the bottle one last time, then sighed and turned to face Mees. "Tell me, does the book hold any worth?"

Mees placed the book on his knees and clasped his hands together. "It's... hard to say. I think so, yes. If the word of this 'Lucio' is to be believed."

"Summarise it for me."

"Well, the book is not quite a book, but rather a journal of sorts. It was written by a man named Lucio Markov and details his life from the years forty-four AS through to fifty-three AS."

"Fifty-three After Sundering? That's the year of the Burning, yes?"

"Correct."

"Then how did his book survive?"

Mees stared at the wall as if he were turning pages in his mind. He had a copy memory, could recall any event in detail since he was a young child, a trait Myddrin often put to good use.

"There is a footnote, at the end of his work." He physically opened the book now, opening it up to the last page.

Myddrin hovered over his shoulder and scanned the contents. "Clever bastard. He wrapped it in a waxed casing and buried it under a tree. How in the world did it end up in the vaults of Drin?"

Mees shrugged. "Your guess is as good as mine, Master. Eight-hundred years is a long time."

"I suppose so. What do his notes have to say?"

"Well," Mees continued. "Lucio claims he was apprenticed to the Mage of the First King of the Gracelands. He was too young to have been alive during the Sundering, but he goes into detail about the battle between the great god brothers Aen and Axel, and how they fought for dominion over both this world and the next. There's nothing too revolutionary in his notes. Most of it we are already familiar with."

"Yes yes. The two gods created man. Aen ruled over the land of the living, while Axel ruled the land of the dead. Axel thought we were broken, wanted to kill us all. The two fought, Axel got in over his head, went kersplatt, but before he passed, he cursed us with this stupid magic we've been viciously fighting over for the past millennium."

Mees raised a single eyebrow at him. "You know, for a scholar, you have a rather stale take on the history of the world."

Myddrin just shrugged. "What else does he have to say?"

"Well, this is where it gets interesting. You see, the current-day church teaches us that Anmendo, the first king, upon his discovery of the transference of souls and the 'abilities' one could acquire through said process, wanted to hide this knowledge. He sought to hold dominion over it, to use it to rule the Gracelands and beyond.

"While this is the generally accepted motivation for the Great Burning, this 'Lucio' speaks of another reason, one not taught by modern day priests."

Myddrin leaned closer, but Mees paused as if something had caught in his throat.

"Go on," Myddrin pressed.

"Well, you see, this is where his tale becomes a little 'far-fetched'."

"All of history is exaggeration and hearsay, until it isn't. I would hear what he has to say and determine for myself if there is any truth to it."

"Very well, Master. Lucio believed that the city of Athedale was," he paused to clear his throat, "was built on-top of the dead body of a god. Axel to be specific."

Myddrin's mouth hung dry. "It can't be. We would be aware, surely."

Mees opened his palms and shrugged his shoulders.

"Give me that," Myddrin said, snatching the book from Mees. He began flipping pages without care.

"That's not all. He says there are souls down there, beneath what we now know as Stonekeep. Thousands of them. Says they are trapped."

"Impossible," Myddrin said, still flipping through pages. "The souls of people who pass naturally from this world are taken to the *otherside*. They live in the Promised Land. Only souls tainted by murder's touch remain within the cage of a human."

"Perhaps," Mees said. "But think about it. We take magic from the *otherside*. We take, ostensibly, from the Promised Land. Wood, stone, sand, steel. We can even take the flesh and bone of animals, mould them to our needs. But never humans. Have you ever heard of a mage crafting the image of a human?"

"Well, no, but if what Lucio says is correct, it would mean there is no Promised Land, or at least if there is, it's blocked to humanity."

Mees nodded. "What it would mean, is that the church has been lying to us."

# Chapter 11
# - Will -

Will traced the patterns of his grandfather's shield. Over and over and over he ran his fingers through the intricate designs etched into its metal surface. Of all the students who took the Passing, why did it have to be Rath who claimed his grandfather's life? The thought of his grandfather's soul dwelling inside of that monster made his stomach churn.

He kept thinking his father would come through the door, scolding him for staying in bed too long, but he never came. He had only his thoughts for company.

They were all gone.

Will was alone.

He didn't know where to go from here. Only the Knights remained.

He flipped open his sketchbook and searched for his special page. He brushed a finger against the charcoal drawing. His mother stared at him in all her beauty.

It was a good drawing, one of his best, sketched two years prior. She had posed for it, asked him to make it. Will had refused, initially. He remembered grunting and moaning at her, telling her he had better things to do. But she had been stubborn, his mother. A trait he had inherited, unfortunately.

Now though, Will found himself so glad to have drawn it, for it was all he had left of her.

He tucked it away and began to gather himself. He pulled his legs out of the comfort of his bed, got dressed, and began walking, one slow step at a time, towards the initiation.

He took the shield with him, hugging it to his chest, unable to let the memory of his grandfather go.

His legs grew numb as he walked. They moved, but they felt disconnected, as if he shouldn't be wasting time with the effort of moving them. He should be grieving. Why was he moving when he should be grieving?

Because he had promised. Promised he would put their deaths aside, become the man he was supposed to be. Why then was it so hard? Why could he not part them from his thoughts?

After walking up the city's incline for who knew how long, Will looked up, his mind forced to make a conscious decision.

The Mage-Way towered over him like a giant bridge. Large, circular pillars lined both sides of the structure, and Will could see the flat stone underneath. At this particular point, the bridge split into three separate paths. If he continued straight, he would end up at the keep. The path to the left led to the church, and the right led to the garrison.

Will turned right. You needed permission to travel atop the Mage-Way, so he was forced to trudge on beneath it, meandering around the various obstacles in his way, be they houses, trees, or people.

Eventually, the overhanging walkway levelled out, and Will made his way over to where two metal-plated soldiers guarded the path beneath a huge archway. He clutched his shield closer to his chest and moved to pass through. He was expecting them to stop him, to at least ask who he was, but he kept walking and no such question came.

A large building greeted him upon entry. Will pushed open the door and immediately wanted to turn back and run.

Dozens of people his age were spread out across a small, oval field. Some sparred, their feet dancing as practice swords clashed.

Others huddled together in groups, mingling. Will recognised most of them from the Passing.

He walked onto the oval, not quite sure what to do with himself. Not a single soul failed to notice him as he strolled onto the grassy soil. Those sparring dropped their swords. Those in conversation ceased, instead whispering softly into the ear of the closest person before standing there idly. Everyone had heard his tale, and any who hadn't were surely being informed. He couldn't hear them, but he knew what they were saying – that he shouldn't be here. How could they trust someone like him?

Will ignored them and bowed his head low.

Everybody seemed to have already formed their own social groups, gathering in clusters of three to five. Will walked past a couple of them, but all shied away, turning their heads as if his presence was poison.

As he stared at his feet, the rough grating of boots on dirt caught his attention. Will turned to see Rath standing next to him, looking smug in his leather tunic. A crowd of three stood behind him, blocking out the sun.

"What a waste of magic," he said with a derisive snort.

Will looked up from his shield. "What do you mean? How can someone waste magic?"

Rath laughed, then broke away from his group to take a step closer to Will. "Not someone, you. You're a waste of magic. You shouldn't be here, kin-killer," he said, spitting on the grass at Will's feet.

Will felt the energy of his souls stir within.

*Kill him,* one whispered.

*Take his souls*

*He stole from you*

*Took him from you*

*Take back what's yours*

*Let us out and we can help you*

Will flinched and took a step back. "Leave me alone, Rath." He turned, slung the shield over his back, and began to walk away.

"That shield," Rath said. "It was your grandfather's, no?"

Will stopped.

"Ha! I knew it," Rath shouted. "He speaks to me, you know."

"That's a lie!" Will said, turning. "He would never."

"He's nothing more than fuel now, destined to feed me power for the rest of his existence. I was hoping to be matched with him, you know."

Will rapped his beat of five on his leg and began whispering the names of his favourite Knights.

Rath only laughed in his face. "This again. I saw you doing it at the trial. You're weak, Will. This order, it's only for the strong. You have no idea what's outside those walls. Having someone like you fighting by our side will only get us killed. Your grandfather would be—"

"Shut up!"

Will looked up to see Rath on the back-foot. He quickly straightened, however.

"What was that?"

"I said shut up! You don't know anything. You're the weak one, using words to put people down. There's no strength in that."

Rath bit hard into his lip. The people behind him covered their mouths with their hands. One slapped Rath playfully on the shoulder, but he quickly brushed it off and closed the gap between him and Will.

"Watch your mouth, kin-killer." He was close enough now that Will could smell fish on his breath. "You killed your own mother. Who does that? Then your father covered it up. He deserved what he got. You whole family deserved—"

Will's world went blank. His body moved on its own. He angled his head back and quickly thrust it forward. Bone crunched and blood spattered.

Rath reared, holding his nose with one hand.

Will drew a series of heavy breaths. All he could see was red. All he could think about was the hatred he had for Rath. How could someone be so cruel? As far as Will was concerned, in this moment Rath was responsible for it all.

Rath raised a fist and swung at him.

Will's body reacted on reflex. His mind recognised the pattern immediately. Rath's arm had pulled back too far, and the angle of his fist was too low. Will lowered his centre of gravity and shifted his torso to the right. As predicted, Rath's punch met empty air.

Will countered, thrusting a closed fist into Rath's exposed stomach.

A crowd had gathered, though to Will they were mostly just blurred shapes. He thought he heard laughter, and assumed they were making fun of him again.

Rath doubled over and gasped. He rose soon after, his mouth frothing with spittle and blood. Dark eyebrows knit, and the leaf shaped scar around his eye crinkled.

Will didn't give him the chance to recover. His body moved on its own, his rage encouraged by his inner voices, his movements honed through years of training and pattern recognition. He threw a right hook that smashed Rath right on top of the scar. Will followed it with another strike to his mid-section. Rath tried to counter, but Will knew his movements even before he made them.

Blood trickled from Rath's chin as Will struck again. He felt a weight around his arms, then he was dragged backwards by unseen assailants. He shrugged them off, slipping past one and pulling at the arm of another to launch them over his shoulder.

*Yes!* he heard an inner voice say.

Will's gaze settled back onto a dizzy Rath.

*Use us*

*Take from the otherside*

*Kill him*

Will's chest began to flare. He ran at Rath, no longer in control of his body. Rath had to pay. He couldn't get away with what he'd said about his family. There needed to be consequences.

Suddenly, he crashed into something hard. He bounced backward, head ringing from the unexpected impact. He looked up to see Rath through a vibrant blue wall of translucent energy that had emerged before him. It stretched the width of the circle made by the gathered crowd, rising twice as tall as Rath at full stretch.

"Enough!" a voice bellowed, silencing everyone.

A figure emerged as the blue image-wall vanished into mist. Estevan towered above them all, casting his scowl over Will and then Rath as he knelt helpless on the ground.

"What is this madness?" Estevan said. "The Gracelands are a place of peace. The Knights are a symbol of strength and prosperity. I will not have our name sullied by two apprentices."

"But Father, he—"

"Be silent when I am speaking!" Estevan said, thrusting an arm toward his son. "You shame me. A Knight must become a master of their emotions. You think you know the world? You know nothing!"

Will's mind began to calm as he forced himself to take deep breaths. The magic within his cage subsided, and he hoped no one had seen what he had been about to do.

Estevan straightened, wiped his cloak clean of dust, and took a steadying breath. "As for the rest of you, I expect this display to be the last. You are not each other's enemy. The real enemy is out there," he gestured in the direction of the Harrows. "Do not expect that just because you have taken the Passing you are ready. I assure you, you are not. Your mentors are waiting, follow me and we shall get started."

He took one last look at the dishevelled form of Rath and turned to leave.

Will stayed behind a moment as forms moved past, purposefully avoiding him. He looked down to his bloody fist. Was this who he was?

It wasn't the first time Will had lost his temper. It used to happen all the time when he was little. His mother had thought that with time his anger would dissipate, but lately he found himself becoming more and more frustrated, with no outlet for his rage.

He focused on his breathing, a trick his grandfather had coached him through over and over and over again. It certainly helped, but only if Will consciously thought about it. When he was finally calm enough, he decided to follow Estevan's crimson cape like the rest of them.

They were led through a large set of double doors and into an adjacent building beyond. They walked a set of narrow corridors ending in a wide, vaulted room. It looked like a monastery. Stone columns rose from the hardwood floorboards. At least fifty chairs were placed around the overly large room, lined up perfectly before a raised platform.

Estevan gestured for the students to take their seats, and they did so. Will placed himself on the opposite side of the room from Rath, whose nose was still caked in blood.

Estevan stood atop the platform, and at his signal the rear doors swung open, an assortment of Knights walking through them. Will gasped. These weren't just Knights; these were some of the most prestigious Knights in all of the Gracelands. They oozed experience. There had to be at least fifty of them.

Will spotted both Thane and Ophelia among their ranks. He wondered if he would have the chance to meet them. He had so many questions, having followed their careers since he was old enough to walk and talk. A thought struck him, his earlier rage steadily replaced by a layer of excitement. What if they chose him to be their student?

He quickly quashed the idea though, remembering his circumstances. He hadn't even taken the Passing. Why would they want someone like him as their student? Why would anyone want him?

Estevan raised a hand for silence. "Welcome, apprentice Knights. You may believe yourselves already powerful. In a sense this is true, but believe me when I say that raw power is nothing without control. We will teach you how to use the magic gifted to you by those who gave their lives to ensure the future of the Gracelands is a bright one. I implore you, do not waste this gift, for we will not hesitate to take it away if we deem it necessary. If you fail to meet expectations, or your mentor judges you unfit to hold such a vast amount of power, you will be put to death, and your souls given to another."

He paused, giving time for his last few words to sink in.

"You may think this harsh," Estevan continued, "but we are not in the business of wasting souls. The magic you now have within your soul-cage has been accumulated over centuries. Each generation becomes more powerful than the last. Do not waste this chance.

"The Knights behind me will each take on a single apprentice. Once chosen, your mentor will be your instructor and sole confidant. They will make sure you have all the tools necessary to become a full member of our order. Only once they are satisfied may you truly become one of us, and begin to take contracts of your own. For some, this can take as little as a year. For others, much longer.

"You may occasionally be required to attend group excursions, though all of this information will be relayed to you at a further date. I will now take my leave and allow time for my Knights to choose their apprentices."

The apprentice Knights erupted into a frenzy of whispered conversations. They were soon hushed, however. The platform shook as the bulky Knight known as Thane walked up to the podium.

"Rath Torbane," he said.

For a long moment nothing happened. The room grew silent. Then, slowly, Rath rose to his feet and walked over towards Thane.

Will's nails bit into his palms at the thought of Rath being paired with one of the most powerful Knights in the Gracelands, but there was nothing he could do about it. He watched in silence as more names were called, each respective apprentice standing and taking their place behind their new mentor. The numbers thinned quickly, making him wonder if he would even get picked. Eventually, only three remained. Will surveyed the platform. Three Knights still stood without apprentices, meaning everyone would be given to someone.

He breathed a sigh of relief, though his throat tightened again as a lady made her way to the centre of the platform. She was tall, slender, and her eyelids were lined with dark paint, making the violet within pop as they stared into the emptying hall. A broad smile stretched the length of her cheeks and she practically skipped along the platform.

"Will Harte," she called out.

A sigh of overwhelming relief left Will's lips as he moved to take his place by the side of this mysterious woman. She smiled at him, black lipstick stretching high into her cheeks. "Welcome, Will. My name is Crisalli."

# Chapter 12
## - Tvora -

Black clouds hung above the city of Tal Varoth, blending in with the black stone walls that rose high into the sky, blanketing the surrounding plain in shadow.

Lucia and Cecco by her side, Tvora descended the great mound of earth leading towards the thick iron gates. Tal Varoth was set between two mountains, carved into the middle like an impenetrable fortress of rock and stone. A moat surrounded the city's base, stretching as far as her eyes could see to both the east and west. She looked down at the murky water below, grimacing as the stench of what could only be dead flesh filtered up to her nostrils. A drawbridge lowered, and faces appeared on the crenelated battlements above. She held her nose as she walked past a pike tied to the railing before the archway.

Impaled atop the pike sat the severed head of a man. His face was fixed into a wide-mouthed scream, his eye-sockets picked clean by scavenging birds.

*That is the head of Tashir Stormwater,* Cecco said from his perch atop her shoulder. *I recognise him from my studies. Did you know, there is a theory that speaks of a man still being conscious up to thirty heartbeats after losing his head? Can you believe it, thirty heartbeats! That is why heads often have such angry expressions when they finally pass, they seek retribution even after death.*

Tvora ran a hand over his smooth feathers. "No need to be nervous, Cecco, we can handle whatever lies within these walls."

Together, they made their way through the high archway of

the front gate without hindrance.

She was quickly reminded why she hated cities. People stared at her as if she had the black death. Those who weren't caught up in the magic of her companions made themselves scarce, barring doors and shutting windows.

"Seems we are not welcome here," Tvora whispered to Lucia.

*Don't fret,* the panther said. *Tal Varoth has been a victim of more than one usurping. It's no wonder they fear magic.*

"Then why live here?"

*Where else would they go?* Lucia said, turning her head to face Tvora. *There is no safe place in all of Otor. At least here they have a wall to protect them against the outside world. They need only worry about what ventures within.*

Tvora frowned, walking past an alley where a boy poured what could only be piss and shit from a bucket down a drain. She didn't know where she was going, but if this 'Carthon' was emperor, then she assumed he would place himself inside the giant, black stone keep at the highest point of the city.

Tvora was used to walking, it was all she had ever known, even as a child. She had fragmented memories of the matron of the orphanage using her as a runner to give and receive messages to the more distant parts of the village, so the climb up the stone-carved stairs of the mountain gave her little trouble.

The open cage inside of her shirt continued to pulse. The sensation was like a constant push and pull. The souls within wanted release, wanted to enter her mind. She couldn't hear them anymore, her friends blocked them out, but she could feel their need. If she wasn't careful, they would consume her. She couldn't let that happen, not again. The only answer was to find more, to feed her friends, to keep them strong. That way they could fight them together. It seemed a double-edged sword, but it was her only option.

The black keep towered over the wide city below. No guards were posted, no escort was given. She simply walked through the front door and into a large room. Several corridors sprouted off in different directions, each as lengthy and empty as the last. She thought of shouting a greeting and listening as her voice echoed through the castle, but she had been invited. If Carthon truly wanted her to join him, he would come to her.

Twin staircases lined the outskirts of the room, curling around the edges of the structure and joining as one at a balcony in the centre. Cecco flapped his wings in warning as Tvora's head snapped to its wooden railing. A hooded figure sat atop it, legs dangling over the edge. She cursed inwardly for not noticing the figure's presence before.

Her hand inched toward Naev, fingers caressing the hilt. "Who goes there?" she said, eyes narrowing.

The figure lifted itself off the railing and moved down the staircase, hooded gaze fixed on Lucia and Cecco beside her. Her first thought was that it was Carthon, but its features were too slim, its movements too rigid.

"Remarkable," the person said, rounding the wooden stump at the bottom of the stairs and stalking towards her.

He bent down to where Lucia sat, the panther's deep snarl only audible in her own mind.

"Don't touch her!" Tvora said, half-drawing Naev from its sheath.

The figure withdrew a gangly hand, moving backward with a loose-jointed awkwardness. "You must be Tvora," the figure said, drawing back its hood. He was male, and pale as the moon. His skin looked flaky, as if it might fall off with a light scrub. His angular smile stretched wide, too wide. It made Tvora cringe just looking at it.

"I'm here under invitation from Carthon. Is he here?" Tvora

asked.

The strange man seemed more interested in Lucia, bending down to a crouch. Lucia retreated, curling around her leg in a protective curve.

"This, this is perfection!" The man said. "The movement, the texture, the weight. I have never seen such a complex image as complete as this. And your bird, it shines scarlet, while your panther shines violet. Usually, a mage is fixed to one colour, the colour of the host's soul and eyes, but yours shines with a second."

Tvora winced. She didn't quite know how to react to this strange man, nor whether he was friend or foe.

"She is magnificent. I must admit I didn't believe the rumours about you. A child killing the soul-hunter responsible for destroying her village is hard enough to believe. Then to reclaim your sanity after breaking from the strain? It is unheard of. But now that I see you in the flesh, perhaps the rumours are proven true. Your eyes do not lie."

Tvora's grip on Naev relaxed.

"Mantis!" came a shout from the top of the staircase. "Step away from our guest. She isn't a specimen for your research."

Another man walked down the stairs. He was huge, larger even than Carthon. He seemed to have forgotten to wear a shirt. His rounded pectorals sat like twin barrels on his chest. He wore tight leather pants, and a silver sword dangled from a buckle at his waist.

Mantis moaned. He rolled his eyes and fixed his mouth into a fake smile, turning toward the newcomer. "Ahh, Glock, always one to ruin my fun. Don't you have some important battle to lead? Knights of Aen to kill?"

The man named Glock harrumphed. "The Knights in Drin fled. Got myself a reward though."

Tvora hadn't noticed it before, but Glock had been holding a brown sack in his hands. He reached into the sack and withdrew a severed head. He threw it onto the ground before her and Mantis.

"My my!" Mantis said, bending over to study it. "Is that Calder?"

"It *was* Calder," Glock said. "Now it's just his head."

"You seem awfully proud of yourself. Calder is quite the prize indeed. One of the Knights' prized pets. You might be strong enough to rival even Carthon now, if it was indeed you who struck the killing blow."

Glock merely grunted.

"I was just welcoming our guest here, before your brutish presence ruined the mood," Mantis continued.

Glock had made his way down the stairs now. He walked up behind Mantis, stopping briefly to admire Lucia's form before settling on Tvora. He had curled locks of blonde hair so bright it was almost blinding. "Welcome, Tvora Soul-Broken, to Tal Varoth."

Tvora grimaced.

"My name is Glock, and this here is Mantis. We are the emperor's Reapers."

Tvora snorted. "Is this it? Just the two of you?"

Glock cleared his throat with a laugh. "No. There are three of us in total, four if Lord Carthon decides you are to be the fourth."

"I didn't come here to be put on trial," Tvora said.

Glock smiled. Tvora actually found him quite handsome. "You are not in the Gracelands. There are no trials here. You simply are, or you are not."

Lucia hunched her shoulders, making her look even bigger than she actually was.

"And if I'm not?" Tvora said.

Glock slowly drew his silver sword from its scabbard. A sharp ring resonated around the hall. He pressed the flat against his lips and closed his eyes. He seemed almost in prayer, whispering inaudible sounds into the blade.

His eyes came alight with a pop of colour, as if he had just woken from a deep sleep. "Galvandier believes you are to become one of us, and I'm not one to argue."

Tvora scrunched her brow. Maybe she did belong here after all.

Glock turned and waved. "Come, I'll take you to our lord."

She followed Glock and Mantis through a series of winding corridors, eventually coming to a stop outside a thick wooden door. Glock pushed it open, his muscles tightening with the effort.

Together, they walked into an open room, lit with dozens of flickering tallow candles and oil lamps. At its centre was a large throne made up entirely of human skulls. Tvora stared into the empty eye sockets, wondering if she had made a mistake coming here, if her skull would be the next added to this throne. She hardened her stance. She wouldn't let that happen.

Resting leisurely on the throne was Carthon, deep in conversation with another figure.

A dark energy filled the room as the embodiment of hundreds of thousands of souls met, screaming at each other in greeting and in warning. Despite the nature of the people in the room, Carthon seemed composed. He moved with slow gestures, each action purposeful and languid, not a hint of concern in his posture.

Glock coughed, and Carthon's attention turned away from his conversation and toward her.

"You're late," he said, plucking a baby tomato from a plate beside him and shoving it into his mouth.

Tvora said nothing. She would not be intimidated, no matter how powerful these men were.

The man beside Carthon glowered at her, his hateful scowl biting into her side with malicious intent. Long, damp hair ran down to his cheeks, framing an angular face with dark, ruby coloured eyes. "She doesn't belong here, my lord. She's an outsider. She can't be trusted with our title," he said, lacing each word with menace.

Carthon held up a hand. "Be quiet, Septus. Tvora is special, and she will be treated as such."

The man named Septus grit his teeth but made no comment. His face twitched, and despite being able to speak coherently, he looked on edge, as if he might burst into a fit of rage at any given moment.

Tvora shouldn't have been surprised at the make-up of the room, no single person could gather such a collection of souls and keep their sanity. She need only look at herself as an example.

Carthon rose from his throne and walked toward her, huge, booted feet cracking skulls with each step. His forearms were the size of Tvora's thighs. He carried with him no weapons, though that quickly changed as he pulled from the *otherside* without even breaking stride.

A long, black sword materialised from thin air. His control over his magic seemed unrivalled. Even Tvora had to strain every time she called her friends' spectres from that plane of existence.

"Kneel," Carthon said, pointing the tip of his conjured sword at her.

Tvora hesitated. Around her, Lucia's paw took a step forward. To Carthon's credit, he didn't waver.

"This is why you have come here, yes? To become one of my Reapers? To swear fealty to me?" Carthon said.

Tvora's eyes narrowed. Despite her better judgement, she drew Naex and slapped the black of Carthon's blade away. "I'm no one's slave. I'm my own master."

Part of her yearned for a fight, for Carthon to be offended, to strike at her, but she knew he wouldn't.

Instead, he lowered the blade and laughed. It was a deep cackle of mirth. A laugh of mutual respect.

"Good!" he said. "We are no Knights of Aen. We do not serve. We take. What we want, and when we want it. Tell me, Tvora, what is it you want? What do you desire most in this world?"

Tvora didn't answer. She wasn't about to reveal her secrets, though she had a sinking suspicion this man already knew them.

"Do you want respect? Position? Acknowledgement? Fame?"

Tvora's foot shifted, and her jaw clenched.

"No," Carthon continued. "None of that matters to you, does it. You want only one thing. You need only one thing. Power.

"It burns in your soul. You crave it, are consumed by the desire. And you shall have it. My gift to you. The opportunity to take back what this forsaken world has ripped from you. Become one of my Reapers. Take what is rightfully yours. Join us, and you shall have what you desire and more."

Tvora shivered. Her breathing doubled. This man, this beast… despite barely knowing her, he could speak her heart. She couldn't deny the truth. She wanted more souls. No, she needed more souls, for her friends' sake. There was only one response to give.

"I accept."

# Chapter 13
# - Myddrin -

Myddrin palmed through Lucio's journal for the fourth time in one day. He reached for a bottle to his right and tried to take a swig.

It came up empty, and he tossed it aside with a sigh.

He couldn't even stay sober for one day. Not a single one.

His mind had grown foggy, and his movements were disjointed, but in this moment he didn't care. His work was too important.

Mees. Where was Mees? He had to see Mees. Mees would help. Mees would know what to do.

"Mees!" he said, looking up to see the helpful Hand entering the room. "There you are!"

Mees wore a hardened scowl. He stared down at him, hands on hips. "Have you been drinking? What happened to quitting? You told me yesterday you wanted to stop, because of the boy."

Myddrin held up a hand and pressed his forefinger together with his thumb. "Just a smidge. This is important research. Yes, very important research," he said, pausing afterward to hiccup.

Mees walked over to the bottle and lifted it up. "Since when does a 'smidge' consist of an entire bottle of vintage Kastarian wine?"

"It was a big smidge," Myddrin said, shrugging his shoulders. "You're not my father, get off my back, would you." He returned his attention to the journal. "You were right, Mees, they're lying to us. Lying they are. The church. Hiding things, secret things." He paused to hiccup again. "What should we do?"

Mees sighed. "There's not much we can do. If you storm into the cathedral screaming heresy, they'll put you in a cell quicker than you can down another cup of wine."

Myddrin smiled. "You underestimate me, Mees. The king!" he shouted, shifting topics. "I must see the king. He will know what to do. Wait. Does he know already? Hm…"

Myddrin tugged at a silver strand of his beard.

"That's a terrible idea," Mees said. "If the king is privy to such knowledge, then it means he is colluding with the church on this cover-up—"

"The king! Let's go see him Mees."

Myddrin rose, tucked Lucio's journal into his cloak, and was already halfway out the door when Mees shouted something over his shoulder.

"Myddrin, you can't go and see the king now! You're drun—"

His voice cut out as the door closed behind him.

Myddrin stumbled his way through Stonekeep. He heard Mees scuttling along behind, though he paid him little regard. He had to see the king, had to do something. He was sick of doing nothing, of running into dead ends.

He rounded a corner without looking. His foot hit something hard, and Myddrin tumbled over. He rolled several times, moaning as he went. He arched his back and placed a hand over a sore spot.

"What in the — you!"

Myddrin tried to rise. His back felt like it was on fire. He lifted his head to see long silver hair surrounding an oval-shaped face with a short, flat nose and thin lips.

Myddrin laughed to himself as the man's features began to blur together. He shook his head clear and rose fully to his feet.

"Halvair. Nice to see you," he said, lacing his words with what he hoped sounded like sarcasm.

Halvair leaned forward and sniffed him, causing Myddrin to recoil. The silver-haired Knight scoffed. "Drunk, again. Typical. Go home, Myddrin, and I don't mean to your room. Go home to your island. Return to your hole and don't come back. You're not needed here."

Myddrin sucked in some air. "That's not what the king thinks," he said.

"You're nothing but a drunken fool. A thief, and a waste of souls."

Myddrin patted at his cloak and attempted to straighten his back. "Why do you still hate me Halvair? The past is the past. We can't change it."

A thick vein appeared above Halvair's left brow, the only blemish on an otherwise picture-perfect face.

"The past is a lie. A lie you continue to live," he said. "You may have everyone else here fooled, but you and I know the truth. You're nothing but a simple schoolteacher who happened to fall upon a mountain of gold."

"And what would you have had me do, hm? Kill myself? Submit to your sword? What's done is done. There's no changing it, no going back in time. You don't…" A wave of dizziness overcame him, and he nearly lost his footing. He steadied. "You don't want what I have. It's not a blessing. No one should 'want' this. I want to end it. All of it."

"And what then?" Halvair said. "Say you manage to put an end to magic. What happens next? The armies of Mirimar outnumber us five to one. The Skull Thrones have united. The Knights of Aen are the only defence we have against them. Our strength of soul is all that protects us. You think war will end if our ability to touch the *otherside* fades?

"Magic was born because of humanity's insatiable lust for war. Taking it away won't fix that, it will only lead us to ruin."

Myddrin fixed Halvair with an intense glare. "What if you found out there's no afterlife?"

Halvair arched a confused brow.

"What if you found out everything is a lie?" Myddrin continued. "That there is no Promised Land. That every living soul, whether their death be natural or through the actions of another, is trapped here, never to leave. Never to find peace."

Halvair shook his head in disgust. "You speak in riddles. It seems drink has made you delusional. I'll say it again, go home Myddrin, for the good of us all."

"What goes on here?" came another voice. Myddrin turned to see King Anders standing crownless in the hall. He wore an elaborate maroon robe and nothing else. His feet were bare, his hair a tangle of brown curls.

When no one answered, Remen continued. "Well? Explain yourselves. I can hear the racket of your argument from my chambers, and if I can, I'm sure my daughter can too. She's just in there practising her letters." He gestured to a door right next to them.

"Myddrin was just leaving," Halvair said, fixing Myddrin with one of his steely glares.

"M — My king," Myddrin stuttered. He blinked through tired eyes, suddenly wishing he'd listened to Mees and not had so much to drink. He lowered his voice to a whisper "I've found something, something important."

Myddrin reached from within his cloak and pulled out Lucio's journal.

The king took a few shuffled steps forward, and Halvair bit his tongue.

"What is it?" King Anders asked.

"It's a journal, from before the Burning," Myddrin said.

The king's eyes immediately went wide.

"It speaks of a place, right here, beneath Stonekeep. The author, he was apprenticed to the Mage of the First King. He says things, terrible things. Speaks of a well. A prison. He says that the passage to the Promised Land is blocked, that Axel's curse prevents us from entering."

The king rushed forward. "Where did you get this?" he snapped.

Myddrin gulped. "It was in the pile of books… the ones from Drin."

Myddrin paused. He had a growing suspicion Remen knew everything. No. He was certain. Even with a full bottle of wine rushing to his head, Myddrin knew the look of a guilty man.

Remen fixed his face into a forced smile. "Halvair, would you leave us please."

"My lord, I don't think that's wise."

"I said leave us!"

Halvair's lip twisted. For a moment Myddrin thought he might strike at him, but he bit back whatever retort he was formulating and bowed his head low before departing, leaving Myddrin alone with the king.

Myddrin stretched his head around lazily to search for Mees, though the Hand had made himself scarce.

When he turned back around, he immediately jumped.

Remen pressed close, his pretend smile replaced by a fierce scowl. "Where did you really get this?"

Myddrin scratched his head. "I told you, the collection from Drin."

The king's eyes thinned into slits. "I don't know what you think you know, but—"

"It's true, isn't it," Myddrin said. He took a step back,

realising he had interrupted a king. Then he retraced his step, standing tall. Maybe it was the alcohol speaking, but Myddrin didn't care anymore. He needed to know the truth, needed to understand the true nature of the magic which had plagued this land for the better part of a thousand years. Maybe then he could figure out how to end it. Maybe then his wife could rest in peace.

The king hesitated. His aggressive demeanour faded with a sigh. He looked over his shoulder, then back to Myddrin. "Not here," he said. "Follow me."

He led Myddrin down the hall and into his personal quarters. A brightly lit room greeted him. The drapes were open, and Myddrin could see the tightly packed houses of the West Quarter of Athedale beyond the balcony.

He gestured for Myddrin to take a seat, then he paced the length of the room. One hand covered his mouth, the other fidgeted nervously.

Myddrin went to sit, but his chest suddenly tightened. He panicked, thinking his souls were readying another assault.

No.

Not here.

Not now.

His chest expanded, and he prepared his mental defences. Then he exhaled, and a loud, obnoxious burp came out. He covered his mouth, looking up to see the king still pacing the room, somehow oblivious to his misdemeanour. Myddrin relaxed and his panic subsided. His chest no longer pained him, and he felt much better for it.

The king turned to him. "What does the book say?" he asked.

Myddrin summed it up for him. Remen took in the information with a kind of stoic indignation. If any of the knowledge surprised him at all, he didn't show it.

"I see," he said when Myddrin finished.

"Where is it?" Myddrin asked, not giving him time to deny the revelation. "I want to see it. I *must* see it."

Remen's first reaction was to make himself seem taller. He squared his shoulders, hardened his expression, and took a closing step towards Myddrin.

Then something changed. His shoulders slumped. His face slackened, and he sunk into the chair beside him. He seemed almost... relieved?

"You don't know how long I've had to hold this," he said. "The Promised Land," he paused to laugh. "A lie. There is no afterlife. Just a prison."

Myddrin leaned back in his chair. He felt as though he had just been kicked in the guts by a horse. "The people need to know, Remen. They need to know their life is a lie."

"No!" the king exclaimed. "You must promise me you won't speak a word of this to anyone."

"It's not fair. People need to know that their lost loved ones aren't at peace. They need to know —"

"They need to know what?" Remen interrupted. "That there is no hope? That they're all as affected by Axel's curse as the Knights are? Why? Why should we subject them to that knowledge? What good would it do? Doesn't the threat from Mirimar already cause enough fear in their hearts? They don't need to fear a simple death as well. Tell me you understand this, Myddrin."

Myddrin paused. The king was right. It wouldn't help. "I understand," he said, dejected. "But there must be something we can do. This could be good. If there is indeed a well full of hundreds of thousands of souls beneath this city, we could use this information. We could find a way to reset the world, end this curse for good."

Remen shook his head vigorously. "You don't understand.

The well is sacred. Even I have only seen it once in my life. The church has kept this secret for hundreds of years. Not even the Knights of Aen know the truth."

"Then do something about it, change the future. Aen's balls you're the king! You have the power."

"Watch your tongue, Myddrin!" Remen snapped. "I *am* the king, and you would do well to remember it."

Myddrin complied.

"The matter is more complicated than simply 'doing something' about it. I overheard your conversation with Halvair, and he's right. Even if there was a way to somehow end this curse, then what? The armies of Mirimar are still coming. They still want to pillage. Our lands are green, Myddrin. Theirs are black and grey. People want what they can't have. They will come for us, take our women for their own, enslave our children, and kill the rest. The magic in our souls might drive them now, but there was war in these lands long before Axel decided to curse us. Our Knights are currently all that separate us from the forces beyond our borders."

Myddrin sighed. Had he been so blinded by his ambition that he had failed to see beyond the scope of his own objective? "I want to see it," he said after a time. "I won't act upon anything, I promise, but I need to know if there is a way. Perhaps," he paused. "Perhaps when the war is won, we might reassess, make a plan for the future. A plan for the end of magic."

The king merely laughed. "I hope I've done the right thing confiding in you Myddrin. And I trust this conversation stays between us."

Remen moved as he spoke. He began rifling through a dusty chest on the mantle. "I can't let you see the well. I'm sorry, but there's nothing I can do on the matter."

Myddrin started to protest, but stopped himself. This was the king after all.

"Now, if you don't mind, I need to use the privy," Remen continued. He finished rifling through the chest, issued a half bow, then made to leave. "I trust you can find your way out on your own?"

He turned to leave, dropping something as he departed that landed with a metallic clink. "I really hate this keep sometimes," he said while leaving. "So many stairs. I feel like all I do all day is walk down. Down, down, and down some more."

He half turned, smiled, then left the chamber, leaving Myddrin to twiddle his thumbs. It took him much longer than it should have to notice the object the king had dropped.

It was a key. An old key. A very old key, long and rusted.

Myddrin shook his head in amusement.

"I guess I'm heading down."

# Chapter 14
# - Will -

Crisalli bent to a crouch. She tilted her head, then pinched him on the cheek. "So young!" she said. "Youth is a beautiful thing, not to be rushed through."

She leaned forward, examining him. "You have nice eyes, Will, son of Alina."

Will looked to the ground, embarrassed.

He had followed this woman — Crisalli — all the way back down the city slope to her home in the Eastern District of Athedale.

Will looked around. Her place was spotless, everything arranged in an orderly fashion and placed as though every piece of furniture and every object had a distinct reason to be there.

He sniffed the air, then scrunched his nose. He knew that smell, hated it. Mint and rosemary.

"What's wrong, Will? Is my home not to your liking?"

"It smells like mint. I hate mint."

Crisalli leaned back and laughed. "Ha, it's good to see Alina wasn't lying when she talked about you. You're definitely an odd one, aren't you."

Will frowned. He had only pointed out a truth. She had asked his thoughts and he had given them. How was that odd?

Something else caught his attention, however.

"You knew my mother?" he said, opening his posture.

"I did, yes. Very well, actually. Alina and I were once great friends."

Will scratched his head, racking his brain to try and remember a time his mother had mentioned Crisalli.

"She never mentioned me? I don't blame her, I suppose. We had our differences, your mother and I, though we knew each other quite well. We were contracted together. Spent a whole winter in Sunmire fighting some foolish noble's war. I was distraught when I found out what had become of her, been blaming myself ever since. I should have seen the signs. She used far too much magic fighting over there. It eats at you, Will. Every time you push yourself beyond your limits, the voices within grow more and more persistent. They build and build until one day you can't take it anymore."

"Is that why you chose me?" Will said. "Pity?"

Crisalli paled. She offered Will a seat at her table, then took the one opposite him. "I suppose you could say I owed your mother, yes. But pity has nothing to do with it. I've heard a lot about you recently. I was there in the court when Myddrin stood for you, when your father was sentenced. Your mother was strong, extremely strong. Much more so than most of those who gave their lives to the Passing. You now possess her strength. All that she once had is now yours, both in your character and her collected souls. I won't fail you as I did her."

Will averted his eyes. Holding her gaze made him uncomfortable. "I don't quite understand. What if it's too much? Isn't my mother's problem now just mine?"

Crisalli sighed. "In a way, yes. But also no. The human mind, it's fickle. Once souls transfer from one host to another, they kind of reset. Yes, it can be a lot, especially when they first enter a new soul-cage. That's why we have new hosts take seed of the poppy after the passing. It slows their mind, negates the initial influence. From what I heard, you passed out after..." she paused. "After what happened. That's likely why your mind wasn't influenced by Alina's souls straight away.

"Once settled inside a new host, the accumulated souls have to start all over again, trying to influence a brand new mind to set them free."

"I see," Will said.

Crisalli shifted her chair and jumped on top of it, crouching like a cat and placing her elbows on the backrest. She stared at him though purple eyes.

"So, are you ready to begin your training?"

Will almost fell off his chair. He straightened, tensed, then issued a confident nod. "I am! I want to become strong, like my parents, like my grandfather. I want to become a Knight they can be proud of."

"Good. Before we start, you should know a little about the life of a Knight. Most of the time we're free to take on contracts of our choosing. Outside of these walls is a whole different world, Will. One where innocent people suffer. They have no one to help them, no one to call on when a soul-hunter ravages their village. That's what we do. We prevent evil. We fight to stem the flow of the curse that holds Otor hostage. But to break a curse we must first become cursed ourselves."

"I see."

"Outside of these contracts, the church – and technically the king – hold ultimate power over our actions. We go where they say, kill who they ask us to kill, and do what they ask us to do."

"That seems a little controlling," Will replied.

"It is. It's also something you need to remember well. We may have the position of a Knight of Aen, but we are still just pawns for the crown and the church to utilise as they will."

Crisalli leaned on the unstable chair and reached for a bowl on the mantle. She plucked an orange candy out and shoved it into her mouth, crunching on the sweet while she smiled.

Will flinched. Each crunch sent his mind into an angry spiral. "Can you stop that?"

Crisalli paused, her jaw coming to a slow halt. She jumped down from the chair. "Mint, and loud crunching. Anything else I should try to avoid around you, hm?"

"Yes, many things, actually. I don't like smoking, the smell makes my nose twitch. I don't like eyes, they're too big and make me uncomfortable. I don't like bugs. I like most animals, but not bugs." Will shifted in his seat. "And I don't like this chair, the cushion makes my skin itch."

Laughter filled the air, though Will couldn't understand why she was laughing.

"Oh, this will be fun, very fun indeed," Crisalli said. "My life has been a little boring of late. You know what, Will? I think we're a perfect pairing!"

Will looked up and offered a weak smile.

"I'll ask you this only once," Crisalli said, her voice shifting to a deeper tone. "Are you willing to do whatever it takes to make it? Are you prepared to overcome your fears and become a true Knight?"

"I am."

"Good, because tomorrow, your training truly begins. Go home, rest. Meet me here at first light, then we will see your words tested."

Will sat, blindfolded, in a chair so uncomfortable it made him want to tear out his skin. Sleep had eluded him for much of the night, but eventually he'd managed a couple hours of rest, only to make it back to Crisalli's and be greeted with… this…

"How do you feel?" a voice sounded from the opposite side of the room. He knew it to be Crisalli, but with his eyes covered, his world was dark.

"I—"

His voice cut out as the sound of another chair grated against the floorboards.

Will immediately covered his ears at the sound. He shifted his feet. Something began crawling up his leg. Will kicked his shoeless foot in a panic.

He sniffed the air. His nose twitched as a minty aroma began to filter into his nostrils. He removed one hand from his ear and pegged his nose.

"What's going on?!" he cried out. "I don't like this. I want to leave."

He removed the blindfold.

Crisalli stared right at him, her big eyes unwavering. Will looked around. The room was dark. He could see the faint outline of potted plants filling the windowsill, though the window was mostly blacked out, as if someone had thrown a layer of black paint over it but left a few gaps here and there.

He looked down and gasped. Hundreds of ants, cockroaches, and the like crawled around his feet. He made to move, his back itching as it rubbed against the uncomfortable fabric of the chair.

"Sit down," Crisalli said.

Will obliged.

"I hope you weren't under the impression I was going to take it easy on you?" Crisalli continued, then laughed. "Oh no, that's not my style. You see, I take pride in what I am, in making people the best they can be. You must understand, to become a true Knight is to become a master of your emotions. The voices inside our heads, they don't go away. They don't stop, ever.

"They come, and come, and come again. We, as Knights of Aen, must be strong. Physically strong, yes, but our mentality must be concrete. In your old life you might have been able to hide from your fears, from your irritations. You could blanket them, even run away from them. But now that your souls are active, there is nowhere to hide.

"You need to train your mind, Will. You need to build walls, to build your tolerance."

Will rapped his beat of five on his chest. Crisalli reached for a bowl in front of her, picked up another orange candy, and shoved it into her mouth.

Will shifted in his seat again, and the fabric grated against the skin of his arm. He took a deep breath, but all he could smell was mint and smoke. Bugs continued to crawl on his feet.

"Calder, Silas, Ophelia, Thane, Myddrin.

"Calder, Silas, Ophelia, Thane, Myddrin.

"Calder, Silas, Ophelia, Thane, Myddrin.

"Calder, Silas, Ophelia, Thane, Myddrin.

"Calder, Silas, Ophelia, Thane, Myddrin."

"Let us begin my first lesson," Crisalli said, ignoring him. "The primary tool at every Knight's disposal is their source of souls. Your souls can be a double-edged sword," she continued.

Will strained. He wanted to run, to leave this room and never come back, but he forced himself to stay, to fight through the irritations and listen.

"They will gift you the ability to touch the *otherside*, to pull forth material from another plane of existence to be used and crafted into something real and tangible on this side.

"But just like you, they tire. They are limited. They feed off your life energy, your food, your drink, your rest. If you overuse them, they will fail you. On top of this, most – not all, but most – will try and break you. They will whisper thoughts into your ear. They will tempt you, plead for you to give up, to set them free. If you break, they win. You've seen it happen. It happened to your mother. It happens to the best of us. When the souls take over…" she paused.

"When the souls take over there is no coming back. It's nearly impossible to find yourself again after breaking, so all of our training goes into the act of preventing it."

Will squirmed, though he tried to keep still. "My grandfather, all of those others at the Passing. They were close to breaking, weren't they?"

"Correct. There comes a time in any Knight's life where the strain becomes too great. Usually this happens when our own bodies start to deteriorate. When we age, we lose the ability to keep our souls healthy. The Passing, as brutal as it may be, can be a mercy, in a way. No one should have to go through the breaking of their soul."

"So, our lives, they're limited, aren't they?" Will said. "We won't live to see old age."

Crisalli took a deep breath. "Unfortunately not, no. A sacrifice we make, for the good of the Gracelands."

For a moment, Will forgot about his surroundings, finding a deeper respect for his elder Knights.

"Now, I want you to try to form an image. But remember, the more magic you use, the more opportunities you allow for the voices to gain influence over your mind. Never make something you don't have the energy to create. We'll start with something small, then build up into larger images over time until you master how much you can and can't take.

"I want you to focus, call upon your souls, create something familiar. Something you know. To master image-magic, you need to be familiar with your creations. You need to know its make. You must study its texture, its weight, its size, and if you want a more complex image, its movement and properties."

"I don't — this is too much — I can't."

"You can! You already have. Start with your grandfather's shield. Picture it in your mind. Hold it, feel its weight. Steel. Call upon your souls, they will find it, take it from the *otherside*, and mould it into a physical creation."

As Crisalli spoke, an image appeared before her. At first it looked like a dozen shimmering ghosts, completely see through and without any real weight. Then the image began to change. The texture glowed a vibrant violet. Curved wings sprouted and then solidified into the form of a dozen hand-sized butterflies. Their wings beat, and the air around them buzzed with a slow vibration. They took flight, moving much like a butterfly might, with short and sharp movements, dropping low and then rising high again as they circled him. One landed on Will's shoulder before diving off, only to regain its momentum and rejoin its caster.

Will closed his eyes, trying to concentrate.

"You must clear your mind," Crisalli said. "Start with the bigger design, then begin to fill in the detail. Once the ghost of the image rises before you, tighten your hold on it, solidify your claim and your intent. Will it to be real, and it will be so."

Will inhaled, though the smell of mint distracted his mind. He shifted, and his back itched from the chair. A bug had made its way to his thigh, causing him to squirm.

Crunch.

Crisalli bit on another candy.

*There you are*

*We found you*

*Let us out*

*This can be over if you want it to be*

*You can escape*

*Set us free*

"No! I won't let you!" Will shouted.

"Will," Crisalli said. "Fight the voices! Create the image! Do it, do it now!"

Will tensed. He focused on his grandfather's shield. The pattern, he knew the pattern. It came easily, formed in his mind. He opened his eyes. The ghostly image of the shield was there, in front of him. He pulled on it, forced his souls to craft it, to solidify it. The shield glowed bright blue. He reached out to touch it.

LET ME OUT

Will fell off his chair. His hands squished several bugs. His mind raced. His breathing tripled.

"Make them go away!" Will screamed. "I can't! Take them away!"

There were thousands of voices now, all whispering, pleading for control, to be set free.

"Please," Will pleaded. "Make them go away!"

His shield disappeared, and Will rolled onto his back, ready to give in, to allow them control.

He felt Crisalli's hands cradle his head. She shoved something into his mouth, his mind too occupied to even comprehend its taste as a liquid flowed down his throat.

Slowly, Will drifted off. He faded into a dream-like state, his head lolling to the side as whatever Crisalli had given him took effect. The voices subsided, replaced by an overwhelming wave of dizziness. Will welcomed it, allowing his mind to fall into the comfort of sleep.

# Chapter 15
# - Tvora -

Tvora's mind rattled with a thousand thoughts that weren't her own. Her body shook as it always did in the mornings. Her cage pulsed, buzzed with activity. Until she brought her friends into reality, she felt vulnerable, susceptible to the hunger of the dead souls inside of her.

But she had to wait, to suffer through it until she had enough strength…

Finally, she could wait no longer this day, and summoned her companions. Immediately, all of her pain washed away as their presence brought her much needed comfort and resistance. Together, they were strong. Once their minds connected, the pull of the dead was nothing but a distant beat in the background.

She spent the day in Val Taroth observing. At first, she clung to old habits, hiding in shadows and avoiding conversation. Hiding came naturally. It was also necessary. At least, it had been. People reacted a certain way when they saw her eyes. In the past, most had run outright, avoiding her at all costs.

Here, it was different. People still had a reaction, still noticed, were still wary. But they respected her, understood her position. Here, everyone was just as crazed as she.

The city of Val Taroth had become a magnet for the strange and powerful. The unification of the Skull Thrones was no joke. She didn't know how he'd done it, but Carthon had rebuilt his father's army, calling upon old alliances and even forging new ones. They all held a common purpose; they feared and hated the

Knights of the Gracelands, wanted their blood and their souls.

Tvora watched from the balcony as men and women wearing pale, horned masks marched the streets.

*Those are soldiers from Tak Berath!* Cecco said from his perch atop her shoulder. *Did you know that in Tak Berath they use real goat horns as currency? You'll notice the richer ones wearing belts full of them, showing off their wealth and fortune for all to see.*

Her current position made it too hard to see properly, but Tvora was inclined to take Cecco's word for it.

More figures congregated on the eastern side of the city. She spotted the tattered black and red crossed banner of *Val Kadeth* in the distance.

*Impossible*, Cecco said. *The Thrones of Tak Berath and Val Kadeth have been at odds since their formation over one hundred years ago. Not even Doonaval managed to unite them in his time. Carthon must have done something bold to get them to work together.*

Tvora remembered something. "Wasn't that head on the pike at the gates King of Val Kadeth? Tashir something or other?"

*Ah, yes, indeed he was. Tashir Stormwater. Perhaps that has something to do with it then. Though I—*

"Please, no! Spare them, I beg of you," came a call from within the keep.

Tvora turned and followed the voice to the throne room. Carthon reclined on his throne of skulls once again, but this time more people were present. Skullsworn soldiers lined the outskirts of the room, dressed in scavenged armour that didn't seem to match at all. One even wore the breast plate of a Knight of Aen, though the white paint had been overlapped by a mixed spatter of dirt and blood.

Two men knelt in the middle of the room, both under heavy chain. One of them bent over and placed his hands flat on the marble floor. His fingers touched a human skull which had fallen from the throne, but it didn't seem to deter him. The man kept glancing to the side.

Tvora circled the room, wondering what he was looking at. She gasped when she noticed. A woman stood within the circle of guards. Tears stained her mud-caked face, and she clutched two children, a boy and a girl, in her arms.

Tvora's hands inched towards Naex.

"Please, spare them. Take me," the pleading man said. "I offer myself. I have no souls save my own, but take it, it's yours. Just please spare my family."

Carthon stood and walked down from his throne and into the circle. He noticed Tvora, and the corner of his lips rose in acknowledgement before he returned his attention to the pleading man. He nudged him softly in the ribs with his boot.

"Get up. Stand up, now." Carthon took in a deep breath and let it out in a long sigh. "You misunderstand," he said. "I have no intention of killing you, or your family. In fact, you are free to go. All of you."

The pleading man made a sort of choking gasp. "I — I don't understand. Then why am I here?"

Carthon laughed. "You think your single measly soul interests me? No. You are here because I want to offer you an opportunity. You are a simple man, a family man, correct?"

"I — uh, yes sir, Lord," he corrected. "I'm a simple blacksmith. I fashion weapons, good ones! I promise, that's all I am, nothing more. Arthur here is to become my apprentice when he comes of age." He gestured towards the boy, who seemed no older than Edith had been.

"Good, good," Carthon said, pacing the circle now. "Well, 'simple blacksmith', it must be hard living in this city, knowing that any day could be your last. I fear for those down there, truly. The world, it is not made to be easy, not made for the weak. The price for protection alone is enough to cause a strain great enough to break a family. Wouldn't you rather have the ability to protect yourself? Wouldn't you rather not be forced to rely on another to protect your wife and two children?"

"I — we manage what we can, Lord."

"But is that enough? Today it is I who holds your family hostage."

Carthon held up a hand as the man began to plead again. "Relax. I am a man of my word. You are all free to go, that is my promise, but let me finish. Today, it is I who holds your family hostage, but what of tomorrow? What of the next day?

"There is no safety besides what we ourselves make," he continued. "Now I come to my offer. This person next to you is marked for death. Where you hold only a single little soul in your cage, this man beside you holds hundreds, perhaps even thousands!"

Tvora took a moment to observe the second prisoner. His eyes were blindfolded. His knuckles grew white as he clenched them. Tvora also noticed Septus edge his way into the circle, red eyes alight with energy. The Reaper licked his lips as if he were enjoying every moment of this performance.

"You'll never get away with this!" called the blindfolded prisoner. "My men will never join you. The Kingdom of Kane will forever remain independent. I won't let you ruin us like your father tried to!"

Carthon laughed again, this one deeper, coming from the belly. "You don't understand. They already have. Kane is mine. Your soldiers fight for me now. They understand this world, unlike you. They follow the strong.

"Now, simple blacksmith, back to my offer." Carthon moved to one of the soldiers in the surrounding circle and pulled a sword from their sheath.

Carthon took the torso-length sword in two hands and offered it to the blacksmith. "The choice is yours. Kill this man, take his souls, and use them to defend your family, or leave. You are free to go, as promised. You and your family. Free to live your lives, however long they may last…"

The blacksmith looked at the sword. His hands shook. He kept glancing from his family and back to the blade. Then his gaze lingered on his family for an overly long time, his bottom lip beginning to tremble. Suddenly, his entire body tensed as his resolve turned to iron. He took the blade by the hilt, rose, and walked over to the blindfolded man. He spared one last look to his wife over his shoulder, then rammed the point of the blade into the blindfolded man's chest.

It took a moment for the killing to be complete, but when it was, the man's souls flowed from his body in a rush of colour. They slammed into the blacksmith, rocking him almost off his feet.

The blacksmith dropped the sword, and for a long moment the entire chamber was filled with nothing but his ragged breathing as he revelled in his new power. Once he had steadied, he looked to his family, and then ran to embrace them.

"What was that all about?" Tvora said once everyone else had gone.

"You think it a waste of souls? You wonder why I didn't give them to you instead?"

Tvora scoffed. "I didn't come here for handouts. I earn my keep."

"Good. There will be opportunity to earn it soon enough, I promise."

"If that man was a traitor, why not simply kill him yourself?"

Carthon relaxed his shoulders. "What do you know of the

origin of magic?"

Tvora raised a brow. "I know a little, what does that have to do with this?"

"It has everything to do with this. Why do you think Axel cursed us? Why do you think he gave us this ability? He did it because he knew what we are. He knew the true nature of what he and his brother Aen had created. Think about it, Tvora. It's the perfect curse. The perfect way to prove his point.

"Axel wanted his brother to see that what they had created was flawed. What better way to do that than to tempt us with a power born only through murder? He knew what he was doing, what he was encouraging. I just proved it to you."

Tvora tracked Carthon as he began pacing.

"It's a game I play. Every time, Axel is proven right. When faced with the choice to either greater oneself, or remain as they are, people always choose more power. Time and time again humanity's greed wins, proving we are nothing more than broken toys.

"The Gracelands may be better at hiding their greed but believe me, they are just as broken as we are. Why not embrace it? Why not live and breathe Axel's vision? I want to smash the mask the Gracelanders hide behind. I want them to bleed. I want them to feel what we feel, to hate like we hate. Only then will they realise they are the same as us, puppets in a play, at the mercy of beings greater than themselves."

Tvora scowled. She didn't much care for the fate of the Gracelands, never had. She'd never been able to think beyond the scope of her village, beyond the Harrows. She just wanted the power to sustain her friends, to give them back the lives she had cost them.

"I know what you're thinking," Carthon said. "You have no business involving yourself in such affairs."

Tvora's scowl deepened. She hated someone being able to read her so readily.

"Our motivations are aligned, Tvora," Carthon continued. "Our goals are the same. The Gracelands have what we both seek."

"You're powerful," Tvora said. "What's to stop me from killing you in your sleep? Then I'll have all the power I want."

Carthon chuckled. He crossed his arms and laughed. "Nothing. There's nothing stopping you. In fact, I encourage you to try it, if you dare.

"But there's more to the Gracelands than Knights to feed upon. They horde something. Something vast, powerful. My father sought it, yet failed to obtain it. A power so unimaginable that a simple taste of it would be enough to feed your 'passengers' for the rest of your life."

Tvora tensed. Her mind raced with a thousand possibilities. Eventually, her thoughts settled on a single realisation. "That's why you wanted me as a Reaper," she said. "You don't think you can handle it. You want to know what I know — how to reclaim yourself if you break."

Carthon bit his lip as he smiled. "Yes, you're right. I would like to know how you did it, how you managed to find yourself again once the tide of souls had consumed your mind. It's a feat worthy of recognition, and replication. If I can manage to take a step into the next world and keep one foot in this one, the opportunities are endless.

"But that's not the sole purpose for your recruitment. I saw you in the pits. You truly are the embodiment of Axel's vision. I watched you kill, witnessed you harvest those souls. You're just like me, Tvora. Proof of a broken world."

Carthon moved towards the balcony and looked over the parapet, placing his hands on his hips. Tvora moved to his side and watched as the Skullsworn gathered below. His smile widened at the sight.

"Tomorrow, we march."

# Chapter 16
# - Will -

Will smacked his hands together and wiped his charcoal-stained fingers clean. His once long stick of black was growing small. He had been drawing all morning, sketching anything that came to mind, everyday objects, weapons of war, even people he had encountered. He flipped through the book, stopping here and there to add a finishing touch. He made a mental note to seal them with a varnish later in the day.

The after-effects of whatever drug Crisalli had given him left him with a nasty headache, making continuing to draw difficult. He hadn't tried to craft any more images today, and thankfully the voices had left him alone, for the most part.

He wandered out of his new bedroom and into the spotless home of his mentor. Will noticed the distinct absence of the smell of mint this time and wondered if the omission had been purposeful.

"What's that in your hand?" came a voice to his right.

Will looked down at his sketchbook and clutched it to his chest.

Crisalli walked over to him and held out a hand.

Will frowned and gripped the book tighter.

Crisalli sighed. "I'm sorry for yesterday, truly. It was too much too soon. I shouldn't have pushed you that hard."

"No," Will found himself saying. "Don't be. Sorry I mean. You were right to push me. I need to be stronger. I want to be stronger. I just... I can't help it sometimes. I can't help the way I feel, the way things affect me."

"I think you're in a much better situation than you think," Crisalli continued, causing Will's brow to crinkle. "To be a Knight is to be a master of resistance. I haven't known you for long, but I can already see your potential. Think about it. All of those sounds, the smells, the sensations that affect you, they've haunted you your entire life, haven't they?"

Will slowly nodded, unsure where this was going.

"You've already developed a resistance to them, a way to cope, to manage everyday tasks around them. That's exactly what Knights do with the voices, how we live day by day. We manage, we tolerate. In a way, you're already ahead."

Will scratched at his temple. He'd never thought of it like that before. Is that what his grandfather had meant?

Will handed his sketchbook to Crisalli. "It's just some drawings. A hobby I like."

Crisalli took the book and began flicking through it. Her eyes grew wider and wider. She flipped through most of the pages quickly, though she stopped on one page for an overly long period of time. Will didn't need to see to know which one it was.

She continued flipping all the way to the end before snapping it shut. "These are incredible, Will. Truly. You have a talent. A talent I intend to put to use."

"Put to use? What do you mean? What do my drawings have to do with magic?"

Crisalli's smile widened. "They have everything to do with it. Do you think us mages just conjure whatever we like from the otherside?" She shook her head. "To take from the *otherside* is to take from a plane of existence similar to our own. We have to know what we are making. It can be changed, morphed into something of our own creation, but first we must understand it, know the patterns of its creation intimately.

"Your shield," she continued. "Those carvings, the patterns on the rim, the lion-head boss, that's a complicated image. Especially for your first one. Why do you think it comes to you so freely? It's because you already know its make. These drawings," she held up his book for him to take back. "They're evidence you already know the make of these objects. More than that, they show that you're capable of analysing and projecting detailed designs. You can use this, Will, both the skill and your knowledge, to create."

Will took back his notebook and stared at it. "So, I should keep drawing?"

"Yes, definitely. More than that, you should practice making some of your drawings sometimes. I'll show you how to do it, what to look for and how to change it. We'll go over basic movement skills once you've managed to craft a few images, as well as some advanced breathing techniques to quell the rising voices. You've a good start already, and with a family like yours I'm sure you're well versed in breathing exercises. Nevertheless, we'll go through it."

"Can we start now?" Will said, bouncing on his feet.

"Unfortunately not, no. Today, your time isn't mine."

Will frowned. "What do you mean? How can time be a possession?"

Crisalli wrinkled her brow the way people usually did when Will said something silly. "We'll, uh, have to work on your social skills as well. That might be harder than I think." She scratched her head but continued. "What I meant is that I won't be able to teach you today. Someone else is."

"Who?"

"Well, it's not just you. They're teaching all of the new apprenticed Knights. It's an excursion of sorts."

"Excursion? To where? Why? Who's taking us?"

Will found himself getting simultaneously excited and nervous.

"Slow down, Will. In truth, I can't tell you. I want to, but I can't. I've sworn not to. Please, be careful. Where you're going it will be safe, but…" she paused. "Just try to keep a cool head."

"A cool head?" Will replied, feeling at his forehead.

"Uh, sorry. Just, when you see what's in there, try to stay calm. Try not to overreact.

"That's all I can say," Crisalli said, speaking before Will could ask where 'there' was.

W ill followed a single file line of apprenticed Knights up a rocky outcropping. A waterfall cascaded down the slope, dampening the hard stone beneath his feet and making for a difficult climb.

The mysterious priest, who had introduced himself as Beyan, had said little so far, only asking that he be followed. Will hid his sketchbook deep within the confines of his uniform. He dreaded the water, or more the thought of water soaking through his precious drawings. In a way, they were all he had left of his former life.

He followed the footsteps of another apprentice, placing each foot in front of the last with care.

"Excuse me, do you know where we're going?" he asked, tugging at his sleeve.

The apprenticed Knight turned. He had a heavily pockmarked face, and thick eyebrows that were practically joined. The monobrow inverted as he looked Will up and down. He huffed a derisive sigh, then turned back around.

Will bowed his head, suddenly remembering his altercation

with Rath. Everyone had seen. Everyone had witnessed him lose his temper. Were they scared of him? Had Rath already managed to alienate him to the point where no one would even talk to him?

Will turned to the person behind him and asked the same question. He was met with narrowed eyes and the shift of a head. "Leave me alone, kin-killer," the apprentice said, refusing to even look his way.

Will frowned. He turned back around and kept to himself the entire trek up the mountainside.

They rounded a bend and Will could see the crystal blue of the Mirror Sea past the mountaintop. He had climbed this mountain before, or rather the other side of it. It was where he had first used his magic and met Molde.

He wiped a bead of sweat from his brow as they came to the mouth of a cave carved into the stone beneath the waterfall. A steady stream of water flowed over the arched entrance, splashing against rock before continuing on its course downstream.

Muffled murmurs made their way through the line as people bunched up and guessed at their purpose here. Will saw Kalle, her hand draped loosely over Rath's neck as the two of them chatted idly with some of the other apprentices.

Everyone continued to avoid Will. He just wanted to talk to them, to connect with someone his age, but he supposed the lack of friendship was nothing new, just another irritation to get used to. It would make him strong, or at least that's what Crisalli had said.

Beyan led them into the cave. Darkness replaced sunlight, the cavern lit only by a few scattered torches.

They hadn't ventured far before Beyan ordered them to a halt. They stood in a large semi-circle three rows deep, watching as the priest positioned himself before them.

"You are all here because you have taken the Passing," he

said, voice calm and collected. "The Passing is only the first step in a wide journey. Many of you have trained your entire lives for this privilege, and by now you have no doubt seen the power you are capable of harnessing. What you have not seen, is the price one must pay."

People began whispering to one another as two figures emerged from the darkness, their features slowly becoming apparent as Beyan continued his speech.

"You will learn what — oh, Cardinal Adralan," Beyan said, pausing mid-sentence as another cleric clapped him on the shoulder. "I did not expect you here today."

Beyan wavered. From the way he shied from the Cardinal's touch, Will thought he actually seemed scared of the man.

The priest was the same man who had spoken during the Passing. He had a prominent, hooked nose and an asymmetrical face that made Will uncomfortable. His left cheek seemed to droop, making his eyes uneven.

Will straightened as the second figure stepped into the torchlight. He towered over the two priests, making them seem insignificant. Two thick hands clasped together as Thane presented himself. Will tried to control his breathing. Thane was a war hero. His hero. Said to have slain countless soul-hunters on his excursions into the Harrows and beyond. Will had drawn him a dozen times over in his sketchbooks.

He had an odd, wide-set double chin surrounded by a short layer of stubble which kind of looked to Will like hairy knuckles. He wore a studded, sleeveless cuirass which seemed almost too small for him. Thick, corded arm muscles stood out like boulders on a mountain.

Will averted his gaze as he remembered that Thane had taken Rath as his apprentice.

"We can take over from here," the Cardinal said, pressing a

light hand against Beyan's shoulder. "Your services are no longer needed."

"But I am to show the apprentices—"

"What do you not understand about no longer being needed? This order comes direct from His Holiness. Thane and I will take over from here. Off you go," he finished by brushing his hand through the air in a shooing gesture.

The younger priest paled and obliged, edging his way through the gathered apprentices and heading back down the mountain.

"Now," the Cardinal said, fixing his face into a smile so crooked Will regretted raising his eyes to look. "Where were we?"

"Such youth!" he continued. "It is a beautiful thing to be young and untainted. But you are Knights in the service of Aen now. I come here to remind you of that. You serve the church first, and the crown second. Aen comes before all, for it is He who created us, and He to whom we owe our lives. Remember this well, young Knights.

"Knighthood comes with a price, and here you will find out what those who can't handle that price become. But I won't lecture you on that which I myself don't know. Thane here is the expert on all matters of the soul-broken. I'll leave this lesson to him."

The Cardinal took a backward step, allowing Thane to come forward.

"Make no mistake," Thane said, his voice as loud and deep as his physical stature would suggest. "The souls within you are not dead, not completely. Every time you touch the *otherside*, they will help you, lend you their strength. But they will also try and take from you. They will eat at your sanity, perhaps slowly at first, but the more you draw from the *otherside*, and the more souls you take upon yourself, the more difficult it becomes to defend against them.

"In time, you will learn how to temper the voices. You will learn strategies to fight against them. But today we look at something different. Today we learn what is to become of us if we fail to keep the voices at bay, and what it means to become soul-broken."

Will felt his heart rate triple. He was filled with an overwhelming urge to run away and not look back.

A shriek sounded in the background, splitting the air and causing heads to turn. Will tensed. His fingers curled into fists as the shrieking became louder, more consistent. It echoed around the cavern like a cat being strangled. Chains rattled in the near distance as something drew closer. Two forms appeared from the depths of the cavern.

They stepped into the light and Will could see two men standing about five paces apart. They each held a metal chain. Behind them trailed a third figure. A woman, if she could still be called that. Her hands were cut off at the wrist, stumps of flesh remaining in their place. The metal chain was wrapped around her waist, jolting as the figure within the bonds jerked back and forth.

Her entire left breast was one massive hole. It looked as though it had exploded from within. Surrounding it were jagged lines of cracked skin. Within the hole swirled hundreds of multicoloured globes of bright energy.

Her souls…

Will recoiled as the woman shook, her head twisting unnaturally. Her eyes were wide open, revealing the milky white within. Only a faint ring of black remained. Whatever colour her eyes used to be had faded.

Even though there was no direction to her stare, no pupil with which to focus, Will felt her looking at him. His breathing doubled, the sight of someone broken bringing back memories he would rather forget.

The woman jerked again, her face stretching into an impossibly wide grin before her head rotated to an almost full right angle. It snapped back into an upright position with an audible crack. Her expression briefly returned to that of a normal, calm human before twisting again. She let out another shriek, her blank eyes now seeming to focus on an apprentice in the front row. The apprenticed Knight almost tripped over her own feet as she backtracked into someone else.

The two soldiers holding the chains pulled and spread out, pinning the soul-broken woman in place. She clawed at the air to no avail.

"This is what will happen to you if you allow those within to consume you," Thane said over the commotion. "Consider this a warning. Allow your thoughts to turn on you, and your soul will break."

"Who was she?" called a voice from the front row.

"Her name is not important. She was a Knight, just as you all are to be. Eventually, she will be sentenced, once an appropriate vessel has been chosen."

Will began rapping his beat of five. It felt odd to chant Thane's name in his presence, but he did it anyway.

"Calder, Silas, Ophelia, Thane, Myddrin.

"Calder, Silas, Ophelia, Thane, Myddrin.

"Calder, Silas, Ophelia, Thane, Myddrin.

"Calder, Silas, Ophelia, Thane, Myddrin."

He couldn't part the vision of his mother from his mind. Every time he looked up, he saw her. She'd had the same blank eyes, the same crazed expression. Was this what she would have turned into? Was this what she was in the end?

The broken Knight suddenly shifted, lifting her head into the air. Will staggered back as she charged, pulling the soldiers off their feet. She ran straight at the apprentices, at Will. Others moved out of the way, but Will's feet wouldn't budge. He froze. All he saw was his mother, come to claim her revenge, to kill him like she would have if he hadn't acted as he had.

Foam frothed at her jaws as the woman swiped at him. Will closed his eyes. He opened them to see a thick chain made entirely of magic wrapped around the broken Knight. Thane's dark, hazel eyes bore down on him from behind her. He pulled, and the Knight was constricted.

Will panted. His vision was a blur, and he felt the voices within call to him once more. Everyone stared at him. He couldn't breathe, he needed air. His head ached, and the confined space of the cave seemed to narrow in on him.

Ignoring Thane's call, Will turned and ran. He couldn't be there any longer, not in the presence of that woman.

The light was easy to find. He reached out for it, racing out of the cave and down the slope, no destination in mind, just away from this place.

He tried to slow down on the water-slick rocks, but slipped, his foot dragging along stone. He hit hard, scraping his leg and drawing blood. His momentum carried him tumbling over and he used his arms to brace for impact.

He landed on a small knoll of grass overlooking the waterfall. His head dangled off the side, giving him a good view of what had almost been the end of his life. He pressed his palms against the soil and forced himself upright. He fumbled around in his waistcoat, fingers coming up empty.

"My sketchbook, where's my sketchbook?" he whispered franticly to himself.

He looked over the edge of the waterfall, then bent to a knee, and wept.

# Chapter 17
# - Myddrin -

"You are still as stupid as the day you left."

Myddrin held his head in his hands, heavily resisting the urge to scream. His Mother had come to see him.

"I don't have time for this. I—"

"Of course you don't. You've barely said two words to me since coming home. Ten years I've been waiting! Not even an explanation. Ten years spent wondering if my only child was even alive. And now you palm me off like some common maid."

Myddrin made to spark a light. He needed a hit right now.

"Stop that! Stop that now!" Molde slapped his hand and flakes of moss were sent spiralling into the air. "What have you become in my absence? This all stops now."

"Mother you don't understand. I need—"

"No, you don't understand. Do you know what people of the court are saying about you? Myddrin, the Doonslayer, the hero turned coward, a drunkard and addict. Those pompous nobles care more about gossip and intrigue than they do about actually protecting the people they govern, but they're right. My son is a derelict. That all changes now. There will be no more smoking, and no more drinking. You are to present yourself as someone befitting your status."

"Mother, stop."

"No, you stop, and you listen."

"I said stop!" Myddrin yelled.

Molde froze, and Myddrin realised this was the first time he had ever raised his voice at her. "I don't do this for pleasure," he said. "I do this because if I don't, I'll shatter. Either the souls inside will break me, or the grief of... the grief of losing her will consume me. I can't stop. I want to, I should, but I can't. I've tried. Many times. Every time I fail. Every time I'm sober, I feel her loss anew. I see the blue of her sphere vanish, her soul flow into that monster. Every time..."

Molde edged closer and reached out a tentative hand. "Myddrin, I..."

Myddrin looked at her then. She hadn't aged well. Her back was crooked, her skin frail and wrinkly, and her once pleasant facial features were worn with hardship.

"It's okay," Myddrin continued. "And I'm sorry, truly. Sorry for leaving you alone. But I can't be the hero everyone expects me to be. I just can't. I want it to stop, all of it. I have to try. For Ismey. I have to try to end it all."

Molde grasped his hand in her own. "I..." she choked on her words, as if they didn't come easily. "I'm sorry. I suppose life hasn't been easy on you. I only wish I could have been there for you, helped you through this."

Myddrin waved her away. "There is nothing you could have done."

"I understand," Molde continued. "I understand why you are the way you are. Just please, please take care of yourself. Your father is long gone. You're all I have left."

"I will, Mother. I promise."

The two continued to talk for a little while longer, this time in a much more pleasant and measured manner. Molde eventually left, leaving Myddrin to ponder his thoughts.

He reached for another bottle of wine and unstoppered it. He went to pour himself a glass, but stopped short. He set the bottle aside and pushed the glass away. Not because he had made the decision to quit, but because he wanted to remember her. As he sobered, he welcomed the pain, the heartbreak. He allowed the memory of her death to overcome him.

Myddrin let himself cry, let himself grieve, and within the storm of emotion something new emerged. Along with her death came the memory of her life, of their marriage and courtship. For the slightest moment, his mind was completely absent of pain. He knew it wouldn't last, that the ache would return, but he didn't care, because for the first time in a long while, Myddrin felt at peace.

Later that afternoon, a knock sounded from beyond the door to his personal quarters. Myddrin rose from his chair. He spared a glance at the still empty glass, proud of himself for not touching it. Mees was off making him some food, so he opened the door himself.

"Glade? What are you doing here?" he said.

Glade bit hard at her bottom lip. She seemed jittery, head jerking from left to right as if she were a misbehaving student trying, poorly, not to look guilty. "Can we come in?" she asked.

Myddrin was about to gesture for her to enter when he noticed. "Wait, we?"

Glade turned to the side and, sure enough, another figure stood behind her. He seemed familiar, though Myddrin couldn't quite place him. His head was completely bald. His hands were clasped together, and he wore the blood red robes of a priest.

"Myddrin, this is Beyan. You've met before, he's on the King's Council. Please, can we come in?" she asked again, sparing a look over her shoulder.

"Of course, yes. Come in. I remember him now."

The two followed Myddrin into his quarters and took a seat

on the sofa where Molde had sat not too long ago.

"What can I do for you?" he asked, sharing a subtle look with Glade that said, *'why did you bring him'*.

"Have you read the book?" Glade said bluntly.

Myddrin coughed. He looked to Glade, then to Beyan, then back to Glade.

"My connection…" Glade said, gesturing to the priest.

Myddrin exhaled. "I see. This is turning into quite the conspiracy. I assume you've read the journal as well?" Myddrin said to Beyan.

The priest nodded. "And more of the like, yes."

"Aren't you, you know, one of them?"

Beyan seemed to deflate a little. His shoulders drooped as if he were ashamed of his own position. "I have been a devoted servant of Aen my entire life. I have prayed, I have taught, and I have even imposed Aen's principals upon others. But something is amiss with this journal and the church's actions.

"Their control of the Knights, it is… too concrete. They horde power, every year growing stronger. I'm afraid that soon they might use this power for something bad. I fear the church has lost its way. I fear for the future of the Gracelands. And now with this information about Axel and what Lucio claims rests beneath Stonekeep… it is too much. I need to know for myself. I need to see with my own eyes if there is any truth to my suspicions."

Myddrin picked at his favourite beard hair, idly twirling it in his fingers. He had a sinking feeling that King Remen had been worried about the exact same problem, though he didn't want to say it out aloud.

"Let me guess, you want my help to find out if there is?"

Beyan paled, though he made a confident show by nodding his head. "We do. Glade and I, we have no magic of our own, no means by which to understand what we might see should Lucio's words prove true. I understand you share the same desire for knowledge. So, I ask you, will you help us?"

Myddrin held back a laugh. He reached inside his coat pocket and felt at the cool metal of the key before brandishing it between his fingers. "Help you? I'll lead the way."

Mees caught up with him as he walked, the Hand's calculated footsteps pattering beside him.

"Skipping dinner, Master? That's unlike you," Mees said.

"My belly will have to wait a while longer, unfortunately," Myddrin replied, rubbing his stomach.

The evening had mostly consisted of reconnaissance. Myddrin had instructed Glade and Beyan to acquire as much information as possible about Stonekeep, specifically any information hinting towards any underground pathways or hidden passages.

Glade had returned with a schematic, detailing the entire layout of Stonekeep. Myddrin didn't ask how she had acquired it.

It took them a good chunk of time to understand what each line and diagram meant, though fortunately, Glade was much better at this than him.

Following the king's vague hint, Myddrin instructed her to look for the lowest possible point one could get to. Of course, there wasn't any indication of a possible vault or cavern below the surface, but if it did indeed exist, they wouldn't expect to find it drawn out for them.

They had already tested several promising passageways. All turned out to be loose ends, either dusty basements full of ageing wine and stored food, or those places nobody ever talked about where the piss and shit ended up.

Myddrin reached for his pipe, but his hand came up empty. Regret filled him as he remembered he'd left it in his quarters. His splitting headache reminded him he hadn't had a puff or a drink all day. In a way he was proud of himself, though he was also feeling the inevitable pull of the voices beginning their whispers.

In order to remain inconspicuous, they had to traverse around the keep separately, meeting up at chosen locations only once all prying eyes were gone from sight.

Coincidentally, this latest meeting point was directly beneath Myddrin's own given quarters. Could that be what Remen had meant? Myddrin huffed, cursing himself for not pressing him for more clues.

"Myddrin? Is that you?" came a voice.

Myddrin looked up from the dark to see vibrant auburn hair appear from within the tunnel, lit only by a few fading wall-lamps. "Glade, it's me, yes. Have you found anything?"

Beyan made himself known, appearing from her shadow to the right. "Nothing, no," he said. "Maybe it's time to call it a day? Try again tomorrow?"

Myddrin sighed. He'd known it wouldn't be easy. "It's a maze down here, no wonder it's been kept a secret for so long."

"Unless the journal's a fabrication?" Beyan said.

Glade took on a hardened stance. "We have to keep looking. We owe it to—"

"Shhh," Myddrin said, holding a single finger to his lips.

Sure enough, footsteps sounded in the near distance.

The four of them clung to the damp wall like frightened cats as the footsteps from around the corner drew closer and closer. A figure stopped at the edge of Myddrin's periphery. Another person converged on his location, their steps ringing much louder.

"Thane! You're late. Were you followed?" came a voice. It sounded squeaky and high-pitched. Myddrin risked a glance. He quickly jerked his head back into the shadows as the bulky Knight known as Thane looked over his shoulder.

"Of course not," Thane said.

The second figure snorted. "Fine, let's just get this done. Follow me."

Myddrin had only had a second to look, but he knew the blood red robes of a priest when he saw them.

Slowly, the two newcomers departed down a dark corridor.

"We need to get out of here," Beyan said, breathing as though he had just run three laps of the keep.

"No, we follow," Myddrin said, already moving.

"You can't be serious, that was Thane! He's one of the most powerful Knights in the order."

"And I'm the most powerful," Myddrin interrupted. "Now, are you coming or not?"

Beyan gulped, but obliged.

"You said you wanted the truth. Well, they're hiding something. I'm sure of it."

They kept a lengthy distance, careful not to allow their own footsteps to betray them. Eventually, Thane and the priest disappeared down a passage to their left. When Myddrin reached it, the way was barred by a large, black gate. He smiled to himself as he noticed the keyhole. He fingered the king's key before placing it into the lock, half expecting it to be the wrong fit. He breathed a sigh of relief when he heard the satisfying click.

"And where exactly did you find this?" Glade asked.

"You have your connections, I have mine," Myddrin said.

Stone walls, thick with lichen, greeted them on the other side. The narrow pathway continued downward, lit with lanterns. Myddrin fought down his claustrophobia, reminding himself who he was and what he was capable of.

Eventually, the walls began to widen, and the passage opened enough for him to breathe comfortably. A dark aura surrounded the cavern, only growing more potent the deeper they ventured.

It was like a thick, invisible fog pressing against him, urging him to turn back and run the other way.

Myddrin squinted, feeling the pressure begin to build in his mind as his souls rebelled against him. It was as if they could sense a power lurking ahead. Water dripped from a series of stalactites above, the icicle-shaped formations of stone like a rain of arrows threatening to drop. They followed Thane and the priest deeper and deeper, clinging to shadows as they watched them enter a large chamber.

Myddrin felt more than saw the contents within the chamber. His trapped souls surged, throwing themselves against his insides. He couldn't tell if they wanted to flee, or join forces with whatever lay inside, but he pushed ahead

"Take only what you can handle," he heard the priest saying to Thane. "No more than necessary. I won't have you or the others breaking before the Skullsworn come. Do not make me regret this."

Thane seemed to stop and stare for an overly long time. Then, the brute reached down and began to glow. Lights surrounded him, became him. Were they souls?

Myddrin had stepped too far out into the chamber. He turned back, but realized that there seemed to be only one way in or out. They'd be caught for sure if they stayed there. He crept over to a large boulder, hid behind it, and gestured for the others to join him.

"What is it?" Glade asked, placing her back to the stone. "What did you see?"

"I don't..." Myddrin said through laboured breaths. "I'm not sure. Whatever it is, we have to wait."

Every second that passed felt like agony as their party waited patiently for whatever was happening inside the chamber to finish and for Thane and the priest to depart. Eventually, their voices subsided, and he heard them stalk quietly back the way they had come.

Myddrin let out a long-held breath, then crept out into the cavern.

Torchlight was no longer needed, as a crystal-clear lake shimmered in its centre, illuminating the chamber like one giant ball of light. Not a ripple broke the water's surface, not a single fish swam within its depths. Not even vegetation grew within. Rock and stone were the only friends to this mystifying force of nature.

Hard, black stone segmented the lake from the rest of the world, cupping it into the centre of the chamber. Myddrin moved to get a closer look, noticing that what lay within wasn't water at all. Hundreds of thousands, perhaps even millions of intangible globes swirled inside. They had no direct form, no shape to them, just a coloured stream of radiant light which acted like a tail as they moved around the well.

The well itself was huge, stretching further than his eyes could see. "It's real," Myddrin said. "Lucio's journal. It's all true."

He paced the stone barricade. Myddrin spun in a circle. The voices in his head calmed as his emotions were replaced by sheer awe. "This can't be real," he said to himself more than anyone else.

He turned to Beyan. "These are human souls. How is this possible? This whole time we were led to believe the dead were at peace, when in reality they were here, just as trapped as the souls inside of me."

He waited for a response, but Beyan seemed in even more shock than him. The priest bent down to his hands and knees on the edge of the well. His breathing was ragged, and he looked as though he were about to vomit. "This… can't be," he whispered. "They lied to us, lied to me. This whole time. There is no Promised

Land. Not for us. No afterlife, no peace. This is where they all end up. Every death not tainted by murder goes here. This... this is Axel's true curse."

Myddrin leaned forward and touched the *otherside*. There was definitely another plane of existence, his magic came from somewhere. If that was so, then it was just as Lucio had said, humanity could no longer travel there, only reach into it temporarily. The air beside him rippled, and he conjured forth the image of a knife. He pulled on it, solidifying its emerald surface. He grasped the hilt and pointed the sharp end at his own wrist. "So, if my blood spills here, my souls enter the well?"

"Myddrin! What are you doing!" Mees said. It was always Mees stopping him.

Myddrin had pulled the knife out to make a point, but now that it was before him, it would be so easy. So easy to end his life, to end his suffering. All he had to do was cut, and there would be no more voices.

He felt something hard tug on his wrist, and the knife fell from his grasp, disappearing into mist. Mees stood behind him, his grip like an iron shackle. "It's not your time yet," is all he said.

Myddrin knew it to be true. What would be the point? He would still be trapped here. Nothing would change. Not really.

"Are they alive?" Myddrin said, struggling to comprehend what that might mean, to be trapped here for eternity, never able to leave.

Glade stepped up, hand over mouth. "My mother, my father, they're here somewhere, they must be!" She began to run her hand over the misty balls of light. They reacted, swirling around her arm.

"Glade don't!" Myddrin said, pulling her back. "It might be dangerous."

He realised how stupid that sounded given what he had just

thought about doing.

"Dangerous? They're taking from it Myddrin! You saw him. Thane took from the dead! That's what they've been doing, secretly bolstering their strength, garnering power. Are they all in on this? Does the king know?"

Myddrin held up a hand. "He can't approve of it either way. Otherwise, he wouldn't have helped us and given me the key. There must be a way to free them. We have to find one, at any cost."

Myddrin took three steps back. He waved his hands in a semi-circle, attempting to comprehend the scope of the cavern. He moved to the wall and placed his hands upon the stone, dragging his fingers along the surface. "This is man-made," he said.

He continued along the outskirts of the cavern, studying the texture, the craftsmanship. The entire cavern was built by humans, at least this part of it was. The stonework seemed old, extremely old, but sturdy. It was built like a dome, the stone arching high overhead, holding strong for what was surely the base of Stonekeep itself. He turned back toward the well, though it was more of a lake. Nothing about it screamed man-made, it was all natural.

A thought struck him like a hammer. His mouth hung wide as the exultation of his epiphany took hold of him. "It's a crater."

His mind raced, recalling years of study all at once. Of Aen and Axel. Of their battle over humanity. All knew it. All spoke of it. But the details were always foggy. Even Lucio hadn't known everything, his notes written more as speculation or second-hand knowledge than experience.

This was where he fell. This was where Axel died. A god.

A commotion sounded from the other end of the cavern; voices, torchlight. People were coming.

"Myddrin, we have to leave, now!" Glade said, already

moving towards the exit.

He heard, but didn't care. He needed to know, needed to see if he was right. He turned to his companions. "Go, I'll catch up."

Beyan and Glade hesitated a moment, though the fear of getting caught shook them, and rushed away.

Mees stayed behind. Mees always stayed.

Myddrin leaned backward and drew power from his trapped souls. He concentrated on an image. The large, emerald-coloured form of a mallet flourished into existence. It stood at least six times the size of a human and hovered in the air above him.

He thrust his hands forward, and with a whirl of motion, he brought the hammer head of the mallet down on a column of stone. It shook with the impact. Stone cracked in several places. The voices in the distance grew louder and Myddrin could see figures starting to emerge beyond the green glow of his mallet.

Glade and Beyan were already gone. He knew he should have left with them, that he should have fled this place, but he didn't care. He needed to know.

He waved his hands again and pulled forth a wall of stone from the *otherside*. All images were transparent, and he could now see the startled faces of priests shouting beyond his emerald wall as he barred their passage.

The internal voices returned, but he pushed them away, his purpose too strong for them to gain any kind of momentum against him.

Once more, the head of the mallet cracked against the rocky surface. Myddrin continued his assault, heedless of the damage he must be causing to the sacred site. Dust flew into his face and mouth as part of the column collapsed. Rubble tumbled around his feet, spilling a few strides short of where the lake began. Myddrin coughed, covering his mouth with his sleeve. He waved his hands in the air, brushing the dust aside as he took a peek beyond the rubble.

A white column stood firm behind the grey of the stone. Myddrin reached a hand into the hole he had created, feeling at the texture.

Shouts continued behind him as more forms appeared. He could fight them, could easily kill them all, but he wasn't that person. He didn't kill simply because he could. Besides, they had seen him, knew who he was. Everyone knew who he was.

He dismissed his image-wall and allowed them to rush him, rush Mees. They seized him by the shoulder and forced him roughly to the ground. He no longer cared. A wide smile stretched the length of his face. He had found the bones of Axel.

These souls…

This well…

It was a giant soul-cage.

Axel's soul-cage.

# Chapter 18
# - Tvora -

Carthon's army trailed behind them like an enormous, flowing river. The main body consisted of Skullsworn soldiers, each separate kingdom making up part of the whole as they crossed the barren plains of the Harrows. Any locals living in settlements in their path had either fled before their arrival, or they joined with the travelling army in hopes of attaining a measure of notoriety amongst the Skullsworn.

Good.

Tvora didn't know if she could sit and watch if this army decided to set ablaze every town and populated village they crossed.

But wasn't that what she was about to do to the people of the Gracelands?

*There's no room for doubt*, Lucia said, padding up beside her. *To doubt is to show weakness. To show weakness is to dig yourself an early grave.*

Tvora bit her bottom lip. Lucia was right. She had made her choice, now she had to live with it. She clicked her tongue as a group of power-hungry soul-hunters sauntered past, eyeing her with malice.

"I hate them," Tvora said. "Hate them all. They do nothing but kill, burn, and rape. I hate even more that we're one of them."

*We are what the world made us*, Lucia said. *Nothing more. When this business is done, we can do what we like. Be what we like. When we have what we need, we can leave, find a home, start an orphanage of our own. We can be better. But for now, we need them. Fight as a monster today to become something greater tomorrow.*

Tvora found Lucia's words soothing. She always felt better when her friends were out. She was weak without them; exposed, vulnerable. Together, they were strong. If only Gowther wasn't so stubborn, she would ask his thoughts on the matter.

"Do you think Carthon is right about the Gracelands?" Tvora asked Lucia.

"The Gracelands are a poison," came a voice to her side.

Tvora tensed and Lucia bent her hind legs, ready to pounce as Tvora spun to see Glock walking up to her. Even exposed to the elements, the Reaper refused to wear a shirt. She was beginning to think that tight leather pants and a long silver sword were his only possessions.

"What do you know of them?" Tvora asked.

Glock harrumphed. "Everything. I was a Knight of Aen, once."

Tvora gasped. She went to probe him for more information when he drew his sword and placed the flat on his lips. He closed his eyes and began whispering to it again. His eyes opened with a pop of sunflower yellow. He smiled.

"Ah!" he said. "Galvandier tells me we will have a great victory here. Yes. More than that. You will spill the blood of my former compatriots. You will reap and harvest their souls tonight, Tvora Soul-Broken."

Tvora winced. She hated that name.

"Why do you fight for Carthon against the Knights?" she asked, ignoring his comments.

"Because I hate them. More so than Carthon, I think. They are a lie. False. They covet power under the pretence of sanctity. I've seen what they keep. What they hide. What they protect.

"At least out here, I know what people are, what to expect of them. The Knights are inconstant. You never know what intentions hide behind their false ideals."

There was more to this story, more to uncover about Glock's true reason for hating the Gracelanders, but Tvora wasn't about to pry. She had her own problems to deal with. There was no room for letting anyone else in. Selflessness in the Harrows always got you killed. She had learned that the hard way.

Not long after, they crossed into Gracelander territory. She stood atop a wide ridge. Beside her stood her fellow Reapers: Carthon, Glock, Mantis, and Septus.

Below the ridge stood half of their army. There wasn't as much infighting as she had expected, and there was a kind of formal ranking system where captains would keep their formations in check. Further down the field lay the city of Kildeen, the Gracelands' outpost, built to keep them safe from the dangers posed by the Harrows.

Kildeen sat at the back of a huge bowl, surrounded on three sides by steep cliffs at least two hundred feet tall. A series of fissures cracked the surface behind the tall, stone walls of the city. The narrow canyons had to be their connection to the Gracelands and the city of Athedale, as well as their main supply route.

Cecco glided through the wind, flapping his great wings before landing on Tvora's outstretched forearm.

"What did you see?" Tvora asked.

*The city is a marvel. I had always dreamt of coming here, but to actually see it... The place is majestic. It's a city in a bowl Tvora, can you believe it? A city in a bowl!*

Tvora sighed. "I meant what potential weaknesses did you see?"

*Oh, of course. I almost forgot that our purpose was to destroy it. Their defences are strong. Their walls are high, and I see no clear way down the cliff-face. The only way in or out is through the tunnels at the* castle's rear. They are well stocked for a siege.

Tvora reported Cecco's findings to Carthon, who took in the information with stoic resignation.

*They know we're here*, Cecco continued. *They are prepared to defend. I can't be sure, but they look to have at least one hundred Knights of Aen among them.*

Tvora repeated Cecco's inaudible words again. Carthon nodded, giving her a sceptical look, as if he weren't quite sure how she'd acquired this information.

"Septus!" he called. "Prepare the men."

Septus made his way down the ridge, spitting orders to those who would listen.

Tvora studied the field below, wondering how it was possible to even get troops down to start the offensive.

"Piss off," she heard one of the soul-hunters say to Septus. "You don't be tellin' me what to do. I'm—"

Tvora gasped.

The soul-hunter's head dropped to the dirt. Blood spouted from his neck as the now decapitated body dropped to its knees and then fell on its stomach. A few dozen souls flowed from the corpse and into Septus. The soul-hunter's death had come so fast that Tvora hadn't even seen how he'd done it.

Carthon just stood and watched, his arms crossed over his chest.

"Is he... always like that?" Tvora asked.

"Do you know the story of the Blood Mage?" Carthon asked, not even bothering to face her.

Tvora winced, suddenly flushed with a fractured memory of her Over-Mother at the orphanage whispering that name at night in order to keep her from wandering off. "You can't expect me to believe he's the Blood Mage. The Blood Mage is a tale from before I was born. He's said to have killed hundreds, even thousands of innocent people. Septus looks no older than thirty summers. He can't be him."

Carthon grinned. "You're right. Septus is not the Blood Mage. He's the man who killed him."

Tvora shuddered, looking back to Septus with new insight. "H— how?" she said.

"Killed him in his sleep. Just eight years old when he did it," Carthon said, shaking his head as if he still couldn't believe it. "He's been carrying the burden ever since."

"That's... disturbing..."

Carthon began to move. "Walk with me," he said.

Tvora obliged, matching his stride as the pair paced the edge of the ridge and stared down at the city from their vantage.

"Have you ever seen a battle of this scale?" he asked.

Tvora went to speak, but Carthon interrupted her, waving his hand.

"Not the kind of fight you experience in the pits, no. I'm talking thousands of soldiers."

Tvora shook her head.

"These soldiers are merely fodder," he gestured towards the gathered soul-hunters and newly acquired Harrowers. "They are expendable. The strong may survive, perhaps even grow stronger, but the majority will fall. You'll soon see that a single regular mage is worth a hundred foot soldiers on the battlefield. And you, Tvora, are no regular mage."

Tvora ruffled Cecco's feathers as he perched on her shoulder. "Wont they just give your enemies more strength? If you send them to their deaths, I mean."

"*Our* enemies," Carthon corrected. "I suppose you could think of it that way, yes, but the result is the same, in the end. That's why I have you."

He turned to face her now, a pleased expression crossing his firm jaw.

"You mean for me to specifically target their Knights?" she said.

"You are perceptive. Yes, I do. I admire you, Tvora. You are the first I have met to cross to the *otherside* and return with your sanity. Well, mostly," he added, nodding at Lucia and Cecco. "This fight won't be won through numbers alone. They're simply a distraction. Do you think I could trust a pack of starving Harrowers and greedy soul-hunters? No."

"Yet you trust me?" Tvora said.

Carthon drew in a long breath through thin lips. "Do you believe I should trust you?"

Tvora tensed. "I've learned never to trust anyone."

Carthon laughed. "And you would be wise not to. No, I don't trust you. I don't need to. My trust lies in motivation. As long as I know what motivates a person, I know how they'll act."

Tvora ran her hand through Lucia's violet coat, lending her a measure of comfort.

"We are one and the same, Tvora," Carthon said. "Like you, I grew my strength in the pits. My magic was born there, moulded in the darkness. I wasn't wrapped in wool like the Gracelanders. I was the son of a great king who didn't give a shit about me. Now I'm the son of a dead king. In Athedale, I would have risen to the title. In Mirimar, I was thrown to the wolves, cast away and forced to fend for myself. I forged my own destiny, fought for my own magic, and I intend to use it to accomplish the feat my father never could."

Tvora didn't react, just listened. Carthon's arm tensed, blue veins popping out like twin rivers. She only now noticed his arm for what it truly was, a canvas full of scars. Ridges of pink skin protruded from his forearm like a lattice, running almost all the way down. It made her wonder how many more just like them were hiding behind his clothes.

Carthon followed her gaze. "I know you think me a monster," he said. "Perhaps you're right, but this world breeds monsters, needs them. We are the same Tvora. It's just that, where your soul was broken from the inside, mine was beaten on the out."

"You don't know me as well as you might think," Tvora said.

"I know what you desire, and that's enough for now."

Tvora scoffed. In the background, Septus had gathered the majority of the Harrowers and bunched them into a group. The Skullsworn that made up the main mass of the army held back.

"Aren't you afraid they'll turn on you?" Tvora asked, motioning towards Septus.

Carthon's lips twisted into a smirk as he began to tremble. His body shook, and his chest emanated a shadow black as night. Tvora recoiled as the sheer magnitude of power resonating from his body grew too much for her to handle at such a close distance. "Oh, Tvora. I have nothing to fear from him. It is he who fears me."

Carthon raised two arms into the air. A swirl of black shapes began to surround him, growing larger as he called upon his souls and drew from the *otherside*. The entire ridge shook as he solidified his image.

She arched her head and stared in awe as an enormous black bridge stretched the width of the standing army. It ran down the cliff like a second wall of stone, its slope much more forgiving than the steep edge of the original.

"You're kidding me," she said, turning back to see Glock standing with hands on hips. "No one has the power to create an image that large."

Glock simply drew Galvandier from its scabbard and pressed it to his lips again.

Tvora squinted, trying to get a better look as the gates of

Kildeen opened, and a rush of blue-clad soldiers came forth, hugging the stone walls and forming into orderly ranks at least fifty men deep. "Why do they come out to face us? Why not hide behind their walls?"

Glock began to stretch, flexing his toned muscles and cracking his stiff neck. "Magic is hard to use at longer ranges. I would think they believe their mages of more use in an open field. I suppose they always have a wall to retreat behind when they fail."

Tvora went to join the army moving down Carthon's black bridge, but Glock grabbed her arm. "No, it's not our time to fight yet."

Tvora spun. "What? The army is moving. I didn't join with Carthon to sit idle."

Glock remained impassive. "Trust me. You'll get a full belly's worth of souls to fill your cage by day's end."

She didn't like it, but she waited, and she watched.

The war cry was deafening. Thousands of men and women descended the bridge, weapons raised as they flooded out over the plain below. The earlier sense of order among them that she'd observed seemed almost non-existent now as bloodlust took hold. Man fought against man as they strived to be the first to meet the defensive wall of shields the soldiers of Kildeen had prepared for them.

As the two armies drew closer, the Harrowers began to sling what little magic they could at the shield wall. Tvora saw the distant glow of image-weapons as they manifested in the sky, only to be hurled at the defenders a moment later. She spared a look toward Glock, who pointed, motioning for her to watch.

Just before the oppressors met the wall, an image appeared. It stretched the entire length the battlefield. A multicoloured scythe joined together by the combined might of what she guessed to be at least fifty Knights.

It hovered in the air a moment, and then released. The scythe sliced through the front-line attackers, cutting them in two for a least a hundred yards before losing momentum and disappearing as if it had never existed.

Blood drenched the dirt that made up the battlefield. Thousands of indistinct globes she knew to be human souls zipped around the field as they flowed into whichever new host had been directly responsible for the previous host's demise.

Just like that, the offensive broke. Arrows rained down from the castle walls as more soldiers dared to brave the barrage. Despite the initial slaughter, hundreds of Harrowers still stood between Carthon and Kildeen. Many began to flee, turning back to the bridge and what they thought to be safety. Septus met them where the black of the bridge met stone.

He drew from his cage and cast a thin veil across the platform at the base of the bridge. Men congregated there, banging on the solid veil as they fought desperately to flee. Carthon ordered them to return to the castle. Those that refused were met with a steel ball to the skull as Septus took material from his conjured wall and threw it at them with the speed of a freshly loosed arrow.

Confused, the soldiers turned and ran in the only direction they could. Some deviated, deciding the edge of the bowl was safer than the defensive wall of Kildeen, but they were picked off by arrows from Carthon's own men.

"Now we move," Glock said, motioning for Tvora to follow him down the bridge.

"What's happening?" Tvora asked. Lucia rushed to her side, sensing her anxiety.

"Everything is going according to plan," Glock said. "Now is our turn to enter the fight."

"Enter the fight? That was a slaughter, how could that possibly have been the plan?"

Glock offered an amused smile. "I can explain it to you if you like, but we're wasting time."

"Explain," Tvora said, her voice raised. "I won't commit myself to whatever this is without knowing what I'm walking into."

"Very well, if you insist. Let's walk and talk, we're expected on the front lines soon."

Tvora followed. "Stick close to me," she whispered to Lucia and Cecco. The image-panther brushed against her leg as they walked, and the hawk found his usual perch on her shoulder.

"Magic isn't infinite," Glock continued, "as you well know. It has a limit. There comes a point when a mage's source of souls will run dry, or tire if you will. Those soldiers are nothing," he said, gesturing to the fleeing men and women on the other side of Septus' veil. "They are dregs; murderers, rapists. They're worth nothing. Their job is to tire the Knights' magic, to wear down their defences. If they fall, that only means there's more souls for us come the end of the day."

Tvora hesitated. This was slaughter for the sake of slaughter.

*We're missing out. Let's go*! cried Lucia, already several feet ahead of her. *Part the brutality from your mind. None here would think twice before doing the exact same to you. This is what we came here for, now get yourself together.*

Tvora calmed, focusing as she and Glock stepped onto the bridge. She drew Naex and Naev from their respective sheaths and followed Glock down the bridge. Septus dismissed his shield as the bulk of Carthon's army followed him toward Kildeen.

The remnants of the initial assault were still hassling the front lines, most throwing themselves at the shield wall and either being beaten back or let through to be impaled on the point of a spear behind.

Septus solidified an image, or rather hundreds of images.

Hundreds of tiny red steel pellets lit up the battlefield, hovering before the charging army. She almost stopped to watch, but Lucia's urgency tugged on her mind. The panther rushed ahead to meet the enemy.

In one whoosh of motion, Septus sent the red pellets streaming through the air. Tvora heard more than saw their impact as cries echoed around the base of the castle. The metal pellets ripped through armour, skin, and bone, decimating the shield formation.

She barely had time to take in the spectacle before a whirl of green blocked her vision as Mantis solidified his image. True to his name, a giant version of a praying mantis came to life. The image-insect was tall, its long, narrow body stretched in the middle. It turned its large, triangular head toward her. Two huge compound eyes stared blankly, scaring Cecco off her shoulder as the bird took flight. Although fascinating, the image seemed distorted, as if the user were trying to create something too complicated and had instead filled in the finer details with a sort of blank slate.

The effect was the same, however. The enormous image-bug crawled on four legs toward the blue line of shields, two oversized appendages lined with razor sharp spines raised and ready. It crashed into the wall, breaking it and allowing troops to flood in through the gap.

Soldiers who were unable to wield magic were quickly overrun, cut down by tools brought forth from the *otherside.* Souls flowed everywhere, scrambling to find their new hosts.

Tvora ducked as a defender thrust his spear at her, rolling to the side. Lucia came from behind to swipe at her assailant, ending his life with one claw.

Glock charged to her left. A yellow suit of armour surrounded his body, his bare chest still visible through the bright hue of the transparent suit. He held Galvandier, the suit morphing and changing around it, allowing his arm to move unhindered. He spilled gouts of blood as the silver sword cut down defender after defender in his way.

A new resistance formed as the remaining Knights banded together. Tvora found herself on the back-foot, deflecting projectiles as a group attempted to block her advance. Cecco whirled around their flank and cut in at a sharp angle. He ripped through the shoulder of the closest Knight.

Tvora rushed forward, using Naev to finish him with a strike through the heart. She felt her body convulse as at least a thousand souls rushed into her. She was used to the feeling, but such a quantity all at once was a new experience. It filled her with renewed energy, with raw power. Not since her first kill had she indulged on so many souls.

The Knight's body crashed to the ground, joining the other dead. Tvora hungrily looked for her next victim. She sought out the one who looked strongest and charged. Naex bit into flesh and she kept going. She whirled, ducked, lunged, and sliced. She cut all in her path. Blood splattered, caking her face, but she didn't care.

She felt her cage nearly double. This was what she wanted. This was what she needed. When her souls recovered, she might be able to sustain Cecco and Lucia indefinitely now, perhaps even Gowther too.

No.

It wasn't enough.

She needed more.

She turned, ready to reap whatever poor soul dared to stand in her way, but found none remaining.

Carthon split the gates with some concoction of his own making that she likened to a battering ram. Just like that, Kildeen fell, overrun by the sheer power of Carthon and his Reapers. It took her longer that it should have to comprehend that she was one of those Reapers. There was no doubt in her mind now that she had chosen the winning side. Carthon would destroy the Gracelands and take his bounty. Tvora would get all she desired and more.

# Chapter 19
## - Will -

Will slapped the water, watching as a ripple crashed against a jagged stone.

He needed to find his sketchbook. He needed to look at his mother, to replace the broken memory of her in that state...

He had to see that she had once been whole, that she had been kind and loving and not the monstrosity she had turned into in her final moments.

He wandered down the mountain, searching anywhere and everywhere. He knew it was hopeless, that the pages were likely drenched at the bottom of the ravine by now, but he couldn't give up.

He sat on the edge of the stream, taking a short break. He looked up and watched as clouds broke and reformed, hoping for a miracle.

Something smacked against the hard stone behind him.

Will turned to see the brown leather cover of his sketchbook sitting idle directly beside him. He shifted sideways, his body straightening. He reached for the book, hands cupping it cover to cover. He flipped through the pages. The only sign of water damage was a slight damp patch in the corner of a lone page. He flipped through until he found her. He stared for a while, then hugged it to his chest and breathed a long sigh of relief.

Will started to stand as he tried to piece together how this was possible. He turned without looking and smashed his head on something hard.

"Oww!" came a feminine cry.

Will recoiled, feeling at the top of his head. "What the... Oh, I'm sorry!" he said, moving to place a hand on the shoulder of the girl he had just inadvertently headbutted in the face.

The girl retreated a step, holding a hand to her nose and tilting her head backward as blood trickled between her fingers. "Is this how you repay a debt?" the girl said, her speech muffled.

Will stumbled for words, still trying to understand what had just happened. The girl had auburn hair that ran in waves down her shoulders. Blown by the wind, it curled around her chest, some of it sticking to her face as she struggled to swipe it clear.

"W — what do you mean?" Will finally managed to say.

"The debt," the girl said. "For your book. It's what you were looking for, right? Before you started hurting the river with your fist."

Will scrunched his face into a ball. "You can't 'hurt' a river. It's water."

"I'm made of water," she said, "and you hurt me..."

Will's scowl deepened, though his fingers curled around his sketchbook. That's all that mattered. He looked from the book to the girl. "You found this?"

The girl nodded, stepping forward with an outstretched hand. "The name's Olive. Nice to meet you."

Will went to take it, but stopped when he noticed the fresh blood on her open fingers.

Olive recalled her arm. "Let's, uh, save the hand shaking for another time. Though you owe me twice over now. One for the book, the other for the nose."

"Sorry about the nose. My name's Will. Are you alright?"

"I'll survive. What are you doing all the way out here anyway, you know your group is up the mountain right?"

Will's eyes narrowed. "How do you know who I came with?"

Olive shrugged, flicking her hair in a coy shift of her head. The bleeding had subsided, and Will managed to get a good look at her now. She was around the same age as him, and quite beautiful. Her face was spotted with freckles, five of them forming into a familiar shape just above her right cheekbone.

"I like your freckles," Will said, moving forward to examine them closer. "Five of them form a star. Did you know that? I like stars."

Olive laughed. Her smile was infectious as she batted her lashes in a playful gesture. "You're an odd one, aren't you."

Will bowed his head. He'd heard that before. This was usually around the time people started ignoring him. Either that, or the abuse would begin. He had come to expect it, though he never really knew why it happened.

"I like you," she said.

It took Will an extra moment for her words to sink in. "You, uh, what?"

"I like you," she said again. "I think you're sweet. A little awkward perhaps, but sweet all the same. I want you to teach me."

"Teach you? Teach you what?"

Olive's expression changed, a subtle tightening of the jaw. "I want to learn about magic."

Will had to hold back a laugh. "You want me to teach you how to do magic?"

Olive shook her head. "No. I want you to teach me *about* magic."

Will raised a brow. "Why?"

"What does it matter why? You owe me a debt, and I want to collect."

Will mulled the thought over, studying Olive with intent this time. "You followed us here, didn't you?"

Olive ignored his question. "You're a Knight, correct?"

"Apprentice Knight," Will managed to stumble out.

Olive paused. Her gaze shifted to the mountain above. "What was in there, in the cave? It must have been something bad to scare you like it did."

Will grimaced. He looked to his feet as if they would provide him comfort. "I don't want to talk about that."

Olive didn't press the issue, a fact he was thankful for. "I saw your drawings. In your book, I mean. You're quite good! Is that what all Knights do? Does it help with your magic?"

Will placed a hand over his chest, feeling his sketchbook through the fabric. He hated the thought of someone else seeing his drawings. They were for him alone, some of them more personal than others. "No," he said. "I haven't seen anyone else doing it, at least. But my mentor says they're useful."

Olive perked up. "Well maybe you can teach me to draw too, that can be the payment for your second debt to me."

Will frowned. "I'm sorry about your nose, but I can't teach you. I don't even have any knowledge to teach."

"Of course you do. You're a Knight, aren't you?"

"*Apprentice* Knight. I'm still learning."

Will watched as Olive's face dropped, her once bright smile fading into a frown. It was almost enough to retract his previous statement altogether. It didn't last long though, and she quickly perked back up. "Then you can teach me as you learn. Who knows, maybe I can even help."

"Why do you want to learn about magic anyway?" he said. "Magic is dangerous."

"Well, that's exactly why I need to know what it is," replied Olive. "If what you say is true, and it's so dangerous, wouldn't it be even more dangerous to not know about it? To live in a world dominated by it, yet be helpless against it?"

Will went to retort, to fight for his case, but nothing came out. He couldn't fault her logic. He said nothing.

Olive sighed. "If you must know the reason, I'm writing a song about magic," she continued. "Figured I needed to learn what it actually was before I start smashing words together that don't make any sense."

"And that's all you want me for?"

"Exactly," she said with a smile.

Will nodded. That made things easy. A simple exchange. She had helped him find his book, so he would help her. No complications. No wondering if they were friends or not. No lingering threat of betrayal.

He slumped his shoulders and rocked backward on his feet. "Fine. I'll teach you what I know, but only if you promise me to never act on your knowledge."

Olive took two steps forward, snorting at his comment. "Don't worry, I know the basics at least. I'm not going to go round murdering the first person I meet. I told you, I just want to learn, not to act."

Will studied her, searching for any sign she might be misleading him. "Meet me back here just before sunset tomorrow. I should have some spare time then."

Olive's smile returned, and Will almost spilled everything he knew then and there. "Great, it's a date," she said.

Will froze, staring dumbly at Olive as she skipped towards him. "Oh, relax! it was just a jest. You should see your face right now. Priceless! You really need to lighten up, else those frown lines will stick."

She skipped past him, bouncing on the balls of her feet. "Don't be late! See you tomorrow, Will."

# Chapter 20
## - Myddrin -

Myddrin sat in a prison cell, handcuffed and blindfolded. He rubbed his head against the cold stone in an attempt to push aside the fabric over his eyes. If he could just move it another inch, he could get himself free in an instant.

Hands and fingers gave a mage a sort of focus, a means with which to direct and control their creations. Even so, an accomplished mage could still make and manipulate their images without the use of their hands. Eyes, however, were vital instruments for touching the *otherside*. Myddrin didn't know exactly how it worked, but a person's eyes were directly linked to their soul. Without sight, there could be no magic.

His head throbbed. His tongue felt dry, and his fingers itched. It had been two days since he'd last had a drink or a smoke. He'd already vomited once. The stink of it lingered, and he regretted having eaten fish for his last meal.

Beyond his fatigue burned a deep-seated hatred for the church. It only seemed to grow the longer he was kept here. He couldn't believe it. The world was a lie. People believed in the afterlife, thought that once their life was over they could truly rest. But this whole time their souls just ended up here, beneath Athedale, to be forever hoarded in the cage of a dead god.

And now he'd found out the church not only knew about it, but were taking from it! A thousand questions buzzed around in his mind. Why would they hide this? Who was involved? How much did the king know? Why hadn't he done something? Had

Beyan and Glade been caught too? Was Mees safe?

He heard the cell door click, and two sets of footsteps stopped before him.

"So, you're the man who defiled our sacred site," came a squeaky, high pitched male voice. Myddrin thought he recognised it, but he couldn't quite place it.

"The Doonssslayer," the man continued, emphasising the 's' as if he had a lisp. "You should never have come back."

Myddrin fixed his lips into another fake smile. He remembered the voice now. How could he forget? It was the same man who had spoken at this year's Passing. The same man he had seen with Thane. Cardinal Adralan.

"Welcome, Your Holiness," he said. "If I had have known you were coming, I would have fixed the place up a bit." He nodded to where he was sure his vomit still sat at the Cardinal's feet. "Please accept my sincere apologies."

"You arrogant, selfish, fool of a man. Do you know what you have done? Do you know what your... your... your..."

"Discovery?" Myddrin interrupted.

"*Recklessness* has caused?" Adralan continued. "The well has sat undisturbed for centuries. Its contents are hidden for a reason. Now an entire section sits beneath a pile of rock and stone. You should not have been in there. You are not meant to know of such things, Doonssslayer."

"Undisturbed?" Myddrin said. "You're taking from it. I saw you with Thane. I know what you did. What you're doing. Why?"

The cardinal was silent for a time. Myddrin knew he should have kept his mouth shut, that he was just making things worse for himself, but he had to know. He needed to know why they would hide such a huge part of their religion.

"You know, for all of your knowledge, you still have no idea how the world works, do you?" the cardinal said. "What do you think would happen if people lost faith? If they knew the truth? Is the world not plagued enough by Axel's stench?

"We have faith in Aen," he continued. "I have faith in Aen. One day he will fix this curse. He will return to us and correct his brother's wrongs. He will free those souls from their prison. Until that day, I will protect this secret with my life. The few lie, so that the many may thrive."

Myddrin slackened. He hated the fact that Adralan was right. What good would it do if people knew the truth? If people knew that their soul was destined for such an afterlife, there would be anarchy, rebellion, chaos. There would be no incentive to follow the rules, to abide by the church's teachings, to be kind.

Something still itched at him though.

"That doesn't explain why you're taking from it," Myddrin said. "Why you're using the souls from the well to bolster the strength of your Knights."

Myddrin listened as Adralan sighed. "I told you, until Aen returns, I will do whatever is necessary to protect what is down there, and our religion. After that vile man whose name you bear invaded, I have lost confidence in those in charge of protecting this city. We are not strong enough. I take no joy in disturbing the dead, but we need them to protect the living. Thus is my duty fulfilled."

"And does the king see it this way?"

Adralan grumbled.

"What if I could fix it?" Myddrin said.

"Fix what?"

"The world. The souls. The well. What if I could find a way to correct it now? We wouldn't have to wait for Aen to come and save us."

"Ridiculous. We are not gods. We have no say in such matters."

"Have you even tried?" Myddrin pressed. "There must be a way. If you would but allow me to study it, to experiment…"

"Absolutely not!" Adralan snapped. "You may hoard the most souls out of any other living human, but do not think yourself so mighty as to be greater than a god. You are nothing. A drunk and a drug addict. Nothing more. Thane, ready the poker. Burn out his eyes."

Myddrin's entire body stiffened. The second pair of footsteps… Thane was here.

He wriggled in his bonds to no avail. He was no fighter. Without the ability to touch the *otherside*, he was nothing, just a common citizen.

Although, without his eyes, would the pain inside disappear? Maybe it would be better this way. Then he could be free of this torment.

No.

This wasn't the answer. The voices wouldn't stop. His pain wouldn't end. He needed to get out. He needed to fix it, fix the world.

For Ismey.

He heard the sizzle of metal over a fire. He felt Thane's thick hands grip his shoulder, grip his head, holding it tight. Myddrin waited for the blindfold to lower. He would only have a moment. He had to make it count. Did they not realise who he was? The danger he posed? He readied himself to end them, to kill them both. All he needed was a sliver of light. He felt his souls begin to churn inside.

*Do it*
*Kill them*
*We will help you*
*Release us*

Then the blindfold lowered.

"What is the meaning of this?" came a shout from behind Thane before he could act.

Myddrin could see. The blindfold had fallen below his left eye. He could end it all now.

"Explain yourselves!"

Myddrin froze.

The king stood behind Adralan and Thane, a trio of blue-clad guards at his side. Myddrin saw Beyan behind them, his bald head bowed low. A silver-haired individual walked into the light as well. Halvair.

If looks could kill, the king would be dead right now. Adralan flushed with fury. His nostrils flared and his arms stiffened. He turned to face the king. "This man has been caught desecrating the Providence. That is an unforgivable crime. It is well within my jurisdiction to punish him as I see fit."

The king sighed, though it came out as more of a grunt. "Release him," he said.

"I will do no such thing. King you may be, but this falls beyond even your power. I will see this man punished for what he has done to my tomb."

"This is a time of war!" Remen shouted. "I will not have my word challenged. Not here, not now."

"You would deny the authority of the church?" Adralan said.

The king turned, letting his hands rest on his hips. "This is not a matter of rebellion against the church. A more pressing situation has arisen and I need his help. Kildeen has fallen. Carthon and his Reapers have taken the city. My brother has trapped himself in a dome of magic while crossing the Penella Pass. Reports say he has ten of his best Knights with him, but I don't know how long their magic will hold."

Adralan scoffed. "This man is my prisoner! I have every right to—"

"I am the king and I say this man is to be released into my custody!"

The tension continued to build as Thane took a step towards Remen. Halvair took a step forward of his own.

Myddrin had stopped listening after 'Carthon'…

He was coming. The man who held his wife's soul. He was here, within reach. Myddrin tingled with a mixture of excitement and anxiety. This was his chance to free her. He had to go. Needed to go.

"I'll do it," he said, breaking the stand-off. All eyes turned to him. Adralan flushed even redder, but there was nothing he could do about it.

"I'll rescue your brother. But first, I need to know if Mees is safe."

# Chapter 21
# - Will -

Will took a deep breath in.

"Deeper," Crisalli called from her rocky perch. "Keep those eyes closed. You want to feel your belly steadily expand. Relax every muscle in your body. Imagine your breath is made of light, and that light is healing every part of you wherever it goes, including your thoughts and emotions.

"Now share that light with everything around you. Allow it to consume you, become you."

Will did as he was told. He had practiced these breathing techniques with his grandfather every day after training. In a calm setting, he could comfortably meditate for hours.

Nothing was calm anymore. Everything had changed.

*You're not strong enough*

*We can feel your weakness*

*You will break*

*Let us out*

Will felt his throat constrict. He began to struggle for air, his breaths coming short and sharp. Eventually, he gave in and lost control of his thoughts, his emotions. He lost his posture and began taking ragged breaths as he gasped for air.

"I can't," he said, angry at himself. "I can hear them. I can always hear them. They know. They know I'm weak!"

Crisalli came down from her rock with a thump and pressed close to him. "You're not weak, Will. You're strong," she made a fist and squeezed it tight. "Try again. This time, allow the voices to speak. Don't let them in, just listen to what they say."

"What?" Will said. "You can't be serious?"

"I'm very serious. If your mind becomes crowded, I want you to observe. Allow them to enter without fight or judgement. Observe the reactions they evoke in you and let those reactions occur without struggling against them. Then, when you're comfortable, allow them to gently disappear.

"You need to develop patience. Patience brings harmony, and once you've achieved such a state, you'll become comfortable with the voices and, more importantly, confident in your ability to quash them."

Will didn't like the idea. It scared him. Terrified him, even. The thought of being consumed by the voices, of breaking and turning into whatever horror he had seen atop that mountain sent a shiver down his spine.

But he was no coward. He was a Knight. How could he expect to live up to the standard set by his heroes if he didn't even have the courage to face a few voices?

He repositioned himself. He crossed his legs and placed the tips of his thumbs to his index fingers.

"Focus," he whispered, before sucking in another deep breath.

He did as instructed, feeling the light of his breath warm his body. He waited for them to come, keeping his breathing pattern steady.

*It won't work,* came a single voice.

*You can't fight us*

*We're inside you*

*We are you*

*Let us out*

Will's first reaction was to cut them off, to swipe at them with an invisible claw. He wanted to distract his mind, to silence them.

He acknowledged that reaction, then dismissed it. He felt his confidence begin to grow. He allowed them to speak again.

*You think yourself clever*

*You're nothing*

*Worthless*

*We will break you*

Each voice was distinct in its own way. Some screamed loud. Others whispered. Some he had heard before. Others were new.

His breathing staggered, but he kept listening.

*You're not strong enough*

*You're weak*

*Pathetic*

*Let us out*

*Let us out*

*Let us out!*

*Let us out!*

LET US OUT!

LET US OUT!!

"AHH!" Wil screamed. He gasped, trying to suck in some breath, but it wouldn't come. He clawed at the air, trying to force it into his throat.

Pain lanced across his cheek. The voices vanished, and his ability to breathe returned.

"You slapped me!" he said, only now realising what Crisalli had done.

"Pain resets the mind, shifts its focus. You let them consume you," she said.

Will looked to the ground. "I'm sorry. I tried. It was working, but I couldn't do it for long."

"We'll try again tomorrow. This is something you must master. If you don't, you'll break. I want to build up your tolerance. Eventually, I'd like to try it while you're surrounded by your irritations, though I think I'll build on them gradually rather than throwing them at you all at once again. Then I'd like to try it while you create images. The voices always scream the loudest while you're using their souls."

Will nodded. "I'll practice every spare moment."

"Don't push too hard while I'm not there. If you break, you'll be a danger to anyone around you. You'll be put down."

Will gulped. He had always respected the Knights, but it was only since he had become one of them that he truly appreciated what they did. What they sacrificed.

He had to be careful.

He had to be better.

Will scurried up the side of the mountain as the sun descended to meet him, dipping just below the peak. He'd spent the entire day training, and now he was late. He'd promised Olive he would be here. He owed her a debt, one he intended to repay.

Will panted, hands on knees. His legs already ached, and his body yearned for sleep. Nevertheless, once he hit the clearing, he straightened and scanned the area.

Light was fading quickly. He rounded a bend in the cliff-face and was greeted by the wide sea beyond. The clouds were painted with changing colours as the golden disc of the sun melted into the sapphire blue current below. A ship was returning to port, and people dotted the coastline, bustling about in preparation.

Through the silence of the sunburned sky, he heard a voice. At first, he thought it was directed towards him. He turned and focused but saw nothing. The voice continued, and now its nature was clearer. It was a person singing.

It sounded distant at first. Will followed it, drawn to the melody. As he drew closer, the singing grew louder, more distinct. It was beautiful, feminine, reminding him of his mother when she used to sing to him at night before bed.

Through the hum of the soft lyrics there was a sadness to the song. Olive sat on the edge of the cliff, legs dangling off the side as she sung and watched ships sail in the distant sea.

*Ships in the night*
*Where lights shine blue*
*Ships in the night*
*Where dreams come true*

*Ships in the night*
*May you weather the storm*
*Ships in the night*
*May the nights keep you warm*

*Ships in the night*
*Where the ocean is clear*
*Ships in the night*
*Where people disappear*

Will tripped over a stray rock and tumbled out into the open, causing Olive to pause. She turned, covering her mouth with her hand to stifle a laugh. She stared as he awkwardly flapped his arms in apology.

"I — I'm sorry! I didn't mean to interrupt," he said, holding one arm with his opposite hand to stop it from moving.

Olive rose and moved to meet him. "You're late."

Will exhaled. "I know. I'm sorry, again. I was held up. But I'm here, as promised."

"Right, well, shall we get started?"

Will obliged, making himself comfortable on the cliff's edge. "Where did you learn to sing like that? It was beautiful."

"Oh, that? I'm not sure, I suppose I've always been able to sing. Kind of have to practice as much as I can if I want to sing my songs throughout all of Otor one day."

"All of Otor?" Will questioned, puzzled at just how she might accomplish that feat given the state of things.

"Yes, why not? I'm composing a medley of songs. When complete, I plan to leave Athedale and the Gracelands. I want to ride across the Harrows and sing in the slums of every passing village. I want to sail across the Mirror Sea and grace the halls of En Belin with tale and song. I want to visit Ganta, to learn, to experience, to write. Even the Black Keep of Tal Varoth must be in need of music. Surely the wicked can soften with a tune and a dance."

"You're insane," Will said. Though even he had to admire her passion, however unrealistic her goal might be.

"Perhaps," she replied. "But then again, we live in an insane world."

Will couldn't fault her there.

"What do you want to know then?" Will said.

"Hmm. Do you really take from another world when you make things? Like, can you see inside of it or something? The dead place?"

"The *otherside*," Will corrected. "Yes, we do take 'things'. But no, we can't see inside, at least, I can't. It's more mental than anything else. We picture what we want, the air kind of ripples, then it just appears."

"So, you can just make whatever you want?"

"No, not at all. There's a limit. You also have to know your object's precise make in the real world, though it is possible to change it, add to it. And I guess you can make your own creations, but I haven't got that far yet."

"What do those colours mean?" Olive continued. "I've always wondered. When you Knights make things, why is everything a different colour?"

Will groaned. "You really don't know anything at all, do you?"

Olive shrugged. "Not really. My father keeps me away from it as much as possible, says I have no business knowing it."

Will nodded. He could understand a father's pressure.

"Well, the colours are linked to your soul. Everyone's soul has its own colour. It's the same colour as your eyes, actually. That's why my images shine blue."

"Oh, cool! I want to see mine! Can you teach me how to make something?"

"Uh, it doesn't quite work that way. You need more than one soul to take from the *otherside*. And I'm sure that even you know what that means…"

Olive's cheeks flushed. "Maybe magic's not for me then…"

Will laughed. He told her of the voices next, of their continued presence inside of him. He told her of the first time he'd made an image, defending the bird from Rath. He told her about what happens when you overuse your souls. Finally, he told her of what he'd seen in the cave the other day, though he left out the part about his mother. He wanted to tell her, to trust her, but it was too soon. What if she saw him differently, as so many others before her had? What if she thought him evil, tainted? The thought swirled in his mind, slowly consuming him until the voices within threatened to take advantage.

He snapped his eyes shut tight and then forced them open again. None of that mattered. They weren't friends. This was just a mutual exchange. Nothing more. It was safer that way.

Olive yawned. "I think that's enough for today. I'll see you tomorrow though, right?" She held out her hand for him to shake. "Friends?"

# Chapter 22
# - Myddrin -

For two days and a good portion of two nights, Myddrin had ridden on horseback. His bottom ached. Every inch of his body rebelled against him as the company of Knights tasked with the duke's rescue pushed him beyond his physical limits.

He hadn't ridden a horse in years. When they stopped beneath the shadow of a large tree for respite, Myddrin wasted no time unstopping his wine cask and downing the contents.

He bent over, hands on knees. Wine dribbled down his chin. Two days sober in captivity had been good for him, but it had also been terrible. He had been in pain the entire time. He knew two days wasn't enough, that if he truly meant to quit, he would need to stay sober for much longer. This wasn't the time for that.

Carthon was out there, within reach. He couldn't risk changing his routine, not now.

He rose to find Mees' arm hovering in front of him with a small cask. Myddrin smiled and grabbed it, quickly downing its contents.

He gagged, then spat it out. "Water? I wanted more wine!"

"You're not in Athedale anymore. Out here, the weather is harsh. You'll die without it. Now drink."

Myddrin grunted and took another sip, this time keeping it down. "I should have let you rot in prison."

The plains beyond Athedale were flat and devoid of vegetation. He had never liked the Harrows. The constant fear of ambush was ever-present in his mind, though he doubted anyone lingering in these lands would dare try to take on a heavily armed contingent of Knights of Aen.

A man named Edlian led the charge. He was a brute, and a hard task master. Myddrin remembered the name from his youth. He had fought in the war all those years ago, earning himself quite the reputation among the order.

"How much farther?" Myddrin asked Edlian, mounting his horse again.

"Kildeen lies just beyond the fissure ahead. This will be our last stop. Keep vigilant. We don't know what horrors lie within the cracked lands."

Myddrin looked to the horizon. The flat of the plains morphed into a wall of segmented plateaus, each broken into sections as if they had once been whole, and then were cracked in the centre by the hammer of a god.

Shadows closed in as he rode into the crevasse. The narrow corridor barely allowed three horses to ride abreast, so the company was forced to split, snaking in a double line after Edlian as they navigated the maze that was the Penella Pass.

Myddrin's anxiety deepened the further they ventured. The Knight riding by his side shuddered. He began hyperventilating, struggling to take a proper lungful of air.

The horses had slowed to a walk, so Myddrin unhooked his wine cask from his belt and offered it to him. The Knight grabbed the cask and took a lengthy swig. Myddrin rolled his eyes, already regretting wasting so much of his supply on him.

"T — thanks," the Knight said, finally taking in some deep breaths. "One last drink before I die."

"You're not going to die," Myddrin replied, though his tone didn't convey the confidence he had intended.

"This is a suicide mission. All know it," replied the frightened Knight. "The city was attacked a ten-day ago. There's no way the duke could survive this long. The whole thing is probably a trap."

"Quiet!" snapped Edlian from atop his horse in front. "We are Knights of Aen, not frightened children. We have been given an order and we will see it through."

No one spoke for the next hour after that. They continued into the fissure, its end out of sight. Night began to fall, and darkness consumed them. Torches were lit. Expressions were hardened. Myddrin tensed, expecting the shouting to begin at any moment.

Everything stilled.

A faint, blue glow emanated from the distance. It was indistinct, but Myddrin knew the hue of magic when he saw it. He went to inform Edlian, but the hardy Knight had already focused on it. He waved a hand, cautioning silence and ordering the company forward.

Before they drew closer, they dismounted, deciding a silent approach would work best. Myddrin crept quietly, hunching his shoulders and hugging the wall like a common thief.

Ahead, rubble blocked the way forward. Stray blocks of stone lay strewn across the crevasse as if someone had tried to cave in the entire fissure. The blue glow shined bright like a beacon between the dark shapes of fallen rock.

Myddrin stopped. Muffled voices sounded from beyond the blockage.

Edlian frowned and pressed his ear to the stone, then motioned for men to begin clearing the rubble. Knights busied around him, quietly removing pieces of stone and fitting them neatly further down the path.

Myddrin waited as men continued to clear the way. He thought of joining them. It wasn't as though it was beneath him, but he had a sinking feeling that he needed to save his strength. The men knew better than to give him dirty looks, for they knew he was their only hope of returning safely to their families.

Myddrin pulled his pipe out to have a smoke when the distinct sound of shouting sounded from beyond the rubble. It was soon followed by a loud thump that shook the fissure. Stray pieces of rock tumbled from the top and nearly knocked the pipe from his hand.

The quake continued like a continuous drumbeat. It felt as though someone were running a battering ram into the wall over and over again. Edlian's Knights quickened their pace, practically throwing chunks of stone out of the way as they fought to see the other side.

With a great effort, a team of about twelve managed to remove one of the larger pieces, giving Myddrin a clear view of the spectacle beyond. The blue glow was, indeed, a domed image-wall. On Myddrin's side, the transparent wall of magic was thin, perhaps only two layers deep. On the opposing side there rose a thick, multi-layered barricade erected by the souls of at least eight Knights. Differing colours of magic overlapped each other, creating what seemed to be an impenetrable barrier.
Just over a dozen figures lay within the dome structure. They looked exhausted.

Two men lay dead on the ground, their throats slashed. Dried blood stained the ground in pools around their bodies.    Over half a dozen Knights still stood inside the dome, their hands raised in an attempt to hold the wall as something clobbered against the barrier from the opposing side, while the rest of the people cowered.    Duke Christoval of Kildeen lay sprawled in the centre, his golden coronet hanging loosely from his head. Dirt muddied the crimson red of his royal uniform.

Edlian shouted something over Myddrin's shoulder, causing the duke to turn and almost sprint in his direction. His voice was muffled through the conjured wall of stone, but Myddrin understood a plea for help when he saw one.

"My name is Edlian, commander of the sixth brigade of the Knights of Aen. We were sent by your brother, King Remen Anders, to see you safely back to Athedale."

The duke mouthed a 'thank you' before turning to shout orders to the others trapped within the dome.

A boy not quite old enough to have taken the Passing was the most active, rising to his feet and practically carrying two men who had collapsed to the rear side of the dome. The blue wall fell on Myddrin's side, allowing the exhausted duke through to collapse into the arms of one of Edlian's men.

"What happened here?" Edlian asked as three women rushed out of the dome to safety, followed by the boy and the two he carried.

The duke rose to his feet, his voice hoarse as he called for water. Edlian obliged, handing the ageing duke a canteen and watching as he gulped it down in one go.

The duke took a steadying breath. "Kildeen has fallen. We tried to escape but they caved in the fissure. My Knights have kept them at bay for ten days, but their magic is nearly depleted. We already lost two, their souls broke," he gestured towards the two dead bodies. "We had to slash their throats," the duke said between breaths. "Thank Aen you're here, I doubt we could have lasted another day."

Just as he spoke those words, another crash sounded on the other side of the dome as their assailants doubled their efforts.

Myddrin rushed toward the duke. "Carthon, is he here?" He had to calm himself. He noticed how he must sound. His eyes were wide, and he was practically grabbing the duke by the scruff of his neck.

The duke shook him off. "Who are you to speak to me in such a way? My city may have fallen but I am still a duke."

Edlian stepped between them. "This is Myddrin, Hero of

White-Rock."

The duke's jaw went slack. "The Doonslayer." He seemed almost in a daze before recognition stuck and he jolted back to reality. "I haven't seen Carthon since the city fell, but he was there. These people are savage. They trapped their own men between my army and their own and sent them to a slaughter. They have no honour, no morals. I will see my people avenged."

Myddrin wandered into the dome. People may have been calling for him to stop, for him to come back, but the voices inside spoke louder.

*He's here*
*We can feel him*
*Go to him*
*Claim your revenge*
*Claim her*
*Use us*
*Release us*

Myddrin continued forward, driven by his desire to see Carthon. He watched as the Duke's Knights struggled relentlessly to keep their defensive wall standing. All manner of offensive magic was being thrown at it. Myddrin couldn't discern any faces out there, they were all just shapes muddled together beyond the assault.

Step by slow step, Myddrin inched closer to the wall. He could feel it in his heart, Carthon was here. It was an ache that would never stop. The man who held Ismey's soul stood beyond that wall.

Myddrin had never killed for pleasure before, only ever in self-defence. His conscience was far from clear, but he had always held himself to a certain code. Carthon would be the exception to this code. Myddrin would rip this man limb from limb. He would tear him apart if it meant he could recapture his wife's soul. He refused to even imagine how she must be feeling, her essence trapped within the body of such a foul creature.

His chest flared as he reached for his souls. Edlian's deep voice rang in his ear, calling for retreat, but he paid it no mind.

The assault on the wall ceased as a black silhouette appeared, the figure's features hidden behind the thick veil of image-stone and shrouded by a cloud of dust.

Myddrin stared, unmoving, unwilling to back down. He could feel him. Feel her.

Carthon was baiting him. He knew it, he just didn't care.

"Let down your defences," Myddrin snarled at the eight remaining Knights holding up the wall.

They stared dumbly at him, their faces strained with the effort of holding the image up. They ignored him.

"I said let down your defences!" Myddrin shouted with more authority than he knew he had. "They will leave you here to die." He motioned to the duke. "Is that what you want? I can handle them. Go, be with your families."

The Knights remained still, burdened by duty and likely unsure who Myddrin even was. He could see that they wavered, they just needed a push.

Myddrin called upon his souls and ripped into the *otherside*. A giant wall twice as thick as their own appeared. He turned. "Take the duke and return to Athedale. I'll hold them here," he shouted, though Myddrin had no intention of holding the wall.

Edlian seemed to listen. He ushered Christoval onto a spare horse and departed without another word. The Knights beside Myddrin followed their duke, sparing a thankful look his way before fleeing through the rubble and down the fissure.

That left him alone to face the wrath of Carthon and his army. He knew it was stupid, that he should turn and flee. Despite what he would like to think, he was not invincible. But a hatred he thought he had buried rose to the surface. He wouldn't hide any longer. This man needed to pay for what he had done.

He resisted the urge to lower his wall, giving the duke enough time to flee. While he waited, he swore he could hear laughter from the other side. A deep, cackling bellow. He clenched his fist. The man was teasing him, baiting him.

Once the duke was out of sight, Myddrin waved his hand, opening a gap in his wall. He held a firm stance as the face of his enemy revealed itself. Carthon stood within the emerald light of his image, looking down on Myddrin through dark, beady eyes the colour of coal. Carthon's features blurred as Myddrin's mind replayed the image of his wife's blue sphere being consumed over and over and over again by the black death that was his magic.

"We have history, you and me," Carthon said, taking a step forward.

"You die here today," Myddrin replied. "Return what you took from me."

Carthon just laughed. "So, you have come to kill me. I knew you would. People told me you were soft. They said you fled, ran all the way to the middle of the Mirror Sea to hide. Poor little Myddrin just wants to fix the world. It's what she wanted, isn't it. To rid the world of magic."

Myddrin's whole body seized. His arms and legs stiffened, though his eyes followed the huge Reaper as he paced the inside of the dome.

"I'll let you in on a little secret. Magic's not going anywhere. This world is broken, and you are proof of it. All it took was a little bait. You just couldn't help yourself, could you. The chance for vengeance, it called to you. The chance to kill me, to free your wife's soul. I don't blame you. The need for revenge is natural. It's part of who we are. It's why Axel didn't want us. Why he tried to end us, to start anew. It's why he cursed us. And he was right, even the purest of souls can be corrupted."

"Shut up. I'm nothing like you."

"Oh, but you are, you just can't admit it to yourself." When Myddrin didn't respond, Carthon continued. "She speaks to me, you know. Ismey. Sweet, sweet Ismey. She was a pure soul if I've ever seen one. But it's as I said, even the purest of souls can be corrupted. She hates me, tries to break me every chance she gets. She's stronger than the rest. Much, much stronger. But her efforts are in vain. She is nothing but a power source for me. Speaking of which, how's my father doing? He's still in there, no? Hello Father!" Carthon said, bending down and waving at Myddrin's chest.

A solitary tear ran down Myddrin's left cheek. His fists clenched. His arms tensed. His souls churned. His head ached. "Enough!" he screamed.

"That's it!" Carthon said. "There's that anger. That need. That desire. It burns inside all of us. Embrace it. Fight me for her! Do it. Fight. Kill me and she shall be yours!"

Myddrin didn't care anymore. He gave in to the rage. The hatred. He dismissed his dome of magic and in the same moment pictured his dragon in his mind. The emerald dragon he had named Shirok crystallized in mid-air motion as Myddrin pulled from the *otherside* faster than he had ever done before.

Shirok swooped. Its long and powerful snout opened wide, revealing a set of razor-sharp teeth, each the size of a dagger.

Cathon reacted. He drew from his own cage and created a scaly image of his own in the form of a giant basilisk. The black serpent matched Shirok in height, slithering forward and wrapping the dragon in a tight embrace, immobilising the creature, rendering them both useless.

Usually, Myddrin would have let it be, would have given up on Shirok in favour of another image, one much less soul-consuming, but he wasn't in his right mind. He dismissed Shirok, only to recreate it free from the basilisk's embrace. Myddrin's souls worked feverishly, drawing substance from the *otherside*, stitching sinew and muscle, scale and bone.

The new Shirok startled the self-proclaimed emperor, sending him retreating onto his back-foot. Carthon managed to produce a shield-wall in time to parry the dragon's second assault, but Myddrin was wise to the trick. He changed the trajectory of Shirok's descent with a wave of his off hand. The dragon whipped its tail around the black wall, snapping into Carthon's rear and sending him crashing head-first into his own creation.

Carthon staggered and snarled in disbelief. Myddrin didn't relent. He pressed his offensive with a variety of creations, this time in the form of spears. He hurled spear after spear at the now retreating Carthon.

"Give her to me!" Myddrin shouted above the commotion as the green of his weapons met the black of Carthon's. Dust swirled around their feet.

Myddrin's chest heaved. He ceased his assault, panting heavily. When the light of his images faded, his world darkened once more.

He heard laughter from multiple directions. Torches lit, highlighting distant forms. The fissure widened, and Myddrin found himself suddenly surrounded.

Skullsworn.

He grit his teeth and pulled on his souls once more. Shirok returned to him. The shadowed forms revealed themselves in Shirok's light. There were dozens of them, looking down at him with smug grins from small ridges set on the edges of the fissure.

Myddrin hated them. All of them. They would pay for taking Ismey from him. Carthon began to rally, to reshape his basilisk, but Myddrin wasn't about to wait. He threw both arms forward, commanding Shirok towards the mass of snickering Skullsworn.

The dragon smashed into them, sending some sprawling through the air, and squashing others. A number of fresh souls filtered through the rising dust and flowed into Myddrin's cage.

Carthon cried out in pain, much to Myddrin's delight, as Shirok landed heavily on his leg.

Another form sprinted past Myddrin's image and began to hurl pebble-sized projectiles at him. It all happened so fast he barely had time to raise his defence. A blood-coloured pebble skimmed off the tip of his sloppily solidified shield-wall and sank into the flesh beside his left collarbone.

Myddrin flew backward as the force of the blow sent him reeling. He landed with a thud. He felt at his shoulder, fingers coming away red.

A cloaked figure emerged within the swirl of light. His face twitched, a sure sign of a soul on the verge of breaking. The pain in Myddrin's shoulder caused his vision to turn foggy as the crazed man stepped over his prone form. A little red image-ball hovered above him, ready to kill.

"Septus, no!" came a call from behind. "Myddrin's soul is mine to take!"

The crazed figure hesitated, but didn't look as if he was about to stop. The red ball inched forward. Myddrin made to form an image, to defend himself, but the pain was too great. He couldn't focus, couldn't picture what he needed, not in time.

A blur of movement came from his side, a shape leaping from the shadows. A man. He stabbed the crazed Reaper in the ribs and kicked him in the chest. The Reaper wailed, clutching his side as he attempted to crawl to safety.

The newcomer turned, and Myddrin let out a groan of both pain and relief.

"Mees," he said.

Mees had brandished a long glaive, born of his magic. He twirled it in his hands in a marvellous show of skill before posing in a defensive stance over Myddrin's prone form.

"About bloody time you showed up," Myddrin said, spitting blood on the dirt.

An array of soul-hunters pressed the offensive, their confidence bolstered by their numbers. They were no match for Mees, however. The skilful Hand cut them down with strikes so precise that Myddrin couldn't even see where they were cut before they fell.

Myddrin's hold over Shirok subsided, and the dragon turned to mist. This allowed more soul-hunters to enter the fray, forcing Mees to retreat. He continued to defend Myddrin as if his life depended on it, which it did. He recreated and dismissed images as easily as if he were breathing. All of Mees' images were perfect replicas of what he intended to create, his copy memory allowing him to recall even the most minute detail.

He bashed a particularly eager soul-hunter over the head with an image-hammer and dropped a boulder the size of a small house on top of another, crushing him beneath its weight. He turned toward Myddrin. "What are you waiting for, fool? Christoval left us a horse. We must get out of here."

Myddrin reacted. Moving through the pain, he rose to his feet and hobbled toward where they had come. He found his horse tied to a post driven into the ground. He untied the rope and placed a foot in the stirrup, then forced his weight over the horse's back.

The Hand bolted toward him, turning only to brandish a solid wall of stone of his own making. As Mees mounted, Myddrin tucked in awkwardly behind him, his head slumping on the Hand's shoulder. Mees kicked the horse into action. Myddrin spared a bitter glance behind, watching as the Skullsworn attempted to penetrate Mees's wall. Carthon was somewhere behind it, alive, Ismey's soul still trapped inside of him.

# Chapter 23
## - Will -

Crisalli's earlier warmth had all but vanished. Her lessons had once again grown harsh, bordering on cruel, mostly because Will hadn't progressed as much as she would have liked. He still couldn't produce an image other than his grandfather's shield.

He dangled from a branch that overhung a cliff, harsh winds cutting through his bare skin as Crisalli launched pebble-shaped missiles in his direction. He looked down. The drop wasn't enough to kill him, perhaps not even enough to break a leg. The fear of falling didn't come from the dread of landing though, but rather from the punishment Crisalli might have for him. Cuts had already ripped through his skin and healed over in the past ten-day. The rigorous exercise took a heavy toll on his body.

A pebble struck hard on his left knee-cap. Will gasped as the impact of rock on bone sent a jolt through his leg. His grip on the branch faltered, slipping an inch.

"You're sloppy today," Crisalli called, her voice ringing in the distance above the rapid gush of circulating wind. "Focus on your defences, call upon your souls. You're their master, not the other way around."

Will grimaced. He focused on his training, going through a number of mental exercises Crisalli had taught him. He took a deep breath through his nose, following the air's path as his belly expanded. He relaxed his muscles, releasing the tension in each of them save for his arms and fingers, which were nearly at their limit of exertion.

Following Crisalli's instruction, he listened to the voices. Instead of running away from them, he tried to pay attention, to find out which ones were the loudest.

He opened his eyes just as Crisalli's arm thrust forward. He called upon his souls and the ghost of his shield appeared in the air before his right shoulder. When he tightened his hold, it shimmered into physical existence. Crisalli's pebble crashed into the sapphire-coated replica and Will watched it fall into the muddy puddle below.

"Yes!" Will shouted, letting his lips sneak into a smirk, only to have the smile wiped from his face a moment later as Crisalli conjured at least a half dozen pebble-sized images from the *otherside* and hurled them toward him all at once. He tensed, desperately trying to bring forth a second image-shield to protect his prone body but there were too many, he didn't have the time. His grip on the branch faltered and he fell into the mud pile, knees bending as he rolled into the landing to soften the impact. His ankles ached as he sprawled onto his back, panting heavily to recapture lost breath.

He heard wet footsteps making their way over to him. He tried to get up, but found his arms and legs were bound by what looked to be some form of *otherside*-born branches. They wrapped around his entire body, holding him in place even as he squirmed, letting out a defeated yelp.

Crisalli's smoky, violet eyes bore down on him. She crossed her arms and shook her head. "Smugness will only get you killed in open battle. When in combat with another mage, you must always think three steps ahead. Don't get complacent. Learn to cast multiple images at once. Defensive tools can be effective, but you can only do so much with a shield. Think about how you like to fight and create an image that will best compliment your style. Stick to something simple for now."

Will felt the pressure ease as Crisalli dismissed his bonds. He sat up, feeling at his wrists before cracking his neck and wiggling his toes.

"I want to do what you can do! Create what you create. Teach me how, please."

Crisalli shook her head. "You're not ready for the more complicated images. Creating the image of a living organism requires finesse, as well as practice."

"Then let me practice!" Will insisted, sitting up.

"You've yet to even master the basics. Only those who have uncountable souls to call upon may form such delicate images through force of will alone. If you don't know what you're making, your creation will sap your souls' energy quicker than you can speak your own name."

"But it is possible?" he questioned. "To make the more complex images, to recreate the tissue of a living organism without the need to study for a lifetime?"

The crease on Crisalli's brow darkened. "The magic of imagery isn't necessarily a recreation. You're drawing from another plane of existence. In a sense, some images are very real. To answer your question, yes. It's possible, but also extremely soul-consuming. The better you know your subject matter, the less of your souls' energy you'll consume. There are Knights capable of crafting images beyond their skill level, even some who concoct their own twisted forms, re-imagining something through their own vision, but this method can be extremely taxing. I wouldn't recommend it, especially not when your mind is ill-prepared for the drawbacks."

Will gulped. It all sounded so complicated. He felt as though he hadn't even scratched the surface when it came to what he might be capable of.

"Before you learn to create the more difficult images, you

must learn the basics of movement," Crisalli continued. "Movement usually requires a focal point. Your hand and fingers are the most appropriate things for the task. They aren't necessarily required though."

As she spoke, she created an image of her own, another pebble. Will squirmed, expecting her to shoot it at him.

She shifted her left hand and Will watched as the pebble changed positions according to her movements. "Your hands may have control over it but, in reality, a mage's eyes hold the power. Take away a mage's sight, and they may as well just be a regular soldier running around blind.

"Most mages stick to a select few creations. If one decides to make something new in the heat of battle, their lack of preparation may cause their downfall. If you want to learn to move your images, practice different hand gestures."

Will went to speak but was stopped by his mentor's upheld hand.

"Complex images require a different skillset altogether. Take animals, for example. All are entirely possible to recreate, but almost all of them are completely different. They move in different ways. Some crawl, some slither, some fly, and some swim. If you want to learn a more complex image, I suggest you start with something small. Learn its make, its movements. Images are rarely perfect replicas, but the more you study, the more effective it will be, and the less soul-energy it will require."

Will's mind buzzed with activity. He wanted to do it now. To create something of his own. He let out a frustrated groan and began rapping his beat of five. He wasn't progressing as fast as he would have liked. He felt like a failure. He had all the power in the world, yet lacked the ability to do anything with it.

What would his grandfather think? What would his father think?

"We're done for the day," Crisalli said. "I suggest you take the rest of the evening to work on your simple creations and movement skills. I'm sorry if I've been extra harsh on you lately, but the Skullsworn are coming quicker than anticipated. We've been asked to accelerate our programs."

Will clenched his jaw. "Do you think I'll be ready to fight them?"

Crisalli's glare lingered. "That remains to be seen. War brings out the fight in us all. It's my job to prepare you, but it's yours to make sure you have enough grit in you to avoid an early grave."

Will sat at the foot of the mountain, atop a boulder overlooking the ravine. Olive was late. The two had spent nearly a dozen sessions together now, and she was usually punctual. As he waited, Will stared at the stump of a recently-felled tree.

He pressed his face closer, observing an ant as it moved across the wood. He watched it stop and start. It took off in one direction, only to stop and move again in a different one. It irked him. There was no clear pattern to it.

He wondered if there was a specific reason for the way they moved, a purpose. He couldn't find one.

"That's a funny looking stump. Anything interesting down there?"

Will jumped backwards, tripping and landing hard on his side. "Where'd you come from? You scared the soul out of me!"

Olive stood not three feet from him, hands on hips. She extended an arm. Will took it and she pulled him up.

"You know, for a Knight, you don't have very good awareness. Anyone could have snuck up on you just then."

"I know. I just get distracted easily. Come and look, can you see it?" he said, pointing at the stump of the tree.

"See what?"

"The pattern."

Olive looked at him the way his father used to whenever Will would try to show him something he found interesting.

"Look here," he said, tracing his hand around the one of the many concentric rings that made up the top of the stump. "You can see how old the tree is by counting the circles. The light ones form in the spring. They're usually thicker because the tree is growing quickly. The thinner, darker ones form in the fall, when there's not as much growth."

Olive followed his gaze, then bent down until she was level with him. "Oh, you're right! That's pretty cool. How do you know all of this stuff?"

Will shrugged. "I just do. I know no one else really cares. I know you probably don't either. I just… I find it interesting."

"I like that," Olive said. "And I do care. Probably not as much as you, but you know you can always talk to me about things that interest you, right? That's what friends are for. To listen, no judgement."

Will stiffened. He made to speak, but when only a gurgle came out, he resorted to a slow nod instead.

"You really like your patterns, don't you," Olive continued.

"Y— yes. It's how I make sense of the world. Everything has a pattern, a reason for existing, for acting a certain way. Some are just harder to find than others."

Olive looked him up and down. "I see. You look horrible by the way. Did something happen?"

Will groaned. He had managed to bathe himself, although he still bore dozens of cuts and welts from where Crisalli had worked her magic. "It's nothing," he managed to say.

"Not likely," Olive said. "You should tend to them. Your cuts, I mean. Lest they fester."

Will nodded, knowing full well they would just be replaced by new ones come tomorrow.

"Are you sure you're up to teaching me today?" she asked. "I won't hold it against you if your mind is elsewhere. The last thing I want is for my teacher's soul to break. Then how will I learn to use my soul-energy?"

Will's eyes grew wide. "What? Tell me you haven't. Olive, tell me you haven't!"

Olive rolled her eyes. "You're really that gullible, aren't you. I swear, I get you with that trick every time. No, I haven't killed anybody. Not yet anyway," she said with a wink.

Will frowned. "Are you here to jest? Or are you here to learn? Sit down."

Olive obliged, sitting cross-legged on a softer looking patch of grass by the riverbank.

"Where were you, anyway?" Will asked. "It's almost sunset."

Olive shrugged. "My apologies. My uncle came to town."

Will lifted his chin. This was the first time she had spoken about even having a family. Up until now he believed her nothing more than a lost child living in the slums beneath the city. He decided to press the issue. "Who's your uncle?"

"No one important," she said.

"Then where has he come from?"

She paused. "He was living in Kildeen, before the city fell."

Will paused. The thought of an entire city being overrun by Skullsworn made his skin crawl. "Were there many survivors?"

"There were lots who fled before the invasion, yes."

"Will I ever get the chance to meet them? Your family, I mean."

Will regretted saying it the moment the words came out of his mouth. He was here to teach her, nothing more. But they were friends now, weren't they? Friends talked about family.

Olive's cheeks flushed. She quickly turned her head. "I don't like to talk about my family. I'm just here to learn about magic, if you don't mind."

Inside, Will hurt. This was what he'd been trying to avoid. The pain. The betrayal. He pushed it aside. He was being stupid. All she had said was she didn't want to talk about her family. He had to respect that.

He gestured for her to listen. "I don't have much to teach you today, unfortunately. I'm not making much progress. I still can't make any images other than my grandfather's shield and a few smaller objects. And every time I do, the voices inside my head just get worse and worse. I'm afraid… I'm afraid if I don't get better soon, then I'll be left behind. Left for dead…"

Olive pursed her lips. "Hmm. These voices, do they have a pattern?"

"W— what?" Will stuttered.

"A pattern. You said everything has a pattern. So, I thought maybe the voices do to. Maybe you can find it, use it somehow. It's the same with your images. Surely they must have a pattern too."

Will thought for a moment. He stopped to consider it. He had been so focused on avoiding the voices, on praying they wouldn't come, wouldn't consume him. Maybe this was what Crisalli meant by listening to them. Maybe he could do more than that. If he could find their pattern, decipher which of them screamed the loudest and when, maybe he could stop them.

"Olive, you're brilliant!"

Olive shrugged. "Really, Will, for someone so smart, you make it very hard for yourself sometimes."

She reached over and flipped open his sketchbook, which had been resting on the stone by his side.

"What are you doing?" Will said.

"Here. Try this."

"Huh? Try what?"

"This!" she said, shoving the open book in his face. The page showed an older drawing he had made of a hummingbird. He remembered sitting there for hours, observing the creature in its natural environment, figuring out the best way to represent it on paper.

"Make it," Olive pressed.

Will took the book from her, then studied the page. He knew the bird's pattern like the back of his hand. It's movements, its features, even the sounds it made.

"Close your eyes and pretend you're drawing. I've seen you do it. When you draw, the world around you may as well not exist. You become focused, entranced. Think of the pattern, then draw it in your mind."

Will obliged. He closed his eyes and pictured the bird the day he'd drawn it. Once the image was clear in his mind, he opened his eyes and began to project it. He felt his cage bubble beneath his chest as his souls leant him their power. He tensed, bracing himself for the inevitable pull of the voices. They came, of course. Hundreds of them. All whispers. He listened for the loudest, welcomed them.

*Nothing comes free*
*Our souls have a price*
*Your mind will break*
*Let us out*

Will flinched, but he didn't close them off as he might have before. He knew them, had heard them time and time again. He found their pattern, or at least some of it.

Will refocused, shifting his attention back to his creation. He waved his hand as he would a stick of charcoal. In a flash of light, the sapphire image of a hummingbird began to appear. He didn't need to finish it, as he would a real drawing. Now that he had a clear image of it, it blossomed into existence in its entirety. It hovered in the air, tiny wings beating. Its needle-thin beak poked at him as he moved to cup it in his hands.

"You did it!" Olive said!

"I — I did!"

"Maybe *I* should be *your* teacher from now on. Aen knows I have a knack for it."

Will laughed. "Maybe you should."

He continued practising for a while longer. He found Olive's presence helped him. Usually, he found other people irritating, distracting, but not her. He felt comfortable, as if the two of them were in a little bubble and the world surrounding them didn't exist.

"I have to get going," Olive said after a time. Will looked to the sky, which was steadily growing darker and darker. She was right. Descending the mountain's slope was not a task one wanted to attempt in the middle of the night. "I'll see you tomorrow, won't I? Same time?"

Will smiled and nodded. "Same time. And Olive," he said, catching her by the wrist as she made to depart. "Thank you. For today."

She smiled back at him, then began skipping away, dancing to a music-less tune as she went. "Bye, Will," she said, waving a backwards hand at him as she left. "Until tomorrow."

Will stared as she left, watching as she tripped and then rose again, curtseying to an invisible crowd as if she had meant it all along.

"Until tomorrow," he whispered under his breath.

# Chapter 24
# - Tvora -

They left the dead to rot.

Tvora stared beyond the stone parapet of Kildeen's broken wall. The dead just lay there, staring up at her with their empty, colourless eyes. The metallic tang of spilled blood mixed with the acrid scent of burnt embers flowed down the wide streets of the city, a reminder of the brutality which had taken place over the past few days.

Tvora felt renewed strength running through her veins. The souls of the Knights she had felled bolstered the reservoir of her soul-cage like no victory in the pits ever could have. How many had she even killed? Seven? Eight? Nine?

It didn't matter. They were all in the grave now.

She still remembered the face of the first Knight to meet her blade's bite. It flashed over and over again in her mind. It wasn't the look of a starved man who would kill anyone for the slightest taste of magic. No. It was the look of a man desperate to defend his country, to protect those he loved.

She tried to force the picture away. This was the hand life had dealt her. It wasn't her fault this was the way of the world.

Lucia prowled up behind her, Cecco flying just above. The sun was beginning to set. They had been with her half the day now. This was the longest they had ever been out without fading away, without her cage running dry.

"When will it be enough?" she said to Lucia.

*We're not done yet*, replied the panther. *We need more still.*

*Enough to sustain all three of us indefinitely. We're nearly there, I can feel it. Keep going Tvora. You owe us that much.*

Tvora's jaw clenched. It was true. She did owe them. How was it fair that she'd left their village with her life when the rest had burned? She owed it to them to give them their lives back, even if in the form of a spectre.

Something was bothering her though. Tvora enjoyed battle, enjoyed the thrill of taking her life into her own hands, but after what she'd seen in Kildeen, she worried that Lucia enjoyed it too much. She worried it would consume her, become her.

She made to voice her thoughts but Lucia spoke first. *Have you tried reaching out to Gowther yet? We'll need him for what's to come.*

Tvora turned her head away from the dead below. "I tried, yes. He wouldn't answer. I don't understand. We have the power now to sustain him, all of you, at least for a time, but he won't respond. It's as if he's withdrawn his consciousness from my mind."

*Hmm,* Lucia mused. *He'll come. Just give him time. Gowther won't abandon us. I'm sure he's just being stubborn as always. When the need arises, he'll waken.*

"YOU WON'T BREAK ME!" came a shout from beyond the battlements. "I OWN YOU!"

"What was that?" Tvora said, hand instinctively reaching for Naex at her hip.

Cecco flew to her then, landing atop her shoulder. *It's Septus,* the bird said. *They've returned from the Penella Pass. He's injured.*

Tvora didn't waste any time. She leapt down the fractured staircase three steps at a time and made her way over to the western gate, which had already been splintered open.

Skullsworn filtered in through the gate. Their heads were down, their shoulders slumped. Four figures carried a crazed and wounded Septus, one man for each limb.

Matted hair clung to a face contorted with pain and madness. Septus' piercing ruby eyes glowed with feverish intensity, a blend of defiance and derangement that sent a shiver down her spine. He clutched his stomach. Blood oozed between his fingers, staining the ground with each faltering step taken by the Skullsworn surrounding him.

"YOU WON'T BREAK ME!" he bellowed, his words reverberating off the walls like a haunting mantra. His voice held an unsettling blend of anguish and madness, as if the very core of his being resisted the forces trying to subdue him. "THIS IS MY BODY. MINE! GET OUT, BLOOD MAGE. YOU WILL NOT BREAK ME!"

Tvora shuddered. She remembered what Carthon had told her about Septus and the Blood Mage. If he broke here, it could be dangerous for them all.

She watched as Carthon followed them through the gates. He clutched at a wound in his side as well, though it didn't seem as severe as the one Septus had received.

"What happened out there?" she asked, more to herself than anyone else.

She continued to stare at Carthon's back as he made his way up the street and into the keep of the conquered castle.

The new residents of Kildeen refused to sleep. Skullsworn roamed the streets, drinking and partying as if they had conquered the entire Gracelands already. Fights were frequent, for though the Skull Thrones were united in theory, old grudges had not been forgotten.

Tvora watched from a high perch as a man was stabbed in the back. He bled out slowly. The man responsible seemingly took pleasure in watching him crawl around on the ground, begging for his life. Tvora thought about intervening, but why bother? Eventually, he died, several souls flowing from his corpse and into the aggressor.

Is this what the world would become?

It didn't matter. Destiny had given her a role and she would play it. One person couldn't change the fate of the world, so why should she try?

The city's population grew by the day. Kildeen had become a kind of rallying point for the wicked. More men of the skull filtered in every day. Soul-hunters from the Harrows continued to pour through the gates, unable to forgo the opportunity to finally hunt down some Knights of Aen.

Carthon had locked himself deep within the keep for several nights now. Tvora decided enough was enough, she needed something to do. She was sick of waiting. Making her way into the keep, she walked past several guards wearing animal skulls as masks, half expecting them to stop her.

They didn't.

She closed in on the locked antechamber within the refurbished great hall. The cold stone walls surrounding her echoed with hollow stillness. She walked silently, her footsteps muffled by the torn and tattered tapestries that flapped like mournful ghosts in the gentle breeze brought in by the shattered windows.

Tvora stopped at the door and listened as voices were raised beyond it. She couldn't decipher what they were saying, but from the general tone, it couldn't have been a pleasant conversation.

Heavy footsteps approached the door, and Tvora took two steps back as it swung open. Glock stood before her, his square jaw locked in place, his cheeks flushed red. He eyed her cautiously, made a loud snorting sound, then brushed past her and proceeded down the walkway. Tvora turned, watching his bare back disappear into the distance, wondering what must have happened in there to cause his temper to rise so.

Lucia and Cecco by her side, she entered the gloomy antechamber. Dim light filtered through a high window. It cast a long shadow of the toppled throne, now just a shattered relic. She walked along the opulent red carpet, now stained with blood and dirt, its fabric worn and frayed.

Carthon stepped from the shadows and into the light. "Curious," he said. "I was told there were three passengers, yet so far I've only seen two."

Tvora tensed. "The third will show himself when the need arises."

Carthon snickered and relaxed, uncrossing his arms and taking another step closer. "Well, I should very much like to meet him one day, if only to sate my curiosity."

"Not many have seen him and lived."

Carthon laughed. "And these 'passengers' of yours, they have names?"

Tvora narrowed her eyes at him. "What business is that of yours? Speak plainly, what do you really want to know?"

Carthon chuckled through closed lips. "Very well," he said, exhaling slowly. "The time has come. I want to know how you did it, how you found yourself after breaking."

Tvora grimaced. It wasn't a subject she liked to talk about. "Why?"

"Why? Because knowledge is power. I want to break the threshold. I want to surpass what we think human minds are capable of. I want to ascend past what we think we know."

"You want the voices to stop," Tvora said plainly.

Carthon smiled. "Magic can be… complex in its nature. Take the breaking of one's soul, for example. A certain person's soul might break with but a few others whispering sinister thoughts into their mind. Another might have thousands of trapped souls all wrestling for control, yet never break. While it's true and proven that the more souls a person hoards, the more likely they are to break, it's also true that mental fortitude plays a pivotal role. The stronger you are of mind, the easier it is to control the power without suffering the ramifications.

"I don't just want the voices to stop. I want to dominate them."

Tvora listened, recalling the moment she had been consumed by those within her. "You want to know what it's like to have your soul break?" she said. "You're both there and not there, aware but unaware. A passenger in your own body, watching as others fight for control. It's like being held down by a weight you can never remove."

"Ah, but you did remove it," Carthon responded.

Tvora snapped her head to face him. "Only because I had help. Only because my friends were stronger than I. Their minds were iron, their strength unequalled. If they hadn't joined me, if we hadn't fought together against the tide, then our souls would all be lost to a thousand hosts.

"If you're searching for a plan to recover yourself when it's your turn to break," she continued. "I suggest you instead build your internal walls higher, and pray the day never comes when they should fall."

Carthon crossed his arms again. His expression gave away nothing. She didn't know if he believed her or not, nor did she care.

He took a closing step towards her and spoke softly but with purpose. "You say this word, 'friends', as if it has meaning. True friendship does not exist in this world. It is a false ideal. There is no such thing as a selfless desire. All turn on you eventually, if given enough time. You will see."

Tvora spared a look at Lucia, who curled around her leg in a show of strength. She frowned and decided to change the subject.

"Did Septus succumb?" she asked, genuinely curious.

Carthon walked to a table and began pouring himself a drink. "Not yet. He still has a role to play. As for you," he continued. "I have a task for you, one I believe you'll enjoy."

Tvora spared a look over her shoulder, remembering the angry Reaper who had just left this place. "One Glock didn't agree with, I presume?"

Carthon sighed. He didn't look amused. "This particular task proved too..." he paused, searching for the right word, "personal, for Glock to handle. That's why I've chosen you."

Tvora inclined her head, intrigued.

"There's a man in Oskon Corr, the city beyond the Hilt. An extremely powerful man. A Knight, actually. I need him eradicated."

"Just one man? How can his death be so important?"

"Never underestimate the power of an accomplished mage. Humans are a fragile species. There are few capable of defending their mind against the press of the dead for such a prolonged period of time. I have my reasons for wanting him dead, but you don't need to know them. All I need from you is to kill him. Can you handle that?"

Tvora felt Lucia draw closer, sensing the opportunity for more souls to feed on.

"What's his name?"

"Cerak."

"And what is his connection to Glock?"

Carthon smiled. "He is Glock's twin brother."

Tvora gasped. "You want me to murder his brother?"

Carthon opened up his palm, suggesting she was correct.

"And Glock won't intervene?"

"He will do as he is bid."

Tvora withdrew inside herself. This was what she wanted. What was Glock to her in the face of her real friends? Nothing. She hadn't come here to play nice, she had come for souls. Now Carthon offered her a chance, a target. Why should she not take it?

"When do I leave?"

"Right now. I'm assigning Mantis to accompany you. Be careful, his hunger rivals your own. The two of you are forbidden to attempt anything on the other. If you should return here alone, I'll assume one has taken the other's souls, and your life will be forfeit."

# Chapter 25
# - Myddrin -

Myddrin groaned. It was the kind of groan that shook mountains. He rolled around in something soft, wincing at a pain in his side. He felt as though he were floating in a cloud, his mind drifting.

He saw Ismey. Sweet Aen, she was beautiful, her soul as pure and radiant as a sunrise. Long locks of golden hair swayed all the way down to her hips. She stared at him as she always had, bright eyes promising the world. Her cheeks were flushed and her lips full. He reached out an arm to touch her, to hold her.

"Ismey," he whispered, beckoning her over, but she only strayed further away, light footsteps taking her into the distant background of nothingness.

"Ismey!" he called, louder this time, but received the same, unheeding response.

Myddrin sat up in a rush, his breathing heavy, legs damp under sweat-soaked sheets. The alluring vision of his lost wife vanished, replaced by the dry wall of his bedchamber.

Head still in a haze, he looked down upon his half-naked form. His shirt had been removed, and some white bandages were tightly wound around his shoulder and upper arm.

"How do you feel, Master?" came a voice.

He turned to see Mees standing by his side, long hands curled around what looked like a hot cup of broth. Translucent lines of steam flowed from its top.

Myddrin clutched his shoulder before placing a weak palm

over his forehead. "I feel like someone jumped inside my mind, brandished a bag of rocks, and started beating me with it. What happened? Did you give me something?"

Mees didn't respond, which Myddrin took to mean he had done something he shouldn't have.

"Mees," he said again, with sudden concern. "What did you give me?"

Mees clasped his hands together. "Seed of the poppy, Master. There was no other choice."

Myddrin forced himself upright, bent over, and thrust two fingers down his throat. He retched, but nothing came out, just dry spittle.

"It's no use," Mees said. "The poppy has already passed through your system."

Myddrin growled and glared accusingly at Mees. "Why?"

"It's like I said, there was no choice in the matter. Your shoulder was maimed. It was a two-day journey back to Athedale, three with you tied to my back. Without the poppy, you would either be dead, or soul-broken."

Myddrin rubbed at his temples, still trying to piece together the events of the past few days. Wine and moss were two crutches he had been unable to do away with, but poppy was a drug he had left behind long ago. Not since a year after her death had he indulged in the addictive substance.

The fact that Mees had carried it with him all this time irked him deeply. "Why do you even have it?"

Mees went silent. He didn't back down though, didn't shy away or show any sign of regret for his actions. "Because you can't die," he said after a time.

Myddrin sat for a moment, thinking about all Mees had done for him. Without him, Myddrin would have died long ago.

"Destroy it," Myddrin said. "It will be the end of me, Mees."

Mees just nodded, then placed the warm broth on his bedside table.

"Why did Aen choose me to play such a role in this world?" Myddrin continued, taking a sip of the broth.

"The Lord works in mysterious ways," Mees said. "Our lives are short in comparison to the span of the world. Often, we don't understand His reasons until long after we have passed."

Myddrin slumped further into the covers of his bed. "Sometimes I wonder if it's all worth it. If humanity is even worth saving."

The two of them were quiet for a time, then Myddrin continued. "I hate Carthon, hate everything about him, but what if he has a point? My hatred exists, and I'm not alone in it. These emotions – anger, resentment, indignation – they existed long before Axel cursed this world. What if we're not worth it?"

Mees moved to sit by the side of the bed. "I want you to think back to your time with Ismey," he said. "Not the day of her death, but the days of her life. Were you not happy then? Was she not content? Think about your time teaching the young, the joy you brought them with tale and story. That's what we must fight for. To create those moments for the rest of the world. For future generations to live free of our burden. We fight not for ourselves, but for them."

Myddrin looked at his Hand then. No. He looked at his friend. "I'm glad I've had you by my side all these years. Without you… Without you, I don't know what I would have become. For that, I thank you."

In a rare show of emotion, Mees actually smiled.

"You know, I didn't realise until just now," Myddrin continued, arching a brow, "but you have an awfully ugly smile."

Mees paled, and for a very real moment Myddrin thought he was about to be assaulted. When no such assault came, he relaxed, sinking deeper into the comfort of his silk-covered pillow. "I'm surprised the church hasn't come for my head yet."

"They did try," Mees said. "The king wouldn't let them. He hasn't allowed a soul save myself and your mother to visit since your return."

"My mother was here?"

Mees nodded.

"How did she seem? Disappointed? Annoyed?"

"She seemed sad, Master."

Myddrin sighed. He wished he had more time to reconnect with his mother. He owed her that much. He promised himself when this war was done, he would put in the effort, would be a better son.

The door abruptly swung open, causing Myddrin to jolt upright.

In walked the king, white gold crown shining bright atop his greying head of hair. His eyes flared as he noticed Myddrin's conscious form. "Ah, you're awake. This pleases me greatly," he said.

Myddrin feigned acknowledgement. He wondered who the king had back there, waiting to end his life if they decided he wouldn't pull through. Halvair, perhaps? Or someone else entirely, ready to take on the mantle of 'World's Most Powerful Mage'.

"Your Highness, you needn't have bothered yourself with me. I'm sure you have more pressing matters to attend to."

"Nonsense," the king said, walking deeper into the room. "I am told I have you to thank for the safety of my dearest brother. Christoval would be here himself, but he is still overseeing those who managed to flee Kildeen before the invasion."

Myddrin baulked, then gestured towards Mees. "Thank him. Mees is the one who held them back. I was stupid. Stupid and careless."

The king feigned a smile, as if he didn't know what else to do, then he bowed to Mees. "Well, I thank you too then. Though I think you understate yourself, Myddrin. My brother told me what you did. It takes a bold man to become a hero, but to become one twice over, that takes real courage."

Myddrin harrumphed.

Remen moved to the door, spared a look outside, then closed it tight. "There are matters that need discussing. Private matters. Can your Hand be trusted?"

"There is no one I trust more than Mees," Myddrin said.

Remen settled into a seat beside the bed, though Myddrin cut him off before he could speak. "I think I know why you wanted me to find the well," he said. "You've known about it for years, haven't you? Since you became king. Known, and been unable to tell a soul."

Remen took off his crown and held it in his hands. "You don't know the burden, the weight of this thing."

"I know something about it..." Myddrin said, not bothering to explain himself.

"You're right, of course. I've been aware of this lie half my life, unable to do anything about it."

"You wanted to reveal its existence, but couldn't do it yourself," Myddrin continued. "I don't have all the facts, but you used me to put pressure on the church, didn't you?"

The king gave an exhausted sigh through thin lips. He nodded. "We used each other, yes. Don't pretend I didn't give you exactly what you wanted. I didn't ask you to start smashing the place apart. That mess is on you."

"Does it have something to do with what they're doing down there? Taking power from the well?"

"That was just a suspicion," Remen said. "A suspicion now

confirmed. The church has grown too powerful over recent years, too ambitious. Their control over the Knights is too strong. I feared that soon they would have no need of me. I fear I'm turning into a puppet with no real say in my own Kingdom.

"Events didn't go exactly as planned. I thought perhaps if they knew the Hero of White-Rock knew about their secret, then they would be wary and back off. Fortunately for me, you brought two Council members in on your adventure. Thanks to Glade and Beyan, the whole King's Council now know about the well, and Adralan's little experiments down there.

"The court is very tense at the moment," he continued. "But now that the church is exposed by someone other than myself, the playing field is more balanced."

Myddrin grunted and turned his head. "This isn't the time to be playing politics. If you haven't noticed, there's an army out there. Trust me when I say they don't give a shit about who's friends with who. They will murder everyone and anyone in their path."

"Then work with me. Stand by my side at Council meetings. Show the church we're united, and then we can focus on what's outside those walls."

Myddrin scoffed. "Don't you already have Halvair for that?"

"I need you both. I don't care if he hates you. He'll have to put up with it."

"And I'm supposed to just trust you?"

Remen straightened. "You want an end to magic, don't you? You want to find a way to release everyone's souls, correct the world? I want that too. I have no magic of my own, no souls in my cage. The Knights are the ones with the power, not me. When the war is over, I'll do everything within my power to help you. I'll grant you access to the well to conduct your research, test your theories."

Myddrin tried to sit up. He shifted his shoulder and bit his lip in pain. His head still throbbed, but he looked Remen directly in the eye. A sudden anger rushed through him. "Ten years ago," he said.

Remen raised a brow. "Excuse me?"

"Tell the truth, and I'll trust you. Ten years ago, during Doonaval's assault, the Mage-Way collapsed before we could retreat to the keep. Was that by your hand?"

The king froze. He tried to keep a straight face, but Myddrin could see the nervous lump he gulped down his throat. He was sure the king was about to lie.

Then Remen squared his shoulders. "Yes, that was my decision. The walls were breached, and the Skullsworn were making their way down the walkway too fast. I ordered my men to cut them off. For the good of the Gracelands."

Myddrin's arm tensed. He remembered the children, forced to endure the horror of that battlefield. There was no regret in the king's tone, but neither was there pride. Myddrin didn't like it, didn't agree with it, perhaps even still hated him for it, but he had told the truth.

"You have my support," he said. "Though, if you don't mind, I need to rest."

# Chapter 26
# - Will -

Will couldn't sleep, he was too excited. He flipped through his sketchbook. The possibilities were endless. What should he create next?

He decided on something practical. A spear. Crisalli had told him to focus on his offence. He studied his picture, memorising its pattern. He closed his eyes, pictured it, then began to sketch it with his hand. It came easy to him this time. He felt his souls go to work, drawing power from the *otherside* as they created the spear.

It hovered in front of him. Will grasped the sapphire imagewood. It felt real in his hands. Even the weight felt similar to what he would expect. He let go, focused, and shifted his hand to the left. He watched with glee as the spear moved upon his instruction.

The voices were still there. However, he had begun to recognise them, understood which ones would speak the loudest and when. Just like an opponent with a sword, they were predictable. When Will could predict something, countering it became simple.

He dismissed the spear and it turned to mist. He began flipping through his book again. His fingers rapped his beat of five at a rapid pace, this time out of excitement rather than nervousness.

His beat stilled when he came upon the picture of his mother. Could he?

No. Crisalli had said it was impossible. Human creation wasn't forbidden, it just wasn't a possibility. Curious, Will tried it anyway, if only to see what would happen. He felt his heartbeat quicken at the possibility of seeing his mother again, even though it was a slim chance.

He closed his eyes, pictured her in his mind. He was met with immediate resistance. It was as if there was a wall blocking his connection. Where before his souls could reach freely into the other realm, here there was nothing. The image wouldn't form, couldn't form.

He released a long-held breath, exhausted, and decided to give up on the act. Maybe it was for the best that he couldn't recreate her. She wasn't fully gone. Her soul rested safely inside of him. That was enough, wasn't it?

Will continued practising until morning broke. His eyes were bleary, and his head throbbed from lack of sleep, but that couldn't dampen his excitement. He wanted to learn. To experience, to become better.

He made his way out of his new room to see Crisalli already awake. She sat on the dining table, already dressed.

Will studied her expression and posture, using what his grandfather had taught him to try to figure out her mood. Her shoulders were slumped, her gaze was unfocused, and her lips were pulled tight. Could she be sad? Frustrated? Annoyed?

Had Will done something wrong?

"Crisalli?" he said, taking a cautious step towards her.

She looked up, eyes popping open as if she had only just noticed him.

"Oh, you're awake. Come, sit," she said, gesturing to the empty chair beside her.

Will did as he was told.

"I have some unfortunate news. I'm afraid I won't be able to train you anymore. At least, not for a while."

"What! Why?" Will said.

"It's nothing to do with you, honestly. I've taken a contract."

"I thought all contracts were voided to prepare for the invasion? That's what you told me."

"They are," she continued. "But this is a contract only I can complete. There yet remain a number of Knights on active duty across the Harrows and beyond. Some of our best warriors are scattered around Otor."

"And what? You're going to fetch them?"

"One of them, yes."

"Can't they just send someone else?"

Crisalli shook her head. "No. This has to be done by me. There is no choice."

"So, they're forcing you to go?"

"In a sense, yes. But they're right. I'm the only one who can bring him home."

Will moaned, scrunching his face into a ball. "Then bring me with you. I can help."

She waved off the comment. "No, Will. Oskon Corr is no place for an apprentice. Not to mention I'll be travelling across the Harrows during an invasion. You won't be safe."

"And where is safe? The Skullsworn are coming, you've said it yourself. Soon they'll be at our doorstep, then I'll be forced to fight them anyway, only I'll be less prepared because I won't have you here to train me."

Crisalli didn't say anything, only stared at him blankly.

"Please," Will said. "I want to come, to learn. I'm better now. I practised last night. Watch."

Will concentrated and tapped his souls. He brought forth the image of the spear, then began moving it with his hands, following its path with his eyes. He thrust his arm forward, and the spear shot into motion, knocking several pots from the once clean bench before embedding itself into the far wall.

"That's... actually impressive," Crisalli said. "The other day you could barely form your shield. What happened?"

Will paused. He hadn't told her about Olive just yet. He hadn't planned on keeping it a secret, the two of them just didn't really talk about much outside of training and magic.

"I found a trick to it. It's all a pattern, you see. I just have to find the elements of what I want to make and stitch them together like a drawing."

Crisalli rose up out of her seat now. Her intensity changed, as if she'd been shaken from her sleepy daze in a heartbeat. She smiled, then shook her head. "I knew there was something special about you. Your mother... she told me there was."

"She did?"

Crisalli nodded. "She once said you would become the greatest Knight who ever lived. I met you once, actually, when you were just a small child. I thought she was crazy. You were always more interested in your drawings and plants and animals than anything to do with playing soldier. But your mother told me, said you'd make it, she was sure of it."

Will took a step closer. "So, I can come then? You'll take me with you?"

Crisalli rubbed at her brow. "Only if you promise to stay by my side no matter what."

Will bounced around the room, unable to contain his excitement.

"You must promise me, Will. Anything I say, you must do; without question, without comment. Am I clear?"

"Yes. I promise," Will said as he beat his rhythm of five on his chest.

Olive was the one waiting for him this time. She sat on a rock at their usual meeting place, idly twiddling her thumbs and whistling a tune he was unfamiliar with. Her face lit upon his approach, which he assumed meant she was happy to see him. It was a surreal feeling, someone the same age as him excited about his company. Growing up, he had always been alienated, shunned from social groups. He had never known how to act in front of other people, especially his peers.

"Will!" Olive cried as she pushed herself down from the rock and skipped over to him. She wrapped her arms around his neck and pressed her head against his shoulder. Will blushed, hands awkwardly hovering in the air, not knowing what to do with them. Her scent flooded his senses, the smell of lilacs soothing him.

She pulled back, eyebrows knotted. "Why so glum?"

Will hesitated. "I — I won't be able to teach you for a while," he said.

"What do you mean? Have you grown bored of me already?"

"No!" Will almost shouted. "No, it's not that. My mentor, she's taken a contract."

"A contract? Weren't all contracts voided due to the coming invasion?"

"This is different, it's for the cause." Will paused. "Wait, how do you know that?"

Olive took a backward step, scratching at her temple. "Oh, nevermind that, my uncle told me, I think."

"Oh, right! Well, anyway," he said. "This will be our last lesson for a while."

"Do you know where you're going?"

Will racked his brain. "Not really. Crisalli told me it's a place called Oskon Corr, but I don't really know where that is. I've never been more than a few miles from Athedale."

"Really!?" she cried, closing the distance between them in an overzealous leap. "Wow, I can't believe you get to go to the Corr. I've never been there myself, not many people have. Hard to get to. Have to go through the Harrows and cross the Hilt first. My uncle told me none of the Knights have been allowed there for at least a decade now."

"You seem to know a lot about the world for someone who was raised in Athedale."

Olive shrugged. "It's on my list of places to sing in one day. Let me know if they have a good theatre, will you please? When you come back, I mean. I want to hear all about it."

"Uh, sure. I can do that!" Will said.

"And make sure you draw lots of pictures too. I want to see everything. The Harrows, the Corr, all of it!

"Oh, that reminds me," Olive continued, reaching for a pack she had at her feet. She withdrew a leather book and marker. "This is for you. Think of it as a present for all you've taught me so far."

Will couldn't believe his eyes. "Is that a graphite marker?"

"Sure is."

Will took it and held it in his hands. "These are extremely rare, how did you come by one?"

"My uh — my family own a bookshop down in the western quarter, but I don't want to talk about them now. It's good, isn't it? I thought you could use it to make quick sketches, with less smudge and all that. The book is empty as well. I thought you needed a new one. Not to replace the old one, but maybe this way you can keep your old one in a safe place. You know, so it doesn't fall down another waterfall," she said with a wink.

"I — I can't accept this. This is too much," he said, pressing them back into her hands.

"Nonsense. It's nothing, really. It's what friends do. You are my friend, right?"

Will's heart sunk deep into his chest. "Right, of course."

He thought about asking her if she was sure, if she truly meant what she said, but Olive was already off, pirouetting through the air before taking her place on the grassy knoll where Will taught his lessons.

"So, what am I learning about today?" she said.

Will proceeded to show her all he had practised the night before, highlighting his progress and stating her as the reason for it. She smiled at that, then proceeded to place her hand on his chest.

"Does it hurt?" she asked. "To draw from your cage, I mean?"

"It's like a weight pressing on my mind. It gets heavier the more I draw from it, then fades when I stop."

"What happens when you draw too much?"

Will paused, his thoughts turning unpleasant. "Then I break. Or I collapse. Whichever comes first."

"Like the lady in the cavern?" Olive questioned.

Will paused, assaulted by a memory he had been constantly trying to suppress. He doubled over, head throbbing.

"What's wrong?" Olive questioned. "Are you okay?"

He righted himself and shook his head clear. "It's nothing, just a bad memory."

"Your mother?"

Will's head snapped into focus. He stood and backed away. "You know?"

Olive stuttered. "I — I was told, yes."

Will bent over, head again riddled with an agonising throb. "How? How could you possibly know that?"

"I — I'm sorry Will. I shouldn't have said anything, I just

know.

Of course she knew. The whole world knew, for all he was aware. Rath probably hand-delivered letters to every home in Athedale, such was his hatred for him.

Will steadied, breathed. He used Crisalli's techniques to calm himself, focusing on his breathing, circulating the air through his belly and then his entire body. He thought for a moment. She knew, yet she was still here. She hadn't run at the sight of him, seemed to even like him. That had to mean something, didn't it? "You don't care? About what happened I mean. What I did?"

Olive moved a step closer and raised a tentative hand to clasp his own. "From what you've told me about someone breaking, there was nothing to be done. She would have killed you, and your father. Possibly dozens more until someone strong enough finally came to help. I know it's hard to hear, and I know it doesn't help, but you did the right thing. You saved lives, Will."

"Then why does it hurt so much?" he said, beginning to sob.

For some reason, he began to turn away, to hide as he always had to when he tried to find comfort in his father, only to be scolded and pushed aside. But Olive didn't push him aside. Nor did she scold him. She held him.

For a long moment he stood there, crying into the shoulder of a stranger. Only she wasn't a stranger. She was a friend.

Slowly, Will parted, face still wet with tears. "If you want to bring joy to people's lives through song, then you're studying the wrong subject. There's no joy to magic, only sorrow."

Olive stared at him for a moment that seemed to stretch, then she spoke. "A joyful song can be a powerful tool when sung to the right crowd, but even more powerful is finding solace through one sung in sorrow."

Through the tears Will smiled. "Well, when I come back, I'd like to hear it then."

# Chapter 27
# - Myddrin -

There was something wrong with the stew. Myddrin could tell just by looking at it. The colour was a dull brown, the texture a slimy mess of undercooked meat with chunks of beef floating at the rim. He sniffed the air and thought he smelled copper. He dug in with his spoon and lifted the liquid to his lips before taking a mouthful. It went down like a cup of salt water, and he had the sudden urge to skip a meal for perhaps the first time in his adult life.

His muscles all screamed in pain. His shoulder felt like it was being prodded by a hot poker every time he moved. He couldn't sleep, and he had been practically shitting straight water for the past two days.

Mees stared at him from across the table. "It's just the after-effects of the poppy, Master. They'll die down in a few days."

Myddrin froze. Hot stew drizzled from his lip as another spoonful hovered by his mouth. His stomach gurgled. His cheeks expanded as he tried to keep down the steaming mess of what passed for stew in the capital.

He failed.

Spittle frothed from his lips as his chest convulsed. A half-chewed lump of what he assumed to be beef flew from his mouth, landing in the lap of his friend.

Myddrin centred himself, straightening a crease in his coat. "Sorry about that."

Mees's frustrated scowl loomed over him like an angry

thundercloud.

A knock came from behind, breaking the tension. A face emerged, and a pale man with heavy, sunken eyes walked into their private room. He looked as though he hadn't had a lick of sleep in months, which, due to the coming war preparations, he probably hadn't.

"Ahem," he said, clearing his throat. "His Majesty awaits you in the great hall."

"Can His Majesty not wait for me to finish my supper?" Myddrin replied, staring back at the bowl with renewed hunger.

The king's herald just stood there, looking as though denying the king five minutes of his time was heresy of the highest order. "I am afraid not, the War Council has already convened. I would have thought you might hold the defence of our kingdom as more important than a couple mouthfuls of stew."

Myddrin stared at him as if the man had just slapped him in the face. He rose, bowl of stew in hand, and pushed it, stew first, into the herald's chest. "The taste was a little off anyway," he said as he brushed past with casual, mocking grace.

The herald didn't retaliate. He'd been bold to openly mock the most powerful mage in Otor. Would have been bolder still to challenge him. Myddrin grinned, taking pleasure in the perks of his status. A pang of guilt soon wrenched its way through his gut though, followed by regret.

"Was that necessary?" Mees asked, catching up to him.

Myddrin rubbed at his temples. "Probably not, no, but what's done is done.

"This whole war," he continued. "What if none of it's necessary? If I could go down to the well again, perhaps I could find a way to remove the stain of magic from these lands. Then the king could sit pretty while Carthon tries to climb the city walls bare-handed, one stone at a time."

"Be careful what you say in there, Master. There are those who dwell behind the safety of these walls who still don't share your view. Magic's very essence is ingrained in our society. Those with all the power won't be so willing to give it up without a fight."

Myddrin exhaled, trying to think of some clever retort, but was unable to dispute the Hand's logic. Corruption was everywhere, even in the hearts of people who claimed to be righteous. Maybe he, too, was corrupt. His perception of right and wrong in this world had been skewed long ago. His wife's death and the depression that followed had beaten his conscience down to an all-time low. It had taken every ounce of effort he had to claw his way out of that hole and into the somewhat reasonable man he thought himself to be today.

Leaving Mees at the door, he tripped over a small stair and stumbled into the great hall. He managed to catch himself before completely falling over, but the resounding echo of his entrance was enough to turn every head in the room.

He flattened his coat and fixed his face into a smile before moving to his place at the round table. He pulled an empty chair from beneath, the heavy wood scraping noisily on the tiling below, causing those nearest to cover their ears in displeasure.

"Master Myddrin," the king said. "How good of you to join us."

The king sat at the head of the table, or rather, rose above the rest in a high chair.

"Apologies for my tardiness. It seems as though your herald had some kind of accident with the stew."

Beside the king, Halvair scoffed. His silver hair ran down his cheek to brush against the slab of oak that made the top of the table.

Myddrin was already in a bad mood, and he was sick of being

slighted by this man, even if his hatred was warranted. Against his better judgement, he decided to stand up to him.

"Is there a problem, dear friend?" he said, directing his words at the cold-faced Halvair.

His words seemed to affect all those in attendance except for the man in question. A series of half-concealed audible gasps sounded from around the table, as if Halvair was some kind of god, and insulting him was off limits. Halvair didn't react immediately, however. Instead, he clasped his hands and leaned his elbows on the table. His eyes rose to meet Myddrin's, his steely gaze enough to smite a man on its own.

"My problem is you," he said, his heavy voice calm yet binding. "You are a bumbling drunk who stumbled into a power you have no idea how to use. You long ago abandoned your oath to this country and are a danger to yourself and those around you. I do not see you as an asset to the defence of Athedale, I see you as a liability. What's inside of you is a weapon lying dormant, one that I would rather oversee than have taken by the enemy."

"Halvair!" the king said, his tone hushed yet aggressive. "You will not speak to our guest in such a manner. Myddrin is here at my invitation and will be treated with due respect."

Myrddin's mouth hung dry, and he sat almost too stunned to respond. He had always known Halvair to hate him, but this was a level of hatred he had not predicted, one born through betrayal and left to simmer for far too long.

The others began to murmur quietly, nods of either approval or shakes of disapproval beginning to form. Myddrin's line of sight came to rest on Adralan, the gangly looking Cardinal somehow having earned himself a seat on the War Council. By his side sat the silent form of Thane. His arms were crossed, his face painted with an angry expression that seemed to be a permanent feature.

Halvair sat back in his chair, content to let his words hang in the air. It was Adralan who spoke next.

"Halvair speaks the truth!" he said, standing and planting two palms on the table. "Myddrin already showed his colour by desecrating our sacred shrine. The church will not stand for his presence here in this city. I demand he return to his hole in the middle of the sea at once!"

"A shrine you've kept hidden!" came a voice. Myddrin looked up to see Glade on her feet. Her fists grew an angry white in contrast to her auburn hair, which curled around her waist.

"That is the church's business."

"The church's business!" another called. This time it was General Strupp. He slammed a meaty hand onto the table. "Bah! Sounds more like all of Otor's business if the rumours hold any truth."

Adralan's eyes narrowed onto Myddrin.

If the noise before was a murmur, then what followed was a storm. Voices clashed as the room erupted into angry conversation. Myddrin just sat back and waited.

There were exactly ten people currently present on the Council, Myddrin included. The king was working hard to quell the rise in emotion caused by the Cardinal's accusation. General Strupp and Estevan were active, though whether in agreement with each other or not, Myddrin couldn't yet discern. Beyan and Glade became involved too. It seemed as though Adralan was on the back foot, though Thane's presence and the knowledge of who they might be offending prevented any violence.

It was Christoval whose voice boomed the loudest, however. The Duke of Kildeen stood, silencing the bickering Council members by thrusting a fist into the centre of the table, making the small black figurines representing Athedale's troop distribution jump, some toppling over and rolling across the wood.

"Enough!" he screamed, his eyes finding Adralan. He pointed an accusatory finger. "If these rumours are indeed true, and the church has been lying to us all these years, I would hear it from your mouth."

Adralan paled, tensed, then relaxed again all within a few heartbeats. He bowed his head, then rose to speak. "I see we can hide from you no longer. Yes, the souls of the dead yet linger beneath this very keep, where they are safe."

"Safe?" It was Estevan who spoke up this time. "I'm head of the Knights of Aen. How is it I wasn't told of this?"

"You are what we made you," Adralan said. "Who do you think formed the Knights? What do you think would happen if people knew the passage to the Promised Land was blocked? That their loved ones slept beneath their feet rather than in the heavens. There would be pandemonium. Chaos. We formed the Knights to keep the Gracelands safe, and for hundreds of years we have done so. You can accuse us all you like, but we do what we do for the good of us all."

His words ended in a long silence as everyone tried to collect their thoughts.

"Is it true you can draw souls from this well?" Estevan said after a time.

Adralan's left cheek twitched. His eyes shifted towards Thane, then settled on Estevan. "That is not your concern."

Estevan rose. "Of course it is! If it's true, why not make use of the well ourselves? Drawing power from it may give us the advantage we need against Carthon. We have a ready weapon literally sitting idle beneath our feet. Let us use it."

Adralan looked as though he was about to faint. "You misunderstand, Knight. The well beneath our feet is not merely a place for the dead to congregate. It is the Providence. Athedale is the location of Axel's death, and the place of magic's birth. We cannot simply take what we want and expect to leave without consequence."

"But you do take from it…" Myddrin suggested, looking at Thane.

Adralan sucked in a deep breath. His fingers twitched, and Myddrin was sure he was picturing throttling him with them at this very moment.

"We take only what is necessary," Adralan said. "Nothing more. The church is higher than even you, Doonslayer. To question our actions is to question Aen himself."

A thought struck Myddrin then, one he kicked himself for not thinking of before. "The Providence. The well, that's what Carthon wants, isn't it?"

Another silence filled the room as everyone began assessing the ramifications of the idea.

"Tell me," Myddrin continued. "Does anyone else know about its existence? Maybe someone took too much from it in the past? A greedy Knight, perhaps?"

"I don't answer to you, Doonslayer," Adralan spat.

"I would hear your answer!" the king said, interrupting. "If this information is to impact the defence of my city, I would know, Adralan."

Adralan pursed his lips and grunted. "Very well. Yes, there was a man, years ago. His name was Glock. He took on too much power and turned against us."

"I'll bet my life Carthon has him now," Myddrin said. "He knows."

"I've heard enough of this!" Adralan said, rising to his feet. "The Providence is not to be touched, nor is it to be spoken about. It was kept a secret for a reason. I don't know how you all managed to stumble upon it, but ask yourselves this, do you really think the truth of the fate of the dead will help the people of the Gracelands? Do you think they will be better off with such knowledge?

"There is no more discussion to be had. No one is to touch what lies beneath our feet, nor is anyone to speak of it. If we find out any of you have done either, the consequences will be severe."

With that, he and Thane rose, leaving without another word.

With Adralan's departure, the tension in the room began to dampen. Everyone stared awkwardly at their hands, not quite sure how to proceed.

"I suggest," Remen said, releasing a sigh, "we return our focus to the defence of this city. General," he said, directing his words to Strupp, "how fare our numbers?"

General Strupp straightened, his bulging shoulders almost edging Estevan off his seat as he leaned forward to speak. "My men are ready. Many lost loved ones in the siege of Kildeen. Others hold within them a long-lasting grudge against Mirimar and those who would prey on the weak. Currently, the garrison holds at fifteen-thousand strong, with several thousand more due to arrive from Spree and Kastar in the coming days."

The king nodded. "Estevan, how many Knights can we count on?"

Estevan let out a long, exasperated breath. "We lost just under one hundred in Kildeen, a heavy loss that only bolsters our enemy's strength. We number just above seven hundred now. Every one of my Knights are worth ten of those foul soul-hunters Carthon has under his service though. A call has been issued, and the Knights out on contract should be making their way here if they're not here already. The most notable being Cerak. I sent out an envoy to Oskon Corr to retrieve him, though after hearing what Adralan just told us, I'm no longer sure that was wise. Cerak is Glock's twin brother…"

"Cerak can be trusted," Myddrin said. "He's not the same as his brother. Before my wife met her end, she and him were close. I know him. He's a good man, and a powerful Knight. You'll need him."

Remen nodded. "I'll take your word for it."

"Glade," Remen continued, "how fare our siege provisions?"

Glade looked up. "We're well provisioned. Supply lines from Kildeen have been completely cut off. Carthon has stalled, giving us plenty of time to gather crops and grain from the harvests. We can survive for up to a year in the case of a siege, maybe two with proper rationing," she said.

"There will be no siege," Christoval said, his voice again taking command of the room. "You were not there in Kildeen when Carthon's legion came. They won't wait us out. Their army is made from those who would just as likely kill each other than wait for us to crumble. I've seen how he operates. His tactics are ruthless. He sacrificed the weakest of his own men just so his mages could grow stronger. Carthon himself brandished a bridge, black as night, and led his men down the slope of Kildeen's plateau. Our walls won't scare him. That I promise."

The duke's words lingered like a cloud ready to weep as a sense of foreboding dread swept the round table.

"Then we need a plan," Remen said. "Any suggestions?"

Myddrin walked out of the throne room sometime later with tired eyes. The plan they'd come up with was actually quite clever, perhaps even enough to stop the assault before it truly began. Myddrin wouldn't underestimate Carthon though. Not again.

He met with Mees on the way back to his room.

"What was the outcome, Master?" Mees asked.

Myddrin groaned. His throat tickled, and his mind and body yearned for some wine and a smoke. "Well, Adralan's an ass, but we already knew that. Also—"

Myddrin ran into something hard. He stumbled.

"What the—"

He righted himself, then looked up to see Thane towering above him. Adralan stood by Thane's side on the wide staircase, as well as half a dozen other people Myddrin assumed to be Knights of Aen under the direct service of the church.

"What's this all about?" Myddrin grumbled.

Adralan smiled at him through thin lips. It was the kind of smile Myddrin hated, one that, when seen, never ended well for him. The Cardinal's gaze shifted from Myddrin to Mees. "We are just reclaiming an asset of ours," he said.

"What do you mean? What asset?" Myddrin replied.

Two of Adralan's Knights moved beside Mees and grasped him by his arms.

"Mees is a valued member of the church," Adralan continued. "And since you are now returned to Athedale, his duty to you is fulfilled, and his service to us is reestablished."

Myddrin took an aggressive step forward. "Mees is my Hand! Always has been and always will. You have no right—"

"*Was* your Hand," Adralan interrupted. "Mees is a part of the Church of Aen. He was sent to the Mirror Sea a decade ago to ensure the man who smote Doonaval did not get himself killed. He has completed this task, and seen you returned here safely. Now he is once again ours to do with what we will."

Myddrin's mind buzzed with activity.

*Kill him*
*Take his soul*
*He deserves it*
*Let us out*

*We will kill him for you*

His chest glowed a deep green as the souls within began to activate.

"I wouldn't do that if I were you," Adralan said. "Kill me now, and your life will be forfeit. Your wife's soul will remain in Carthon's possession, and everything you desire will be gone. Don't make an enemy of the church, Doonslayer."

Myddrin's hand visibly shook. His fingernails bit down on his palms so hard he thought he might draw blood. "Don't do this," he said as the Knights began escorting Mees way.

"It's already done," Adralan said, lips twisting into that same sinister grin.

"Mees!" Myddrin pleaded, reaching out a tentative hand.

"I'm sorry, Master," Mees said, turning his head. "Please, forgive me."

# Chapter 28
# –Will –

Will stood by his bed, fretting over what to pack for the journey. His hands wavered over his sketchbook. He wanted to bring it more than anything, but then again, he didn't want to lose it a second time. It would be safe here.

No.

He needed her close. He didn't know what awaited him out there. If he was going to die, he would have her picture nearby. He tucked it away beneath his cloak. He had also packed his new, empty sketchbook given to him by Olive, as well as the graphite marker. He was eager to test it, though it would have to wait.

"We're leaving!" Crisalli called from the other room.

Will wiped some dust off his grandfather's shield and hauled it over his shoulder. At least he would have a piece of him on this journey.

He moved into the living room to find Crisalli waiting. She held something in her hands. A strip of cloth covered it, though he could tell by its shape it was something long and flat.

"What's this?" Will asked, taking a step towards her.

"It's for you," she said. "Open it up."

Will obliged. He slowly pulled at the cloth, revealing the shining blade within. It had a small, curved cross-guard with an intricate ring on each side. Within each ring was carved the spiralled symbol of Aen.

Will's eyes widened. "This is my father's sword."

Crisalli nodded. "Now yours, if you want it."

Will took the blade from her hand and lifted it into the air. "Where'd you get it? I thought they took all of his belongings when…"

Will's throat caught, remembering what had happened to his father.

"They did. I talked to them, asked if you could have it."

Will inspected the blade again. He swung it in a downward arc. It was light, easy to swing, and razor sharp.

"Thank you," he mumbled. Haylin hadn't always been the best father. He had always struggled to understand Will, though he supposed the feeling had been mutual.

In the end, he had died protecting him; had sacrificed himself so Will could have a future. Will owed it to him to become something, to not let his sacrifice be in vain. He gripped the hilt tighter. Now he had a token from each of the men who raised him. They were dead, but not forgotten. Never forgotten.

"I assume you know how to ride a horse?" Crisalli said.

Will bounced on his toes at the mention of horses. "I do! Ma taught me when I was young. I love horses. I love all animals, well most animals, just not bugs, though I do still find them interesting. Some of them move in the strangest patterns. Did you know that ants—"

"Will," Crisalli said, holding up a hand. "We really need to get a move-on."

"Right, of course."

Will trailed Crisalli down the winding streets of Athedale. Some people gathered to watch them go, gawking at them from their homes. Others minded their own business, wanting nothing to do with the Knights.

Once at the stables, Crisalli led him to his horse, a beautiful mare of chestnut brown.

"Does she have a name?" Will asked as he fed her some hay

from his palm.

"Her name is Fix. You'd better get used to her, nothing worse than a horse on the road that won't listen."

Will's attention drifted back to Fix. He looked her in the eye while stroking her side. Fix leaned into his hand, which he took to mean she approved of him. He pressed his head into her coat, listening to the sound of her heart thumping in a relaxed rhythm. She was already saddled, so he tied his shield to her side and jumped onto her back. She staggered a little, but looked comfortable enough.

Crisalli mounted her own charcoal-black stallion, a larger breed than Fix, and led them towards the gates that had been his safe-haven all his life.

"So, are you going to tell me who this Knight is that we're going to find?" Will asked once the gates of Athedale were a mere silhouette against the horizon.

Crisalli went silent, her face twisting into a knot.

Will frowned atop his mount. "Why is your face all weird?" he asked.

His mentor's expression tightened even further. "His name is Cerak," was all she said.

Her horse pushed forward at a slightly faster pace, causing Will to press Fix into a trot to catch her. "Did I say something wrong?"

Crisalli waved him off. "No, it's nothing you said."

"What is it then?"

Crisalli shook her head. "You're just like your mother, did you know that? Inquisitive to the bone."

Will shrugged. "You still didn't answer my question."

She sighed. "He's a very powerful Knight who could play an important role in the safety of the Gracelands."

"If he's so powerful, why is he all the way out in the Corr?"

"Cerak's brother had a run-in with the church. A bad one. He got caught in the middle. Instead of turning against them like his brother, he chose to take a permanent contract in the Corr. We haven't heard from him in a few years. In truth, I don't even know if he's still there..."

"Can you promise me something?" Crisalli continued.

Will nodded.

"I know you're excited, and I know you're eager to prove your worth. But this isn't the place for it. The Harrows isn't safe, the Corr isn't safe. Not for anyone, and especially not for us. If I say run, you run. If I say hide, you hide. Do you understand?"

Will tensed, gripping Fix's reins a little tighter. "I understand. I promise I'll listen. But do you think we'll run into much trouble on the way there? It looks empty so far."

Crisalli gazed at the desolate open plain of dirt beyond and shrugged. "The most powerful foes will be cooped up in Kildeen with the rest of Carthon's army. We'll try to avoid that route as best we can. But this is the Harrows. Always sleep with one eye open in this place."

The first five days and nights passed with little trouble. Will refused to drop his guard, heeding his mentor's warning and clinging to the thought of becoming fuel, forever trapped inside a madman's soul-cage.

They slept in shifts, not daring to brave the night without at least one set of eyes to look for danger.

His fingers itched to busy themselves, so he spent what little spare time Crisalli allowed him by the fire, idly sketching in his new book.

The Harrows was vast. From what he could gather so far, it seemed to be made up of hundreds of small hamlets and communities, spread thin throughout the landscape.

The two of them took a long detour north before heading west, an agreed upon necessity with Carthon having taken Kildeen. Luckily, with most of the would-be murderers joining his army, there would be few left to trouble them as they passed through.

Will shifted in his saddle. His thighs felt as though they were on fire. He knew it was only chafing, but he couldn't part his mind from the feeling. Then there was Crisalli's horse, which kept trying to chomp at Fix. Will steered her away, only for Crisalli to harp at him to stay close and on the path.

"Control your horse then!" Will snapped, his frustrations hitting their limit.

"Relax. It's just a playful bite. It means he likes her."

Will steered Fix away again. "Well, she doesn't like him. Are we close to the Corr yet?"

"Yes, actually. Sniff the air. Tell me what you smell."

Will obliged and sucked in some short breaths through his nose. "Smells like fish."

"Exactly. We're near the ocean. See that path down there?" she said, pointing with her arm. "That leads to a valley, the valley leads all the way to the Hilt, and beyond it, Oskon Corr. The Corr is surrounded on all sides by sea, though I wouldn't be caught sailing in those waters. The Islanders to the north have a knack for pirating."

Will rapped a nervous beat on his chest as he thought about being taken by pirates. The thought of ships made him think of Olive. She wanted to travel the world, sing anywhere and everywhere. Maybe it wasn't such an impossible dream. Perhaps he could go with her one day? When the world was a little safer.

They made camp that night within the valley, overlooking a ravine. His legs ached and he hadn't eaten all day so he got a fire started and dug into some of his rations, taking first watch while

Crisalli slept. A few hours after dark, Fix issued a nervous neigh, drawing his attention towards where the horses were tied. He rose, eyes darting in the darkness. Fix wasn't one to startle easy.

An eerie silence crept through the valley, and he leaned over to gently rouse his mentor. Crisalli woke with a gasp, her knife sliding from its sheath with a sharp ring. "What do you see?" she asked before Will could get a word in.

"I — I don't see anything, but Fix seems nervous. That's unlike her."

Crisalli rose and began rolling up her sleeping pallet. "Gather your things, we're leaving. The Hilt isn't far. From there it is less than a day's ride to Oskon Corr."

"But it's the middle of the night…"

"Don't question, just do as you are tol— watch out!" Crisalli screamed, pushing him hard. Will fell as something dark whistled past where he had just been.

"Soul-hunters," Crisalli whispered. "They've found us. Get to Fix, now!"

Will wasted no time, sprinting to his horse as more arrows clattered on the stone next to him. He slashed through the hitching rope rather than taking the time to untie it, then mounted Fix and kicked her into motion.

Crisalli stalled, closing her eyes in concentration. Soon after, a flutter of colour lit up the valley as hundreds of tiny violet butterflies were born from Crisalli's magic, concealing their position. Then she followed.

The two horses galloped along the ravine. Will spared a look behind, watching as the butterflies dissipated, out of range for Crisalli to keep control.

"Should we not stand and fight?" Will called over the gush of wind in his face.

"No. We don't know their number. Never rush into a battle

when you don't know who you're fighting. We ride for the Corr."

Will wasn't about to argue. Instead, he focused on staying mounted. He hadn't yet reached full pace when he felt something whistle past his flank. He turned his head, then veered sharply to the left as another projectile narrowly missed his chin.

Off-balance, Will was forced to jump off the side of his horse, landing in a tumble. The wind was driven from his chest, and he was left watching Fix continue riderless into the dark. He rolled around in the dirt, gasping for breath. Figures surrounded him, and he thought he saw Crisalli begin to wheel her stallion around.

Breathless and blinded by the dark, Will regained his footing. His shield wasn't there, still hooked to Fix's back. He reached for his father's sword and drew it from its sheath.

"Ambush!" he heard Crisalli cry. "Defend yourself!"

The first assailant reached him before Crisalli could finish her warning. A shadowy figure slashed at him with a clumsy wave of his sword. Will sidestepped and followed its arc, waiting for the inevitable over-extension, then used his opponent's lack of grounding to his advantage by darting past his attack and sticking his own blade deep into the soul-hunter's chest. The hunter gasped, choking out blood, then fell dead at his feet as Will withdrew his blade.

Will's chest glowed a deep blue as the hunter's dozen or so souls flowed into his cage. The souls were nothing compared to what he already had. Will just stared dumbly at the corpse.

He had made that. He had killed someone.

Crisalli had reached him now, engaging in her own melee from atop her mount. At a quick glance, he counted at least six other assailants, three of which moved to entrap the charging Crisalli. That left three for him.

He remained frozen for a moment longer, eyes glued to the man whose life he had just ended. He looked to his blade, which was slicked with blood.

"Will! Get a hold of yourself!" he heard Crisalli shout at him.

He shook his head clear, then managed to batter away an uncontrolled incoming strike. He kept his distance, expecting a magical assault. When none came, his confidence grew. Crisalli had said that most of the soul-hunters left to join Carthon's army. That meant these bandits mustn't have magic yet, or at least not enough to sustain a proper image.

Will raised his sword as the next bandit came at him. This one was more competent than the last. His footwork was solid, his cuts smoother and more accurate, although he quickly became easy to predict. Will parried his first few strikes. The hunter even threw in a feint or two, realising Will's defence wouldn't be easily broken. Will found him easy to figure out all the same. His pattern was simple. He would only slash from two angles. He had no variation, no technique. Will waited for his arm to begin its rise to make the same slash he had done the six times prior. With a flick of his sword, he sliced through the hunter's unarmoured ribcage, exposing the glow of his souls within. They too joined his own.

If the two remaining soul-hunters were worried about their companion's injury, they didn't show it. One brandished a sinister smirk, as if he relished the boodlust.

He looked to his standing companion. "These two're Knights. Bet they've souls aplenty." He licked his lips before spitting onto the soil. "The boy's mine. Stand back, Hetch."

Hetch snorted, brushing past his companion. "Get lost, Mort! I'm due for some fresh souls. Slim pickins out here recently. Imagine what Ma would say if I came home with that much magic juice. Get me back in her good graces that's for sure."

Will didn't wait for them to finish their argument. Instead, he used the time to run. He wasn't scared, surprisingly, but he didn't favour fighting two-on-one either. He bolted for Fix, who had thankfully not abandoned him and had wandered back.

"Take your horse, get yourself out of here, make for Oskon Corr!" he heard Crisalli scream over the clash of swords. "I'll hold them off!"

He turned just in time to see a soul-hunter fall, blood gushing from his stomach where an image-sword had made its home. The sword disappeared, its purpose served.

Will was readying himself to mount when he heard the hunters rallying, preparing to come at him again. He watched as one conjured a spear of solid magic, the shaft hovering in the air. Will cursed. That meant he had at least some souls to draw from.

Will stopped short. He could easily dodge the spear, but he was standing in front of Fix. If he moved, the spear could hit her. He grit his teeth, riddled with indecision.

His assailant didn't wait. He pushed, and the spear shot forward, its copper glow barely visible in the night. Will panicked, scared more for Fix's life than his own. Something within him awakened. It was like that day in the forest with Rath when the bird's life was in danger. Power came to him freely, and he felt his stolen souls feeding him all of their strength. He opened his arms and his grandfather's shield appeared before him, only this time it was almost five times its natural size.

The spear splintered against its blue-glowing surface, falling useless at his feet. Will held the shield with his mind, keeping it in place. He remembered Crisalli's teachings. Using his two arms as a tether, he thrust the shield forward.

The two soul-hunters tried to run, but the shield caught them, its impact sending them reeling. Their fragile bodies flailed as they were thrown into the air and sent plummeting into the ravine.

Will caught his breath, staring at his own hands as if he couldn't believe that power was his. He felt a few more souls flow into his cage.

More deaths by his hand.

He turned to find Crisalli and saw that more soul-hunters had joined the hunt. Their numbers had swelled to nearly a dozen, surrounding his mentor and taunting her with feints and jests.

To her credit, Crisalli didn't waver. She stood her ground, though her mount now lay dead at her feet. Will's heart lurched for the dead animal. He hadn't much liked the horse, but such a beautiful creature shouldn't have met with such a cruel end. It wouldn't be forgiven.

He reached into his soul-cage and drew every scrap he could garner. He followed his breathing techniques, fighting off the voices as they made to consume him. He prepared himself to release it all. He didn't know how yet, but his body was acting on its own.

Before he could manoeuvre himself into position, however, a hail of arrows rained down from above, skewering at least three soul-hunters and halting their advance.

Will looked to the sky, but could see nothing, only a blanket of black, spotted with stars. More arrows came down, their aim indiscriminate, one thudding into the earth beside Crisalli's feet. She reacted, summoning three violet shields which surrounded her body.

Soul-hunters fell, and Will heard a distinctive whistle followed by a shuffle of footsteps and the sound of tumbling stone. Within moments, all of them were surrounded by a line of pointed spears. It was hard to see in the dark, but a flicker of torchlight within the ranks highlighted green surcoats.

Will stopped pulling on his souls and surveyed the newcomers. Each was fully armoured and armed for battle, with thin veils covering their faces. Were they more soul-hunters? If they were, he didn't stand a chance.

"In the name of the king of the Corr, surrender!" one called, though Will couldn't discern who.

One stupid soul-hunter broke into a run, charging at the nearest soldier with a fanatic war-cry. He was met with a spear to the chest, his lone soul flowing into the spearman.

"I won't ask again," the same soldier called. "Surrender, and you will be taken to the capital. Refuse, and you will die here."

Will looked to Crisalli. Her shields were still fixed in place. She took a wide glance at her surroundings, then dismissed her magic and placed two hands above her head before taking a knee.

Others followed suit, not wanting to end up with a hole in their heart.

Will felt the butt of a spear poke him in the shoulder. "Kneel. Don't be foolish now."

Will obliged, dropping to his knees.

"Filthy soul-hunters," he heard another soldier say, spitting at the foot of Crisalli. "You lot have no right to roam these lands. Put double watch on this one, she has a strong cage to draw from. And get the sacks, we'll see how well their magic works blindfolded."

Heavy hands gripped Will's shoulders, immobilising him. He moved to struggle against them when a sack was thrown over his head, plunging his world into darkness.

# Chapter 29
# - Tvora -

Lucia scouted ahead. As the quantity of Tvora's souls had increased, the range of her magic had expanded. Lucia and Cecco were becoming more independent by the day, less reliant on her.

In a way, this was good. It's what they wanted. Tvora relished the fact that she was now able to give them some semblance of freedom, even if it was finite. They were still a part of her though. Lucia and Cecco's physical forms weren't actually alive. They could experience their own senses, see with their own eyes and feel their own pain, but they were still connected. Each cut dealt to Lucia or Cecco would have a mental repercussion for Tvora.

Cecco flew the skies, searching for threats from beyond, and Lucia stalked the ground, finding what Cecco couldn't.

*The road ahead is clear, nothing but rock and stone,* Lucia said, her voice resonating inside of Tvora's mind.

Beside her, Mantis cracked his long fingers. Thin lips stretched high into his cheeks every time Lucia was in his presence.

*He stares any harder and I'll turn that smile into a whetstone for my claws,* Lucia said.

Mantis continued to stare, unaware of her remark.

"Keep your eyes on the road, where they belong," Tvora said instead. "The path forward is clear."

Mantis craned his neck. "They're just so... so... perfect," he said, moving his hands as if to cradle Lucia's head.

Lucia snapped at him and he jumped backwards, cackling as

he went. "Ha! Did you do that?" he looked to Tvora, then back to Lucia. "How? The texture, the muscles, the fur. The fangs! All such minute details. How is this possible? I need to know, I must know."

Tvora grimaced. She caressed the hilt of Naex. "Save the dissecting for your own experiments. Our bond is none of your business."

"Your bond? You really believe that, don't you," Mantis said. "Fascinating."

Tvora scowled. "Focus on the task. Carthon said neither of us could claim the other's souls, but he said nothing about taking a few fingers."

As she spoke her last word, Lucia swiped at the empty air an inch from Mantis' hand, causing him to jump again. Once he realised his fingers were still attached, he burst out into another round of deranged laughter.

Tvora rolled her eyes. She wondered at the wisdom of pairing the two of them. Did Carthon not think her capable of performing the task on her own? Perhaps this was his way of testing her skill, of forcing her to prove herself worthy to stand by his side without having to admit she was being tested.

To see if she could be trusted.

She laughed at the thought. There was no trust out here, only knives left in backs. Even so, she couldn't deny the opportunities serving such a man brought her. Even now she could feel the warmth of her new souls feeding her strength, making the strain of each day a little easier.

Lucia wanted the power, was driven to it, her every action dictated by it. Deep down, Tvora knew her to be jealous. She wished it were her with the physical body and not Tvora.

Tvora didn't resent her for it. She couldn't possibly imagine her pain.

Cecco swooped in a moment later, the red-hued hawk flapping his wings furiously as he hovered just above her eye-line. *I found it! The city is just beyond the rock formation.*

Tvora looked up. "Great work, Cecco, ride with me the rest of the way."

Mantis gave another curious look her way. She had been alone for so long she'd forgotten how she must seem to others, having conversations with her friends as if their thoughts were voiced aloud.

She ignored him, stroking Cecco's wing as he landed on her shoulder.

*Did you know,* Cecco started, *that the city of Oskon Corr was once in alliance with Athedale? They fought together in the early Soul Wars against Mirimar, before even Doonaval's time. The growing emergence of soul-hunters and the harsh terrain of the Harrows eventually rendered their alliance no longer viable. Now, the Corr isolates itself. It's often referred to as the Island City, but it's not actually an island. Did you know—*

"Cecco!" Tvora said. "You're rambling again. How is this relevant to our task?"

*It's not. I simply wished to share my knowledge with you.*

Tvora held up a hand. "If your knowledge isn't relevant, then keep it to yourself. I have more important things to worry about."

Cecco went silent, which for him was as rare as the sun shining in the night. He took flight again. *Very well. I shall leave you to your important matters.*

A pang of guilt wrenched its way through Tvora's gut. "Cecco come back, I didn't mean…"

Cecco left, flying off to who knows where. Her only comfort was the knowledge that he couldn't get far without his form fading, though she soon realised this wasn't a comfort at all. Just like Lucia, Cecco was trapped. They were all trapped. All in this together.

"Shit," Tvora said, kicking at the dusty road. She'd never had a problem with Cecco's ramblings before, why had it bothered her so much now? She pondered her feelings for the next few miles, keeping her distance from Mantis.

The foggy blue of the ocean illuminated the distant horizon as Tvora stepped out from a valley and into the open. To her left and right stretched a symmetrical rock formation which ran the length of her vision. It looked like the hilt of a sword, true to its name. In front of her extended a thin strip of land ending in the city of Oskon Corr, which sat nestled at the back as if cradled in the pommel of the sword. Surrounding it on all other sides, the sea raged.

Strong winds buffeted her every step as she and Mantis walked towards the city. As they drew closer, the area became more populated. Rather than a single gate, the city's boundaries were defined by a vast moat. A series of sturdy stone bridges arched over parts of the moat, presenting several points of entry. People gathered around each bridge in haphazard lines. Pack animals such as camels and horses were plentiful, even a few donkeys were present, their owners having filled their backs with goods to trade.

Thankfully, Cecco returned to her without deciding to hold a grudge. He and Lucia allowed themselves to fade, the trio deciding not to attract unwarranted attention. Carthon had planned for their entrance into the city, providing old papers and false identities for the two of them. Oskon Corr was not as strict as the Gracelands. Where Athedale refused admittance to anyone born outside of their borders, this city welcomed all, provided they paid the price in coin and gave reason for their stay.

After a short wait in line, Mantis tossed the guard a hefty bag of coins, three times the cost of admission. The veiled guard weighed the bag in his hands, sparing a quick peek inside before slipping it into his jacket pocket and nodding his approval.

Tvora kept her head down and her hood low, concealing her eyes. A rough hand gripped her arm, and she had to fight down the urge to draw Naev and cut his throat.

"Show me your face," said the man who had taken the coin.

Tvora didn't respond, prompting Mantis to come to her aid. "Take the coin and we'll be on our way."

The man gripped her tighter and made to lift her chin with the other.

Tvora raised her head voluntarily, fixing the guard with a fierce glare.

The guard's eyes grew wide, and he released his hold on her immediately.

"H — h — hollow… They're hollow…" the guard mumbled, taking a step back and reaching for his sword.

# Chapter 30
# - Will -

A sudden pulse of light flooded Will's vision, shapes blurring together as the sack was lifted from his head. He tried to rise, but found himself unable. Two hands gripped his shoulders, pressing him down with impressive strength. He felt something cold and sharp against his throat, causing his muscles to seize up.

"Try to create an image and I'll make one of your blood," came a feminine voice from in front of him.

Will tried in vain to steady his breathing.

"Calder, Silas, Ophelia, Thane, Myddrin.

"Calder, Silas, Ophelia, Thane, Myddrin.

"Calder, Silas, Ophelia, Thane, Myddrin.

"Calder, Silas, Ophelia, Thane, Myddrin.

"Calder, Silas, Ophelia, Thane, Myddrin."

The woman just stood there, knife drawn, staring. She wore dark clothing under a mossy-green coat. Black, knee-high boots scraped against the cold stone floor as she turned to a figure behind her, whose features were hidden in shadows. "What's wrong with him? Is he broken?" she asked.

The second figure approached, arms crossed and held tight to his chest. "Mmmm, I don't think so. His eyes are sky blue. Too much colour in them to be broken."

The woman edged closer to Will, her dark hair brushing against his cheek. "Tell me," she said, twirling a knife around her knuckles, "what's a soul-hunter like you doing so close to our border?"

Will grimaced. "I'm not a soul-hunter!" he almost shouted, half rising from where he knelt before being shoved back down.

The woman's eyes rolled. "Don't lie to me. You're young, but lie to me and you'll pay for it. I saw you use magic in the valley. The souls required for an image that size is quite significant. That kind of power isn't attained through an innocent life. Now, I'll not ask again, why did you come to the Corr?"

Will felt his heart quicken. He didn't know what to do. Should he tell the truth? He found himself hating Crisalli for not giving him more information. If he told them who he was, who they were, would that then condemn them, or save them?

Whatever the answer, he had no time to ponder it any longer. "If you saw me using my magic, you would have seen me fighting against the soul-hunters, not for them."

The woman frowned. "It's not uncommon for soul-hunters to fight amongst themselves, it's expected even. This proves nothing."

Will grit his teeth, left with no choice. "I'm an apprentice Knight from Athedale. I came here with my mentor on a contract for the capital."

If this information resonated with her, she showed no hint of it. "What was the contract you were tasked with?" she said, her voice calm.

Will hesitated. "I — I'm not sure. I wasn't told anything."

A droplet of blood dripped from his neck as the knife-wielder pressed harder.

Will clenched his fists. "We were sent to find aid. Some man, someone powerful."

"What was this man's name?"

Will fumbled for words. "C-Cerak. His name was Cerak."

The woman relaxed. The grip around his shoulders eased. Will collapsed onto his hands and knees, panting, sweat dripping from every pore.

"Come with me," she said, turning her back to him.

Will rose, suspicion slowing his movements. His captor unlocked the door and motioned for him to follow. A hand shoved him in the back, causing him to stagger, but he managed to catch his feet before he tumbled.

Shoulders slumped and hands still bound, he followed her down a narrow corridor lit only by a few incandescent candles. They continued up a winding staircase and through another narrow corridor even darker than the last.

They came to a halt before a metal cage, similar to the one Will had been kept in. He took a peek inside.

"Crisalli!" he called, pressing his face into the bars.

She looked up, her head still covered by a black sack.

A guard removed it, revealing her face. Her hair was a dishevelled mess and her eye make-up had run down her cheeks, leaving inky black stains. She rose. "Will, you're alive!"

Their jailer smirked. "Seems you may not be a lying weasel after all."

Crisalli snarled through gritted teeth. "I told you no lie. We are Knights of Athedale, here to see Cerak. He's still on the council, yes?"

Will issued a sigh of relief, glad he had chosen to tell the truth. The jailer plucked a key from her waist and unlocked the cell.

"Place the sack back on and follow me," she said.

"Get your hands off me!" Crisalli grumbled as a third guard entered the cell and pushed her forward.

"Come, the king awaits."

Will watched as Crisalli's face twisted into a knot. "The king? I didn't come here to treat with kings. I came here for Cerak. Take me to him."

The jailer just smiled. "Are you going to come willingly? Or shall I present you to the king unconscious? Make your choice."

Crisalli looked as though she were about to murder the jailer out of pure spite, but after a tense moment she relaxed, allowing the rough hands of the second guard to clamp the sack back over her head.

Will held a breath as his world again grew dark. They were led down another series of winding passageways and spiral staircases. It became impossible to discern any sense of direction with his face covered by cloth.

Eventually, they came to a rest. After being forced onto his knees, the sack was removed. His shackles were unlocked, and the jailers made themselves scarce. Will shared a confused look with Crisalli, who just rubbed at her wrists.

They knelt in the centre of a circular room with a large, domed ceiling. Splinters of light seeped through glass-paned windows, illuminating parts of the otherwise darkened room.

Crisalli placed an arm across Will as a bout of laughter echoed around the dome. Its tone wasn't cruel, nor was it mocking. It was more of a deep, resonating belly laugh that spread throughout the building, bouncing off the walls.

"Who's there?" Crisalli called. "Show yourself!"

An audible hum sounded, followed by a bright light and then the thud of something hard landing at their feet. The object disappeared as quick as it had come, so Will couldn't discern what it was.

He looked up to see the shadow of a man silhouetted in one of the rays of light, suspended in the air as if by some illusion. The silhouette vanished as quick as it had come, disappearing into the darkness. The laughter returned.

"Stand behind me," Crisalli said, positioning herself in front of him. "Have your shield ready to conjure. Stay vigilant."

Will did as he was told, remembering his lessons and shifting his focus.

A bolt of light struck the ground before them, causing Crisalli to falter. She grit her teeth and shouted. "Show yourself! Coward!"

Before giving their estranged assailant time to react, Crisalli created her thousand butterflies and sent them fluttering. The recreated insects filled the entirety of the room, illuminating it with bright, violet light.

The previously shadowed man came into view, his bulky form hovering on a golden disk.

Crisalli's demeanour changed. Will watched as she… smiled? She took three steps forward and thrust her arm towards their assailant. Her butterflies converged and he cried out in pain.

There was a sudden clap of hands, and fresh light bathed the entire dome, as if some darkness that had covered the windows had been removed.

Bright eyes the colour of molten sunlight stared back at them from a tall figure with an impressive moustache. His chest was completely bare. Ripples of muscle bulged from his arms and shoulders. A golden crown adorned his head, embedded with dozens of jewels that glittered in the light as he descended from his disc and walked towards them. The disc vanished behind him, the image no longer needed. The man puffed out his chest, his smile almost just as broad as he embraced Crisalli in a giant bear hug.

Will reached for a sword that wasn't there. He snarled and moved to wrestle the man off her. He tried to pry away his grip but it was like trying to bend metal, his grip was far too strong.

"Will, settle down," Crisalli said through squeezed lips. The man with the golden eyes released his hold, and Crisalli took in a deep breath. "This is Cerak, the man we came here to see."

Will relaxed, confused.

The man — Cerak — stepped back and laughed again, this time raising his hands into the air. "My love, you've come to your senses and returned to me!"

Cerak looked at his arm, wiping a trickle of blood from an open gash. "Razorblades on butterfly wings, you never cease to amaze me my love."

To Will's surprise, Crisalli actually smiled, a sight he had yet to grow familiar with. "Seems I'm not the only one who changed. What's that piece of junk on your head? Surely it can't be a crown?"

Cerak bowed deeply, the crown falling from his head to land perfectly in his open hand. "You may address me as King Cerak from now on, my lady."

Crisalli shook her head. "There's only one way to wear that crown in the Corr. Tell me you haven't, Cerak. Tell me it's a ruse."

Cerak grew quiet, and a silence seemed to hang in the air. Will still didn't understand what was happening. He wanted to ask, to pry for information, but Cerak spoke before he could gather his wits. "A lot can change with time, my love, though your beauty remains untouched by it," he said, moving to cup her jaw in his palm.

Will's mentor swatted it away with an aggressive flick of her wrist. "I'm no concubine to be swayed by your charms. I came here to bring you back to Athedale on orders from King Remen himself. You're a Knight, and have been called upon to fulfil your duty to the kingdom."

Cerak recalled his arm. His face contorted into an expression Will knew to be anger. He drew a sharp breath. "Concubine? You wound me, my love. Were we not wed? Were we not once in love? Such a feeling does not diminish as easily as people say."

Crisalli angled her head to the side and snorted. "A lot can change with time…"

Cerak grunted. "Remen has grown cold, sending you here to do his bidding. He must be desperate. I assume news hasn't yet reached the Gracelands of my ascendence. I'm no longer tethered to your order. Remen has no sway over me any longer."

"By what right?" Crisalli demanded. "None sworn may forsake their oath!"

"By right of ascendency!" Cerak bellowed. "I am king of these lands now. I rule Oskon Corr. To the soul-grave with the Knights."

Crisalli scowled, her tone growing hushed. "What happened to you Cerak? You were my husband, and you just left? I know something happened between you and the church. I know your brother was involved. But that's not good enough. I had a right to know why the man I loved decided to just up and leave without even a goodbye."

The king's face grew pale. He just stood there, arms to his sides, pouting. "I — I'm sorry," he said. "I had no choice. It's not fair, you're right, but what my brother did, what I became involved in… It was too dangerous for me to stay. You were better off with me gone. I need you to trust me."

Crisalli scowl deepened, her black-inked eyes weapons of their own. "Curse your soul, Cerak! I did trust you. Trusted you not to leave. I won't make that mistake again.

"War has come to the Gracelands," she continued. "If you won't help us, then we have no more business here."

"Wait!" Will said, stopping her as she made to turn. "He's strong, we need him."

Crisalli's eyes narrowed in on him. "Not now, Will. This isn't your fight."

"We can't have come all this way for nothing. Please," he said, turning to Cerak now. "Please reconsider."

The foreign king's eyes settled on Will. "Who's the brat?" His eyes flickered upward in an instant. "He's not ours, is he?" he said, his voice rising an octave.

When Crisalli said nothing, Cerak retreated a step. His mouth went wide.

Crisalli chuckled. "No. He's not ours. Though I should have let you sweat it out some more. The boy's Alina and Haylin's spawn. He's training under me as an apprentice Knight."

Cerak moved a step closer and bent over to examine him. Like Crisalli, he had a strong scent, though his was musky. Will took an involuntary step back.

"I knew your mother well, boy. How is she?"

Will looked to his feet. Crisalli placed a comforting hand on his shoulder and answered for him. "She's since taken the soul-road. Will is my responsibility now."

Cerak nodded, not pressing the matter.

"Well Will, son of Haylin. Have you ever seen the city of Oskon Corr before?"

Will shook his head. "No sir — King."

"Ha!" Cerak laughed. "This boy knows his manners. Definitely not ours," he said, winking at Crisalli.

Will frowned. There was still much about these two he didn't understand.

Cerak offered a hand to Crisalli. "Please, stay for a while. Allow me to show you my city. Despite what you may think, I have missed you."

"Shall I place the sack back on my head, first? Or was that just a formality you greet all guests with?"

"Hah! No apologies there, I'm afraid. Times have been... stressful of late. Soul-hunters have been emboldened by Carthon's movements. Those too scared to join him are fleeing north, and those who remain are having to hunt elsewhere. Slippery pests can sniff out magic like a hound to a leg of ham.

Lost many brave soldiers to their raids this past season."

"And yet you're content to sit behind your walls doing nothing to stop him?"

Now it was Cerak's turn to frown. He grunted. "Come, the contests are about to begin. Let me show you my city."

"There are so many people here," Will said, jumping up and down to try and peek over the top of the king's escort. Timber-framed houses flanked cobbled streets that seemed forever twisting. They meandered off into random patterns, though all seemed to somehow find their way back to the main pathway, which Will had since learned was called the Snake-Way.

Markets were prevalent, the streets filled with people selling all sorts of spices and silks Will had never seen before. The salty smell of brine filled the city as fishermen worked the docks. Will jumped again, and he thought he caught sight of merchant ships about to anchor.

"Where are the pirates?" Will asked, turning to Crisalli. His mentor held a stiff posture. Her arms were crossed, and her gaze was fixed to her feet.

"The pirates aren't here, lad. At least, not at the moment," Cerak said, clapping him on the shoulder. He looked to Crisalli. "Still not a fan of tight spaces, I see. Don't worry, we're nearly there."

Crisalli just huffed and made a clicking sound with her tongue.

The Snake-Way eventually led uphill, and before long Will could see the outline of a large circular structure similar to the amphitheatre in Athedale.

Unlike the rest of the city, this building was made with heavy stone. Columns rose into the sky like giant hands, supporting some kind of bowl in the centre.

Cerak turned, his lips widening into a grin. "Welcome, my friends, to the Crucible."

Will gulped, the name of the structure alone was enough for his chest to tighten. He followed Cerak down a narrow path, each step bringing them closer to a growing pounding. A heavy beat of feet on stone surrounded him, followed by the rage of a cheering crowd as Will stepped out into the open.

The roar was deafening. Hundreds, no, thousands of people crowded the auditorium, screaming at the top of their lungs, angry fists raised at some sort of spectacle that was taking place down in the bowl below.

Will's heartbeat raced. He felt both excited and anxious at the same time. His ears rang, the sound too much for him to handle. He reached out a hand and Crisalli took it in her own, squeezing tight. Will relaxed, allowing her to take him into the midst of the crazy atmosphere.

Two rows of soldiers dressed in similar garb to those who had captured him marched in a synchronised pattern. They then parted, allowing Cerak to pass before proceeding to escort the three of them up a flight of stairs to a private balcony.

The king took his place upon a slab of stone overlooking the balcony. He gestured for Crisalli to take the seat beside him, which was almost as high.

Will settled into one of the empty chairs, shifting awkwardly and turning to the 'oo's' and 'ahh's' that demanded his attention. He had to clasp his ears with his hands.

His eyes were drawn to the spectacle below, where a duel took place. Two mages were entwined in an all-out magical battle, throwing their best and most creative images at each other as if their life depended on it. Both were still standing after the latest barrage, though blood seeped through a dozen open wounds.

One competitor had completely lost the use of his left arm, the limb dangling weakly at his side.

Will's head throbbed as the memory of his grandfather's death at the Passing jumped to the forefront of his mind, brought on by the growing sense of dread at the inevitable outcome of the duel. Although he had never fully come to grips with the necessity of the Passing, at least he was beginning to understand it. This, however, was an entirely new form of barbarism.

Below, people were cheering, calling, and lusting for blood. They wanted to see death, had probably paid for it. He could see by the sour twist of Crisalli's face that her thoughts mirrored his own.

"What is this?" she demanded. "Why have you brought me here?"

Cerak remained expressionless, eyes focused on the bout below.

"Answer me!" Crisalli insisted.

Cerak turned his head. "This is law. This arena is all that keeps the darkest among us from committing murder in the streets. Without the games — the entertainment they provide, the safety they instil — our society wouldn't function. Our economy would crumble. We would be at war with ourselves. We would be but another extension of the Harrows."

Crisalli's eyes narrowed. "You speak of 'we' as if you were born here."

"It's as I said. I've been gone for a long time, much has changed."

Will's mentor stood and watched as a man's head was severed from his shoulders. Blood spurted from his neck and his body dropped like a pin. Hundreds of intangible globes of light poured from his corpse, rushing to meet their new host. The victor tilted backward as the souls collided with him. He gasped, then raised a fist into the air and bellowed a satisfied war-cry.

The already on-edge crowd raged into a frenzy. For a moment, Will thought they would riot, break down the barricade, and charge the energized contestant. Will pressed his hands harder against his ears. Cerak motioned with his hand and within seconds, uniformed soldiers all over the stadium brandished a line of spears and shouted a war-cry of their own, forcing the crazed citizens back into their seats.

The stadium began to quiet as a gate opened. Attendants made their way into the pit where the contestants had competed. They hauled the dead body onto a wagon before wheeling it away beneath the cheer of the crowd.

"This is what you call civilisation?" Crisalli said, gesturing to the bed of blood that still stained the ground. "This is no different than a pit-fight in the Harrows."

Cerak scowled. "Don't compare this to life in the Harrows. There's no slavery here. I don't condone the use of shackles. No contestant here competes to fill their belly."

"Why do they fight then?" Will asked, genuinely curious.

Cerak re-settled into his seat and leaned towards him. "You wish to know more about my city?"

Will nodded, making a point to avoid crossing eyes with Crisalli.

"I always do find the youth of the world to be more open-minded," Cerak said.

"They fight for coin, Will," Crisalli said, pulling out a silver piece and twirling it around her fingers. "Money is all that matters here."

Cerak paused to pluck and eat an almond from a platter offered by a young servant girl. He shifted in his seat until he seemed comfortable enough to continue. "Money is important, yes. These games bring in revenue, which we put to good use manufacturing weapons for the defence of our city and acquiring food to feed the people within. But coin is secondary. The real reason for these games is order."

"Order?" Will questioned.

Cerak nodded. "Unlike the Gracelands, Oskon Corr is ruled by the strong, by the Seats of Power."

"Seats of Power?" Will asked, leaning closer.

"There are twenty, plus a secondary council comprised of another fifty lesser seats, to make matters simple."

"So, seventy in total?" Will stated.

"If you believe the lesser fifty to have any influence, then yes. But more than their duty to the safety and longevity of the city, many people see the lesser fifty seats as a formal ranking system, an order for which those may challenge for a Seat of Power."

Will's face contorted. "How do people challenge for a higher seat?"

Cerak gestured to the sands below to where another two contestants were entering the ring.

Will's mouth opened and shut. "They fight for it?"

Cerak nodded. "In order to progress in this city, you must be strong enough to hold your position." He held up a hand, stopping Will's protest before it had begun. "Before you ask, there are rules. One may only challenge a council member of up to three positions higher than their own. If the challenged member refuses the duel, then they must swap with the challenger, no exceptions. If they accept the challenge and perish, then all other members affected progress a seat, and the challenger takes the lowest spot on the council."

Will listened with piqued curiosity. Suddenly, the laws of the Passing didn't seem so bad. "So, who has the top seat?" he asked.

Cerak fingered his moustache before opening his palm and gesturing towards himself. "You're looking at him, kid."

Will stared in awe. "So, you fought down there? All the way to the top?"

Behind Cerak he heard Crisalli scoff. "Fool ass mage. That much magic has more chance of seeing you soul-broken within the next year than keeping hold of that crown. That is precisely why royalty within Athedale are not permitted to wield any magic; too much of it and your brain turns to mush."

"There's been more than one soul-broken king of this city," Cerak said. "The council is not oblivious to the danger. If it should occur, all other members are to turn on the accursed immediately and remove the threat."

"To what end?" Crisalli said. "The cycle will continue. The one who slayed the former will only endure the same painstaking process. This method only delays the inevitable."

"One could say the same fault lies within the principles of the Passing, wouldn't you agree?"

Crisalli didn't rebuke him.

"There are circumstances in which the balance of power can be restored," Cerak continued. "When a soul-cage becomes too full for a person to handle, it's considered honourable for them to take their own life rather than give in to the inevitable pull of the dead."

"How does Myddrin do it?" Will asked, watching as they both turned to stare at him. "He's the most powerful mage in the world. If what you say is so hard, how does he still live?"

Cerak scoffed. "That kook of a man is still alive, is he? I thought he wouldn't last the year after taking on all of Doonaval's souls. Seems my old friend is stronger than I thought."

"You two were friends?" Will questioned.

"Good friends, yes, though that was a long time ago. He's returned at last then, has he?"

Crisalli nodded.

"Good, then you won't have need of me."

Crisalli slammed a fist into the chair. "That's bullshit and you know it. Carthon is every bit as powerful as his father was. He's united the Skull Thrones and has half the soul-hunters in the Harrows at his beck and call. We can't win this fight alone, Cerak. I came here to take you back with me but now that I'm here, now that you're king, perhaps there's another reason for me to be here. Together, we could patch the alliance between the Gracelands and the Corr."

Cerak sighed. "You always were ambitious, my love. I'm sorry. I'm sorry you came all this way for me, but I can't help you. There's too much bad blood between the Corr and the Gracelands."

"You pig-headed fool. What do you think will happen to the Corr if Carthon invades? You think the Hilt will protect you forever? He will carve a path of destruction Otor will never recover from, and you know it. You can't sit on the fence here."

"You don't understand the weight of what you're asking, Crissa. The Corr became independent from the Gracelands for a reason. The men who hold the Seats of Power are ambitious. Many, I suspect, have ties with Mirimar already. I'm doing all I can to prevent the Corr from collapse."

"You are a king. Tell them what to do. If they refuse, take their heads."

"Bah," Cerak grumbled. "Your ignorance knows no end. You forget I was a Knight. Most of the council have lived their entire lives in the Corr. Many were there when the Gracelands betrayed their oath. They don't trust you, and for good reason. Convincing them to turn and fight for a cause they have no stake in wouldn't be easy."

"If siding with Carthon is the alternative, it should be."

Will could see his mentor's temper flaring. He decided to stay silent as the two of them brooded for a lingering moment.

"Then leave," Crisalli eventually said. "Come back with me alone. Forsake your precious new title, or at least ask for a leave of absence. We need a mage like you manning the city walls. Myddrin isn't enough."

Cerak placed a heavy hand over his brow. "If I leave, this city will fall apart. Already, Arber of the Third Seat has eyes for my throne. If he is to lead... I fear for my people."

Crisalli took a slow breath before speaking in a hushed tone. "These are not your people."

Before Cerak could respond, a soldier came to attention beside the balcony entrance. "My king, the competitors are waiting for you," he said.

Cerak rose to leave. He made a half-turn backward. "I'm sorry," he said. "My place is here."

# Chapter 31
# - Myddrin -

"Mees! I need more wine!" Myddrin called across his bedchamber.

When no cry of protest came, Myddrin remembered. There was no one there. Nobody to call him out when he drank too much, to talk him into a quiet rest when he wanted to indulge, to clean up the mess he left behind.

Mees was gone.

Myddrin sat alone. He slumped into his chair, empty bottle in hand. His head throbbed with a constant ache. He felt at his shoulder, fingertips coming away bloody. His stitches had loosened and the bandages were now stained a dirty red.

That wouldn't do. He couldn't live like this.

He rose and opened the door to his chamber in search of the physician. He stumbled around the castle grounds, clawing his way to the medical ward. He stopped as a person wearing the plain brown rags of a lowly priest walked past. They had a bald head and a face like a blank canvas.

"Mees?" Myddrin said, reaching out a tentative hand.

The priest leaned away from him and frowned. He seemed almost scared.

Not Mees.

"Bah," Myddrin said, waving a dismissive hand at the priest before moving away.

Adralan would pay for this. Myddrin didn't know how yet, but the arrogant prick would pay dearly for taking Mees from him. He could obliterate him. Could destroy them all. He felt them churning, his souls. He felt the danger of breaking, more present than ever before. He needed a reprieve. Needed to stop the constant ache, the pain in his shoulder, the voices in his head.

Myddrin pushed open the door to the small apothecary. The physician took three steps back, startled.

"M — master Myddrin. You don't look well," he said. The physician wore a close-fitting linen coif atop his head. A leather satchel hung from his belt containing the essential tools of his trade as well as a few vials of medicinal herbs.

Myddrin grunted and pointed to his shoulder. "Need new stitches," he said, covering a burp with his hand.

"O — of course," the physician said. "Have a seat. I'll get to it right away."

Myddrin obliged, slouching into an uncomfortable chair. He allowed his mind to drift as his shoulder was stitched tight.

"That should do it," the physician said after he was done. "I recommend rest. Your body needs time to heal. I know it's painful, but your wound isn't as bad as it seems. With some proper rest and limited movement, it should be back to normal in no time."

"Bah!" Myddrin spat. "Not possible. Don't you know there's a war coming? I won't get to rest until I'm in the grave."

The physician made a poor attempt at feigning a smile, then nodded and made to leave. "You can, uh, let yourself out. I'll give you a moment to gather your strength."

He left before Myddrin could say anything else. Myddrin shifted, then groaned again. Everything hurt. Why did everything hurt?

He spotted something out of the corner of his eye. Something he knew well. Part of him screamed to get up and leave, to walk away and not look back, but that part of him seemed small and irrelevant right now. He was in pain. War would be here any day. He needed strength, needed a reprieve.

Myddrin rose and walked over to the apothecary's table. He grabbed a handful seedpods, shoved them in his pocket, then left.

He stumbled back to his chamber at a much faster pace. Once inside, he slammed the door and leaned on its frame. He took a deep breath, reached into the confines of his pocket, and looked at the pods.

That small voice returned. Mees' voice. It told him to discard them, that he didn't need it. He was better off without it. Myddrin listened, then pushed the thoughts away. He moved to his table, placed the poppy seedpods in his mortar, and began smashing them with the pestle.

Once he'd scraped out and refined the sticky, tar-like substance, he brandished his pipe. He held onto it for an overly long time. It sat there in his hands, an instrument to remove pain and suffering.

He placed the milk of the poppy into the bowl of his pipe and began to light it.

Before he could change his mind, he took a deep puff, allowed it to fill his lungs, then exhaled and relaxed. He felt his pain slowly begin to disappear, his mind returning to that state of blissful nothingness.

He took another puff, then another. Six times he inhaled. He drifted. The pain vanished, and finally, Myddrin felt at peace.

# Chapter 32
## - Tvora -

Tvora expected the guard to shout an alarm, for her to have to fight her way in. She prepared for it, already reaching inside her cage for souls to generate Lucia. The guard just stood there though. His hand gripped the hilt of his blade, and his eyes went wide, but he seemed frozen. It was as though the sight of Tvora had scared him to stillness.

Tvora tightened the hood around her head. Mantis approached the petrified guard and produced another pouch of coins, this one heftier than the last. "Say nothing, and this is yours," he said, placing the second pouch in his free hand. "Speak against us, and your throat will be the first we cut."

The guard's fingers twitched. He said nothing, took a step back, pocketed the silver and allowed them to pass.

Tvora released her grip on Naev, then walked in stride with Mantis into the bustling city.

Tvora hated crowds. Even before she had become soul-broken and shunned from this world, she had never been fond of them, preferring to keep to herself. She held her cloak high, the hood covering the whites of her eyes from would-be onlookers, but she found she hardly needed it. The 'Crucible', or whatever they called this strange structure in this even stranger city, was packed to capacity. Tvora could have stood up and danced a jig naked and those next to her would have hardly taken any notice, so involved were they in the proceedings below.

"What's the plan, Bug-man?" she said to Mantis, who sat awkwardly on the seat beside her. His chin leant on his open palm as he stared glaze-eyed into the crowd.

"Patience," Mantis replied.

Tvora cracked a knuckle. "I don't want to linger, and my companions are itching to come out. Why do we risk ourselves in public?"

Mantis craned his neck to face her. "There's little privacy in this city. You just have to deal with it."

Inside, Tvora seethed. Why did she have to get stuck with Mantis, of all people?

A bald man in dark brown robes was making his way up the flight of stadium stairs. People ceased their cheering as he passed, as if their mere voice might be offensive to the man and could be met with punishment.

Tvora eyed him as he stopped and turned to face her row. All he needed to do was blink and those in his way made themselves scarce, climbing over seats in order to flee from his glare. Tvora half rose herself, not wanting to draw any extra attention, but Mantis placed a hand on her arm, an act which earned him a hardened scowl.

The bald man took a seat next to Mantis. His hands were clasped over his lap, and his straight-backed posture unnerved her. "My master is ready to speak with you, follow me please."

Tvora shifted uneasily in her seat, wondering if they had been uncovered. However, when Mantis obliged him and rose to follow, she did the same. Her fists remained clenched though.

They were met with a mixture of both curiosity and fear as they walked down the crowded aisle, as if people wanted to know how they were important enough to be chosen, but also feared repercussion if their stare should linger for too long. Tvora tightened her hood anyway and lowered her head.

They were ushered into one of the balconies overlooking the arena. The view from here was spectacular, unhindered by the hundreds of bobbing heads and the buzz of the cheering crowd. Half a dozen people filled the balcony, the most noticeable being a man atop a high chair who had a servant fanning him with a giant leaf.

The man clicked his fingers and the others dispersed, leaving only himself, Mantis, Tvora, and the bald man who had escorted them here.

"It has been a long time, Mantis," the man said. "Last I saw you, you were but a child suckling at the teat of your mother. Now you return here, a Reaper serving the Skull Thrones."

"The Skull *Throne*," Mantis corrected. "The thrones are conquered, only one remains. Val Taroth is the sole power in Mirimar now."

"So it would seem," the man said. "Come, sit by my side, we have much to discuss."

Mantis obliged, moving into the seat opposite him. As Tvora edged further into the room the man rose to greet her. "Forgive me, but I don't believe we've had the pleasure. I'm Arber, holder of the Third Seat of Power. If you don't mind, would you remove your hood? I assure you, there are no secrets here."

Tvora spared a glance toward Mantis, who nodded. She removed her hood and stood tall, showing this 'Arber' character that she was not to be taken lightly.

He tried to hide his shock, but it was there. A twitch in his lip, a widening of his eyes. He quickly masked it, but it was clear he hadn't been this close to someone broken before.

"I see that the rumours, for once, prove true. Carthon has indeed acquired himself a reclaimed soul, and a beautiful one at that," Arber said.

Tvora glowered, his attempt at flattery having no effect on

her. She placed a foot forward and took delight in watching him take a backward step. She could have said something, introduced herself, or even asked what she was doing here in the first place, but she didn't. She decided to trust in Mantis for once, taking a seat beside him.

"Very well," Arber continued. "To business then." He turned to Mantis. "I've been informed that on a certain matter, our interests are aligned. You wish for the king to be removed, and I wish to be king."

Tvora leaned forward. "King? We haven't come here to smite a king."

Arber raised a groomed brow. He looked to Mantis. "Carthon didn't inform her?"

Mantis shrugged, then offered an amused grin. "Tvora will perform the task set, don't worry."

Tvora scowled. She wanted to kill him, kill all of them, cut their smiles from their faces with her blade. Of course Carthon hadn't told her. She was just a pawn to him, a weapon to use.

She leaned back into her seat, reminding herself that she didn't actually care for political games. As long as she got what she wanted, what did it matter who she had to kill?

Arber nodded. "Very well, moving on then. I make no move to hide my displeasure with Cerak's appointment. He is, and always will be, an agent of the Gracelands in my eyes. He doesn't know what it means to be of the Corr. He knows nothing of our sacrifice, of our values. He changes too much, and already many are beginning to listen to his poison."

"Why don't you take his head yourself then?" Tvora interrupted, earning her a leer from their host.

"Despite what you may think, our city is a lawful one. Those who hold one of the twenty Seats of Power may take no action against another. The only way to progress is through directly challenging them to a duel in this very arena."

Tvora scratched at her head, trying to follow. Mantis had explained the basics of their customs on the trek here, but she often grew bored when matters turned political. "He's too powerful for you, isn't he," she said.

Arber leaned back in his chair, hiding his frustration with a forced smile. "It would seem I've grown too comfortable with my head firmly attached to my shoulders, yes. If I were to challenge for the crown, I would surely lose."

"So, you would have us do it for you," she said, fingering her blade from hilt to tip.

Arber offered another forced smile. "That's why you're here, isn't it?"

Tvora bit back her frustration at being misinformed by Carthon.

Mantis gestured for him to continue.

"I can help you, grant you access to the palace when he's at his most vulnerable."

"And after?" Mantis asked. "You'll help us against the Gracelands?"

The mage of the Third Seat paled. "The Gracelands are a stain on Otor," he continued. "We helped them win a war, sacrificed thousands of our own, only to be betrayed and left clutching empty air when it was our turn to request aid.

"But," he continued. "The matter is more complicated than a simple request and answer. Even with Cerak removed, I won't be made king. Coranar will take the title. Perhaps I'm strong enough to challenge him for it, but even then, there is the matter of convincing the council to come to your aid. Not all wish to see the Gracelands burn as I do."

Mantis offered an unamused sigh. "Then stop babbling and make your point. You wouldn't have asked me here if you didn't have something in mind."

"Very well. When Cerak is removed, I will make my case to the council. I can't guarantee their co-operation, but I know them well enough to predict which members might support you in your cause. In exchange, of course, for clemency. I want Carthon's word that once Athedale is no more, Okson Corr will remain unprovoked and free to govern itself. I'm not so foolish to expect an alliance, only to be left out of his plans to conquer Otor."

Mantis pondered his words for a time, long arms stretching into the air. "I'll carry your message to my lord. In the meantime, agreement or no, we have a king to silence."

# Chapter 33
# - Will -

"Stubborn fool," Crisalli said, her cheeks flushing an angry red. If it were possible for humans to produce steam, it would be clouding around her like a storm right now.

Will cowered in the corner, not because he was scared — well, maybe he was — but because he didn't know what to say. He didn't know how to cheer someone up when they were sad and angry. His mother and father had argued all the time and he'd never known what to do. Maybe he was just used to hiding, to shying away from loud noises and negative energy. He liked things positive. Negative emotions only led to pain, and pain led to unhappiness.

Crisalli calmed somewhat, resting her legs atop the silken sheets in the room Cerak had provided them for the night. She exhaled, letting her head drop to the comfort of her pillow. "Don't ever get married, Will," she said.

Will skipped a breath. "So, you two are really man and wife?"

"Were," she corrected. "Well, technically I guess we still are, though I may need clarity on the rules for husbands who abandon their wives and never return." She sighed. "It's not all his fault, I guess. Trouble always followed his family. I suppose I knew what I was getting into. I can only blame myself for that."

Will shook his head. "You're wrong. It's not your fault. A man should never abandon his wife, no matter the circumstances. Otherwise, what's the point of marriage?"

His mentor's face began to brighten. She sat up and moved to ruffle his hair. "You're just like your mother, did you know that? She always knew the right thing to say."

Will raised a brow. "Really?"

"Really."

"So, what happens now?"

"Now?" she said, forcing a laugh. "Now we go home. Home to fight a war we can't win."

"We leave empty-handed then?"

"You heard him out there," Crisalli spat. "He won't budge. He's been gone too long, there's nothing left to salvage, neither from our marriage nor his duty."

"That's not true," Will said.

"You a sudden expert on the intricacies of human emotion are you now, boy?"

Will frowned, expecting to be hurt by the jest, but he found his mind suddenly clear, his thoughts forming easier than usual. "I can tell by the way he looks at you," he said. "My father never looked at my mother that way, not toward the end anyway. I may not be good at expressing my own emotions, but I can still see them, sense them. The look Cerak gave you wasn't one of someone who no longer cares."

Crisalli faltered, her once stern and rigid expression melting like candlewax. "I…"

Her face hardened again, firm lines of frustration returning just as quickly as they had gone. "It doesn't matter. The man made his choice. We both need to move on and live with it."

Will said nothing, just slumped his shoulders.

"You should get some rest," Crisalli said. "You'll need your strength for the return journey. We leave at first light.

"And Will," she said, moving to the candle opposite them. "Your mother would be proud of you, of the man you're turning into. I just wanted you to know that."

She snuffed the flame. Will, suddenly feeling the weight of the last few days, collapsed onto his bed, exhausted.

Will woke in a sweat, haunted by the same dream that had plagued him since his mother's death. He wiped sleep from his eyes and squinted through the darkness, expecting to see his mentor. She wasn't there.

He sat up. Her bed was empty, nothing but a mess of ruffled sheets. Will felt alone, like something was wrong. He knew he was probably being paranoid, that his lack of proper sleep was clouding his judgement, but the emptiness of the room unsettled him.

He rose from his bed. He hadn't bothered to change his clothing — a habit he had picked up on the road — so there was no need to dress himself. He wandered into the hallway, searching for Crisalli. Had she abandoned him? Everyone else in his life had left him, one way or another, surely it was no coincidence.

The hallway of the palace was like looking into the mouth of a cave with no end in sight. The sun hadn't yet risen from its rest, evidenced by the slight glow of starlight seeping through a high window.

He thought he caught Crisalli's scent to the west, so he took off that way.

The corridor was narrow and soundless. Each of Will's clumsy footsteps echoed, announcing his presence to any would-be stalkers of the night. He would make a terrible assassin.

He came to a stop outside an old door that was slightly ajar. He thought he heard voices within, and as he crept closer he knew one of them to be Crisalli. She spoke in a hushed tone.

Will poked his head through the door, ready to interrupt.

"I've never stopped loving you," he heard a male voice say.

"Bullshit," Crisalli said, causing any words Will might have said to jump back into his throat. "You abandoned me. After your brother was outcast, there was nothing left for you."

"That's not true!" the male voice said, which Will came to recognise as Cerak's. "I would have flown to the moon and back for you. You must know this."

"Then why," she said, her voice taking on a harsh, throaty sound as tears swelled her eyes. "Why did you not take me with you?"

Cerak didn't reply. He wrapped strong arms around Crisalli and pressed her head into his wide chest.

The two stood for a long time, vulnerable, taking comfort in each other's pain.

"I'll talk to the council," Cerak said, parting from their embrace. "There may be something I can do. To help you. To help the Gracelands. To help us."

Something in the background caught Will's eye.

It was subtle, but unmistakable. A shadow of movement from the balcony. Cerak's quarters were high from the ground, any intruder would have had to scale the building.

The shadow moved, creeping closer, now a silhouette against the stone tiling. A rigid shape began to form, followed by a featureless figure standing against the red of the curtain. Crisalli and Cerak didn't see it, the emotion of the moment rendering them vulnerable.

A flare of green burst to life. Soundless, a crystalline shard formed in the air.

"Watch out!" Will cried.

Crisalli spun. She shoved Cerak hard in the chest. The bulky king crashed hard into the frame of the bed. The emerald shard solidified and split the air as its conjurer sent it spiralling.

Crisalli let out an agonised cry. The shard had sunk into her shoulder right where Cerak's heart had been a mere moment before.

Will rushed into the room, his mentor's pain calling him to action. Several more shards formed as the dark figure growled.

Cerak grumbled like a raging bear. He screamed at the sight of Crisalli's blood, which flowed down her sleeve from a fist-sized hole just above her right shoulder-blade, the flesh torn and bloody.

Cerak formed his golden disk and flipped it around, the oval-smooth surface facing the mysterious assailant.

Shards crashed into the disk, most falling uselessly to the floor. One shard changed trajectory, however, curling around and under the disk to pierce the thick muscle of Cerak's calf. The stocky mage barely faltered. He grit his teeth and pushed his entire arm forward. The disk followed its master's movement, thrusting forward with a burst of speed. It hit the shadowed figure front on, its momentum taking both disk and man into the air, sending him flying off the balcony and into the silent streets below.

Will caught a wounded Crisalli, letting her weight lean on his slender frame. She was still conscious and breathing, which was a good sign. She coughed, and a gout of blood splattered the floorboards. "W-who was that?" she wheezed.

Thick veins protruded from Cerak's forehead as he clenched his fist and spat a string of curses. His attention remained fixed beyond the curtain as another presence made themselves known.

A violet glow illuminated the room in a wash of colour. A paw large as a lion's stalked into view. It was followed by what Will could only describe as a giant panther. Its head was as large as Cerak's chest. Thick, meaty legs took the beast forward as it circled the room. It was clearly an image, made of only a single colour, though Will had never seen one so real. Each muscle had its own individual sinews, bulging and retracting with each careful step.

Usually, images were abstract, devoid of emotion and capable only of following their conjurer's will. But this… thing, seemed alive. Its eyes were wide, two dark jewels that spoke of intelligence. They followed him, never leaving his own, sensing his fear.

"Begone, beast!" Cerak spat, conjuring a spear the length of an oar and grasping it with two firm hands, not trusting uncontrolled magic to be effective.

He lunged violently at the panther, watching as it skipped to the side, avoiding the blow. The panther made no sound, though it didn't need to.

"Show yourself, witch!" Cerak demanded.

Another figure walked into view from the balcony, brandishing two forearm length swords and waving them with a threatening grace. On her shoulder perched a scarlet hawk. It glowed like fire, its features even more intricate and life-like than the panther's.

Will faltered, placing his mentor's head on the floor as the woman in question opened her eyes. They each held a thin, hollow, oval-shaped line of black stitched into a sea of white.

A flare of panic erupted like a volcano inside of him as buried emotions rose to the surface. He clutched his heart, air refusing to come in and out as it should. In this woman he saw only his mother, staring back at him, broken. Memories flooded him, overwhelmed him. Past regrets weighed him down, rendering him unable to move, unable to do anything but watch as this woman did what she had come here to do.

The voices inside of him picked their moment, attacking him in a sudden rush.

*Run*
*Don't let her take us*
*Use us*
*We can help you*
*Let us out*
*Let us out*
LET US OUT

Will clamped his ears with his palms, hoping that would block them out, but the voices were internal. His pain was made worse by his fractured mind. He could barely comprehend his surroundings, though he thought he saw movement, two forces colliding. Cerak must be fighting the stranger. He heard Crisalli's voice, calling to him, shouting instructions like she always had, but he couldn't understand her, his focus fixed on the wave of souls fighting for control of his yet unbroken soul.

He felt the warmth of the floor as his body crashed, his mind wrestling with itself, fighting an invisible force. His mentor fought on, battered and wounded, and he just lay there, weak, useless, helpless.

# Chapter 34
# - Tvora -

Mantis plummeted, arms flailing. Tvora shook her head in disappointment. She should have done it herself. She doubted he was dead, no souls flowed into the room. She turned away, he must have crafted himself some sort of pillow to land on.

Although he was out of the coming conflict, he had severely wounded one of her opponents. The woman's presence hadn't been planned for. Cerak should have been asleep, alone. This was supposed to be simple, an in and out job. Regardless, she was here now, and suddenly eager to test her strength.

She stepped into the room, Naex and Naev drawn, acting like twin extensions of her arms. Lucia had gone ahead and was locked in a fierce stand-off with the apparent king.

Tvora wavered, her head twisting as her eyes met with Glock's. Only it wasn't Glock. The resemblance was uncanny. They had the same chiselled facial structure, only Cerak wore a moustache. The same square jaw and blonde hair, only Cerak's was cut short.

She shook her head clear, reminding herself that this wasn't Glock. The task had been set, and she would complete it.

A third presence made himself known. A boy no older than she had been when her village had burned turned to face her. He stared at her if she were a ghost, blank eyes shaking with horror.

She thought about ending him. It would be easy, just one slice from Naex. But he was no threat, and she was no child killer.

He seemed to be doing her work for her anyway. He bent to

a knee, mumbling a string of inaudible words. She knew straight away what was happening, had been through it herself. He could be a problem if his soul broke. Those freshly broken were erratic, unpredictable, and above all, powerful.

Cerak shouted at her, demanding she face him. Lucia swiped her paw, slicing through his spear, which re-formed a moment later.

"White-eyed assassin," Cerak said, edging in front of the wounded woman. "Who do you work for? Why have you come?"

Tvora ignored him. Cecco jumped from his perch. In an enclosed room such as this, a real hawk's movement would be limited, but Cecco was more than a simple animal. Creating his own momentum, he swooped from above and crashed into Cerak's exposed chest. The impact was deafening, and the woman that Mantis had wounded let out a shrill cry.

Cecco retreated to his usual position at her shoulder, though no blood slicked his scarlet feathers. Cerak bent to a knee, gasping for breath, but his flesh remained unmarred.

A golden light began to flutter out of existence where Cecco had landed.

*His reflexes are fast,* Cecco said. *His shields strong. This won't be easy.*

Tvora snarled. "We'll batter him down."

*Are you sure it's wise?* Cecco continued. *The palace will be alerted by now. The plan's failed, Mantis saw to that. The blame won't rest on you.*

"Blame?" Tvora spat. "You think I care who Carthon blames?"

She closed her mouth, realising she was talking aloud.

"Carthon?" Cerak said. "What does his black heart gain from my death?"

She gave her answer in the form of a forward lunge, dancing

towards him and brushing his spear aside, hoping to land a slash to his torso. Cerak countered, catching her wrist with his off-hand and kicking her hard in the abdomen.

Tvora snarled, preparing to re-engage, but Cerak's rage was unrestrained. He bellowed a war-cry and hundreds of gold nails appeared before him, pointed in her direction.

A flare of panic swelled within her as he let loose. Lucia was before her in an instant, moving with magically-fuelled speed. The nails thudded into her side, into her flesh.

Tvora grimaced. Technically, Lucia couldn't be killed, not unless she herself was to perish. Still, she was more than a mere image; part of her soul was imparted into each distinctive feature. It wasn't quite pain that she felt, but each nail wounded her soul, grating on her mind like a hundred tiny wounds. Whatever Lucia felt, Tvora endured as well.

Cecco felt it too, the hawk flying out through the balcony to avoid the deadly nails himself.

Lucia picked herself up, quick to recover. She swiped another paw, but Cerak was relentless, already charging with his spear. Tvora battered his strikes away, taking a series of backward steps until there were no more to take.

The wounded woman recovered. She was clutching her bloodied shoulder, but had regained her feet and was prepared to enter the fight.

The boy still rolled around on the floor, screaming, his soul about to break.

Tvora grit her teeth and thrust both swords at the approaching spear in a criss-cross action. Her swords cut through the magical spear, and the man named Cerak retreated a few steps.

"We must leave," Tvora whispered to Lucia.

*We can take them,* she reassured her. Lucia began stalking

towards the boy.

"What are you doing, Lucia?"

*Taking what we need.*

Her jaws opened wide, ready to crunch down on the prone boy's neck.

"He's just a child!"

*He's not a child! He's a Knight! And he will die as a Knight.*

Tvora blinked. The wounded woman leapt on Lucia, stabbing her with a violet blade born from the magic of the *otherside*.

Tvora winced at the mental burden of her wounded friend. She shared in her pain, her torment. She screamed.

*Call Gowther!* Lucia shouted in her mind. *Do it now!*

Tvora set her feet and closed her eyes. "GOWTHER! We need you, come forth!"

She braced herself against the wall, ready for the ground to shake, for the beast to awaken.

Nothing happened.

Gowther didn't come.

"Gowther," she called again, a whisper this time. "You stubborn fool, come out here."

She pressed her consciousness onto his. She could feel him there, at the surface. She knew he had been distant lately, but he had always come to her when she needed him, always.

"Where is he?" she asked Lucia.

Cerak reared, preparing another assault with his magic.

"Gowther has abandoned us," Tvora said. "We must leave, now."

Lucia recovered and pounced into the oncoming Cerak, the two of them tumbling into the back wall with a resounding crash. The king pushed her off with brute strength, punching at her side with his fist.

Lucia's body transformed, becoming incorporeal. She reformed herself a moment later, set her hind legs, then changed targets, leaping and swiping a claw at the already wounded woman.

She collapsed to the floor, blood gushing from her chest and shoulder.

"Lucia, what are you doing? Leave them! Let's get out of here, now!"

Her jewelled eyes stared up at her, filled with hunger. *I will not leave empty-handed.*

In one savage motion, Lucia clasped her thick jaws around the wounded woman's neck and twisted.

She shook, and then shook again.

"NOOOO!" came a tear-filled cry from the corner of the room.

But the deed was done. Thousands of intangible globes of light rushed into her in a wave. Tvora became disoriented, overwhelmed by the sheer amount of power, of souls, that she had now accumulated. So deep was her euphoria that she almost didn't notice the room shaking. At first, she thought it to be Gowther coming to her at last, but as her senses returned, she saw it to be Cerak. He radiated power, his chest a beacon of light as he attempted to create an image large enough to fill the entire room.

Tendrils of gold began to form and re-form. This time she didn't hesitate. Leaving Lucia, she sprinted for the balcony and jumped. Cecco appeared before her, expanding his form to triple his usual size. She grabbed his talons, and the feathery hawk took her weight. She spared a look over her shoulder, watching as whatever image the king had conjured made the entire building shake.

She hated fleeing, hated being bested, but she had no choice. Gowther wouldn't answer her call, and Lucia refused to listen, her lust for power proving stronger than their bonds of friendship.

She closed her eyes, wishing for the peace of a unified mind again. It didn't come.

# Chapter 35
# – Will –

Will's mind was a maze, a puzzle he couldn't put back together. He felt his control slipping, as if he were a puppet on a thousand strings. His body moved on its own, though it couldn't choose a direction to go. He struggled against it, using the strategies Crisalli had taught him to try to calm the wave. He focused on the loudest voices, those he recognised from previous assaults.

He pressed everything he had against them. He hadn't broken yet, but his tactics were proving of little use. He quashed one voice, only for another to rise and take its place.

*We're inside you*
*Let us out*
*Give us control*
*You'll be better off*
*We can help them*

He became dimly aware of the fighting taking place around him, though it only saddened him further knowing he couldn't help.

At the back of his breaking mind, he recalled a conversation with Crisalli.

Pain.

Pain could jolt his mind back into a conscious state, could break the crazed souls' hold over him and restore the balance he needed. Myddrin had said the same, reinforcing Will's next decision.

With great effort, Will rose a fist into the air and brought it down on his face. He felt his nose crunch with the impact, and for a brief moment the voices withdrew.

They returned shortly after, however, reinvigorated. He raised his arm for another strike, but found himself unable to bring it down. It was as if it were stuck to the air by some invisible tether.

A crash sounded from his surroundings. He tried to take a look, but all he managed to do was roll over, his back arching from the internal strain.

Through the corner of his eye, he watched as the violet panther swiped at Crisalli, sending her to the floor in a spray of blood.

Will's heart thumped as he lay there, motionless. He wanted to help, wanted to come to her aid, but he couldn't move.

"C — Crisalli..." he managed to say as he tried to crawl towards her.

Internally, he screamed. He tried to force his limbs to move, but he was too weak. "Leave her alone... please," he whimpered.

Whoever had control of the panther didn't listen. Will couldn't even turn his head to look away as teeth sunk into the pink of her flesh, biting down and twisting her neck like a rag doll.

He opened his mouth to tell it to stop, but the voices only took advantage. They pressed on his mind, ready to consume him, to become him.

A violent shout, deep as a drumbeat, split the air. A power he had never before seen rattled the bedchamber, waves of errant energy pushing against him. Tears filled his eyes as the ghost of an image began to appear, though what it was he couldn't discern.

Cerak's rage poured forth, the pressure created by his image pressing against Will's already prone form. Will was losing control, he could feel it, the power he once held over his own body was slipping.

A cackle of laughter that wasn't his own left his lips. The feeling was surreal. He was both there and not there, aware of what was happening yet powerless to stop it.

*Just let go*

*We have you now*

*Let me out*

*Set me free*

Pain ripped into him as whatever — or whoever — was taking him over made their final assault. The realisation hit him harder than the pain. He was going to die. Worse than that, he was going to be forever lost inside of his own body, replaced by whatever crazed souls had dared to overthrow him.

His eyes rolled to the back of his head, and his vision began to fade, replaced by another. Colours formed. He could see the world again, only it wasn't reality. There was no dead body before him, no sounds of battle surrounding him. Was this, the *otherside*?

*Will*

He heard a voice in this place of in-between.

*Will. Can you hear me?*

There it was again. It felt familiar. Kind.

*Son, are you there?*

"Mother? Is that you?" Will said, though he wasn't sure if his words were even audible anymore.

*Yes. I'm here. Will, listen to me. You have to fight it. Fight them. I'm here. I've always been here. There's no time. Please, Will. You're stronger than them, stronger than me. I'm proud of you. Now fight!*

Will pushed against whatever held him. He wasn't sure if his mother's words were real, or just some distant figment of his imagination, but he used them as fuel. He used them to retake control.

His eyes fluttered open again, and the vision of the *otherside* faded, replaced by the horror which had become his reality.

And then it hit.

Whatever image Cerak had been attempting to conjure manifested fully. It expanded quickly, hitting Will head on and sending him crashing into the opposite wall. His head cracked into the wood and the world went black.

Will woke in a haze, his vision a puzzle of fuzzy images. He thought he heard voices, a bunch of inaudible words or phrases.

Was this death?

He moved his arms, spreading his hands out in front of him before wiggling his fingers. He was in control, these were *his* decisions, his body was following *his* orders. He inched his left arm up, wincing at the pain.

Pain was for the living. He searched his consciousness for any sign of the invasive souls who had come so close to taking control. They were gone — or rather, they were still there, but back where they belonged, buried beneath whatever walls Will's subconscious mind had conjured.

He searched for his mother. He remembered hearing her voice, but she was gone too.

A man sat before him. He was weeping. Two giant hands cradled his head as he muttered a string of words into them. He lowered his hands and looked at him, golden eyes filled with despair. Cerak slowly reached for the sword beside him and levelled it at Will.

"What is your name?" he said.

Will shuffled back on all fours, the fear of death returning.

"What is your name, boy?" Cerak repeated.

"W— Will. My name is Will," he stuttered.

Cerak lowered the sword, but his muscles were still stiff with suspicion. "Not broken then."

"What happened?" Will asked, trying to piece together the fragments of memory he had from the previous night — at least he thought it was only the previous night?

"You've been out for two days," Cerak said. "I've been monitoring you to make sure you didn't break. We were invaded by agents of Val Taroth."

A piece of Will's fractured memory snapped back into place. "Crisalli!" he yelled. "Where is she?"

Even as he spoke the words, he knew the truth. Cerak's reaction only confirmed it. He remembered the sound more than anything else. The crack of bone breaking, the rip of flesh parting. The sounds of death.

He began to grieve in the only way he knew how. He sobbed. Crisalli was dead. He hadn't known her for long, but she had been kind to him, helped him learn, helped him grow when nobody else could. And now she was gone, just like everyone else in his life. Gone because of humanity's insatiable lust for power. A power he now held. A power he couldn't escape.

He wiped away the tears and hardened his expression. His father had always told him that to cry was to show weakness. The strong didn't cry.

An aggressive hand gripped his face like a vice. Cerak's thumb pressed into his cheek, his fingers pulling him closer to him like he was on a hook. His cold gaze met Will's own.

"Let it out," Cerak said, his voice heavy and intense. "Let it all out. Don't hold back."

He let go.

"What do you mean?" Will said, holding back another sob and feeling at his cheek.

"Suppressing emotions won't help. It only delays the inevitable, builds a shaky foundation which will crack when tested.

"Crying is healthy, crying is natural. Allow it to happen. She meant a lot to you. Let yourself grieve. Show her how much you care. Just, don't let grief consume you. Never let it consume you. The voices within you have subsided for now, but they will return. Do not make it easy for them. Build your internal walls high. Do you understand?"

Will nodded, then sobbed into Cerak's shoulder.

"What if I stop using my magic?" Will asked, walking in stride with Cerak as they entered through a thick, iron gate.

He waved the question off. "It wouldn't matter. Once a person has tapped into their reserve of souls, they become susceptible to them. Even if you were to never call upon their power again, at most all you would do is slow their influence."

Will grimaced. "So, I'm stuck with these 'things' living inside of me for the rest of my life?"

Cerak sighed. "That's the cost of seeking power. It never comes without consequences. Did Crissa," Cerak paused. "Did Crisalli begin to teach you how to control the voices?"

Will nodded.

"Good. Practice what she taught you every day, and remember to keep your head, even in the most extreme of circumstances."

Will took in Cerak's words stoically. "What happens to me now?" he asked.

"You will remain by my side until I know for certain you won't break. For now, we are going to council, there is a matter I must present."

Will followed him like a lost pup as they walked through yet another set of double doors. The king walked with purpose, his strides wide and his back straight. Whatever he was going to do, he was determined to see it through.

Will froze. He had walked into a room as bright as the sun in a cloudless sky. He squinted, basking in the atmosphere of the windowed ceiling. The room was circular, and it was filled with people. Twenty curved seats lined the outskirts of one half of the room in a semi-circle. Each seat was placed slightly higher than the last, the final one at least two dozen feet off the ground, all supported only by a metallic golden pole protruding from the marbled floor.

Will craned his neck. How did they even get up that high? There were no stairs, no ladders.

Another five rows of perhaps ten people each made up the opposing side of the room, though these chairs were all on the same level. Conversations ceased as all eyes turned to Cerak, who wore a stern expression, eyeing each and every one of them, watching to see their gazes falter.

A strange sensation fluttered in Will's stomach. It was the same feeling he had experienced during the Passing. He was still new to the world of mages, but he was sure it had something to do with the sheer amount of power accumulated in the room. There were thousands of trapped souls here, all mixing into one invisible voice.

Cerak motioned for him to take a seat with the crowd. Only one empty seat remained. Will's heart quickened as he took his place uncomfortably between two shady looking figures. He jerked his head away upon recognising one of them. The victor in the Crucible. His arm rested in a sling, and his hair was slick with oil. He regarded Will with contempt, huffing a derisive sigh before ignoring him entirely.

Will sunk into his chair, watching as Cerak approached the tallest seat in the room. For a moment, he thought him about to look a fool, the chair far too high to be accessible. Then Cerak waved his hands and a golden staircase shimmered into existence, spiralling around the golden pole before solidifying. He climbed the staircase, dismissing it as soon as he had taken his place.

Hands resting against the armrests, he cast his gaze out into the gawking crowd of mages gathered to hear him speak. He let the silence stretch, building both tension and suspense.

"Oskon Corr has come under attack."

Gasps surrounded Will as the crowd rose into uproar. Calls of 'who would dare' and 'agents of Mirimar' rose above others, though he could hear some vocally accusing the Gracelands of the deed as well.

Cerak raised a hand in the air to indicate that he wished to speak. "It was indeed agents of Mirimar who invaded my home and attempted to take my life," he said.

"Preposterous!" came a call from somewhere amidst the fifty gathered seats.

"Lies!" came another, this one from the twenty high chairs.

Cerak ignored them, raising his voice even higher. "While the sovereignty of the Corr is built upon bloodshed, I cannot allow this to stand. An assault on myself is an assault on all of you!"

"I presume then, that you have proof that this was indeed the work of Mirimar?" said another man two seats to Cerak's right, the third-tallest chair in the room.

"Words were spoken from the assailant's very mouth. A soul-broken witch acting as one of Carthon's Reapers."

More gasps sounded, the room descending into a muddle of whispers and murmurs.

"What is it you would have of us, Cerak?" said the man again. "Ride to war against Mirimar because a woman openly claimed, while apparently attempting to kill you, to be from there? Did you not consider that perhaps that is exactly what she meant you to believe? She could just as well have been an agent of the

Gracelands attempting to turn us against Mirmar."

"Watch your tongue, Arber," Cerak spat, his fists clenching and unclenching. "Athedale don't allow those whose souls have broken to live. She was no assassin under their influence."

"A fact you would know well, being from there," Arber said.

"Arber!" a third person said, a portly looking man well past his prime. He sat in-between the two of them in the second-highest chair in the room. "Continuing to interrupt out of turn will see you removed from the chamber."

Arber stalled, but didn't relent. "I merely wish to highlight the fact that Cerak would risk the safety of the Corr by having us rush off to defend his old country. The Gracelands have given us nothing but a cold shoulder ever since we bled for them. I will not hold my tongue if the consequence is another fruitless war defending their outdated kingdom."

Grumbles of agreement reverberated across the chamber, many nodding in approval of Arber's words.

"Stay your hand, Arber," said the man in the Second Chair. "Cerak has not proposed anything as of yet, he has merely presented information. Let us hear what more he has to say." He turned to Cerak expectantly. "What do you propose?"

Cerak leaned forward. "I do not want war. We have suffered enough as a result of our neighbours' savagery. I would not see us through yet another time of hardship. But neither can I ignore what is happening in the world around us. Carthon is moving, he has taken Kildeen and even now gathers an army ready to march upon Athedale. I understand many of you hold a bitter grudge against them, but I ask you this. What if they fall? Where do you think Carthon's eye turns next? Do you think his bloodlust will be sated? Do you think his yearning for power will cease?"

"Then why not align ourselves with Carthon?" Arber said. "Why not aide the winning side? Strike a deal with him. Break away from all ties with the Gracelands."

Will had to stop himself from rising in his chair, though many others did not. The room erupted into chaos, the calls of support for Arber rivalling those against him.

It took a long time and many attempts before Cerak finally managed to quell the uproar.

"SILENCE!" he finally screamed. Amidst the frenzy, the king had conjured his gold skimmer disk, allowing him to stand and hover over his high chair. "You speak poison, Arber. I would remind you that I am king. I will not tolerate such ideals in my court. Carthon and his legion are more beast than man! They will not ally themselves with us, nor should we seek their allegiance."

"Your mind is clouded, Cerak!" Arber replied. "You would have us run back to the Gracelands with our tail between our legs. Tell me, did you not host a member of the Knights of Aen this past week?"

"I did," Cerak replied, his voice callous.

"And tell me, who was she to you?"

Will could see the lines forming on Cerak's face. His cheek twitched. "She was an old acquaintance."

"An acquaintance? You deny then, that the two of you were wed?"

Cerak's anger manifested fully now, his shoulders seeming to double in size. "In another life, she was my wife, yes."

"And where is she now, might I ask?"

Cerak paled, unable to hide the sole tear trickling down his cheek.

"Will you not answer this simple question?" Arber pressed.

"She is dead!" Cerak spat. "She died protecting me from the foreign witch."

The strength in Cerak's gaze faltered, overshadowed by the immeasurable grief he must be feeling.

Arber, however, did not let the matter rest. "You bring us here to council today for personal vengeance, then?"

"Watch yourself, Arber," Cerak stated. "You tread a dangerous line."

"These are dangerous times," he continued. "I won't be forced to hold my tongue when the future of my city rests upon the whims of a man grieving his lost whore."

Cerak snapped. Whatever composure had been keeping him in check vanished as he leapt off his disk. He lunged fist-first, knuckles connecting with Arber's exposed right eye with a crack. The mage of the Third Seat tumbled off the back of his chair. He plummeted the near two-dozen-foot drop, caught only by a last-minute image conjured by another member of the council.

Cerak's disk caught him on his descent. He stood, chest puffing, his back facing the angry crowd.

The man next to Will grit his teeth and charged. Images formed as the man compensated for his broken arm by using his magic. He shot forth a series of half formed images angled towards the oblivious king.

"Cerak! Watch out!" Will called, taking a stand.

Cerak's golden disk slid from his feet and shot backward all in one motion. Everything happened so fast. The disk crashed into the images, deflecting their path, and it didn't stop there.

For a long moment everything was still. Silence hung in the air as the crowd grew quiet.

Then his head dropped from his body.

The man who had been next to Will collapsed, dead, the golden disk now slick with his blood. Souls flowed from the bloody pool and into Cerak.

The king turned, his eyes wide with horror.

"The king has violated the law!" someone called from the crowd. "No mage shall harm another member of the council outside of the Crucible! He must answer!"

The room erupted again, this time calling for Cerak's head. Another man beside Will rose, raising an angry fist as he spat insults at the man who was supposedly his king.

"You are all fools!" Cerak shouted.

His words were left unheeded. Will looked for an exit, panic rising in his chest. He suddenly knew what was happening. It was obvious most here didn't want Cerak to rule. He was too powerful. In order to progress, one needed to challenge for a seat above them. Cerak had won his place as king. None could best him. All knew it. Arber had just given them their opportunity to bypass this obstacle. Cerak had broken their law, and they weren't about to let it slide.

The portly looking man from before rose in his chair, legs resting against an emerald image of his own creation. All conversations ceased as they allowed the second-in-line to the throne to speak. Unlike most in the room, he didn't look smug. He showed no sign of pleasure at what he was about to say.

"Cerak, you have broken the first law. No man shall harm another outside the sanctity of the Crucible. With the authority of the council, I hereby denounce your claim to the throne, relinquish your seat of power, and sentence you to death."

Will gasped.

Cerak stepped onto his golden disk and allowed it to take him high into the air. He puffed out his chest, hands in tight fists. He thrust an arm forward. "You listen to this man," he said, pointing at Arber, "and you will all die. Carthon isn't the answer. You think he will give you independence? Then I say you are all fools."

"Kill him!" came another cry.

"Take his head!"

Cerak laughed, thrusting his head backward in an overzealous show. "Come on then," he said, sounding almost crazed. "Who will be first? You want my crown? Come and take it."

No one moved, not a soul.

Cerak floated around the circle, gaze unfaltering, daring someone to take him, to challenge him. When no challenge came, he stopped at Will, offering him his hand.

"Come on, Will, we're leaving. My time here is done."

# Chapter 36
# - Myddrin -

Myddrin sat on the top of White-Rock. His legs dangled off the edge as he watched the city prepare for what was coming. The stone itself was an oddity, a lone protrusion stretching like a finger into the sky. It stood paramount, a majestic force of nature overseeing the entire city.

Hundreds of tiny dots were hard at work below, fashioning steel and armour, hauling carts of grain through the streets, spending last moments with loved ones…

Myddrin leant backward, his mind in a blaze. The pain in his shoulder was gone. The voices were nowhere in sight. The memories which had haunted him for so long were still there, but they felt distant.

He exhaled, puffing a ring of smoke which filtered into the sunny landscape. This was where his journey had started. This was where his life changed. He wondered what his life would have been like if he hadn't been holding that spear. Then these souls would have been someone else's burden.

Behind the layer of fog clouding his mind lingered a gnawing guilt. He felt like a failure, a disappointment. He felt weak. He had given in to the allure of escape. Resorting to poppy once more after so long without it cut him deep, though it was also a necessity. It was the lesser of two evils, or so he told himself. Take a little poppy now to avoid breaking his soul and rampaging across the capital…

It seemed logical. It was enough of a reason to stop him from completely falling into a pit of regret and remorse, though only barely.

"I hope I'm not interrupting," came a call from behind, causing Myddrin to jolt to his feet.

Halvair stood but a few feet from him, his silver hair blowing in the wind. "Relax," he said. "I'm not going to push you. Though that would be a fitting end." He laughed at his own jest, stepping towards the edge of the rock and staring down.

He shook his head. "Baffling, isn't it? I managed to overpower Doonaval, the most powerful mage Otor had ever seen, only for him to land on a spear held by a lowly educator like you. I mean, what are the odds? Magic truly is a fickle concept, don't you think? A minuscule detail such as which wound fells a man last can be the difference between a wealth of power, and none at all."

"What do you want?" Myddrin said, stifling a cough.

Halvair took in a deep breath, exhaling it all at once. "You know, Myddrin, as much as I despise you, I have actually come to rather admire you. At first, of course, I was consumed by hatred, for you took everything from me. I believed you to have professed the glory for yourself, to have shunned my accomplishment and claimed it as your own. I now see that this was not the case. You were just a bumbling fool, unaware of the circumstance of your reputation's birth."

Myddrin scowled as Halvair paused to laugh. "But that's not why I respect you," he continued. "I respect you because you have survived. I respect you because despite the fall of your false reputation, you found a purpose. You wish for an end to magic. An admirable goal, albeit an impossible one. To bear the burden of magic's taint is no small task. I know well what you have had to endure. I continue to be surprised that your soul has not yet broken. Alas, I find your purpose to be a futile one, and that brings me to my point."

"Speak your poison," Myddrin said.

Halvair shook his head and sighed. "Do yourself and everyone else a favour, and when you get home, look in the mirror. Ask yourself what you see.

"Because what I see is a broken man. You've had a hard life, Myddrin, but right now, you're washed. You're in no state to protect this kingdom."

"What do you want, Halvair, I don't have time for—"

"I wish for your permission for me to kill you."

Spittle spouted from Myddrin's mouth as he gasped. "You… what?"

"I wish to claim your souls, publicly, and with your permission."

"Has your soul broken? You're insane."

"Perhaps, but what do you have to lose? You have no family ties, save for your mother, who you have my word will be well compensated and cared for. You no longer have your little Hand following you around. And the church despises you. The Gracelands need strength in this time of jeopardy. You're no warrior, you never have been. Look at the people down there. You're responsible for all of their lives. All of those families rest upon your ability and skill with magic. You don't want this burden; I see it in you. You want only to rest, to be free. Let me carry it for you. Let the responsibility fall upon someone capable."

Myddrin withdrew inside himself, angry that some part of him saw sense in Halvair's words. He wanted to rebuke him, to fight him, to challenge him. He wanted to tell him that he was wrong, that he was capable, that he could help them. But nothing came out. He just sat there, mouth dry, no words forming.

Halvair held up a hand. "Don't answer now. Have some time to think on it." He turned to leave. "But don't think for too long. There's a war coming, Myddrin. Do what's right, for the good of us all."

# Chapter 37
# - Tvora -

Tvora lay sprawled atop a giant rock. Her arms ached from holding Cecco's talons and her fingers were numb from the cold of the night. She felt exhausted, yet even through her exhaustion she felt a new strength. She unbuttoned the top of her shirt and pulled it open. Just above her breast, her open soul-cage swirled with the unfamiliar weight of thousands of new souls. Her well had swelled significantly.

With this new power came a sense of regret. She felt herself changing, morphing into a person she neither knew nor understood. Was this who she was now? She summoned Lucia, the violet panther manifesting as a light in the dark of the night.

*Do you feel it?* Lucia said. *The power, this is amazing. If every Knight in the Gracelands holds this many souls, we'll soon be able to hold our forms forever! No longer will my presence fade as the sun begins to sink.*

Tvora sat up, her jaw fixed into a grimace. "You shouldn't have done that, Lucia."

Lucia's head twisted in confusion. *What do you mean? Can you not see the power I've brought us? With this we can do anything! We can go anywhere we wish. No longer will we be challenged because of what we are. Those who refuse to accept us will tremble beneath the weight of our magic.*

"I don't know how much more my conscience can take. When will we have enough? When can we stop?" Tvora asked.

Tvora felt at her cage. She thought of Edith, of the poor

children from the orphanage. Of the blind woman. Their souls slept inside of her, fuel for her friends. Was Tvora becoming the same as the person who had killed them? Was she a monster too?

*Conscience?* Lucia snapped. *You overestimate the value of a human life. These people are rotten, they deserve to be purged.*

"He was just a child, Lucia! A boy! You nearly killed him. He was no threat."

*He was not a child!* Lucia spat. *He was a Knight. He had countless souls sleeping inside of him, and he was about to break. If he had, he could have killed us all. I make no apologies.*

"I just, I feel as though for every soul we gain I'm losing part of my own. I don't like who I'm becoming, who we're becoming."

*That woman and the child would have killed us if they had the chance. It was us, or them. It has always been us against the world. You need to purge this weakness from your soul. It has already cost me one life, I won't have it cost me another!*

There it was. Lucia's words hit Tvora like a punch to the gut. She did blame Tvora for her death in their past life. Worse, she resented her for it.

She found herself suddenly angry, furious even. She rose and balled her fists. "Do you think I wanted you to die? You're my best friend Lucia! Do you think I asked for that soul-hunter to come to our village and take Gowther away? I did what I had to. I stood up for what I believed in."

*And look where it got us*, Lucia said. *Our village burned because of what you did. Me, Cecco, Gowther. We all burned because of you. Yet you survived, all because the hunter wanted you to suffer. He wanted you to live with the pain. Because the world is rotten!*

Tears fell from Tvora's cheeks now as she recalled the torment of her past life. Her throat constricted and she began to choke.

"But I found him!" she said. "I grew strong. I tracked him down. I avenged you. I brought you back!"

*We brought ourselves back. We saved you from your own broken mind. I know you did your part, Tvora. But it's not enough.*

"Then when will it be!?"

Cecco flew between the two of them then, flapping his scarlet wings. *Stop it you two! You mustn't fight like this! Let the past be the past, please!*

Tvora just stood for a moment, shaking. "I need a break," she finally said. "A break from you," she looked to Lucia.

Inside her mind, Lucia growled. For a long while nobody said anything. The two of them stared at each other.

*Very well,* Lucia finally said. *I'll give you some space. But war is coming. We can't miss out on this opportunity because of your frail conscience. Summon me again when this crisis of character is over.*

Then she left. Her form turned first to mist, then to nothing at all.

Cecco landed on her shoulder. *Would you like me to go as well?*

Tvora pet the hawk's feathery side. "Just for a little while, I promise."

In a whoosh of motion and a flash of colour, the hawk disappeared as well, leaving Tvora alone with her thoughts.

She found Mantis on the road, riding atop a giant, green image-bug. The beast traversed the rough plains of the Harrows with relative ease, six legs propelling the creature forwards. Only Mantis' pride had been injured in the confrontation with Cerak, and Mantis preferred not to speak of it.

Any sign of pursuit had long since been quashed. Once they passed the border into the Harrows, any trackers would find themselves hard-pressed to follow.

"Where are your passengers?" Mantis asked.

Tvora glared at him and said nothing. The two of them didn't say another word the entire trek back to Kildeen.

The desolate plains soon turned into a bustle of activity, as tens of thousands now camped outside the stone walls of the keep. Camp-fires littered the surrounding plateaus as the various tribes of the Harrows gathered in support of Carthon and his legion.

Skull-crossed banners fluttered in every direction. She could be angry with Lucia all she liked, but there was no hiding from this. It was happening whether she wanted it to or not. The lines had been drawn, and people were taking sides.

Carthon was waiting for them in the throne room, sitting expressionless on his stolen throne. Septus seemed recovered and sat by his side, though his attention constantly wavered. His eyes darted to all corners of the room, as if the control over his souls was slipping by the day.

Tvora looked to her shoulder, expecting Cecco to make some nervous quip, but it never came. The bird wasn't there.

Carthon clasped his hands, welcoming her with a warm smile. "My Reapers return at last."

Tvora tensed. She'd been dreading reporting of her failure. Her first true test as a Reaper and she had failed. She wouldn't cower before him though, wouldn't beg forgiveness. No. If he was displeased with her and made to act on it, she would show him what she was truly capable of, even without the help of Lucia and Gowther.

"Is Cerak dead?" he asked in a way that suggested he already knew the answer.

"He livesss," slurped Septus. The crazed Reaper wiggled his fingers in front of his face, staring at them as though they were the most fascinating fingers in the world. His head snapped to the side in a sudden jerk of movement, causing Tvora to shift her feet. "You ssshould have let me kill him," Septus said, jerking his head back towards Carthon. "I would have ssstabbed him good."

Carthon held up a hand.

"Did you know he was a king?" Tvora said.

Carthon offered an amused smile. "Perhaps."

"Then you sent us there to die," Tvora spat. "You knew we couldn't defeat him."

"To die, you say? You are a Reaper of Mirimar now. If you can't handle yourself, you don't deserve the title. Besides, I see new strength in you. You must have had some success."

Tvora frowned.

"Tell me," Carthon continued. "Who did you kill? It must have been someone important."

Tvora straightened. Her thoughts turned to Lucia as her mind replayed the vision of the woman's neck snapping. "It was a woman. A Knight, I think."

"Did the king care for this woman?"

Tvora flinched. "Yes, a great deal. He wasn't happy when Lucia ended her life."

The grin on his chiselled face stretched even wider. "Ah, well there you have it, results," he said.

"I — I don't understand."

"You're a brilliant soldier, Tvora, but you have not the mind nor the temperament for politics. You may have failed to end his life, but you have planted the seed, a seed I intend to see quickly grow. You have done all I needed you to do, both of you.

"Go," he continued. "Sharpen your blades, summon your spectres. Soon, we march to Athedale."

# Chapter 38
## – Will –

Will flew through the air, damp hair sticking to his face as wind blew against him. His stomach sank, levelled out, and then sank again as Cerak steered his flying disk at a furious pace. Despite their situation, and despite the growing anxiety clawing its way through his insides, Will found his current situation thrilling. He couldn't believe it, they were flying.

"Why don't all mages travel like this?" he shouted over the howling wind. "This is amazing!"

Cerak slowed his pace, dropping the hardened disk to a lower height that was less nail-biting and more manageable. "Not all mages are strong enough."

"It doesn't seem that hard," Will prodded, tapping his knuckle against the solid disk below their feet.

Cerak huffed. "It's not just the size of the disk you have to factor in, young one. It's the motions, the weight, the control. All of this must be accounted for, and even then, most mages don't have the souls to sustain and control the image for long enough to ride it."

Will thought it over, the words making sense. "Just how strong are you then?" he asked.

Cerak shook his head in a slow, defeated motion. "Not strong enough."

Will wanted to comfort him, to ease his pain, but what was he to say? Sorry your wife is dead? Sorry your country wants to kill you? He opened his mouth, about to say it, but stopped himself.

In a way, Will felt closer to Cerak now. They shared a familiar pain.

"We'll be in Athedale by morning, I suggest you take this time to rest," Cerak said.

"What will happen in the Corr?" Will asked, biting his tongue one moment too late.

"Ulver of the Second Seat will take over as king in my absence. He is capable, careful. He holds no love for Mirimar and knows well the stench of Val Taroth. My purpose there has ended, perhaps it was never truly there to begin with."

"So, you'll help us in the war?" Will asked.

"That, I've yet to decide. First, let's get you home. Crissa should never have brought you to me."

Will deflated at the mention of her name. Perhaps he was right. As the initial thrill of flight subsided, Crisalli's absence became all-consuming. He hadn't noticed how much he had come to care for her, to rely on her. He tried to push those thoughts aside, but they were always there, like another voice scraping at the edge of his busy mind.

He couldn't help but feel responsible. She died protecting him. He had just lain there, motionless, unable to help, unable to control the power of his souls. It was his fault she was dead. He had been useless, worthless. He didn't deserve to be a Knight. He needed to be stronger, needed to be better.

He felt like he had betrayed his mother all over again. Crisalli was her friend, and now she was dead. Everyone Will became close to ended up dead…

His mother.

His father.

His grandfather.

Now Crisalli.

He thought of Olive. How had he forgotten about her? He

hadn't touched his sketchbook since setting foot in the Corr. He hadn't even had time to see the theatre as he had promised he would. What if she just ended up dead too?

He tried to push those thoughts aside. They weren't healthy. He knew they weren't healthy, but neither could he deny their existence.

He stared at the bland hills below in search of an escape. All he saw was a broken land, cracked and picked clean by the dysfunctional humans who were responsible for its care.

The Gracelands was not perfect, it had its problems, but nothing was worse than this. They flew over a scattered village, the infrastructure pieced together from nothing but rotten timber and makeshift materials. Cerak hovered low enough that Will could see the faces of the villagers as they stared up into the bleak sky.

They probably thought him a god, come to save them from their misery. That thought was likely quashed as Cerak ignored their curious pointing and shouting, instead continuing overhead.

"There's nothing you can do for them," he said, as if sensing his compassion.

"Why doesn't Athedale help? We're so close to home. Surely they can do something?"

Cerak shook his head. "Beyond those great stone walls, the outside world may as well not even exist to them. Kildeen is the only foothold they keep in the Harrows. With the city now taken and Carthon in control, there's little left out here for those not under his influence. We need to be careful here to avoid his scrying eyes."

The rest of the flight went by unhindered, though he could see the strain the magic was placing upon the former king. He made no comment about it, but his eyes constantly wavered, and his muscles were pulled taught. He was stretching his limit, the energy from his souls was running thin. If he didn't rest soon, they would fall.

Fortunately, the familiar flash of the colour of his homeland touched the edge of the horizon. The walls of Athedale loomed like a giant nest at the peak of a large rise. On one side was nothing but steep cliffs falling into the blue gulf. To the city's right rose the twelve fingers of the Ash mountains.

A horn blasted from the battlements as those below were alerted to their presence. Bows were trained on their location as Cerak descended. He came in slow, levelling the disk so all could see him. By the time the disk hit the stone, at least forty soldiers were upon them. Some leveraged a line of pikes, others held longbows, fingers pulled tight around the string as they prepared to loose.

"Who goes there?" a man shouted, likely a captain by the blue sash covering his plated shoulder pad. "Name yourself!"

Cerak placed a hand on Will's shoulder, his wide frame shielding him from view. "I am Cerak Bane, Knight of the Fifteenth Division."

The captain bit his lip, gaze not faltering. "Rolland!" he called without looking away. "Get the charts.

"Why do you not use the proper channels?" he asked, his question directed at Cerak now. "Even Knights must report through the western gate."

"Do your eyes not see?" Cerak spat. "There's a war coming. Step aside, I must speak with the king."

"The king? Just who do you think you are? Step back!" he screamed as Cerak motioned forward.

"Sir!" came a call from the gathered soldiers. The voice was deep, his tone thick with age. "This man is who he says. Been missing for a dozen years or so, but aye, I remember him well."

The captain relaxed a touch, but didn't relent. He turned

slightly to receive a piece of parchment, pausing to unroll it. He scanned the contents, eyes darting from Cerak to the paper and back. "Who's the boy?" he asked.

"His name is Will, apprenticed Knight to Crisalli Bane."

"And where is she then?" the captain questioned.

Cerak sighed, bowing his head.

"What's all this fuss about?" came another voice, a commanding voice. "The forces of Val Taroth are twenty leagues out yet."

Will stepped out from beneath Cerak's shadow. This was a man familiar to him. "Estevan!" he called, glad to see a familiar face, even if it was the father of the boy who held his grandfather's souls.

Estevan turned, crimson cape swirling. His face shot to life as he shifted from Will to Cerak. "My eyes must be deceiving me," he said, moving a step closer. "Crisalli was successful then. I'm grateful you held true to your oath."

Cerak only grunted in response.

"Tell me, where is Crisalli? I would like to speak with her, there is much to report upon."

Will felt his nails biting into his skin. His face contorted with the effort of holding back tears. Cerak looked to his feet and made another grunting sound.

"I see," Estevan said. "Come, the both of you. Walk with me."

Will stepped cautiously past the captain who had questioned them, trailing Estevan's cloak as he and Cerak conversed. "It's been too long, brother," Estevan said. "I'll admit, I was beginning to wonder if you still walked Otor. It's true then, Crisalli is no longer with us?"

Cerak turned and nodded, his face a mask of grief. "Her life was stolen by an agent of Tal Varoth. One of Carthon's own Reapers, a soul-broken witch with hollow eyes."

Estevan stopped in his stride. "So, the rumours prove true, Carthon has won himself a returned soul."

Again, Cerak nodded.

"I would hear it all, if you are right of mind to tell me."

The trio continued towards the keep's gate, down a series of winding cobblestone passageways, and then eventually up a set of stairs leading onto the Mage-Way.

Will peaked over the edge, marvelling at the infrastructure. He turned again to follow and nearly ran into something hard. He stepped back, mouth opening wide as a stone statue stared down at him. He looked around. Dozens of statues lined the outskirts of the Mage-Way, their stone faces sculpted with a skill beyond Will's comprehension. They stood frozen in time, postures fixed into fighting poses capturing a moment of perpetual battle-readiness.

Realising he had fallen behind, Will ran to catch up to Cerak and Estevan.

Cerak turned to him at the foot of the keep. "I must go alone from here."

Will gasped in protest. "You're leaving me? Where am I to go?"

It was Estevan who spoke. "You've done well, Will, making it back here after such an ordeal. Return to Crisalli's hold for now. I know it must pain you, to lose a mentor, but these are times of war. Your resolve must be strong. You have my permission to stay there and rest. I'm sure you're travel weary and sore. I'll send someone for you in the morning and we'll find you a more suitable place to call home. You can relay the events of your travels then. For now, go home, rest."

Will looked to Cerak, as if he needed his permission first.

"Do as he says, but don't lose heart. I'll be around when I can. You're my responsibility now. Keep your head down, and don't let them in," Cerak said, pointing a loose finger towards his temple.

Will wandered the city streets, alone. They had brushed him aside like he was nothing, was of no importance. They had pretended like they cared about him. He knew the truth. He was an inconvenience, a child playing at something that was far too out of his depth. He couldn't blame them, not really. There was a war coming, they had more important issues to worry about than the well-being of an apprenticed Knight. Was he even apprenticed anymore?

He had been back to Crisalli's house, stayed there for several nights. Cerak hadn't come by as he'd promised. He'd likely forgotten Will even existed. He couldn't stay there any longer, couldn't live inside a dead woman's house. Not when every item, every possession would remind him of her, of what he'd lost.

Instead, he found himself traversing the bluffs. He looked to the ravine below, hoping to see Olive sitting there, waiting for him to arrive as she had done before his venture west. Instead, all he found was a blank canvas of rock and stone. He sighed. Would he ever see her again? He might not have the chance, given what was coming.

He sat there, legs dangling over the cliff's edge. He reached into his coat for a sketchbook. He missed drawing. He had so much more material now, so many new sights to bring back to life with his charcoal.

But that would have to wait.

A steady wind drifted in from the east, bringing with it the soothing melody of a voice. It was faint, but the words were familiar. He followed it, moving against the breeze. He skidded down a dirt path, rocks tumbling down the side of the ledge as his weight broke their rest.

The ravine turned and his vision was hampered by a steep cliff shadowing a sharp bend. The voice grew louder, the tone feminine and rich with emotion. A flicker of auburn caught his eye. Will sprinted, ducking under a mound of protruding stone.

Then he saw her. Clothed in a white gown, she sat upon a lone boulder overlooking the flow of water. She continued to sing, unaware of his emerging presence.

He shifted his feet, and her voice stopped. She turned. "Will!" she almost screamed. She stepped down from the boulder, her foot tripping over her dress. Will rushed in and caught her before she fell.

She rose, blowing a lock of hair from her eyes, her smile broadening as her gaze met his own. Before he could offer a greeting, she swung two arms around his neck and pulled his head towards her shoulder. "I thought I'd lost you!" she said. "I'm so glad to see you're safe."

Will stood, awkward, and mumbled a greeting of his own. He couldn't even describe how good it felt to see her again, to know that he wasn't alone, that somebody still cared for him.

"It's good to be home," he finally said. "How did you know to come here?"

She waved him off. "Oh, I heard you'd returned. I've been waiting here every night since. You didn't think to skirt your promise to me so easily, did you? I bet you learned a wealth of knowledge and saw hundreds of interesting places crossing the Harrows. Please, you must tell me all!"

Will paled. His presence meant more to her than simple knowledge, didn't it? His face twisted, and he took a backward step. "How did you know I was back?"

Olive's smile faltered, though it was soon replaced by her

characteristic enthusiasm once more. "Don't worry about that. Come, tell me of your travels."

Will bowed, the thought of retelling his mentor's death weighing on him.

"What's wrong?" Olive said. "Is something the matter?"

Before Will even knew what was happening, he felt a tear making its way down his cheek. He made to hide it, to wipe it away before she saw, but he remembered Cerak's words of comfort. He was allowed to show emotion, to grieve. Olive was observant. She pulled him in, recognising his pain for what it was. Without another word, he embraced her, his tears spilling into the white of her shoulder. "She's gone," he whispered. "Crisalli, she's dead."

"Oh Will, I'm so sorry," she said, stroking his back. "I don't — is there anything I can do?"

Will gulped a wet lump down his throat and shook his head. As he stood there, weeping onto her shoulder, he began to think. He didn't even know this girl, not really. He didn't know anything about her, her family, her childhood. He only knew for certain that she wouldn't hurt him, that she was a friend, a true friend.

"Can you sing me a song?" he found himself saying, yearning for the sound of her voice.

Olive parted, relaxed. "Of course." She ushered him to a seat upon the nearest rock. "What kind of song would you like to hear?"

Will paused for a moment, then looked up at her. "Do you know any sad songs? I think… I need to let myself grieve, before I can heal, I mean. I need to feel sad, to think about her… think about everyone…"

Olive squeezed his hand, then moved to take her place on the makeshift stage near the riverbank.

"This is a new song, one written with the knowledge you've gifted me. I call it 'Somewhere Between.'"

Will allowed himself to relax, drifting into the slow melody of the song.

> *I'm somewhere between this real world and make-believe*
> *I'm drifting in a stream searching for a place to grieve*
>
> *A power in my soul, these voices in control*
> *Will I ever be whole? It all takes its toll*
>
> *I thought I lost myself*
> *These thoughts keep creeping in*
> *And then I found myself*
> *Though what remained was paper-thin*
>
> *I'm somewhere between this real world and make-believe*
> *I'm drifting in a stream searching for a place to grieve*
>
> *The darkest lies hide behind bright eyes*
> *The warmest smiles make the sharpest knives*
>
> *A sickness in the brain*
> *A silence in the dark*
> *A stillness in the moment*
> *A splinter in the heart*
>
> *I'm somewhere between this real world and make-believe*
> *I'm drifting in a stream searching for a place to grieve*

Will felt the weakness drain out of him, his anxiety washing away with his tears. His confidence began to grow, his resolve strengthening with every note. Olive stopped and made her way back to him. "I'm sorry it's not very long, the second verse is still a work in process."

"It was beautiful," Will said, finding he genuinely meant it.

He wiped his cheeks clean and sat there for a long moment. Something inside shifted, cracked. He placed a hand on his temple as his head began to throb.

"Will, what's wrong? Are you okay?" Olive asked.

Will ignored her, instead focusing on his thoughts.

*You'll lose her too*

*Just like everyone else*

*We can help you*

*Let us out*

*You can be free of this pain*

*Let us out*

"Go away!" Will screamed, swatting the air. He looked up just in time to see Olive gasp. Her face twisted, the pattern of her freckles crinkling as she looked at him with fear in her eyes.

"No, I'm sorry!" Will said. "Not you. Please. Don't go."

*You see*

*She doesn't understand*

*She will leave you*

*Let go of the burden*

*Let us out*

*We can set you free*

Will groaned. He began hitting himself in the head with his palm. "Go away, please. Leave me alone!"

"Will, I'm here," Olive said, grabbing his hand and making him stop. "It's okay. We can fight them together. I'm not going anywhere."

It wasn't enough. What if he broke? What if he changed? Turned into one of them? Became like his mother? He was dangerous. He could hurt her. His friend.

"I can't, I'm sorry. I have to go," he said, standing.

A blaring horn sounded in the distance, the signal thundering over the bluffs. In unison, Will and Olive turned to the commotion. It was followed by another horn blast, and then another. Three blasts, the signal for war.

Will spun, panicked. "I must go, I'm sorry! Please, forgive me..."

# Chapter 39

## - Tvora -

Tvora stood at the foot of an army. Never before had she seen so many people in one place. She could feel their magic, their hunger for more.

She looked over her shoulder at Carthon. Adorned in a thick coat of fur he stood on a ridge, a dark conductor of impending doom. His eyes, pools of shadowed malice, were fixed onto the thick stone walls that stood in the way of his army claiming the souls of the Gracelanders within. A black, jewel-less crown circled his head, its twisted design mirroring the skewed nature of the soldiers under his command.

Skullsworn.

All had come. All had answered his call.

The city of Athedale looked impenetrable. A curtain of stone stretched the entire length of the horizon, cut off only by the raging tide of the Mirror Sea and the high peaks of the mountains.

Tvora was no tactician, had no mind for strategy. She had no idea how to penetrate such a defence. She was but an arrow in Carthon's quiver, a blunt tool. Dependable, but disposable.

Glock came up beside her and placed a hand on her shoulder. "This is the beginning of a new era. Galvandier has assured me of a great victory here today. He never lies to me."

Tvora squinted in confusion before remembering he was talking about his sword, which he then kissed before sheathing. She let herself relax into a laugh, glad she wasn't the only one in this world who seemed to talk to herself.

She looked around. All of Carthon's Reapers were present. Mantis stalked to her right, long fingers cracking as he conjured the image of at least a dozen miniature bugs and began manipulating them to fight each other like they were puppets on a string.

Septus walked up to the ridge to stand beside Carthon. His body visibly shook with each movement. His steps were disjointed, and his head kept swaying from side to side. He reached up a hand and slapped his own face. He said something to himself, but Tvora was too far to discern what it was.

Habit bade her to bend down and pet Lucia's coat, to find comfort, but she wasn't there.

She was riddled with guilt. She'd sent them away. Why? For a little peace of mind? They were her friends. They were all she had. She needed them back, needed them now.

She walked over to a place that was a little more private, then reached inside her cage and ripped into the *otherside*.

Lucia and Cecco appeared a moment later, fresh from their slumber. They were much larger than before, their forms stronger now, with more souls to draw from. Cecco returned happily to her shoulder, and Tvora actually found herself smiling at the comfort he brought.

Lucia, however, turned her head away.

"How do we overcome this?" Tvora said. "I don't wish you to be my enemy. I don't want to part from you."

*Nor I you,* Lucia responded.

"Then can we place our differences aside? Find common ground?"

*That depends on what you see as common ground.*

Tvora sighed. "I see your ambition, Lucia. It is warranted. I've been through all that you have, seen all that you've seen. I know how you feel."

*Do you really, though?* Lucia said. *How can you know how I feel? You walk on solid ground and breathe air that fills your lungs. Me, Cecco, Gowther, we've lost that. Never again will we do as you still do. Being here, right now by your side, this is the best I will ever get. I will do all I can to see we make the most of it.*

"I can't change the past," Tvora protested. "Even if your body's lost, you're still human! You still have a conscience, a sense of right and wrong. I won't sacrifice who we are even if would mean we could be together longer."

Lucia issued a mocking laugh. *Look where you are, Tvora! You think these people care for conscience? The world does not care about us, why should we care about it? You made this choice. You chose this side. You are the body that acts, not I. I suggest you live with it and prepare. We have a war to win. You will find no more goodness that side of the wall than this, I assure you.*

With that, Lucia left to stalk the length of the gathered army.

Tvora's nails bit into her palms. She swiped an aggressive arm into empty air, causing Cecco to fly off her shoulder in fright.

She bit her lip and began to pace the dirt around her. Maybe Lucia was right? What was she thinking? There was no room for conscience in this world. No room for weakness. She had been weak once before, and it had gotten them all killed. She chose this path. She was surrounded by Skullsworn. There was no going back, no becoming someone else. This assault would happen with or without her.

Tvora clenched her fist. She was a Reaper of Mirimar now.

And reap she would.

# Chapter 40
## - Myddrin -

Consciousness clawed at the edge of Myddrin's mind. With a slow, hesitant flutter, his eyelids parted like heavy curtains unveiling a scene of regret. Morning light through the windowsill struck like fire. His head thumped a relentless beat. He blinked, realising he was cocooned in a suffocating warmth — his own vomit.

He tried to move, to inch away, but his limbs felt like lead. He caught a glimpse of an empty wine bottle somewhere amidst the stinking pool of his own bile. His throat burned, and when he gulped it felt like swallowing razor blades.

He tried to rise, to remove himself from this situation, but there was no strength left.

Mees. Where was Mees?

The door opened just as his consciousness began to fade. The blurred shape of shoes walked towards him. He reached a tentative hand towards them, mumbled something incoherent, then his eyes shut fully.

Myddrin woke with a start this time. His eyes shot open and immediately he thrust his body backwards, arms flailing frantically in an attempt to retreat from a mess that was no longer there.

He looked down. He was in his bed, and his clothes were changed. In place of the royal uniform given to him by the king was a simple robe. The stink had vanished, and the room looked... clean?

He still remembered fragments of the night before, of his violent descent into a world where all that existed was a sense of disgust and self-loathing, echoing the inner turmoil that had long plagued his tormented soul.

That world still existed, was still present, only now he was sober inside of it.

"I won't let you do it," came a voice.

Myddrin snapped his head towards it. "M — mother?"

Molde stood in the corner of the room. Instant regret stabbed at Myddrin as he realised who had cleaned him up. She came towards him, her steps slow. She walked with a stick, and her back was bent, a silent narrative of years bearing the weight of life's burdens, the most notable being him.

As she reached him, she tried to straighten, the gradual process like the unfolding of a time-worn book. "I won't let you do it," she repeated.

"Do what?"

"Kill yourself. Or let that man do it for you, the Knight. I won't let you."

Myddrin wiped a drop of sweat from his forehead. He took a sip of water from his bedside, patted his throat, then made to speak. "How do you know about that?"

Molde placed her hands on her hips and grunted. "You still mumble in your sleep, just like you would as a child. I guess some things never change."

Myddrin frowned. He bowed his head in shame. "What choice do I have? Look at me. I'm in no shape to defend a city. I'm a fraud. A pretender. A false hope. Why not let that hope rest in the hands of someone capable?"

"Because you are my son! I won't allow it!"

Silence hung in the air for a long time then, measured in

heartbeats. Myddrin had to bite down on his bottom lip to stop it from trembling. Eventually, his mother came even closer and leaned by the bed. She took his hand between her own ageing fingers. "Listen, Son. Please. Listen.

"When you first came back here, I was appalled. I was glad you had returned, but you were a drunk. You had no manners, no care, no sense of self. I hated who you had become, what you had turned into.

"I was wrong. You told me you sought a way to end it. To erase magic from the world. That was Ismey's dream, wasn't it? Yes, I remember. That's what she always wanted, her life's mission." His mother paused. She looked up at him through tear-filled eyes. "You've dedicated a decade of your life in pursuit of your wife's dream, haven't you? You've sacrificed so much, all for the desire to see her work complete."

Myddrin shied away. There was pain there. Too much pain. He couldn't…

"Well, where does that dream go if you die?" Molde continued. "Who will complete Ismey's wish if you are to fall? Do you think this man who would kill you will have a care for creating a better world? Perhaps he will defeat the evil at our doorstep with the power you give him, but what then?

"No. He's just like any other. He will take what you have and use it for personal gain. They all do. The cycle will never end unless someone stops it, and as far as I can see, you're the only one left trying.

"So, you can't die. Not now. Not until you serve your purpose. Not until you make her dream a reality. I won't allow it."

Myddrin looked to the ceiling, trying but failing to hold back tears of his own. His mother was right. He couldn't give up now. Not to Halvair. Not to anyone.

Yet what could he do? A decade of searching for an answer and still he was no closer to ridding the world of magic.

No.

That wasn't true.

He knew about the well now. The Providence. The birthplace of magic. There had to be a way to use it to undo what Axel did. He just had to find it. But first, he had a war to win.

Slowly, he rose. In the distance he could hear horns blasting, the garrison mustering. Carthon had arrived.

"Mother, I…" he mumbled.

"Take these," Molde said, handing him a freshly washed uniform. "Don't let her down."

Myddrin took the clothes and quickly got dressed, then downed some water and bread. He stopped at the table where half a bottle of wine and his pipe were sitting. He eyed them for an overly long time, then made to take them.

"What are you doing!" Molde said. "Have you learned nothing?"

Myddrin turned and hardened his gaze. He pocketed his pipe and grabbed the bottle. "This is war, Mother. I go out there fighting how I feel right now, and I won't be alive long enough to see Ismey to her dream. I need this. I need my wits. After the war's done, feel free to chain me to the floor until every last drug is clear of my system. But for right now, you need to let me go."

Myddrin waited a moment for a response. When none came, he left in the direction of the Mage-Way.

It didn't take him long to get a quick buzz going. He knew he had to hold back, to not over-indulge, but after a couple of sips here and a couple of puffs there, Myddrin felt back to his usual, mildly-inebriated self. Already the pain in his shoulder and the voices inside his head began to fade as his mind began to both fog and clear at the same time.

He fixed himself into a somewhat reasonable posture, then sauntered down the winding staircase of Stonekeep.

The guards nodded his way, then proceeded to push open the double doors. With a straight back, Myddrin walked through.

He was greeted by at least three dozen soldiers, standing in two rows of neatly organised lines on either side of the Mage-Way. They stood like statues, emulating the stone sculptures on display behind them.

Myddrin saw them for what they were — an escort.

At the foot of the escort stood the king, looking the part in his gold-threaded, embroidered tunic. By his side stood the silver-haired Halvair, and Estevan.

They turned at his approach. The king fixed his lips into an overzealous smile, though Myddrin couldn't part his eyes from Halvair. The mage looked smug, his head held high. The corner of his lips curled upward in a self-assured smile of his own. His eyes glinted with the arrogant confidence of someone who knew they had the world at their fingertips.

This was where he expected Myddrin to bend. This is where he expected Myddrin to fall, to succumb to his will, to die by his sword.

Myddrin forced himself to look away, to avoid his gaze. Instead, he kept walking and took his place on the opposite side of the king.

Out of the corner of his eye he still saw it...

Like a fleeting shadow cast by a setting sun, the atmosphere shifted. Halvair's smug expression wavered, caught by an unexpected gust of cold reality. His eyes flickered with uncertainty, and the swagger in his stance weakened.

Still, he said nothing.

"Glad to have you with us," the king said, motioning for the party to proceed along the bridge.

"Wouldn't miss it," Myddrin replied.

They walked in synchronised silence the entire trek atop the over-city pathway. Before reaching the defensive walls, the way split, snaking into a series of smaller paths leading towards different sections of the wall. The escort continued along one of the central paths until they reached the battlements.

Myddrin walked along with the king's entourage up to the parapet. The city behind was quiet. What lay beyond their walls was most certainly not. Skullsworn blanketed the surrounding landscape. Born from the deepest depths of Mirimar, the horde from Val Taroth sat in waiting.

Their numbers were bolstered by soul-hunters from the Harrows, each and every one of them hungry for souls, jumping at the chance to feed on the previously unattainable meat that was the Gracelander Knights of Aen.

"Myddrin! It can't be," rose a booming voice above the cacophony of sounds.

Myddrin turned to see a familiar face. "Cerak? By the gods, what are you doing here?" he replied, opening his arms wide as his old friend thumped into him, wrapping two thick arms around his back and squeezing tight.

They parted. "How long has it been?" Cerak said, looking him up and down. "Seven, eight years?"

"Over a decade, actually."

"You've grown fat! What are they feeding you over on that island of yours?" Cerak said.

Myddrin just scratched at his head and looked down at his belly.

"Oh, come on, merely a jest." Cerak placed a hand on Myddrin's shoulder and looked him in the eye, his expression turning serious. "I know it's long overdue, but I'm sorry about what happened to Ismey. Your wife and mine... They were close once. It seems we both have someone to avenge today."

Myddrin gathered his meaning. He chose to acknowledge Cerak's pain with a firm nod. "I'm glad to have you with us. I see the Corr has treated you well. Does this mean we have their support?"

Cerak's mood completely changed then. "All is well, until it isn't.

"Just me, I'm afraid," he continued. "But Aen help the first ugly skullfuck who climbs over that wall. I'm here to stay."

Beside them, the king shouted an order. "Estevan, do it now!"

Both Myddrin and Cerak turned to watch as Estevan blew a distinct tune on the horn previously at his hip. What followed was a feat never before seen in the history of magic.

The air outside the city walls rippled with energy. All around him, left and right, pockets of magic began to shimmer into existence, brought forth by a mage temporarily breaking through to the *otherside*.

Gusts of wind whipped at their feet as fragments of colour formed, broadened, and then reformed. There must have been at least one-hundred pieces stretching the landscape. Myddrin angled his head over the parapet. He could see Knights everywhere, standing atop the stone walls, working their magic, tearing chunks from the *otherside* and shaping them.

With a snap of sound, the pieces finally began to click together in a vibrant tapestry of colour.

Though still transparent, it blotted out the sky, the sun.

A second wall.

It made sense. The Skullsworn and soul-hunters were said to be dysfunctional, brought together for the sole purpose of destroying Athedale. Myddrin remembered liking the plan when he'd first heard it mentioned. Carthon might have other plans for this city, but the people following him didn't. Anything they could do to delay them would only serve to sew discord amongst their ranks. Sew enough of it, and perhaps the hungriest of them might turn their attention towards much more attainable prey; each other.

Something inside of Myddrin twisted. His souls churned. A figure caught his eye before the last piece of the puzzle clicked into place in front of him.

The figure still stood there, on his ridge. He was too far to see clearly, but even through the blur of the barrier, Myddrin knew who it was. The keeper of his wife's soul.

Carthon.

Inside his head the voices whispered.

*Let us out*

*We can kill him for you*

*It will be easy*

*Just let us out*

# Chapter 41
# - Will -

Will looked up. A rainbow of colour illuminated the entire horizon. He wasn't alone in his wonder. The streets were full of people leaving their homes to witness the immersive magical feat. The transparent wall shimmered, its weight providing a beacon of hope that was sorely needed for the common folk of Athedale.

He watched as children clung to their mothers' dresses, as a young boy only perhaps three years his junior stood in awe while those on the walls prepared to defend their homes to the last man. Will stood, confused. What role was he to play? None had come for him as promised, the threat at their doorstep seeming to come quicker than they had prepared for.

The fear of those around him was palpable. Many had loved ones atop the walls. Fathers, brothers, husbands, sisters. All would play their part, would try their hardest to keep those they loved safe.

Who did Will love? Who did he fight for? All whom he had come to care for were lost, buried beneath the weight of magic's touch.

Where once he had loved it, now he was beginning to hate it. Nothing good ever came of it. All the childhood heroes he once looked up to he now saw in a different light. Were their minds just as plagued by magic's influence as his had become?

He hated Aen too. What kind of god would allow such a cruel world? How could he believe in the existence of such a deity if this was the outcome of such a belief? He looked to his own hands, clenched them, remembered them covered in blood, someone else's blood. He was a part of the cruelty of this world now, had killed inside of it, and would probably be forced to again.

He unclenched his fists, knuckles white from the exertion. He reached within himself, searching for resolve. He couldn't change the past, nothing he could do would undo what had already happened. He had to look to the future, to carve his own path, create his own destiny. He was done watching events unfold around him. He had been cursed with this tainted power, but he was still human. He was still in control of his actions. He was the one to decide how such corruption would be used. He would be the good in the world he wanted to see. He might not be able to change the course of history, as one such as Myddrin might, but he could damn well make sure that some of these children would see their fathers again.

His mind focused, Will returned to Crisalli's home. He dressed himself in his father's uniform. It felt a little loose, although Will had grown enough recently to make it somewhat comfortable.

He pushed open the door to his room and picked up his sketchbook. He spared one last look at the vision of his mother before pocketing it. If he was to die, he would have her close.

He draped his grandfather's shield over his shoulder and strapped it to his back. Sword in its scabbard, he made for the city walls.

There was a hush about the city, the dreaded silence before a battle he had read so much about in his youth.

He wanted to visit Olive, to fix things, but it would have to wait. When this war was done, he would find her and make it right.

He moved about the streets. Most of the soldiers were already on the walls, though he spotted another contingent marching in their direction. He resisted the urge to catch up and report to their captain, for he feared they wouldn't believe he was truly an apprenticed Knight and turn him away. Instead, he followed.

Athedale was situated against the side of a mountain, therefore the slope was forever a downward spiral, another defensive feature sure to hold any would-be invaders to a disadvantage should they breach the walls. Fighting downhill was by far easier than leading an offensive up a slope. His grandfather had taught him that.

The streets came to an end, and Will came to a clearing. Staring down at him were two walls; one the thick white stone that had stood solid for centuries, the other a colourful mash of images standing taller even than the stone. Soldiers flooded a nearby staircase. Two guards stepped aside to allow them entry as they rose to join their brethren above.

Will motioned to join them, to slip in behind the last of the soldiers as if he were one with their unit, but a firm hand grasped his shirt and pulled him backwards off the steps.

"Where do you think you're going, kin-killer?" a voice sounded.

Will turned to see Rath standing at the foot of the second set of stairs. Will brushed Rath's hand off his shirt before squaring up to him. Of all the people he could have run into in this moment, Rath was the worst of them. He stared down at him from his new vantage on the stair above. Like Will, Rath had grown over the past few months. His shoulders were rounder, his face more structured. His left eye was blackened and bruised, making his scowl even more gloomy.

"Step aside, Rath," Will said with confidence. "What's out there is bigger than you and me. This isn't the time to pick another fight."

Rath's lips angled into a snarl. "You don't get it, do you, Will. You don't belong here. I know you. You're a coward. A few souls in your cage doesn't make you strong. We need capable people on these walls, people we can trust. Go home, save yourself the trouble."

Will's chest flared blue. He was done listening to Rath's dribble. "I won't say it again, step aside."

A man descended the stairs above Rath then, an imposing figure, thick with muscle and sporting no shortage of scars on his face.

Thane.

Will's hand inched to his blade as Thane placed a hand on Rath's shoulder. Will watched as Rath flinched at his touch, one hand reaching for the bruise under his eye.

"Is there a problem here?" Thane questioned.

Will said nothing. Thane was one of his heroes, a man he had idolised, but there was something off about him. Something dark. He couldn't place exactly what it was, but Will had been around Knights and magic long enough now to know that something wasn't quite right about the man.

"Nothing, sir," Rath said.

Thane stared at Will for an overly long time before eventually breaking off. "Come on, Rath, let's go." Thane pushed him hard in the shoulder as he turned, causing Rath to stumble a step and fall over.

He spared a frustrated look towards Will before biting his lip, gathering himself and climbing the steps.

Will frowned. There was something going on there. He'd never seen Rath so afraid before. Despite it all, he found himself feeling sorry for him. There was nothing to be said for it now though, nothing Will could do about it. He needed to move, and quickly. He needed to blend in.

Soldiers packed the city walls, most clad in thick armour of heavy steel.

Wind berated his skin. He could see it all from here. Banners from Kastar, from Spree, from Sunmire. All had come to defend against the threat.

Will didn't know where to go, what to do. The massive image-wall was like a magnet, drawing his attention to the various colours. Up close, he could feel the power. It vibrated with a deep tone, the energy keeping it together almost alive and tangible. How many souls worked to keep this structure standing? How many Knights worked tirelessly to see that this city stood another day?

The city walls stretched far into the distance. He was but one part of a massive whole. He risked a glance over the wall, squishing in-between two soldiers who grew agitated at his insistence. Beyond the wall, through the colour, stood an army. Will had to force himself to breathe, as if the easiest thing to do in life had suddenly become impossible. There were so many of them. How could the world be so full of hatred that this many souls would gather to destroy life? Will steadied, focusing his thoughts. This was the reality. The souls down there had made their choice; they sought ruin. Will had made his; he sought to protect.

He settled himself in behind a row of trained archers, finding a place against the stone where he could sit and wait with the rest of them. He didn't know how long he would be here. Maybe the wall would hold and Carthon's army would give up their efforts. But even Will knew such thoughts were overly optimistic.

There was something more going on along the battlements, something Will couldn't fully understand. The only way he could describe it was a great sadness. He could see it painted onto the men's faces as he studied them. The way they walked. The way they talked. It was as if they had already accepted defeat, already given into that fear the enemy had tried so hard to instil.

The image-wall gave them some comfort, but it wasn't enough. They needed more. They needed hope.

A trumpet sounded, and everyone present turned towards the central pillar, where Myddrin stood vigilant. Another figure emerged by his side. In his hand he held a large sceptre, a crown of white gold circling his head.

The king.

Whispers spread over the gathered soldiers as a third figure emerged next to the king. This one much smaller, feminine.

"The king and princess have arrived!" he heard one of the soldiers comment.

"Bless her," said another. "How brave she must be to show herself in a time such as this."

All of Athedale came to a hush as the king raised his sceptre into the air. Will looked on as the king began his speech, inspiring what he could into the soldiers of Athedale and instilling his faith within them. Will listened, but his attention was drawn elsewhere. The princess stood by the king's side, auburn hair tied neatly into a bun with a strand falling to her cheeks on either side. Will squinted before recognition dawned. His eyes suddenly shot to life, his mind unable to control his body as he shifted from place to place, trying to get a better angle to confirm what he already knew in his heart to be true.

Princess Oliviana.

Olive.

His Olive.

Was the daughter of the king.

She stood proudly by the side of her father, watching over her subjects. Watching over Will. All eyes turned to her as her father stepped back. Not a single soul still stood watching the advancing horde, as all within view stopped and listened when the princess began to sing.

*There's a palace in the clouds where the world gets bigger*
*But to get there means to fly just a little bit higher*
*There's evil out there who will try to take your thunder*
*But to beat it means to be just that little bit stronger*

*So be brave with me because I can't wait to see*
*The day when the world becomes what it was meant to be*

*There's a silence in your heart that may cause you to stutter*
*But to start it means to fight just that little bit harder*
*There's a stiffness in your bones that may cause you to shudder*
*But to fight it means to stand and link arms together*

*So be brave with me because I can't wait to see*
*The day when the world becomes what it was meant to be*

Silence.

Nobody spoke. Nobody had needed to speak as she'd continued to sing, to inspire, to console. Her last notes hung in the air. Will couldn't move. The melody of her song lingered, spread, infiltrated his mind, infiltrated all of their minds. Will watched as shoulders broadened, expressions softened, resolves strengthened. The effect was obvious. People's spirits were returning.

Will looked up towards Olive again, proud. How could a simple song make such a difference?

They were going to win this war.

# Chapter 42
# - Tvora -

The night sky blanketed the plains of Athedale. The starless sea above would have shrouded their army in darkness, but even firelight wasn't needed with the great wall of light illuminating the entire landscape, dwarfing the whitewashed walls of the city in an overbearing show of colour.

Where before Tvora had stood transfixed, now she stood impatient. For two nights the wall had stood relatively unmolested. Two nights that Tvora sat idle while agents of Val Taroth poked and prodded to no avail.

A crack had formed here and there, and occasionally a puncture would be created when enough force was used to break a piece of the magic. But every piece which broke was soon remade. The relentless Knights seemed to be in constant supply of souls.

She hated to admit it, but their tactic was strong. By sheltering themselves like a turtle, they could wait until Carthon's army either starved to death or turned on themselves. There were already signs of in-fighting. The most ruthless and impatient of those he had gathered were beginning to get restless. They had been promised a chance to feed, to freely reap the souls of an entire city. So far, all they had done was pick at a wall.

Despite all of this, Carthon remained unfazed. There was no sense of panic in his demeanour, no rashness to his actions, nor even a change in general posture. If he was at all worried that his army would crumble around him, he didn't show it.

Camps had been set and appropriate rations given, though all here with a lick of sense about them knew that this army hadn't the provisions to survive much longer.

"Do you doubt me?" Carthon said, approaching her for the first time since the erecting of the image-wall.

Tvora scowled. "It's not you I doubt. It's the resolve of your men."

Carthon crossed his arms. "The strong-minded amongst us know not to be unbridled by such a simple wall."

"And what of the weak-minded?"

Carthon smiled. "They'll have a purpose to serve, don't worry. There are many pieces yet to come into play. We just have to be patient until we're ready for them all to fit."

He pointed to a fraction of the wall. "There, do you see how the colours change?"

Tvora had to squint, but sure enough, a chunk of the wall changed colour, or rather vanished and was replaced by another.

"They're taking it in shifts," Carthon continued. "It takes a lot of souls to sustain an image of that size. Souls which deplete over time. I've almost got it, their pattern. Two more days and I'll have it, two more shift changes. Then we can strike when they're most depleted, at their most vulnerable."

Tvora continued to watch, searching for the pattern he'd spoken of but finding none. "Two days is a long time. What if the soul-hunters can't wait that long?"

Carthon smiled again. "Oh, they won't. But that's exactly what I'm counting on."

Another two nights passed and still Tvora waited patiently. Several fights had broken out, mostly between the soul-hunters. So far, they had been quashed by either Septus or Mantis, who bloodied their weapons whenever the need arose. Something bigger was brewing though. She could feel it. Blood would boil soon.

"Summon your passengers. It's time," Carthon said, already walking towards a small hill above the majority of the soul-hunters.

Tvora didn't question. Lucia and Cecco came to life beside her, silent upon their entry.

The soul-hunters gathered, ready to wet their blades on something, anything. She could feel their rage, hear it.

The Emperor of Mirimar opened his arms wide. "For too long the heathens in the Gracelands have spat upon you from their high walls. They dare to think themselves better. The people atop those walls do not know true pain. They have not walked the desolate plains of the Harrows, have not braved the stench of the pits. They do not know what it is to feel fear, to wake up every morning not knowing if it will be your last. This pain, we share," he said, gesturing to all present.

"Now we have opportunity. A chance to strike back at those who would shun us. To break the chain that binds us and shape the world as we see fit!"

Below him, the Harrowers roared. The sound was deafening, resonating across the plains as even those who could not hear his words screamed their agreement.

Carthon waited until they had settled, motioning for them to hush with his off hand. "But our enemy is not without strength," he continued. "Their magic is powerful, and we must become even stronger if we are to break through to their heart. I see your lust for revenge, your desire for strength! Let us first cleanse ourselves of the weak. The world I seek to create is only for the strong! Who among you will answer my call? Who among you will leave here a god?"

The army turned to uproar, fists slamming onto shields, feet stamping on dirt.

"I challenge you, men of the Harrows!" he continued, pointing his hand at the gathered soul-hunters. "Purge the weak from your ranks. Prove your might before me and my Skullsworn and earn your place in my new world. Go forth, those who wish to cleanse. Fight each other before the image-wall! Show Athedale our might! Let all see what will become of them once we are finished!"

Tvora stood confused as a rush of soul-hunters flowed past her, running head-first towards the wall. Not all followed, however. The gathered army was vast, and only those most eager for blood took the opportunity presented. Carthon's Skullsworn held back, as did a number of notable soul-hunters.

On instinct, Tvora moved to follow, Lucia thinking it her right to enter the cleanse. Carthon draped an arm across her stomach.

"No," he said. "This isn't for you."

Tvora turned. "What strategy is this? What sense is there in wasting your army fighting each other? The people on those walls will be laughing at their fortune!"

"Look around you," he said. "These Harrowers mean nothing. They are not special, but just because I don't value them as I do my own, that doesn't mean they don't have their uses."

Tvora baulked. "Forgive me if I fail to see what use this savagery has in your end game."

Carthon only smirked. "Do you remember what I said before about the frailty of a weak mind?"

Tvora nodded.

"Just watch, and you will see the truth. Even the weakest among us may become the strongest, if given the right push."

Silently, she watched as the deranged soul-hunters began to fight each other. Souls zipped around in colourful streams of light, flowing from host to host, from cage to cage as blood soaked the battlefield. The Harrowers were mad. They were out to kill. Who they killed made little difference.

They fought with brutal savagery, now closer to the walls of Athedale than the bulk of the Skullsworn. One crazed soul-hunter plunged her knife into the back of another, thrusting it in and out, blood spraying everywhere even as the deceased's souls flowed into her body. Not long after, she was struck down herself as the thick end of a club smashed into her ear. Her death was instant. Souls which hadn't even made it into her cage yet changed course and flowed into the aggressor with the club.

Coloured images lit up the battlefield as they used what tools they had to gain advantage over their opponents. Most were weak, with few souls to draw from. Several tried and failed to solidify their images. Others ran out of soul-energy in the middle of a manoeuvre, their constructs disappearing before having any effect. A couple stood out among the crowd. One in particular created a sword as long as a ladder. He swept it across his body, felling half a dozen with each swing.

Tvora looked on in horror as those participating embraced the most sinister aspect of human nature. The battle lasted almost an hour. She stood confused, still not recognising the logic of it all. What purpose did this needless slaughter serve?

That was when the first soul broke.

It happened quicker than Tvora remembered. The man with the giant sword. With an eerie screech, he fell to his knees, hands on his head, fingers scratching at his temples. His chest exploded in a burst of colour as the souls within sought a way out.

Tvora felt for her own exposed chest. In that visceral instant, the details of a memory began to unfold before her mind's eye. The soul-breaking moment caught her off guard, hitting like an unanticipated storm. The sights, the sounds, the emotions — all vividly reconstructed as if the wound had never healed. The pain, though dulled by the passage of time, regained its sharpness. It cut straight through the layers of detachment she had unknowingly built up.

Cecco flew to her side then, his presence calming. Even Lucia lingered a step or two closer.

As swiftly as it had emerged, the memory retreated back to the recesses of her mind, leaving her standing, watching.

With free access to their souls, the hosts of someone who had broken could release all their power at once without the need to worry about losing their mind, because their mind was already lost.

The man who had broken screamed. His body dangled as if on a thread, however many hosts had taken control each pulling in a different direction. If there was one thing Tvora knew about those freshly soul-broken, it was that they only had one need, one reason to live. To search for more souls.

They were drawn to the energy created by images. It was like a drug which was impossible to function without.

Splinters of incomplete images manifested into existence, surrounding the broken soul-hunter like fragments of shattered glass. In one thrust the hunter let go of them, sending pieces scattering over the battlefield, felling dozens of unaware Harrowers in one deadly motion. A stray piece of a fractured image nearly felled Tvora, stopped only as Carthon's black wall rose before her, the two constructs colliding before fading as if they were never there.

Another soul broke, then another. Similar scenes unfolded throughout the entire strip of land before Athedale. Chests were ripped apart from the inside. The eyes of the broken turned hollow and white. The souls within were now entirely visible, the spherical lights glowing with vibrant energy as they squirmed, trapped inside until their host perished.

Each of the broken made short work of their surrounding pocket of Harrowers. Before long, only a dozen or so were left standing, each broken, their unfocused gazes broadening as they sought their next source of magic. Each broken mind came to the same conclusion; the massive wall the Knights had projected.

Beside her, Carthon shifted, preparing the real army for an assault.

She watched in anticipation as the freshly broken sprinted towards the wall. Half-formed images she couldn't even describe came into existence, some at least ten men tall. The images crashed into segments of the wall. Over and over again the broken hunters battered it, pieces cracking and crumbling.

Carthon raised a fist, and a wash of Skullsworn began their steady ascent towards the city.

Lucia and Cecco by her side, Tvora followed.

She tightened her grip on Naex. How many souls would she claim this day?

How many souls were enough?

# Chapter 43
## - Myddrin -

"Soul-broken!"

A concussive blast rocked Myddrin off his feet. He scurried to recover, then rushed to the parapet. Huge chunks of the second wall shattered like glass as punctures formed in every direction.

Myddrin watched from above as Knights hurried to repair the defensive wall of magic. They fought a losing battle. The soul-broken demons were drawn to magic like Myddrin was to moss.

He didn't even have time to comprehend and assess the dizzying tactic. The freshly broken came at them without regard for their own flesh. Arrows rained down on the lone targets, piercing the nearest beneath the collarbone. The broken man continued along his path as if the wound were nothing, the pain split amongst however many souls had managed to scrounge control over his physical form.

Dozens of scattered images formed before him, arrows clattering uselessly against the barely formed surface as the assailant used them as a makeshift shield.

A column rose from beneath his feet, continuing to grow as the image stretched, propelling the crazed, hollow-eyed man toward the battlements, where a row of tired Knights stood perplexed.

The array of misshapen images surrounding him split, remnants rupturing the air before shooting towards a group of unprepared soldiers.

Cries of pain echoed from below as death rained. The victims' souls left their bodies, flowing into the broken man's cracked cage even as he made his descent. Shouts of alarm rose as he landed atop the battlement with a resounding thud. Bones snapped and skin tore upon impact.

All Myddrin could do was watch as those not impaled by the barrage of splintered images breathed a short sight of relief.

"Don't be fooled!" Myddrin shouted from his platform above, though his words may as well have been lost in the wind. The broken man rose, his disjointed body moving wildly as he rushed the closest soldier and sunk his teeth into the pink of his exposed neck.

The fallen Knight bucked and kicked, but eventually fell dead on the cold stone. Even more souls gathered towards the broken man, who soaked them in like morning sunlight.

Myddrin grit his teeth, turning to see similar scenes unfolding on the outskirts of the city walls. "Get the king and the princess out of here. Now!" he said, thrusting his arm towards them.

Just as they motioned to move, the air around him split. It crackled with an unnatural energy as a rift to the *otherside* opened and an image appeared.

Whatever it was dropped like a boulder falling from a cliff. Myddrin and Cerak reached into their own cages and a protective dome appeared around each of them.

The boulder crumbled around them, breaking the stone surrounding their feet.

Myddrin pushed against his image, and both his shield and the boulder were sent flying away. He recovered, panic rising as he saw that the place where the king and princess had been standing was covered in rubble.

He gasped.

The rubble began to shake, then burst apart, revealing Halvair inside with the king and his daughter, alive.

Myddrin covered his ears as the soul-broken man cried out, propelling himself forward using his magic like a springboard. He must have leapt the entire length between the battlements, all to get at him and his magic. The hunter's head snapped to the side, the bones in his neck cracking as he tilted his head at an unnatural angle.

He charged straight at them, the allure of Myddrin's magic too hard to ignore.

In tandem, Myddrin and Cerak each conjured an extended sword more than a man's height in width. Together, they swung at their charging foe. Myddrin's cut low, severing his legs from his body. Cerak's sword sliced high, splitting his torso in two.

Momentum took the Harrower several feet beyond their swings, where the parts of his body dropped in a heap, staining the white stone with splashes of crimson.

Myddrin braced, preparing for the influx of souls usually granted to him after such a feat, but none came. Instead, the deceased's souls flowed into Cerak, the former king's strike having landed the fatal blow.

Cerak screamed as enough souls to break a man suddenly became his burden. He began to shake, hands on temples as he struggled to contain it all.

Myddrin gave him some distance, knowing too well the impact such an influx could have on someone. The first few moments were crucial when gathering new souls. If you somehow managed to contain the initial assault, then your chances of remaining sane improved dramatically. Still, managing such a vast amount wasn't an easy task.

After a moment, Myddrin spoke. "Cerak, are you well?"

Cerak took a lengthy breath, placing one hand on his chest as it rose and then fell. He clenched his fist in a show of strength. "I'll manage."

Beyond the wall, more chunks of the shimmering barrier began to fade as Knights were forced to turn their attention elsewhere.

Cerak pulled a golden disk from the *otherside* and levelled it at his feet. "Hop on, we have a job to do."

Myddrin obliged, stepping onto the disk. He spared one last glance towards Halvair, the king, and the princess. Either out of respect or duty, Halvair nodded, lending Myddrin confidence that he would protect them.

Cerak took off faster than Myddrin had anticipated. He clutched onto Cerak's waist as they descended into the throng of battle.

Horns of war blew from all corners of the city wall as troops mustered and defenders engaged with the enemy. General Strupp paced the battlements, furiously shouting orders, runners taking off faster than they had come as they moved to spread his word.

Archers loosed at will, their kills marked by the occasional soul seeping into their bodies. Another two defensive volleys of arrows whistled past Myddrin's head, arcing over the wall before descending on their prey.

The army from Val Taroth closed the distance quickly. With the barrier all but dissolved, Carthon's agents didn't hesitate. Solidified images from both sides flew through the air. Some crashed into stone, breaking chunks of the battlements apart and sending defenders plummeting to their deaths.

One savvy Knight who was still holding onto his piece of the barrier redirected it rather than dismissing the chunk of solidified colour. He shifted its weight, slamming it down on a large portion of invaders, squashing them before they had a chance to scale the wall.

To others, however, there may as well not have even been a wall at all. The enemy carried with them no siege equipment.

Instead, they created their own.

Thousands of crystal-like images formed and solidified at the foot of the city. Ladders, stairs, and columns of elevated stone came into existence as Carthon's army improvised.

Those who lacked any usable magic of their own latched onto other's creations, charging up flights of stairs as tall as the city walls with no regard for their own safety. The initial burst of invaders was cut down like butter, the combination of Estevan's Knights and Strupp's trained archers sweeping the ascending invaders with relative ease.

Myddrin and Cerak sat back for a moment, waiting for a crack to appear, for one regiment to be under more pressure than another. He watched as an arrow pierced the heart of a Skullsworn about to breach the wall. His image disappeared along with his life, the platform he had conjured for himself breaking apart and sending at least fifty climbing Skullsworn plummeting to their deaths.

A black image began to shimmer into existence amidst the centre of the charging army. This image was different, at least thirty times the size of any other on the battlefield.

Myddrin didn't have to see his face to know the man responsible. A platform black as night and wide as a street formed. It arched across the sky, its apex hovering above the towering battlement.

He could do nothing but watch as the black bridge dropped. The entire foundation of the city wall rocked as the bridge slammed into it, creating a pathway directly over the wall and into the city.

Skullsworn surged, led by a man Myddrin recognised. Myddrin reached for his shoulder. The pain of the metal ball tearing into his flesh replayed in his mind as more of the small images formed and shot forward.

There were hundreds of them. They pierced through flesh and armour, felling knight, soldier, and skullsworn alike.

It was aimless destruction.

Estevan repositioned himself. Rallying what Knights were still standing around him, he conjured another defensive wall, partially blocking their advance towards the breach.

Inside, Myddrin boiled. How dare they come to his city. How dare they think themselves able to take a people's lives so easily, with no thought toward the repercussions of their wanton destruction. They ruined without care, without regard, all so they could attain more power and bring about more destruction.

No more.

Myddrin may not have asked for this power, he may have despised it to the very core of his being, but there had to be a reason it had fallen upon him. He hated it, but he would use it. By Aen, he would use it. He couldn't hide any more, couldn't pretend this was someone else's problem. He would kill them all.

He was the Doonslayer.

He was Myddrin.

He was death.

# Chapter 44
# - Will -

Will's senses screamed at him, all of them at once. A whirlwind of sound. Metal clashing. Stone breaking. Men dying.

Blood. Sweat. Tears.

He looked down to see a severed hand scattered across the blood-soaked cobblestones.

Once, the sounds might have overwhelmed him, perhaps they still would, but through it all Will found a sense of clarity, of purpose, of composure.

The broken soul-hunters had come without warning, killing dozens. Then the black bridge fell. Souls flowed, more than he had ever seen before. They changed hosts like wildfire, hopping from person to person with each death.

Sword in hand, Will fought. He slashed man after man as they jumped over the parapet. It was easy, their patterns were simple enough to read. They had no skill, no awareness, just wild aggression. Aggression without purpose was easy to predict.

He stepped to the side as one nearly took him by surprise. Will cut him behind the neck, an undeservedly quick death. Fresh souls flowed into his cage. He breathed them in. Welcome or not, they were inside him now. His burden.

He kicked out with his foot, watching as another hunter's face shifted from confident to petrified in a matter of moments. He fell to his doom.

Will spared a look beyond. Skullsworn were swarming up and over the black bridge like locusts. Many died, picked off by archers and Knights throwing constructs at them, although they were just replaced by more. An endless tide.

Beside him, a soldier screamed his last as the muddied image of a spear pierced his heart. Will had no choice but to step over his impaled corpse.

Estevan began to rally some troops to make a stand on the bridge. Defenders cut, pushed, and scraped at the black substance overextending the city wall, but none of it did any good, the image was as thick as the stone they stood on. The only way to remove it would be to fell its maker.

Will spared a look over his shoulder to where Olive had been standing. He had seen one of the broken hunters land there. Worry itched at him. He wanted to protect her, to see her safe. She shouldn't be here. Not in this...

They had come so fast. He didn't have time. Nobody had time. He just had to hope she was okay, that Myddrin would protect her.

Will turned his attention towards the bridge. A number of Knights had gathered by Estevan, pushing the attackers back. They joined together, exhausting their cages, throwing image after image at the raging tide. Hundreds of Skullsworn perished, their corpses tripping those behind, sending even more to their deaths as they fell.

Will tucked himself behind the Knights, behind Estevan. He drew from his cage, breaking open the *otherside* and using everything Crisalli had taught him. He hurled a conjured spear down the bridge. He didn't even see it hit, though several more souls entered his cage, marking his kill.

Time passed. Seconds? Minutes? He couldn't tell, but they were holding.

In a sudden whirl of motion, several Knights toppled. Will barely saw it, couldn't comprehend it. Their souls simply left their bodies, blood soaking their once white armour as they collapsed, dead.

A figure emerged at the head of the oncoming forces. A red shield floated in the air in front of him.

Estevan shouted, threw everything at him, but still he came.

Closer.

Closer.

Closer.

He was almost within reach when the red of his shield broke apart as several fist-sized balls shot forward like lightning.

Will brandished his grandfather's shield, hiding behind it. He felt something impact. His hand buckled. His fingers screamed in pain. He looked up to see everyone around him dead. Only he and Estevan remained.

The figure kept coming. He looked deranged, his red eyes wide as the sea. Was he broken?

No. Not yet.

He spoke to himself through all of the chaos, all of the killing. He spoke even as he slashed at Estevan's defensive wall, battering it down.

"You won't break me!"

Slash.

"I am in control!"

Slash.

"Go away, Manius!"

Slash.

"Blood Mage, be gone!"

Slash.

Estevan buckled, dropping to a knee.

He was going to die. Will was going to die.

The crazed agent of Mirimar continued to beat at Estevan's wall. Will wanted to help, but he couldn't move. Every time he tried to, his shield would get pelted by more magic.

Will looked behind. Nobody was there. No one was coming. The Skullsworn were encroaching. This was his end.

Like thunder, something struck from above.

Crack.

Will lost his footing and raised his shield. It struck again.

Crack.

He let out a breath, patting his chest and checking on his limbs. They were all there. He was still alive.

He lowered the shield.

The black bridge had been split in half. A giant green thorn stuck out from the surface like the stinger of a bee.

Blood caked the surface of the thorn. The Skullsworn were gone, cut to pieces. Souls flowed, thousands of them.

Only one remained. The red-eyed Reaper. His shield stood strong above him, but he was wounded, his left arm hanging limp at his side.

Will looked up. What had happened? Who had saved him?

Then he saw it. The golden disc.

It descended.

They descended.

Cerak and Myddrin landed in front of him. Beside him, Estevan breathed a sigh of relief.

The Reaper snarled, said something incoherent, then fled, jumping right off what remained of the bridge and back into the gathering swarm.

The two titans of magic didn't stop, didn't even look at him. Together, they destroyed. They swept the battlements clean. Flashes of emerald and gold zipped around the battlefield. Skullsworn died, howled in pain, fled.

Defenders rallied, spurred on by their emergence. Slowly they began to retake the top of the wall.

Myddrin didn't stop. Cerak didn't stop. They leapt the walls, took the fight to them. Two men against an entire army.

And they were winning.

Images formed. Images dropped. Giant boulders of green and gold crushed. Massive scythes cut swaths into the enemy ranks as they put their limitless magic on full display.

The entire battlefield looked like a colourful tapestry as souls flowed and images clashed. Will tried to gather himself, to help, but there was simply nothing he could do. Not against this.

A horn blasted in the distance as a man ran to Estevan, shouting.

"Breach! Breach on the beach. The northern wall," he paused, hands on knees and took a breath. "The Corr. Oskon Corr has come. Their ships… They've taken the northern wall. Strupp calls for reinforcements."

# Chapter 45
# - Tvora -

Tvora stalked the battlement, a phantom amidst the fray. Her blades struck with silent lethality, leaving behind a trail of fallen bodies.

Cecco acted as her warden, Lucia her scout. Those not torn apart by Lucia's claws, Tvora finished quickly. Together, they carved a path towards the centre. While Carthon's black bridge had created an opening, now it stood broken, splintered down the middle. She watched as it faded, the image withdrawn.

Down below, the army of Skullsworn were being beaten. Two figures standing atop a golden disk continued to wreak havoc amongst their ranks. She knew she shouldn't, that she had a job to do, Knights to kill, but it was impossible not to watch.

These Knights, they were on another level. They must have had countless souls to draw upon. She held her breath as one of them reached into the *otherside* and solidified the largest image she had ever seen. There was no function to it, no design, no detail, just a flat piece of stone. Its surface glowed a bright emerald. It shimmered as the Knight literally just dropped it.

The entire battlefield shook with the impact. The image must have just flattened at least one fifth of their entire army in one go.

A whirl of motion sounded behind her.

Tvora grit her teeth and turned to see the tip of a blade halt mere inches from her exposed neck. A body dropped dead at her feet, a hole in his chest. Cecco swooped by, covered in blood.

*Don't get distracted,* he said.

Tvora grunted. He was right, she needed to move. If she could create enough space, kill enough of them, then maybe Carthon could get another foothold, another bridge through to the centre.

Naex and Naev in hand, she ran. She slashed. She killed. Every Knight that fell to her blades haunted her. Every soldier she maimed tormented her. These men weren't killers. These people didn't seek power. They weren't like her. They didn't kill because they could, they did it to protect.

No.

She couldn't think like that, couldn't know that for sure. She cast such thoughts aside. She was here now. She had made her choice. This was who she was now.

She cut another soldier to ribbons. A single measly soul flowed into her cage.

She shuddered, her mind throbbing with a psychic pain. She heard Lucia cry out ahead, saw glimpses of her violet form thrashing around with another foe.

She ran to her, leapt over her form, and spun, blades flashing. They bit into something hard. Not flesh, but another image.

It pressed against her, forcing her back. She retreated. Lucia cried out again, snarling.

A trio of Knights stood in their way. A boy cowered behind them. No, not a boy, a fourth Knight. A red burn mark scarred his eye.

Tvora straightened. She paced the area before them, assessing them, analysing their strength. Their broad-shouldered leader held her steely gaze. His chest glowed hazel. They didn't back down, didn't seem afraid.

She would make them feel afraid.

Their leader came at her, spiked mace in hand. Cecco swept from above, altering his swing so that he missed. Tvora took advantage, though instead of striking at their leader as they predicted, she altered her route, thrusting her blade into the Knight to his right. Naex bit into his neck, killing him in moments. She pivoted and changed target, leaping upon the third Knight just as the larger one brandished a protective shield over himself.

The third Knight didn't even have time to create an image of his own as Tvora stabbed him through the heart.

Tvora froze, realising she had made a mistake, perhaps a fatal one. She'd forgotten about the fourth Knight And now her back was exposed.

"Cecco!" she called.

It was too late, Cecco too far.

Only nothing came. She turned. The fourth Knight stood frozen in fear. His chest glowed, but no image came forth.

Tvora leapt back, out of range of both remaining Knights.

"Thane, I'm… I'm sorry. I couldn't… I…" the fourth Knight babbled.

The senior Knight scowled, head half-turning to face the younger Knight. "You're a coward, always were. Get out of my sight before I kill you myself."

The boy didn't need asking twice. He ran.

The Knight — Thane — shifted his attention back to Tvora. She felt her cage swell with new souls. She felt powerful, unstoppable. This man though… there was something different about him.

He lowered his head, took a deep breath, then released it in one slow exhale. He opened his posture, then looked to his dead companions and puffed out a derisive snort. "Weaklings."

He shifted his focus back to Tvora. His features barely moved, yet there was something sinister in the way his face knotted, something dark.

Together, they attacked. Lucia, then Cecco, then Tvora.

The Knight flexed his entire body. A golden-brown shield

surrounded him in an instant. He pushed outwards and the shield expanded, smashing into Tvora and her friends, sending Cecco spiralling into the air, Lucia tumbling down a flight of stairs, and Tvora into a spin that turned into a roll when she landed, and then a crash as she hit the stone wall.

She gasped and blood splattered the white stone.

She tried to recover, but more images appeared, dozens of them. They took the form of spikes. In a burst of motion, they shot forwards aimlessly, but there were so many…

One clipped Cecco's wing. He cried out in her mind. She felt his pain. It was her pain. Their shared pain.

Anger swelled her thoughts, fuelled her movements.

How dare he.

He would pay for hurting her friends.

More spikes formed, but Tvora was quicker. Lucia recovered. She raced up the stairs, then pounced, finding a gap in his shield. Her jaw bit into his flesh just as Tvora did the same with Naex.

The man cried out. His cage radiated as he called upon more of his souls. His power threatened to explode, to expand and end them for good this time. Tvora struck first, hitting the source. She dug her blade into his chest, into his cage. He opened his mouth to scream but no sound came forth as the souls within him burst apart. Blood dripped, flesh tore. The Knight fell.

Souls entered her. So many souls.

She doubled over, bending to a knee.

The souls continued to come. It hurt, but it also felt so good. Her chest burned.

Just who was this Knight?

Lucia and Cecco felt it too. They came to her, shared in the pain and ecstasy.

Her cage must have doubled, tripled even.

*Tvora, are you well?* Lucia called.

The assault ceased. The souls stopped flowing. Her mind buzzed. Her hands shook. She lowered her shirt and peeked inside her open cage. She could feel their power, their energy, could see them in there, joining with the others.

Tvora steadied, calmed herself.

Footsteps shuffled around her. Tvora turned to face them, to kill anyone who would dare harm her or her friends. She raised Naex into the air, poised for a killing blow. She made to bring it down, to smite another foe.

Her arm stopped mid-air, however, as she noticed the form of a frightened girl. She paused. The girl wore a full set of armour, was clearly a soldier of the Gracelands, but her face... there was fear, so much fear...

Tvora could smell the urine, could see her frozen limbs and terrified expression. This wasn't the face of a monster. It was the face of someone who had no choice other than to fight to protect their land.

"Go," Tvora said, lowering her arm.

The frightened soldier didn't move.

"I said go!"

The soldier tripped, recovered, then stumbled away down the battlement.

*Tvora! What are you doing? She's getting away!* cried Lucia.

Tvora ignored her. She looked to her hands, checked again on her cage. This Knight she had killed, his souls were enough. She felt it. Tvora could go, could leave this place. Could start anew. Lucia, Cecco, Gowther, they could last at least a day now by her side without fading. She knew it in her heart. This was enough.

Something hard crashed into the wall to her right, shaking her from her feet. A cacophony of sound exploded around her. She rose to see a second black bridge overlapping the rampart.

The girl, that was where the girl had run.

She looked down the battlement, ran to the bridge. The girl had splattered, half of her body crushed beneath the weight of the new bridge.

She spared a glance beyond the wall.

Carthon.

She stood in two minds. This was the world. This was life. This was death. She thought of Edith, of the blind Overmother and all the children in her care, all now in the grave. She thought of her own past, of her friends, of their death.

She had what she wanted. She could flee, leave this battle, leave this place, find somewhere quiet, start a life.

*This is not the time, Tvora! We are not done yet!* Lucia said.

Without waiting for a response, Lucia ran down the rampart. She wouldn't stop, couldn't stop. "When will it be enough?" Tvora whispered.

Lucia didn't hear her, didn't want to hear her. She ran.

Tvora had no choice, she couldn't leave her, couldn't abandon her friends. If she left Lucia now, her friend would never forgive her. She needed to see this through, needed to get to the end.

But where was the end?

Not knowing the answer, Tvora followed after Lucia.

# Chapter 46
## - Myddrin -

"Cerak, stop! We weren't done!" Myddrin called as wind whipped at his face.

Myddrin's chest burned. His head throbbed. His shoulder ached. His souls clawed at him, spoke to him, all vying for a piece of him.

Myddrin's resolve was strong though, stronger than it had ever been. He wouldn't break, not now, not while he had purpose. There were more Skullsworn to kill.

But Cerak was flying in the opposite direction, away from the bulk of their army. Myddrin had latched himself to the golden disk, allowing Cerak to dictate their movements while he focused on the destruction of the invaders.

He tried to unhook himself, to jump free, but they were moving too fast.

"Where are you taking us?" he shouted over the gale of wind.

"Look to the coast," Cerak said. There was a harshness to his tone, a determination that matched Myddrin's own current state.

Sure enough, ships dotted the coastline. The disk slowed, and Myddrin caught his breath. He looked to the castle walls, where he could see men fighting, Knights dying.

"What's happening?" he said.

Cerak grumbled. His chest glowed. "The Corr has come. They've joined Carthon."

Myddrin gulped. "What do we do?" He looked over his shoulder. Carthon's Skullsworn were regathering, preparing, but if the northern wall fell to the Corr, the battle would be over. Myddrin knew it. Cerak knew it.

Cerak shot forward as Myddrin held to his hip. Dozens of ships had entered the gulf. Their green sails billowed and snapped in the wind. Their bows darted through the water, breaking waves and driving towards the northern wall, where several had already engaged the city's defenders.

The bulk of their fleet were made even faster by super-sized propellers born from magic and utilised for mobility. The huge, colourful contraptions were larger than the ones he had seen Estevan use. Larger and more practical.

Multiple mages churned through their souls as they worked to turn the great wheels, pressing their ships faster. Soon, all would dock. Soon, the entire Corr army would be upon them.

Myddrin wouldn't let that happen.

Cerak sent his disk forward, out into the open sea. Below him, the tide raged. White foam frothed as waves spat at them. It was as if the sea knew what was happening and had decided to join in.

The cries of the dying roared behind them as defending Gracelanders held against the first of the Corr to land. They would have to hold strong for the moment.

Cerak angled towards the remaining ships, lowering himself into their range. Some noticed their presence and began shooting arrows, shooting magic.

Myddrin summoned a wall that blocked their attempts, but it wasn't enough. He needed to go on the offence. They needed to feel his rage. They needed to know what happened to those who sought to kill the innocent, to stand against the Gracelands.

They needed to sink.

Myddrin raised his hands, drew from his cage. This time he took a leaf out of Cerak's book. His image formed as a thin disk.

He expanded it, thickened its shape, sharpened its edge, then turned it on an angle. It stood twenty times the size of any man. It hovered in the air before them, completely under his control.

Then, with a mental and physical push, he sent it towards the largest ship. He watched from above as the disk cut into wood and man.

Wood cracked and splintered as the ship split. People died. People jumped, preferring their chances with the sea. The propellers faded as the ship sank.

Beside him, Cerak performed a similar feat, though rather than one decisive blow, his targeted ship sank after several strikes of a golden hammer.

Together, they sank three more ships in a similar manner. A single tear ran down Cerak's cheek. It clearly pained him. He had ruled over these people, had been one of them for such a long time. It had to be hard to do this to them.

The four remaining ships made to turn, to flee. Myddrin readied himself to cut them down, to make certain of their victory, but Cerak stayed his hand. "They're done. Let them leave, let them learn. There's only one more soul I need to crush."

He changed course. The disk descended upon the northern wall. People turned at their approach. Friendly soldiers cheered, emboldened by their swift victory at sea. The unfriendly lashed out, even more desperate now to cut down the defenders quickly.

Myddrin landed on the stone. His feet wobbled, but he soon steadied.

Cerak leapt off the disk. Forgoing magic, he tackled another man to the ground. The men of the Corr around them made to help, to stop Cerak. Myddrin blocked them, summoning his emerald wall and watching as they beat at it uselessly.

"Look what you've done, Arber!" Cerak spat, slamming down a fist on an exposed cheek. "Is this what you wanted?"

Crack. Another fist.

"Carthon isn't the answer."

Crack.

"You would never be free of him."

Crack.

"You've led the Corr to ruin."

Crack.

Myddrin thought he would stop, was expecting him to stop, but he didn't.

Fists now a bloody mess, Cerak continued to pound the new King of Oskon Corr. He punched him until his face became unrecognisable. At some point during the beating, Arber's souls entered Cerak. Myddrin could hardly watch.

Finally, Cerak stopped. The entire northern battlement stood silent. Everyone stopped fighting, both sides just froze and stared.

Myddrin dismissed his wall. Cerak rose and turned towards the remaining soldiers of the Corr.

"Leave, now," he said, still panting. "I'll only say this once. Leave this place, and never come back."

Still, nobody moved.

"NOW!" Cerak yelled.

Feet shuffled. Weapons dropped. The soldiers of the Corr ran.

# Chapter 47
## - Will -

Will palmed his way through the throng of dead bodies. The sight of a man cleaved in half turned his stomach. He bent over and spewed his guts.

The stories were wrong. There was no glory in battle, no thrill for the fight or desire to kill. There was just emptiness and regret, knowing that every breath might be your last.

He tried to gather himself. Above the roar of the ongoing battle, a commotion arose. Chunks of stone were propelled into the sky as the top of the wall shattered. A shrill scream split the air. A body soared, then fell. He splattered against the cobblestone path below.

Will's heart wrenched. A second bridge had landed. He looked around. Myddrin and Cerak were nowhere in sight. Where had they gone?

He stumbled up a flight of stairs. He couldn't wait any longer. He needed to see if Olive had fled, needed to make sure she was safe. Surely she would be safe.

He climbed up blood-slicked stairs. People had been here. People had died here.

He climbed faster, skipping steps. Finally, he came to the open platform he had seen Olive sing upon. Bodies littered the stone. Skullsworn.

He heard a cry further toward the city. He could see fighting in the distance, the blurred shapes of images clashing.

He ran. The Mage-Way split in front of him, sectioning off

into different routes that ran atop the entire city.

He listened to the sounds, followed the lights, and chose the middle one. Dead Skullsworn lay everywhere. Dozens of them, completely obliterated, their masks torn to shreds.

The path widened. Flashes of silver and yellow lit the route beyond as two mages clashed.

"Will!"

He spun.

Then he noticed her.

"Olive!"

Will ran over, kneeling beside her. She sat with her knees spread. Blood soaked her once colourful dress. A body lay on the stone before her.

And a crown.

"Are you okay?" he asked, placing a hand on her cheek.

Olive nodded, her face wet with tears. "I'm fine. But my father…"

"Is he?"

"No. He's not dead," she said. "I can feel him breathing, and his soul didn't leave. You have to help me, Will. I can't carry him by myself."

Will nodded, moving to hold his weight over his shoulder. The king's head was soaked in blood from a cut, but the rest of him looked unharmed.

The king groaned.

"What happened here?" Will asked.

"The Skullsworn. They were too fast. Halvair saved us. There's no time, we have to get him to the keep."

Will understood. He pushed off with his feet, taking the weight of her father. Olive helped, lifting him under his other shoulder.

Around them, the clashing mages drew closer. Their fight

took up the entire pathway.

"It's Halvair," Olive said. "He's fighting someone strong. Really strong. He's already injured. I don't…"

"We can't worry about that now," Will interrupted. "We'll have to go back, take another route."

He looked up just in time to see a flare of violet.

A figure stalked the path behind them, sleek and feline. A panther.

Its eyes glowed with an otherworldly gleam. Fangs bared, the panther lunged.

Will pivoted. He dropped the king and drew his sword, raising it in a desperate parry. The violet panther's jaw clamped down on the blade's edge, its feral eyes locked onto Will.

The beast's sinewy muscles rippled as it continued to thrash. Will's hand buckled. His grip faltered. He pushed out with all of his strength and ripped his sword free.

The panther retreated, then circled back around.

Will knew this creature, would never forget. It was the same. The same beast that had killed his mentor.

Another figure walked up behind the panther. She bore the same hollow eyes as his mother had when she met her end. The same hollow eyes which had haunted him ever since.

Soul-broken.

# Chapter 48
# - Tvora -

Lucia continued to swipe at the boy. He looked familiar. She had met him before, in Oskon Corr. He had been about to break. He didn't seem broken now. He seemed strong, defiant, and extremely quick.

A Knight.

He beat back Lucia's attempts again and again, using a combination of footwork and well-timed parries.

A girl sat behind him. A girl and a man. A crown lay at his feet.

Tvora grit her teeth. She wasn't about to leave Lucia to fend for herself. Lucia was her friend, her everything.

She jumped in front of her, blades at the ready. The young Knight leapt back. He stood over the girl, his shield raised high. His eyes darted from Tvora to Lucia. Cecco hovered above, though he seemed too distracted by the fight between Glock and another Knight just beyond them.

Tvora struck, but the Knight was prepared. He shifted his feet, pushed his shield into her blade, and swung with his own. Tvora deflected the strike, then leapt back.

Lucia jumped, sensing an opening. A flare of blue shimmered into existence and the image of a second shield appeared before Lucia. She crashed into it, then landed hard.

Tvora moved in for a killing blow. Naex whistled past his shield. The Knight pivoted, dodged. He dove to the side, his body falling in a heap.

Tvora began to lunge, but Lucia had other ideas. She made to strike at the prone girl kneeling by the side of the wounded man. Perhaps her father?

"Lucia, what are you doing? She's just a girl!"

Lucia didn't listen, didn't want to listen.

The Knight cried out. "Olive, no!"

He jumped to his feet. Leaving his shield behind, he vaulted the distance and placed his body over the girl, leaving his back exposed.

Lucia latched onto the flesh of his shoulder. She began to jerk, to kill.

For an almost surreal moment, Tvora lost track of reality. She closed her eyes, opening them to see herself. She was younger, still a child in the eyes of many. She looked scared, terrified even. Gowther stood in front of her, hands caked in blood. He protected her.

The memory struck like a dagger to the gut. Suddenly everything made sense. A piece in her mind clicked back into place. He had sacrificed his life so that she might live. And what had she done with it? At first, her vengeance had been just, her quest to save her friends had fuelled her existence and given her purpose.

When had she strayed? When had her purpose shifted from mere survival to becoming that which she hated most? This Knight was willing to give his life for the girl. Tvora needed to stop it, needed to break the cycle, to right her wrongs. She needed to find herself, her true self.

"Lucia!" she screamed, covering her own ears.

The cat still didn't listen. She wanted more souls, was driven by the need. She let go, then opened her jaw for another bite, this time on the neck.

Tvora charged. She tackled her friend. Together, they fell.

Together, they wrestled. She held on tight, wrapping her arms around her fur.

"Stop, we're better than this. Please."

Slash.

Claws raked her back, drawing blood. They shared in the pain.

"We're better than this."

Slash.

"WE'RE BETTER THAN THIS!"

Slowly, the fight drained from Lucia. She stopped struggling, stopped attacking. For a long moment the two just lay there, unable to part from each other.

*I'm sorry,* she heard Lucia say. *I'm... ashamed. I can't... I can't stop. It's like a need. This body, this world... I can't do it anymore, Tvora. I can't live like this. I want to go home.*

"You're not in this alone. We're in this together. Lean on me. Lean on Cecco. Lean on Gowther. Together, we'll find some peace in this life we've been given, I promise you. But I can't ride with you on this pathway to darkness. If we continue to act without morality, without mercy, we'll lose ourselves. We'll lose each other."

Tvora felt their bond deepen, their minds begin to unify. She held her tight, lending Lucia her reassurance, proving she would never let her down, never leave her side.

*I wasn't always like this,* Lucia said. *It's this world. It breaks you down. Tears you apart from the inside. How do we stop it? How do we find what you say?*

"I don't have all the answers, but this isn't one of them," she indicated the Knight and the girl. "I know that now. I should have known it all along."

"How touching," came a voice from behind.

A spear pierced though Lucia's violet chest.

Tvora felt as though a part of her were ripped in two. She gasped for breath as if she had felt the blow herself. She rolled around on the stone, turning her head to see Carthon standing behind her, his large frame casting a towering shadow.

"I thought you were stronger than this. It's a shame, really. We could have been something, you and I. I had high hopes. No matter. In this world, there's only room for the strong."

Tvora tried to gather herself but was met with a backhanded fist. She fell to the floor. Cecco tried to come to her aide but was struck down by a magical projectile.

"Cecco!"

Crack.

Carthon's knuckles smashed into her cheek. She fell. Blood spattered and her vision grew foggy.

"Stay back!" she heard someone call. The boy — the Knight.

Through the thin slit of her swelling eye she saw the blue of his image-shield rise.

"Impressive," Carthon said, his voice rising above the hum of magic. "You would make a fine Reaper, child." Even as he spoke, Carthon drew from his deep well of souls, summoning a black spike the size of a small house.

"Give up the king, give up this fight, and I'll let you live," he said to the boy. "You can join me if you wish, or go about life your own way. I'll even let you kill this one," he motioned towards Tvora. "I can tell you want her dead. I can see it in your eyes. Go ahead, kill her. Claim her souls, take her power. It's what everyone wants in the end."

Tvora tried to gather herself, but Carthon kicked her in the stomach. Breath left her body. She gasped, clawing for air that wouldn't come.

She had seen Carthon do this before, had watched as a man had taken a similar deal, killed a much stronger man in cold blood. Taken the power for himself.

The boy looked to her, hardened his stance, then set his gaze on Carthon. "I don't want power. I don't want her souls. I don't want to kill anyone. I want you all to leave. I want to keep my friend safe."

Tvora looked away. She couldn't look at him, not anymore. She felt ill. Here was a boy, forced to become a man. He only sought to protect those he loved. He fought for his friend.

Same as her.

How had she become the monster she sought to destroy?

"A pity," Carthon said, exhaling a breath. "Then you shall die."

The black spike shot towards the blue shield with devastating velocity. It pierced the surface, its tip mere inches from the Knight's chest.

The boy held his ground. There was no hesitation, no moment of indecision. The boy was prepared to die for them.

Carthon withdrew the spike, then thrust it forward again.

The blue shield doubled in size, but another puncture appeared, then another, and another.

Time and time again Carthon battered it down. The boy fell, but still he fought, still he rebuilt his shield. It was only a matter of time. He would die soon. They would all die soon.

His defiance struck a chord within her. She felt something shift.

A rumble sounded deep inside her chest, one she'd thought to be lost. She dug within herself, reaching for and gripping the familiar yet distant sensation. She felt her souls begin to churn as something massive swirled. Her eyes came alight as finally, the sleeping giant answered her call.

It was time.

Gowther had come.

# Chapter 49
## - Will -

The darkness shattered his shield. Cracks formed. The black tip pierced through his veil and into his shoulder. A shallow wound only, though he feared the next one would be fatal.

He looked behind. Olive clung to his leg. She pressed her body over her father's. The king groaned, beginning to wake. Will had to stay strong. He couldn't let them down, couldn't let her down.

He rebuilt his shield, only for it to be shattered again. This man... this power... it was too much.

He bent to a knee, rebuilding his shield one last time, using everything he had.

It broke again all the same.

The darkness came.

Then, behind the darkness, something rose. Something massive, inhuman.

A shade of blue fought the black.

Was that him? Had Will done that?

No. Not him.

The ground shook. A shape formed. Its ghostly coat hardened, taking the shape of a great bear. Giant teeth protruded from a huge maw as the conjured creature let out a soundless roar.

A thick layer of fur covered four meaty legs. The beast slammed a paw into the ground, breaking stone and sending a chunk of the pathway toppling below.

Will angled his head to see the broken woman back on her

feet, both panther and bird surrounding her in a protective ring as the man that could only be Carthon turned to face his new adversary.

"I see you've been holding back," Carthon said. "The stories were true then. The third passenger of Tvora Soul-broken finally makes itself known."

Carthon shifted the shape of his image into a wall of darkness and turned it against the giant bear. The two images clashed. The bear swiped straight through the black, breaking it into pieces. Carthon seemed unfazed. He danced back until he was almost touching Will's foot.

Will's legs shook with the effort of keeping himself upright. He had to get Olive and the king out of here, but the path was blocked on both sides. Halvair and the other Reaper continued to battle behind them, the soul-broken woman and Carthon in front of them. There was no escape.

"You could have had it all, Tvora!" Carthon called over the commotion. "And you would throw it all away over the life of a boy."

The woman who had killed his mentor stepped forward into the shadow of the giant bear. The mage and spectre seemed to share a mental communication of sorts before she turned to address Carthon. "You asked me not long ago what it was like to break my soul. Now I see that yours is already broken. I think it has been for years. Whatever trauma you were forced to endure has scratched away at any lingering emotion. You have no room in your heart for empathy. I know this because I was almost like you. I know what it's like, to lose everything, to love nobody and hate everyone. But when I see these people, human beings just like us, who stay to protect those they hold dear instead of running to save themselves as they should, I see there's more to this world than self-pity and revenge."

The woman turned to look at Will, her empty eyes reminiscent of his mother's the day he had been forced to slay her. He couldn't bring himself to forgive her, not now. She had caused too much pain, too much suffering. She didn't get a free pass just because of a late change of heart.

But what could he do? His life was in her hands, potentially Olive's as well, and all of those still defending the city. He needed to buy them time, and helping her would do it.

Sword firmly gripped in his hand, Will charged.

# Chapter 50
# - Myddrin -

Cerak bent to a knee. His eyes bulged as the onrush of power seeped into his veins and through to the very core of who he was. He puffed out his cheeks. His fingers clenched as he suffocated on the influx of fresh souls. Spittle formed at the edge of his mouth as breathing became secondary.

Myddrin knew this pain, understood this struggle. He drew a knife from beneath his cloak and forced it into Cerak's hand. Their eyes locked. Cerak understood. If he broke here, it could be the end for them all.

Cerak rose. His features calmed. His breathing returned. He still held the knife, but colour returned to his eyes. Still gold. Still sane.

"Not yet, brother. Not yet," he said, re-summoning his disk.

Myddrin relaxed, exhaling a long-held breath. Together, they hopped on the disk and took flight.

With the retreat of Corr, the entire northern border was almost free from assault. The southern end also held strong. The problem was at the centre. With Carthon's second platform providing such easy access, the invading Skullsworn were overflowing the defending soldiers. Parts of the central corridor were already overrun. Friendly soldiers began retreating to a more defensible position. If the aggressive tide wasn't stemmed now, eventually the invaders would spill into each flank and overwhelm the city.

Myddrin grit his teeth as something massive arose from

within the city walls. A giant bear clawed at a wall of black, drawing his eye and causing Cerak to come to a halt. They looked at each other for a moment before Cerak sent his disk into a dive.

Fresh hatred filled him, fuelled him.

Carthon, the man behind Myddrin's continued misery, and the one responsible for this entire forsaken war, stood within reach.

Myddrin gathered his souls. His chest flared a vibrant green. He prepared to unleash it all. This needed to end, and Carthon's death would do it. He readied an image, waiting until he was within range. As he moved to release it, Cerak's disk changed course. Cerak dove, throwing his body without warning and without regard to Myddrin.

He landed atop Carthon's adversary, a woman he couldn't quite place. The momentum of the disk continued, forcing Myddrin to jump. He toppled onto a stone platform, twisting his ankle as he turned to roll into a landing.

The scene he looked up to find was bizarre. Cerak and the woman tumbled over broken stone. Three apparitions followed them. A panther, a bird, and a bear, all of differing colours.

Cerak rained down a flurry of punches on her protected head.

"I'll kill you, witch! You killed her! You showed no mercy, and I shall give you none either."

He thrust his fist down again and struck her on the face.

Claws bit into his skin as the panther swiped. Cerak reeled. He drew from his souls and stabbed at the panther with something sharp. The bird swooped him and he battered it away with a shield he formed around his fist. Then came the bear. It barrelled towards him. Head bowed low, it hit shoulder-first, sending Cerak tumbling over its back.

Myddrin shifted his attention. Carthon's black sword swished through the air, though Myddrin wasn't the target.

A young Knight stood his ground, battering the sword away before thrusting forth his own. It met empty air.

"Will?" Myddrin said, scrambling to cover him.

His eyes widened, taking in the scene. It *was* Will. He stood over someone, protecting them.

The king and princess!

Myddrin didn't waste any more time. He sprang into action, meeting Carthon's black blade with a green one of his own.

The two swords born of the *otherside* clashed. They held together, grinding against one another. Myddrin's eyes narrowed, finding Carthon's. He pushed forward, gaining momentum. He could sense victory, could see the strain in his adversary's expression.

Myddrin would split him in two, right here and now.

A flicker of yellow flashed in his peripheral. It came between them, carved his sword into pieces, bit into his flesh, and severed a finger.

Myddrin cried out in pain. Blood gushed. It trickled between the gaps in his knuckles. He looked down at the gory stump. Half a finger gone, just like that.

He back-pedalled, trying to find the source of the strike. He searched for the yellow and found it in the form of man-sized barrier that stood in front of him. Sticking out from its side stretched a long sword, slicked in blood.

The yellow disappeared, revealing a face he knew well.

"You... must be Glock," Myddrin said through laboured breaths.

Cerak's shirtless twin looked at him above a sinister grin. He placed the flat of his blood-slicked blade to his lips and kissed it.

Carthon laughed. He looked to Glock. "Did you finish it?"

Before he could respond, Will attacked. The young Knight had no fear. He charged the villainous Reaper, forcing him back with his blade. "Leave. Us. Alone," he said, each strike sending Glock back another step.

Despite a valiant effort, Glock battered away his attempts and knocked Will's sword from his hand. The Reaper stepped forward, ready to kill.

Myddrin gathered his wits. He drew from his cage and brought forth his wall. He expanded it, then changed its shape, wrapping it around both Glock and Carthon.

Hand still leaking blood, he squeezed, and the wall tightened. Bones cracked as the two Reapers were crushed together.

Myddrin continued to squeeze, to squash, determined to end this here, to kill them both. He didn't want their souls. Didn't want their burden. But he would take it if it meant the world after their deaths would be a little less dark.

A torrent of black emerged from his sphere of green. Spiked tendrils broke through his cage, expanding it, collapsing it. Myddrin tried to reinforce it, to double down on his prison, but the black proved too strong.

His wall shattered and broke apart, falling to the ground where it disappeared.

Glock and Carthon gathered their breath, then set their focus on him. They came at him in tandem, slicing with both magic and sword.

Myddrin threw up another wall, but it broke down quickly. He bent to a knee, readying himself for death.

After everything he'd done, it wasn't enough. They had him.

Without warning, silver magic bent around his shoulder, shooting towards the two Reapers. Whatever it was pierced through Carthon's shoulder, drawing red. The Emperor of Mirimar wailed in agony. Everyone took a step back, wondering what had just happened.

Myddrin turned to see Halvair standing behind him. His

body was broken. He stood on two feet, but he wavered, looking as though he could collapse at any second. He panted heavily, then bent to a knee. One arm was outstretched, the other...

Was gone. His right arm had been severed above the elbow. Blood seeped from the wound, though he had stemmed its flow with some sort of magically crafted tourniquet.

"You should... have finished me off..." he said.

Myddrin stared for a moment at his rival, at the man who had truly bested Doonaval that fateful day. Guilt ripped through him, gripping him from the inside and threatening to pull him down. Myddrin had caused this. Perhaps Halvair would have already defeated them all if Myddrin had given him the power to do so. If he hadn't been so stubborn...

No.

He couldn't think like that. Halvair was still alive. Myddrin was still here. Guilt would have to wait a while longer.

An enraged Carthon let loose. A tide of black shapes shimmered into existence. He hauled them towards Halvair and Myddrin.

Despite their differences, Myddrin and Halvair fought together. Flashes of silver and green met with Carthon's black. Their world became a mash of colour. Anything else became impossible to see.

In the background, he could still hear Cerak fighting with the soul-broken woman, though even there it became impossible to tell who had the upper hand.

Through the mass of shapes, a figure appeared. Glock charged them, sword in hand.

Halvair stopped him, trapping him in a silver cage similar to the one Myddrin had just made. Before he could escape, Halvair thickened it, pouring layer after layer upon the prison until there was no escape. He squeezed, and then squeezed again.

The black in front of him disappeared, and his vision returned to see Carthon standing over the king, over the boy. Black sword in hand, he readied a strike.

"No!" Halvair said, running to their defence.

"Halvair, wait!" Myddrin called. But it was too late. While distracted, a black spike split Halvair from behind.

He hadn't seen it...

A trap...

Carthon smiled as Halvair fell to his knees. The spike had pierced his heart. He looked up at Myddrin, then to Carthon, and took his last breath.

Tens of thousands of souls flowed from his corpse. They rushed into Carthon in a wave of energy. Only when Doonaval died had Myddrin seen more souls release from a single body.

Myddrin didn't wait for him to complete the transaction. He couldn't spare a tear, not now. Fresh souls or no, Carthon was wounded. Myddrin built a wall between the Emperor and Will, then pulled his hand back. The wall slid along the ground, sweeping Will, the king and the princess out of the way. They rushed towards him, taken by his magic.

Halvair's souls finished entering Carthon's cage. The dark emperor looked at his hands, felt at his chest. His eyes rolled to the back of his head. He went into some kind of trance. He began whispering, muttering to himself. His entire body convulsed. The air around him rippled with violent black energy.

Myddrin went to step closer, thinking him vulnerable, wanting to end him right there and then, but he couldn't. Hundreds of doors to the *otherside* manifested as small tears, distorting reality. If he took another step forward, he honestly didn't know if all of him would be able to return.

Through it all, Carthon remained calm within his veil of chaotic energy. He breathed in slowly through his nose, then exhaled even slower through his mouth. Myddrin didn't know exactly what was going on, but he knew from experience that Carthon was fighting for his sanity this very moment. By the looks of it, he was winning.

All fell silent.

The dark energy subsided, and Carthon's eyes popped open.

Myddrin tensed, preparing himself for the worst, but without another word, Carthon turned and fled. He ran down the Mage-Way, towards the keep, towards the well…

Myddrin made to pursue. He couldn't let Carthon get into the well. He already had enough souls now to potentially end this battle. If he managed to gather and somehow control all of the souls sitting down there, the world would be at his fingertips.

He stopped. Cerak and the soul-broken woman still fought behind him. The king slowly began to wake. Will and the princess were still in danger. He couldn't abandon them. They needed him.

He shifted and brought forth an image. He targeted the soul-broken woman and unleashed.

Colours clashed. Swords swiped. Her apparitions rallied, all of them. They blocked his attempts. Even when her back was turned, still they protected her. It was as if they had a mind of their own. They acted with their own thoughts, their own instincts.

Cerak and Myddrin once again became a team, doubling down on their magical barrage.

Both sides charged, ready to risk it all in one final assault.

"Stop!" Will shouted. He created a wall of his own, separating the conflict. The panther pounced. It changed course mid-flight, using its powerful legs to bounce off the wall and propel itself back to its master.

Cerak turned from the battle, craning his neck to look at the person interrupting his moment of bloodlust. "What is it, Will?"

he said. "This is the woman who murdered Crissa! She took her from us, I won't sleep until her soul is mine."

Will took a step forward. "It doesn't need to be this way!" he said. "She saved me from Carthon. She turned on him. She wants to fight with us."

"You can't trust her! Her soul is broken. Don't be fooled!"

Myddrin watched on, expecting the woman in question to attack, though she made no move to interfere.

Cerak raised his fist, but Will walked in front of him, arms outstretched, placing his back to the woman. "No," he said.

"Will!" Cerak pleaded.

The blue bear moved. It towered over Will. Myddrin readied an image, preparing to intervene.

Will looked the bear in the eye, reached out a hand. He took a step towards it.

The bear… leaned into his touch. It bowed its head, allowing Will to pat its sapphire coat.

"You don't want to hurt us, do you?" he said, continuing to stroke the magical creature.

The bear responded. It shook its head in a slow, sweeping motion.

Myddrin looked from the bear to the woman. Her arms were interlaced, and her gaze was unfocused.

"Your images, they move on their own. How?" Myddrin said.

The soul-broken woman grunted. "We are one. Gowther's soul and mine share both mind and body. The boy is right, the four of us have no quarrel with you, if you do not make one."

Myddrin gasped. The four of them? Sharing a mind? Could it be possible?

"Bah!" Cerak said, taking an aggressive step forward. "Liar! You're a Reaper of Mirimar. You're a murderer. Pet or no, you killed Crissa. I can't forgive that.

"Step aside, Will!" Cerak called. Veins popped from his arms like tributaries. Whatever mental strength had been keeping him in check was dwindling with each passing moment.

"Cerak!" Myddrin said, placing himself in front of Will. "This isn't the time. Carthon is on his way to the well. If this woman claims to want to help, then we may have need of her."

Cerak's fist clenched tight. Myddrin knew this pain. He understood what it was like to lose a loved one, to want revenge. It was a thirst that could only be quenched through one action. Honestly, he didn't know if he would stand down if their places were reversed.

Slowly, Cerak began to lower his guard. His fists unclenched, and his breathing dropped to a slower, more reasonable pace. He eyed Will, bowed his head in a nod Myddrin took to be respect, then turned to face the soul-broken woman and made to speak.

Before he could utter a word, however, his shirt began to change colour. A pool of red formed below his chest.

The sharp point of a sword stuck out from his ribcage as a form rose behind him. They were the same height, the same build, and wore the same face.

Glock.

"Cerak!" Will shouted.

Where had he come from? Myddrin cursed. Halvair's prison. How could he have been so foolish! His death had freed him. He must have hidden, waiting for the right moment...

The Reaper withdrew his sword. Cerak spat blood and fell backwards. Glock caught him and cradled his brother in his arms. "I'm sorry, Brother, but your mind is lost. Let your soul rest inside of me, so that even in death we will not be apart."

Myddrin raged. He poured his anger into a targeted assault, brandishing image after image and sending them whistling towards Glock. It was no use. He used his dying brother as a shield, knowing Myddrin would deflect their course. He backed into the stone railing. "We await you at the well, Doonslayer," he said. He thrust his dying brother forward before vaulting the parapet.

Myddrin rushed to chase him down but by the time he got to the edge, he was already gone.

Cerak coughed blood. Splashes of red trickled down his chin as he tried to speak. His chest convulsed, the overwhelming power within him reacting to the wound, souls pushing with everything they had as they prepared to either seize control, or leave.

Despite all that was happening, Cerak laughed. More blood spouted from his open mouth as the former King of Oskon Corr found what little comfort he could knowing that he was soon to pass from this world.

"B - bastard," he said, his speech laboured. "Always knew he would be the one to do it."

Myddrin continued to put pressure onto the wound, holding onto the false hope he would pull through.

"Cerak, stay with me. Fight it. Come on!" Myddrin said, though even he knew his words to be weak.

"Come here," Cerak spat, eyes focused on the soul-broken woman.

She hesitated, but then took three steps towards him.

"Kill me. Do it now."

Myddrin waved his hand between them. "What are you doing? Have you lost your mind?"

More blood trickled down Cerak's chin. "Quickly... Before my brother gets what he wants. I want her... to kill me."

"Why? For what reason?"

"I want... to be with her. I want... to be with Crissa."

Myddrin closed his eyes. He opened them to see the soul-broken woman show the first sign of emotion he had seen from her.

Her mouth opened. The lines in her forehead deepened and her hands stopped mid-motion. "You want me… to kill you?" she said.

Cerak nodded. He forced himself to sit upright and snatched her arm out of the air. His grip tightened, causing her to pull her blade and level it as his throat.

"Do it," he said. "But be… warned. If you… don't help them. If you…" he paused, choking on his own blood. "If you, turn on my friends. My soul… will find you. My soul… will haunt you."

Cerak's golden eyes shot to life, marking his power. Then they began to fade, and fade quickly.

"Do it now!" he said. "I should have never left her, Myddrin.

"I should have never left her.

"I should… have never…"

The soul-broken woman thrust her blade into his heart.

"Left… her…"

The gold faded, and Cerak's life ended.

His chest erupted. Countless souls exploded out from him in a blinding display of colour. They streamed straight into the exposed and open cage of the soul-broken woman, slamming into her with force enough to knock her off her feet.

She fell onto her back, unable to even scream, so deep was the agony and ecstasy she must be feeling. The three apparitions beside her must have felt it too, for they began to flicker in and out of existence, morphing between corporeal and incorporeal.

Myddrin couldn't look, refused to look.

This world… when did the cruelty end?

A scream split the air, causing him to turn.

"Myddrin, help!" cried the princess. "It's Will! He's shaking! It won't stop! Please, Will. Stay with me!"

Myddrin ran to Will, leaving the broken woman to fend for herself. Will lay flat on the stone bridge, his body in some kind of shock. His legs were stiff as nails, every muscle pulled taught. His right arm twitched, fingers beating a rapid rhythm on his stomach.

He whispered something, repeating the same sentence over and over again. Myddrin leaned closer.

"Calder, Silas, Ophelia, Thane, Myddrin.

"Calder, Silas, Ophelia, Thane, Myddrin.

"Calder, Silas, Ophelia, Thane, Myddrin.

"Calder, Silas, Ophelia, Thane, Myddrin.

"Calder, Silas, Ophelia, Thane, Myddrin.

"Calder, Silas, Ophelia, Thane, Myddrin.

"Calder, Silas, Ophelia, Thane, Myddrin.

"Calder, Silas, Ophelia, Thane, Myddrin.

"Calder, Silas, Ophelia, Thane, Myddrin.

"Calder, Silas, Ophelia, Thane, Myddrin."

"Will!" Myddrin yelled into his ear. "Will! Listen to me. Fight it! You have to fight it!"

Will's eyes flickered open.

The blue. What had happened to the blue?

# Chapter 51
## - Will -

*Another one dead*
*How many more will there be?*
*We could have stopped it*
*Let us out*
*We can fight them*
Will screamed.

He knew his body was on the floor, that he was shaking, but he couldn't stop.

He could hear the voices around him. Myddrin's voice, Olive's voice, but he couldn't register them.

"Will, stay with me! Please, hold on!"

Olive?

Will groaned. His back arched. It was as though a door he thought he had locked tight had swung wide open. The tide of souls came all at once, choosing their moment. It caught him off guard, like an unanticipated storm. They rushed through him, each a chaotic whisper vying for dominance.

His eyes began to blur. Unseen hands tugged at his limbs, pulling him upright. He stood. Through his foggy vision he saw Olive jump back. Was she scared of him?

*That's it*
*Let go*
*It will be easy*
*Give up control*
*We have you now*

"Olive, step back! He could be dangerous!" he heard a voice

call. A real voice. Myddrin?

Will fought. Spittle frothed at his lips. His arm shook. One rose, though he gripped it tight with his other hand and pulled it back down.

*There's no point in struggling*

*We have you now*

*Just let go*

"We have to kill him. He's too far gone. There's no other way. His soul is broken."

Inside, the voices roared all at once. They doubled down on their efforts, sensing this might be their only opportunity. Will took an involuntary step forward.

"No!" called another voice. Olive? "You can't have him, you hear me!"

Two hands gripped Will's shoulders. "I won't let you touch him. Fight it, Will! Fight them."

"Olive, step away from him!"

Another voice. The king?

Still the two hands gripped him, shook him. "Follow the patterns, Will! Remember? Follow the voices, squash them. Don't give up."

Both of Will's arms lashed out. His hands wrapped around something. A neck?

He squeezed.

"Fight… it…"

Will's entire body stiffened as he threw everything against the unseen power which had taken control. He focused his thoughts. His mind drifted back to his training, to his time with Crisalli, to his time with Olive.

Find their pattern. Squash them.

One by one.

*Let us out*

Squash.

Will found the loudest of them, predicted its rise, then saw to its fall. He pressed it down, silenced its voice.

*Set me free.*

Squash.

He found the next loudest, silenced that one too.

Again and again, they came for him, but he knew them, had lived with them. He understood which ones would speak, what they would say. He squashed them all.

His mind floated in this space of nothing. He still couldn't see, couldn't feel. He sensed his mother, somewhere in the distance, watching him, guiding him.

Slowly, his vision returned, though it was different. His reality was distorted. He saw Olive and immediately released her. He saw Myddrin readying to kill him. He stepped back.

He saw blue, so much blue. He saw the world as if through two entirely different lenses. One was the reality he knew and understood. The other was like an ethereal, parallel realm. Everything radiated with a spectral brilliance. Every facet of existence seemed cloaked in a luminous, ghostly blue hue. The sky above shimmered in varying shades of azure. The buildings and structures around him retained their earthly forms, but it was all like one giant dreamscape, the shapes constantly shifting between tangible and intangible.

Where was he?

Was this... the *otherside*?

He walked forward in this unknown space. He reached out a hand, seeking comfort.

Olive grabbed it, held it. She cleared her throat. "Will? Is that you?"

Will looked down at her, shifting his focus back to reality. The landscape remained the same, but her features appeared. It was as if he were stuck in-between one reality and another.

He saw her throat, saw the bruise forming. Guilt riddled him. He looked down at his shaking hands.

"I — yes, it's me. I promise."

"Your eyes," Olive said. "They're glowing."

For a frightful moment Will panicked. He clawed at his eyes and stumbled around. "What colour are they?" he asked. "Are they white?"

"No. They're blue. Bright blue. And your—" she paused to cough, "your chest. It looks like it's on fire!"

Will looked down. He ripped open the fabric of his shirt, thinking himself soul-broken. There was no hole, no open cage, but Olive was right. His entire chest flared with blue magic. Cracks had appeared around his cage, marking his skin, but he was whole.

Myddrin gripped him by the arm. "Will, what do you see?"

Will mumbled. "I — uh. I see blue. It's like everything is on fire, only it's not."

"Can you touch it?

"I — I'm not sure. I'm too scared to try. Myddrin, where am I? What's going on?"

Myddrin exhaled. Will's vision shifted towards the two dead bodies. Both Halvair and Cerak lay motionless on the stone. Unlike the others present, they had no colour, their features completely dark in his new world of light.

Another was there too. The woman. She had recovered, defeated her demons. She began to rise, her passengers close by her.

"I'm not sure," Myddrin said. "But we can't stay here. Skullsworn will be here any moment. I must get to the well and stop Carthon."

"Well? What well? What are you talking about?" Will

questioned.

"There's no time to explain. I have to go." He turned to the soul-broken woman who had taken Cerak's souls. "I could use some help. Are you with me?"

She gave a slight nod.

Myddrin turned back to Will. "I don't know what's happening, but I promise you we'll find out after. For now, I need you to get the princess and the king to safety. Can you do that?"

"I can."

Will stood taller. He looked to his shoulder. It should be in pain. The panther's claws had raked bloody marks into his skin. Why wasn't it hurting?

He moved to aid the king, who was now conscious, but King Anders recoiled at his touch.

"It's okay, Father. Will's a friend. I promise. He's here to help," Olive said, pulling her father's arm over her head so he could lean on her.

"Go," Will said to Myddrin. "I'll get them to the keep. I'm a Knight of Aen. I won't let any more people that I stand to protect die. I refuse."

To his surprise, Myddrin smiled. It was quickly covered, though for a second he had reminded Will of his grandfather. "Why are you smiling?" Will questioned.

Myddrin waved a hand in the air. "Ah, just a twitch in the lip. Don't worry about it."

"What of the bodies?" Will said. "We can't just leave them here."

Myddrin bent down to where Cerak lay. He closed his eyelids. "We'll have to come back for them." He bowed his head in respect. "I'm sorry, friend."

In a whoosh of motion, the soul-broken woman leapt atop her giant bear. "Less talk, more action. Come on. Let's go. Hold onto

Cecco's talons. Do it now. Show me where to go."

It took Will a moment to realise she was talking about the scarlet hawk, which had now doubled in size. Myddrin seemed to clue on faster. He took hold of the spectre's talons and was lifted into the air. "Good luck Will. I hope to see you again soon."

Then they were off. The bear leapt the stone railing of the Mage-Way and vaulted to the ground below.

Just like that, they were gone.

Together, Will and Olive carried her father down the length of the bridge, one slow step at a time. The king kept fading in and out of consciousness, though there were times when he woke fully and was able to walk on his own two legs.

Slowly, they picked their way towards the keep. It took all of his energy to focus on the task before him rather than getting caught up in exploring this strange new world he found himself surrounded by.

Soldiers came into view. Friendly soldiers. They rushed to them and took the king off his hands. They'd made it. Stonekeep loomed above.

A horn blasted from the direction they had come from. Will turned. He could see soldiers running, fleeing. He spotted the red cape of Estevan at their front, leading the retreat.

Other horns sounded. More soldiers crowded the different branches of the Mage-Way, all running to the keep.

In this new state of mind, Will could feel their magic, could see what chased them…

Skullsworn.

The air filled with the cries of the dying as fleeing footmen were picked off one-by-one.

The king took one look and began shivering. He felt for his bloodied head, then fell backwards. "Not again. Not again… I can't…"

"We have to go back. We have to help them!" Will pleaded.

"No no no no…"

Will shifted. He walked to the nearest Knight, pulled on their cloak. "We have to go now! They need our help!"

The Knight brushed him off. He looked to the king, awaiting an order.

The king made it to his feet. He took one last look at the oncoming Skullsworn.

"Collapse the bridges. Do it now. All of them!"

# Chapter 52
## - Myddrin -

Blood slicked the tunnelled entrance to the cavern. Myddrin and the woman — who he had come to know as Tvora — stepped over half a dozen corpses, all dressed in dark robes.

Vacant eyes stared at him from their place of rest. It hadn't even been a struggle. The moment Carthon had entered their domain, they had been marked for death.

He pegged his nose shut. His head began to throb and the ache in his shoulder returned as the effects of his drugs began to pass, and the reality of his struggle became painstakingly apparent.

*You're going to fail*
*You're not strong enough*
*Not without us*
*You need us*
*Let us out*
*We can beat him*

Myddrin slapped himself on the cheek. He hated himself for it, but he brandished his pipe and sparked a light.

Just a couple of quick puffs to keep the voices out. However unhealthy the habit had become, it worked. The voices subsided, and he returned to that state in which he seemed to function at his most capable.

Tvora stared at him and raised a brow, but said nothing.

They continued down the tunnel, coming to a halt to find a scene even more blood-soaked than the last.

This time there had been a fight. Knights of Aen in full plate had been completely brutalised. The walls in front of them had collapsed, though a giant, circular hole split the rubble in the centre. It was as though they had tried to cave in the tunnel, and possibly even succeeded, but Carthon had just blasted straight through anyway.

In amongst the dead Knights, Myddrin spotted the broken body of Cardinal Adralan. He had several puncture wounds in his chest, and a pool of red surrounded him.

Myddrin had no love for the Cardinal, hated him even, but in this moment, he couldn't help but feel sorry for him. All of his preparation, all of that time hoarding souls and lying about the well, and this was the best defence he could muster. His Knights were dead, their souls claimed. Even with the help of the Providence, they weren't enough to stop Carthon.

A moan sounded from somewhere within the rubble. Myddrin moved towards it. Tvora's passengers brightly illuminated the cavern, but Myddrin brandished an image of his own anyway, using its glow to search for movement.

"M — Master. Is that you?"

"Mees!" Myddrin said. He rushed to the rock and started lifting.

"We don't have time for this," Tvora said.

"Mees is my friend. Go ahead if you must, but I won't leave him here to die."

Myddrin continued to lift rocks. He could see Mees now, placed between three heavier chunks of stone. In a way, he'd been lucky, if they'd been any smaller, they would have crushed him.

One of Tvora's passengers walked over to them. The bear pulled at a piece of stone, using his arms as a human might.

Myddrin dragged Mees by his skinny legs from within the depths of the rubble. His face and body were covered in dust. His right leg had been crushed, and was most likely broken.

"Myddrin, I'm sorry… I tried… to stop him."

Myddrin cradled him in his arms. "Shhh, Mees, you don't need to speak. It's me who owes you an apology. I should never have let them take you. I should have stopped them. Done something."

Myddrin pulled Mees's head to his chest, allowing himself a moment as a wave of emotions hit him all at once. He knew Mees was just a servant sent by the church to keep their key asset safe and sane after Doonaval's invasion, but he had become more than that to him, much more. Mees had fed him, had cleaned him up after his many drunken nights. Mees had protected him, both from outsiders and from himself. Mees had killed for him, had sacrificed his entire life so that someone like him could continue to live.

Myddrin didn't deserve someone like Mees. Nobody deserved someone like Mees. Did Mees have a dream of his own? Did he have aspirations beyond being just Myddrin's Hand? Or was Myddrin's dream so all-consuming that Mees had no choice but to be a part of it?

"Go," Mees said. "Go fight him. Go and beat him. I'll manage on my own from here."

Slowly, Myddrin propped him up against the cold stone wall. He wanted to stay, to help Mees as he had so often helped him, but right now there was no choice. He spared one last glance towards his friend, then followed Tvora into the depths of the underdark.

"What is this?" Tvora asked, slinking to a knee.

Myddrin felt it too, the same as the last time he had been down here. His souls churned, reacting to the vast amount of power.

"This is the power of the Providence," Myddrin said. "The might of all the lost souls in Otor linger down here, sleeping beneath the weight of our greed."

He pressed on despite the feeling, unsettled by the thought of what Carthon might do if he was to get his hands on so many souls.

The weight only grew heavier the deeper they ventured. The path widened, and he could see the bright glow of the well shining in the distance.

Together, they walked into the clearing. He could still see the chunk of white protruding from the surrounding wall where he had struck the last time he had been here.

Axel's bone.

Axel's cage.

The Providence itself shone like a beacon. A figure stood belly-deep inside of it. Colour swirled around him, twisting and turning into a giant whirlpool.

Carthon.

His arms were crossed over his chest and his eyes were closed. He mumbled a string of inaudible words.

Myddrin's first thought was that he was broken, though he seemed too composed. The freshly broken were usually erratic and unpredictable.

The ghostly forms of the souls rose. They orbited him like moths drawn to an otherworldly flame, spinning into a vortex. Carthon's chest pulsated, radiating with an eerie darkness. The colours spiralled, drawn to his presence. They began to merge into the inky shadows, becoming one.

His eyes opened, and Myddrin couldn't help but waver. The whites of his eyes had turned completely black, two dark pools of obsidian.

"What have you done?" Myddrin said, unable to look away.

Beside him, Tvora shifted her feet. Her mouth hung open. Like Myddrin, she was unable to look away.

"Can't you see?" Carthon said, his voice deep and heavy, like a thundercloud preparing to clap. "I have achieved it. I have pushed past the threshold. I can see it. The *otherside*. It's all around me."

"So, you are broken," Myddrin said.

Carthon laughed. "No. Not quite. What I am goes beyond being broken. I am both here and there, in complete control of the souls flowing inside me. I am free of their burden, yet they are not free of me.

"My father sought it, this state of mind. He strived for it his entire life, to have ultimate access to the power of one's souls without the consequences that come with it. He failed. He misunderstood the sacrifice needed. You need to be willing to die, willing to lose it all, to risk breaking your soul and losing your mind. It's the only way.

"You helped me see it," he continued, a finger pointing towards Tvora. "You helped me understand the final step required. You were wrong though. I became who I am without the need for friendship, without the aid of another. I did this by myself. Strong of mind and body. Now I am complete."

"So, you would see the world burn just to sate your own selfish ego!" Myddrin called.

"I would see the world thrive!" Carthon responded. "You are naive, Myddrin. Do you know why Axel cursed our souls? It was because we were already tainted! Aen knew this, even your church knew this. Yet they continued to live in this perpetual state of denial when the proof was all around them!

"Humanity is a failed experiment. A broken toy. Axel proved this. He dangled the temptation of greater power on a thread. All we had to do was corrupt ourselves to get it. All we had to do was kill for it. And look what happened… look how the world turned out…

"I am the embodiment of human nature. Why fight what we were made to become? Even you are corrupted by it. That lust for vengeance, that need to see me dead. You can't deny it, so why fight it?"

Myddrin's whole body shook with fury. He hated that part of him agreed with Carthon, even understood his reasoning. But there was an even larger part of him that detested it, that hated the very thought of such a line of action. That light inside of him grew. He needed to be better. He needed to believe that humanity could surpass their greatest weaknesses, could grow to refuse indulgence in their darkest impulses. He had to believe it, otherwise, what was the purpose of his existence?

Carthon laughed. "You can stop searching. There's no light to be found. Now, come. Let us see once and for all whose soul burns brighter, Doonslayer. Prove yourself worthy of the name, or end up as fuel for my fire, just like your beloved wife."

# Chapter 53
## - Tvora -

The cavern rippled with violent energy. A black ghost appeared before Carthon, lit by the colourful lake at his feet. It shifted and hardened, morphing into the shape of a serpent with a tail thrice as long as Gowther was tall. It solidified, and she could see the focus on Carthon's features as he continued to craft a second image born of the *otherside* beside it. A direct replica.

Together, they twisted and squirmed, rising to half the height of the vaulted cavern. Thick fangs protruded from their open mouths, and even though they were soundless, Tvora could imagine their hissing snarl as if they were alive and aggravated.

She took a step forward, ready to call her friends and come to Myddrin's aid, when a silver sword cut a swath of air in front of her.

She turned to see Glock appear out of the shadows.

"That isn't your fight," he said.

Tvora snarled. "This is madness. You would stand and watch as Otor is torn apart?"

"Madness? This is what you were a part of, what you helped us achieve. The plan does not die simply because you had a change of heart. I would have thought you, of all people, would understand. You are more broken by the state of this world than any of us."

Tvora grimaced. "There must be more. There must be more to this existence than pain and torment. I think I've found it. Only a sliver of hope, but it feels good to embrace. To fight for someone else, for something good. I don't know what that means just yet, not fully, but I want to live to find out."

"Hah," Glock scoffed. "You sound just like my brother. You have him, don't you?"

Tvora said nothing. She took a step back.

Glock made another dismissive sound through closed lips. "I suppose I only have myself to blame for that. I was soft. I missed his vital organs. Perhaps that was my subconsciousness' way of alleviating my guilt. Leaving him alive.

"Such weakness. Believe me when I say, it won't happen twice."

Behind him, the emerald shape of something unfathomable began to awaken as Myddrin began to prepare his defence against the black serpents of Carthon's make.

"Your fight is with me!" Glock said, slashing at her with Galvandier.

Tvora jumped back and drew Naex and Naev. She held them aloft, pointing Naex towards Glock even as he drew Galvandier to his lips and began whispering his inaudible chant.

In an instant, his eyes snapped open and a yellow shield curled around his entire body. He thrust his arm down, and his shield shaped around it, morphing with the movement and reforming to guard the place his arm and sword had just passed through. This continued as he moved through a series of formations Tvora had watched him perform every morning before the battle.

Through the yellow, she watched him smile, and then charge.

Lucia dove from the shadows and leapt at Glock's flank, only to be rebuffed as tooth and claw bit into the hardened shield born of material Glock had manifested from the *otherside*.

Tvora grit her teeth as Glock continued his advance, unhindered by any potential threat Lucia might have posed.

Forced backwards, she deflected what would have been a killing blow with Naev just in time. She tried to catch her breath, to find a moment of reprieve and re-evaluate this new threat, but Glock proved relentless. He pressed her with vicious strikes the likes of which she had never experienced in her pit-fights in the Harrows.

Galvandier rained down on her in a flurry, the yellow shield following its path wherever it went, making it impossible to go on the offensive. Gowther and Cecco entered the conflict. Cecco used his speed and Gowther his weight to try and penetrate the sturdy shield. The bodies of her friends crashed into his side. Gowther continued to grow, the bear now rising to a height to rival one of Carthon's black beasts. He stamped a foot on the roof of Glock's shield, but still it held.

Pain lanced through her mind, feeling like a tear in her brain as she watched Glock thrust his sword into the meat of Gowther's giant paw.

He used her pain to his advantage, taking large steps forward, away from the apparitions of her friends and towards her exposed form. Tvora dove, but not before Galvandier sliced into her belly.

She groaned as blood trickled down her shirt. For a moment she thought herself dead, her guts about to explode onto the rocky cavern. But her reflexes were well-trained, and the cut was a shallow one.

Even so, her friends experienced the pain too, and they reacted. They pounced, a flurry of wings, claws, and teeth converging on the Reaper's glowing form.

Glock spun, cutting, retracting, and thrusting in a swirl of movement. All three of her friends cried out in silent protest as their bodies were assaulted. Tvora screamed, unable to hide her pain as the mental toll grew too high.

A heavy crash sounded in the near distance as Myddrin and Carthon's fight drew closer, causing Tvora to leap away from three enormous figures as what looked like an emerald dragon clashed with the twin serpents. She watched the two mightiest mages of this era fight a battle of two fronts. Each of them bled from a number of minor cuts, each had active shields, and where Myddrin carried a green sword three times the length of Naex, Carthon carried his own black blade of death.

Swords rang as metal met metal. The four human figures danced at the foot of the Providence. Glock pressed her again, but this time she managed to beat him back with a deflection from Naex. Still, she could see no way through his impenetrable shield.

*What do we do?* asked Gowther, his voice a welcome intrusion, reminding her she was not alone. *There's no breaking it.*

*We beat him down.* Lucia said. *His shields will break eventually. They must.*

As one, they readied for another joined assault. Gowther hit first, his mountain of a head slamming into Glock's side, sending him off balance. The shield curled around his feet even as they were swept from him. Lucia came next, charging at full speed. She swiped at the teetering Glock. Instead of falling, he rolled. His shield turned spherical, and he tumbled inside even as Cecco crashed into the shield at maximum speed.

Glock rolled into the wall at the edge of the cavern, cracking it and sending rock tumbling over his shield. Still, it refused to break. He regained his footing, a cut lip his only injury. He wiped the blood away with a finger.

In a wave of colour, he dismissed his shield.

"You amuse me," he said, pacing the stone around her. "What would you do, I wonder, if you found out your entire world was a lie?"

Tvora hardened her stance. "Be quiet. Face us and die."

"There's the lie," he said. That word, 'us'. It's truly fascinating the way you have convinced yourself they live. It's amazing, really. You genuinely believe these 'apparitions' you've created for yourself are alive and well."

"Shut up! You don't know anything!"

"Perhaps. I can't begin to comprehend the mindset it takes to convince yourself such a concept is possible. But know that it is all a lie, a lie born to assuage your guilty conscience. You know it's true. Deep down, you know they're not really your friends. You tell yourself they are because it makes you feel better. I know the struggle. I do the same with Galvandier. I know the sword can't speak to me. I know there's no truth in it, but it helps me. Helps keep me sane. It gives me a focus.

"But you... You've gone beyond sanity. Sometimes, our darkest motives conceal themselves from us. They cloak themselves in whatever they must to move us to action. Your friends are your cloak. You use them as a shield, as an excuse, all so you can become stronger!

"You pretend you fight to protect them, but really you fight for yourself!

"Shut up.

"SHUT UP!

"YOU'RE WRONG!"

"Am I?" Glock said. "Then tell me, where did your friends go?"

Tvora froze. She looked to her left, then to her right. "Cecco? Gowther? Lucia? Where are you?"

Nothing.

They were gone.

No colour. No voices inside her head. No one to lean on.

Was that all they were? Just figments of her imagination? Fragments of her past that she had pieced together in order to keep her from going completely insane?

No.

That couldn't be. They had to be real. They *were* real.

"They're dead, Tvora," came a whisper. "Just like you're about to be."

Galvandier sliced at her exposed neck as Glock appeared in front of her. When had he closed the distance?

In a desperate attempt to cling to life, she raised her right hand. Naex deflected the longer sword, though Glock followed with a sharp elbow to her temple.

Tvora staggered, and Glock pressed her. Swords twirled as she went on the defensive, backstepping all the way to the rear of the cavern.

She screamed as she fought. Tears filled her eyes as her mind clouded with uncertainty. How could she doubt? After all this time, how could she doubt?

Her friends were real. They were alive. They were with her.

"Help… me… Lucia…"

Bright violet flashed into existence. In her mind, her friend roared.

Jaws bit and claws raked. Lucia bit into Glock. She shook, jerking her head back and forth, tearing a chunk of flesh from his shoulder.

Glock lashed out, enraged. His sword sliced into Lucia. His yellow shield returned as he kicked her off.

"Cecco!"

Bright scarlet zipped into action. The bird swooped, careening into the bulk of the shield and knocking Glock off balance.

"GOWTHER!"

The blue bear appeared in all his glory. Gowther slammed into the top of the shield, cracking its surface.

Glock swung Galvandier. His shield morphed around the blade's edge, though he only hit empty air. Tvora found her opening, a slight delay before the shield could catch up with the sword's movement. She thrust Naex into the gap.

She felt her blade meet flesh. Glock stopped.

Gowther smashed. He smashed and smashed again. The shield broke. Lucia and Cecco pounced.

Flesh tore and blood dripped.

Glock smiled at her even as her friends ripped his body to pieces. "Hello, Brother," was all he said before he became a corpse.

His body dropped, and his souls became one with her.

# Chapter 54
# - Will -

"Father, please! You can't do this. These people need our help. We can't abandon them!" Olive said, tugging at the king's robe.

"I'm sorry, sweetheart, but this is what must be done. I need to keep you safe. We retreat to the keep."

Anders turned to a Knight. "Do it."

Will, still in his state of in-between, raged. He grabbed the king by his robe and pulled him close. "What are you doing! They'll die! Those are your Knights! Those are the people who have protected you! And you would just throw their lives away!?"

Rough hands grabbed hold of him and threw him down onto the cobblestone floor.

A line of swords levelled at his throat as a number of Knights prepared to end him.

"You are speaking to the king, boy!" said a Knight.

"Will!" Olive called, running to his side. "Leave him alone!"

The Knights wavered.

"Collapse it, do it now!" shouted King Anders.

Will turned to Olive. "I'm sorry about this, but I need to help them. I will make it back. I promise."

Will set his feet, then ran. He knew it was reckless, that he would likely die, but he did it anyway. Why had he promised that?

Images formed behind him as something large loomed. Will ignored it. He ran towards the fleeing soldiers, towards Estevan, towards the Skullsworn.

The ground shook behind him, and he felt his feet begin to give way. He didn't stop. Even as the stone cracked, he continued, looking back only sparingly to see the now distant form of Olive beyond the falling bridge.

He sprang off his feet, landing in a roll. When he rose, he found an entire section of the Mage-Way had collapsed. The support system connecting them to the city wall was still intact, but the one supporting their path to the keep had been completely caved in.

The fleeing soldiers scrambled to a halt.

"We're doomed!" one soldier called out.

"They've abandoned us!" cried another.

Skullsworn stormed up the Mage-Way, edging closer and closer. There had to be at least two hundred defending soldiers trapped there. And Will was now one of them.

He stepped into their ranks. He observed their expressions, searching for strength but finding only despair.

The blue flames of the *otherside* grew brighter. People around him began to stare, to notice his glow.

Will felt strong, extremely strong. He didn't know why, couldn't explain his confidence, but he just knew in this moment that he could help, could do something.

He pushed his way through the throng of panicked soldiers. He found Estevan at their rear, attempting to rally his men and get them into formation. He saw Rath there as well, hiding in the shadow of larger men.

The Skullsworn were here. He could see their ravenous forms. They charged at a full sprint, hungry to feed on their souls.

Will reached for the *otherside* to form an image, but realised he was already there. He pictured the make of his grandfather's shield. It formed in front of him without any real effort. He felt something inside shift. Souls seemed to leave his body. They drifted into the abyss that was this new world of blue. Only a few, but enough for him to notice.

He expanded the shield until it grew large enough to cover the entire width of the broken Mage-Way.

More souls left his body, their power expended.

Were they free now?

Will didn't have time to contemplate it any further. He pushed on his shield, and it shot forward.

It flattened the entire front line of the converging Skullsworn. He pushed again, and the shield continued its trajectory. It carved a swath through their ranks. Some tumbled off the edge to their inevitable deaths, others it crushed on impact.

More souls flowed into him, their power now his to command.

He hated it, didn't want it. He wished the world was different, wished he didn't have to kill. But these people were murderers. They wouldn't hesitate to end the lives of innocents, so neither could he hesitate to end theirs.

The soldiers surrounding him stood in awe. Some even cheered. They began to listen as Estevan set them into formation.

"To me!" he called. "Stand! Stand and fight!"

Skullsworn rallied. They doubled in number, even more hungry than before. Will closed his eyes. He thought of his sketchbook, of the pictures within. He didn't need to see it, he knew his drawings inside and out. He focused on their patterns, all of them at once.

He opened his eyes. In a giant wash of blue, his drawings came to life. Images formed, anything and everything. Weapons in the form of swords, spears, and arrows materialised out of nothing. They hovered in the air, surrounding him.

A forest of life appeared as birds, bugs, a deer, and even a strange looking tree or two came to life through his magic.

More of his pictures emerged as he mentally flipped through the pages of his book, creating drawing after drawing.

He felt the souls used to create each image begin to flow out of his body, to flow into the *otherside*. He *was* setting them free.

It felt good, really good. He was helping them as they were helping him.

He set his focus on the Skullsworn and let loose. A blur of motion blocked his vision as whatever he had created crashed into them. The souls of the dead continued to flow into of him as he killed, gaining more souls than he could expend. With each dead enemy, he grew stronger. With each image created he grew weaker.

But he didn't feel weak. He felt strong. These creations came easier than ever before, his mind in full control.

From within the enemy ranks, two figures emerged, bodies covered in thick shields, one green and one red. They rushed him.

Will jumped back, narrowly avoiding a blow that would have killed him. He fell to a knee. Defenders of Athedale stepped in to take his place, but they were cut down as the two agents of Mirimar sliced them to pieces.

"Cover the boy!" he heard a friendly soldier shout above the chaotic mess of the battle.

Again, soldiers moved to surround him, to protect him.

All died.

"You won't break me, Blood Mage!"

Slice.

They were cut to ribbons as scarlet magic carved through plate and flesh.

"I am in control!"

Heavy, bloodshot eyes met his own as the Reaper from before focused on Will.

More Skullsworn joined the fight now, engaging with the trapped Gracelanders.

Red balls the size of fingernails materialised in front of the Reaper. Even in Will's world of blue, the red stood out like fire in the dark.

Will tried to use his new abilities to stop him, but he was too slow, and the Reaper too quick.

He closed his eyes, thinking this the end.

Nothing came.

He opened them to see more blue. Had he done that?

No.

Estevan stood in front of him, his feet set, and gaze focused. "You've stolen your last soul, Reaper."

He wrapped a sphere of blue around the deranged Reaper and squeezed. A pocket of red formed within the sphere. It pressed against it, forcing it to expand.

Estevan strained, nearly losing composure, and then closed both hands together in one giant clap. The blue contorted. The red vanished.

Soldiers cheered and rallied, spurred on by Estevan's victory.

A vibrant, emerald light rushed through their ranks as what Will could only describe as a super-sized praying mantis tumbled into their defensive line.

Large, compound, lifeless eyes stared down at him. It swung a scythe-like forelimb directly downward.

Will rolled. The limb smashed into the stone where he had been, cracking it.

More emerald images appeared. They took the form of large ants, each the size of a boot. Dozens of them scampered all around him. They crawled up soldiers' legs, bit off limbs.

Estevan's formation broke as men turned and ran, only to turn back once they realised there was nowhere to go.

Will continued to duck and roll as the large praying mantis seemed to target him alone.

He managed to brandish his sword and cut at a limb. The metal sliced into the exoskeleton, severing a leg.

Will scrambled to his feet. He spotted the crooked smile of the controlling Reaper hiding behind two men of the skull. It was the same Reaper who had attempted to assassinate Cerak back in Oskon Corr.

Will called upon his souls. His chest radiated sapphire as they gave strength to his desire. He was done being weak, done watching as people around him died. Never again. Not while he had the strength to stop it.

He brought forth a copy of his father's sword and sent it flying through the air. The tip pierced the Reaper through the eye.

Everywhere around him the green disappeared. The ants vanished. The mantis shimmered out of existence. Souls flowed into his cage, more than ever before. They filled him, fuelled him.

He used their fuel, watching as they took from one reality and created in another. He made hundreds of images in the air, surrounding the Mage-Way in blue shapes.

This time, it was the Skullsworn's turn to run. They saw what awaited them, then decided they would rather hold onto their lives. They ran.

Will let them. He kept his images in the sky, holding them there, daring them to turn back and face him.

None did.

Souls visibly leaked from his cage now. They seeped into the *otherside*, free of their prison. Will rejoiced. Was this what Myddrin had been searching for? Was he the key to freeing the souls trapped inside?

Could this be the beginning of the end for magic?

# Chapter 55
# - Myddrin -

Myddrin projected image after image, solidifying each into tangible objects. In his hand he held a longsword born of his magic. He sliced through blackened shapes one by one as the dark emperor shot them towards him.

Bright stone walls rose and fell, each one of them cut down with a power and force beyond comprehension. Behind them, Shirok continued its battle with the twin serpents. Both Carthon and Myddrin split their attention, each controlling their fictional beasts while simultaneously focusing on each other's movements.

Myddrin had once held an advantage. Now Carthon had matched him, had pushed past him, even. Something inside the man had awakened. Myddrin had seen it before, only minutes ago in fact. Will had given off the same radiant energy.

What did it mean though?

The twin serpents weren't waiting for him to find out. They moved with synchronised accuracy, biting into Shirok's crystallised hide while sweeping their giant tails at Myddrin's legs.

Myddrin jumped, but not fast enough. The tail clipped his right leg, sending him flipping through the air into a somersault.

He gasped. Hard stone awaited him. Myddrin's souls worked feverishly, and a bed of green pillows solidified beneath him, allowing his head to crash into the soft cotton born of the *otherside*.

He bounced, dropping his blade and rolling to the side as Carthon continued his assault, only barely missing him with his dark blade.

Myddrin conjured a column of stone beneath his prone body. The column extended upward, rising to half the height of the cavern.

Beside his own column rose another, this one black as its conjurer's soul. With it came a great bellow as Carthon used it as a springboard, launching himself at the recovering Myddrin.

With a mental order, Shirok came to his defence, slashing at Carthon and altering his course mid-air. Carthon sprang off another image and Myddrin jumped, landing on Shirok's back. One of the serpents leapt upward, wrapping itself around Shirok's leg and dragging them down.

Both Carthon and Myddrin fell into the Providence, their fall cushioned not by water, but by the sheer number of souls within, holding them upright with a density not even Myddrin could fully understand.

Something else was different about Carthon, something he should have noticed before. His body was leaking. Darkness oozed from his chest. It drifted away before disappearing completely.

Were they his souls?

Carthon swiped at them, attempting to claw them back into his cage. "Where are you going!" he shouted. "I didn't say you could leave!"

Myddrin's own souls chose this exact moment to turn against him too, though instead of leaving, they taunted him.

*He's too strong*
*This is your end*
*Let us out and we can stop him*
*If you don't, everyone will die*
*Trust us*
*We can help you*

Myddrin's head surged like never before. His hand shook. His body trembled. He needed more wine, needed more moss, needed more poppy... Anything to make it stop.

He felt them all. Hundreds of thousands of them, trapped inside his cage. Never before had he utilised so many. Never before had he called upon so much power, used so much of their energy.

All power came with a price, and Myddrin wasn't nearly done paying it.

He felt the trapped souls of the Providence flowing around him too. They swirled in an endless pit of nothing, their pathway to the *otherside* forever blocked.

Carthon continued to grab at his disappearing souls, though every time he only ended up grasping empty air. His hand filtered straight through them. "You are mine!" he shouted. "I claimed you. I conquered death to master you."

Again, he grabbed at them. Again, he missed.

"Fine," he said, composing himself. "If you won't stay as my fuel, I'll just have to take more!"

The well vibrated. The whole cavern shook as he extended his arms. The whirlpool returned, whipping into a tornado with Carthon in its eye. Souls flowed into his cage, more than Myddrin had ever seen. The entire Providence seemed to drop a level.

Black images formed around him; at first dozens, then hundreds, then thousands. They had no design, no direct purpose. They were just there, filling the entire cavern.

"Do you see now?" Carthon said, his voice strained and taking on a hard edge. "This is what your church hid from you. There is no peace after death. No rest. There is only the now. We are what the gods made us. We are wicked. Why deny what we are?"

Myddrin fell backwards into the well. There was no fighting

this, no way out of this predicament. He hadn't the energy left to stand against so much hate. He just sat there for a moment, surrounded by the dead, staring at a wall of darkness, thinking.

Was humankind really so broken? Had this scenario always been inevitable? Doomed to repeat itself over and over and over in a never-ending cycle? Or was there an out? A way forward? A way to eliminate hatred?

No.

Carthon was right about one thing. Hatred was a part of everyone. Anger, greed, desire. They were all human emotions. Everyone was capable of feeling them, of experiencing their ache.

What then, was the answer? How did the cycle end? Was there a way? Or was humanity truly broken?

He thought back to something Ismey had once said. She told him that humans were merely products of their environment. The temptations were always present, dangling on threads, ready to be pulled. The trick was in giving someone less of a reason to pull.

Love. Family. Friendship. Duty. Purpose.

Give a person a reason to live, and the temptations start to fade. He remembered her words like she had spoken them yesterday. She had thought about it, what would happen beyond magic, beyond her dream. She wanted to create that environment, had told him that Aen had constructed humans to evolve, to experience, to learn, to teach, and to remember. She held out hope that one day things would be different, that humanity would find the brighter side of their nature, and nurture it. All she wanted to do was set that spark of hope.

That spark began with the fall of magic.

Myddrin might not be able to see that goal through right there and then, but he could absolutely do something to stop Carthon from spreading his destructive influence any further.

He rose to his feet. Still half submerged in a pool of souls,

Myddrin stood and faced the darkness. He called for his souls, as many as would answer, and answer they did.

Vibrant, green energy lit the cavern in bright, radiant light. Images formed. Like Carthon's, they had no shape, no purpose. Calling upon so many at once, it was impossible to manipulate and sculpt them. They were just fractured pieces of another world.

Carthon howled, and the darkness fell.

Myddrin thrust his arms forward and his green met the black.

They came together in a clash of sound. Chunks of magical debris fell from the air. Some landed at his feet, causing him to shuffle sideways, others merely dissipated before hitting the ground, whatever soul was used for their creation now spent.

Through the carnage, he spotted Carthon. His cage oozed darkness. More souls left his body than were filtering through. He seemed distracted by it, consumed by it even. It was as though he had only just realised that his entire vision had been a lie. He had spent his life trying to master his souls, and he had finally achieved it, only to find out it meant setting them free.

That was what was happening, wasn't it?

It had to be.

Myddrin continued his offensive, forcing Carthon to use his souls, as many as he could. He needed to talk to him, needed to convince him to help. Part of him knew it was an impossible task, but he had to try.

And yet to talk to him, Myddrin first had to subdue him. He delved deeper into his cage, drawing more power than he knew he had. He projected a wall as tall as the ceiling and swiped with his arms. All of Carthon's shapes were pushed aside in one fell swoop.

If Carthon'd had his wits, he could have just made more, but his leaking cage preoccupied him. His concentration faltered only for a moment.

Myddrin shot two emerald spikes directly into his shoulders.

Carthon flew through the air, landing at the edge of the Providence. All of his images faded. Myddrin walked over to find him gasping for breath.

"I don't... understand," he gurgled, blood dripping down his chin. "This is not how... it's supposed to work."

Myddrin looked down on him, and in this moment felt only pity. "Your souls. Tell me. Where did they go?"

Carthon's black eyes shifted towards him. "You know... where they went."

"Help us," Myddrin said. "Set them free. You're beaten. Do the right thing, please."

Carthon laughed, though it came out as more of a distorted moan as he coughed up blood. "Of course... mighty Myddrin... the Doonslayer. You would rely on my accomplishment." He paused again to cough up blood. "Your wife is still in here. I could set her free. Is that what you want?"

Myddrin took a step forward, then stopped himself as Carthon held up a weak finger.

"Why should I?" he continued. "They don't deserve to be free."

"Even your heart can't be that black! You're done! Set them free!"

"No!" Carthon bellowed. "Do you know why... your people burned all of your books all those years ago? It was to cover up your sins. Centuries worth of war, of murder, of rape. Centuries of slavery, of starvation, of domination. Human greed... knows no bounds.

"Magic isn't the reason... for our greed. Magic is the proof of it. So, no... I won't help you end it. I won't help you free the dead. The dead deserve to rot!"

Inside, Myddrin raged. This man. This beast. This human… had been broken long ago. There was no redemption to find, no heartstring to tug on. He was simply dead inside.

Myddrin summoned his emerald blade and raised it high above his head. He didn't care if the souls inside would kill him. He just wanted this man, this abomination, to die, to pay for all he had done.

"You see," Carthon said before he could swing. "Even you, Doonslayer, are a slave to the hatred inside of you."

Carthon projected his black blade, and brought it down upon himself.

It pierced his heart.

Souls filtered out of him. They seeped into the Providence, into Axel's cage, into their prison.

Where they would remain.

# Chapter 56
## - Tvora -

Tvora hugged her hands with her knees. She sat on a ledge atop the highest point of the castle these people called Stonekeep and rocked back and forth. She watched as Carthon's once unstoppable force ran for their lives.

Her nails bit hard into her skin.

"Why did I doubt?" she said. "Why do I still doubt? Who am I? Am I truly alive? Was this war even real?"

Her head throbbed as her own intrusive thoughts began to consume her.

*I'm here,* came a deep voice. It rumbled inside of her, reverberating across her entire being.

An image appeared on the ledge beside her, a bear, its form shrunken to the size of a cub.

*We're all here.*

Lucia appeared too, her lithe figure perched on her opposite side. Cecco came next, taking his place on her shoulder, lending her warmth and comfort.

"But I doubted you," she said. "I still doubt you. How do I know? How do I know you're real? That I'm not just chasing the merriment of my past? How do I know I'm not just reconstructing you all from memories to make myself feel whole again?"

Gowther padded closer to her. *You don't know, not truly. I suppose the question you should be asking yourself is, does it matter?*

Tvora recovered from her stupor and looked up at Gowther. "What do you mean?"

*We are here. We are real. We are living inside of you. But even if we weren't, would you be better off knowing?*

Tvora stared absently into the distant sky, pondering the thought. He was right. She needed them. Whether a figment of her imagination or a part of her soul, she needed them. Without their company, without their comfort, she would be truly alone.

"Where were you?" she asked Gowther. "Where were you when I needed you? When we needed you?"

A quiet settled over them, broken by a soft change in the wind.

*I'm sorry,* Gowther finally said. *At first, I wanted to save your strength. With me not around, both Lucia and Cecco could be with you for longer. But then... you started to venture down a dark path, one I didn't want to be a part of. I told myself that you needed to find the right path for yourself, that you needed to do this without my guidance. But now I think I was just afraid. Afraid of facing the reality of my situation. Afraid of facing the tough choices you were confronted with. For that, I am ashamed. I abandoned you when you needed me the most. I won't make that mistake again.*

Relief flowed through her in a giant rush. It was a feeling she hadn't realised she needed. That's all she had wanted, an explanation. Not even that. She just wanted Gowther back. Her friend by her side again.

She reached out for Lucia then, feeling her presence draw closer. "What are you thinking, Lucia? I no longer want to force my opinions upon you, but I wish to know your thoughts."

*I... Like Gowther, I feel shame. It's me. I am the darkness pulling you down, pulling us all down. My greed almost cost us everything. For that, I'm sorry.*

*But,* she continued, *I also don't want to lie to you. That darkness, it's still there. I understand it better now, I'm even willing to fight it, but it's still a part of me. I don't think it will ever disappear, not fully.*

Tvora pet her on the head, and Lucia leaned into her touch. Gowther moved closer too, until all four of them were huddled together on the cold rooftop. "It's okay Lucia. We'll fight it, together."

*What do we do now?* Cecco asked after a time. *We can't stay here. We won't be welcome.*

*We'll find our own way,* Gowther said. *Find a place, a nice place. We'll settle. And we'll live.*

"I'm in," Tvora said, feeling more whole than she had in a long time.

*Me too,* Lucia said.

"What of you, Cecco?" Tvora queried.

*Did you know, that in the coastal city of En Belin, the bond of friendship is marked by sacred rings shared between a group of people. If any of the party are to break their promise, or to lose their rings, it is the responsibility of the others to—*

*CECCO!* Tvora, Lucia, and Gowther shouted in unison.

*Right, yes. My apologies. I'm with you. My wings are at your disposal, for eternity.*

Hiding a smile, Tvora closed her eyes and let the warmth of her friends lull her into a sleep.

# Epilogue (1)
# - Rath -

Rath wandered the city streets in the aftermath of the battle, alone. He felt at his chest-plate, fingers coming away bloody. He paused. Was that his blood? Or someone else's?

He shuddered. Perhaps it was Thane's. It may as well have been. Thane's blood was on his hands either way.

He clenched his stained hand into a fist, coming to the realisation that he didn't actually care. He was glad Thane had died, was glad he'd had a part in it. The man had promised him strength but delivered only suffering. Beating after beating, all because Thane thought he was weak.

Rath was sick of being overlooked, sick of living in the shadow of other men. He wanted real power, more than anything in the world.

Yet the battle had come and gone, and he remained the same.

And now Will was being hailed as a hero. How was that possible? How could someone so frustratingly pathetic turn into the saviour that he should have been?

A figure appeared at the end of the empty street, breaking his line of thought. A familiar red cloak trailed the figure as they walked into an alley.

"Father!" Rath called.

It had to be him. Rath had seen him on the battlefield, had witnessed first-hand as he killed a Reaper. It was incredible, a feat truly worthy of his title. What was he doing here?

Rath was his son, his blood. That had to mean something, had to matter. He wanted to prove himself. He needed to earn some respect, before his father's shadow grew too tall.

"Father!" he called again, following him into the alley. "What are you doing here alone? Let's go. You're a champion. All of Athedale saw what you did. Let's celebrate. Come, Father."

Estevan gave no response. He stood motionless. A breeze drifted through the alley, billowing his cloak, but he didn't so much as flinch.

"Father?"

Steadily, Rath placed a hand on his father's shoulder and began to turn him. Rath jolted backwards. It felt like touching fire. His father let out a cackle of inhuman laughter through twisted lips. Whoever had made that sound, it was not the man Rath knew.

Slowly, the man that should be his father turned fully. He raised his right hand into the air and curled his fingers. He looked at them as though he were using them for the first time.

Estevan's eyes shifted to him, and Rath's heart pounded. In place of his blue eyes was an empty shell of white marked only by a hollow line of black.

Soul-broken.

This man wasn't his father, not anymore.

In his place stood something deranged, something raw and powerful.

"Hello, Rath," the vessel spoke.

Rath took another backward step. From what he knew about the soul-broken, they were dead to the world, their bodies a husk, a host for a thousand voices. But only one voice spoke to him now, and they knew him.

"W-who are you? What have you done with my father?"

Slowly, the man approached. "Your father is here," the voice said again. "Inside of me. As are many more. I have been waiting a long time for this, to return to this place. You are blessed. The first to witness my reincarnation."

Rath found within himself a small measure of courage, stamping a single foot. "What are you talking about? What's your name? What have you done with my father?"

The soul-broken figure paused, stopping to think. "My name? I haven't had a proper name in a long while. Perhaps you might know me by another. You may call me the Blood Mage."

Rath paled. His feet were now frozen. He remembered the name well. But the Blood Mage was just a tale, a story told to frighten small children. He couldn't possibly be real, could he?

However, as this man who had once been his father settled those cold, hollow eyes on him, he knew his words to be true.

"Tell me, Rath. Is it power you seek? Prestige? Reputation? I can give you it all. Beneath the very ground you stand on rests a power beyond anyone's comprehension. Take my hand, and I will show you. Take my hand, and you will receive my blessing. Refuse it, and become as your father, fuel for my rage."

The man who had once been Rath's father extended his hand, and inside, Rath trembled.

# Epilogue (2)
## - Myddrin -

Myddrin opened his eyes. They were glazed and unfocused. Everything around him was a blur.

He groaned and lifted his head, only for it to fall back down on something soft. He felt weak, extremely weak. He moved his fingers and they obeyed. They reached for his stomach. It grumbled, clearly angry.

He tried to speak, but his throat was parched. He attempted to clear it. When that failed, he reached for a glass on the table beside the bed. His bed?

It was filled with water, so he took it and downed it.

His head throbbed like never before. He waited for the voices, expected them even, although he found them to be strangely silent.

Memories assaulted him, memories of the battle. He remembered the onslaught. He had killed hundreds, perhaps thousands. He felt them inside of him, new souls mixing in with his old. He knew how much power lurked within his cage, but in this moment, he didn't feel powerful at all. He felt like a shell.

"Master Molde," a voice said.

Was that Mees?

"For the last time, Mees, I'm not anyone's master. I'm just a lady. Call me Molde."

"Very well, Lady Molde, it's Myddrin. He's waking up."

He heard a groan, and then a shuffle of footsteps.

Fingers clicked in front of his still blurry eyes, and he swiped a hand at them. "I'm awake, I'm awake, get your hands away from me," he said, attempting to sit up. "Where am I?"

"Yep. Still my Myddrin," his mother said. "Here, take this."

She shoved something bitter into his mouth and Myddrin immediately went to spit it out. She held his mouth shut, forcing the contents down his throat.

He turned and spat. "What was that? It tastes disgusting!"

"Just some peppermint oils and dandelion root, mixed in with a few other things. It will do the job. Your body's been through the works these past six days."

"Six days!" Myddrin said. "I've been out for six days?"

Molde nodded.

"What of the war? What of the Skullsworn? What of Carth—"

He paused. Carthon was dead. He had watched him end his own life.

"Not to worry, the war's won," Molde said. "The city is in a pretty sorry state though. The king has people working around the clock repairing the damage and clearing the dead."

Myddrin turned to face Mees. Relief flooded him knowing his friend had survived. His left leg was in a splint, making it hard for him to stand up straight. Currently, he leaned on a tall stick.

Myddrin moved to stand, but his right leg was stuck on something. He pulled at it.

"You can't be serious," he said, looking down to see a large metal chain wrapped around his ankle.

"Deadly serious," Molde said, staring down at him with hands on her hips. "You told me I could chain you down once the war was over, until you recover. Well, the war's done."

Myddrin sighed. He fell back onto the bed. "You're insane, woman."

"Hah! I'm a mother. We're all a little insane. You're not going anywhere, not until I say so."

A knock came at the door then, a quick beat of five.

When no one moved to answer, whoever it was knocked another five times.

Molde motioned towards the door. "It's that boy again. He's an insistent one. Been trying to see you every day since the battle ended. They've even been calling him a hero, can you believe it? Hang on, I'll tell him to come back later when you're better rested."

"No!" Myddrin found himself yelling. "No, let him in now."

Molde didn't move.

"Please. It's important. I need to speak with him."

His mother grunted, begrudgingly opening the door and greeting him.

Will walked into the room and immediately pegged his nose. "What is that awful smell?" he said. "Is that mint? I hate mint."

His eyes found the chain around Myddrin's ankle and he reached for the hilt of his sword. "What's going on here? Why are you in chains? Are you being held prisoner?"

He crouched into a fighting stance, and Myddrin waved a calming hand at him.

"No, no. It's nothing, Will. Please, lower your guard. I'm fine. This is just a precaution."

"A precaution? You mean in case you break?"

"Uh, yes, let's go with that."

Will released the hilt of his sword and turned to Molde. "I'm sorry."

Molde nodded, and Will took another step towards Myddrin.

"What's the matter, Will? What did you need to talk to me about?" Myddrin asked.

"Oh, yes! Something happened to me, back in the battle. I know you were there, you saw what happened, but there was more. When you left, my souls did something strange."

Myddrin sat up fully in his bed, eyes now fully alert. "What is it? What happened?" he asked, even though he thought he knew the answer.

"They…" Will said, pausing. "I think I freed them. Not all of them, but lots. I think they left, to the *otherside*, to the Promised Land. I can't be sure. I've thought a lot on it, but I know what I felt. They were happy to go, to be free of a cage."

Myddrin's heart thumped.

"I came to tell you, and only you, but you weren't well," Will continued. "I don't trust anyone else, only you. I know you were looking for a way to free them all. I don't know if I can do that, but this has to mean something, doesn't it?"

Myddrin looked to Mees, then to Will. He wanted to hug him. "Can you do it again?" he said, speaking much faster than he intended. "This state you were in, can you replicate it?"

"I — I think so, yes. I can't be sure, but my souls feel different now. They're no longer taunting me. It's like they want me to set them free, but I've been too scared to try."

"It's okay, Will. We'll work this out, together."

Myddrin shivered. This could be the answer to everything. How could he have missed it? That state Carthon was in, where his souls were leaking, Myddrin thought that possibility gone, dead with his selfish suicide. But Will had achieved the same feat mere moments before him, only Myddrin hadn't realised it at the time.

"Mees, do you know what's become of the Providence?" he said.

Mees nodded. "No one has been in there since the battle. At least, none that I've seen. With the cardinal dead and half of the tunnels caved in, I don't think the king knows what to do with it."

Myddrin turned his attention back to the boy. "Will, listen to me, this is very important. I know this might seem crazy to you, but do you think you could set hundreds of thousands, perhaps even millions of souls free when in that state?"

Will took a backward step, then retraced it and hardened his stance. "I could try. But why so many? I'm not killing you, you can forget about—"

"No, not me. I won't make you do that. There's something else, I'll explain it on the way. Come, let's go—"

"Absolutely not!" Molde said. "You're in no condition to be going anywhere. And I will not let you use this poor boy in whatever scheme you've concocted. He is a child, Myddrin. You have no idea what the consequences could be if—"

"I'm not a child," Will said. "I'm a Knight. And I want to help. Myddrin saved me when I was young. His wife saved me. I remember. I remember what she said to me, about her dream. She wanted to rid the world of magic, just like you, Myddrin. If I can help you, I will. Tell me, what do I need to do?"

Myddrin looked to his mother, then to the shackle binding his leg. "Please."

Molde exhaled slowly, then removed the shackle. "Fine. But I'm coming with you. Don't even try to question it!" she said, holding up a finger.

Myddrin allowed himself to relax for an instant, then rolled out of bed and landed on his feet. His legs wobbled. He felt as though he were learning to walk for the first time. Eventually, he regained his movement. His chest still burned, and his head and muscles still ached, but in this moment nothing in the world was going to stop him from going back to that well.

It didn't take them long to get down there. Myddrin knew the way by heart now, and Mees had been right about the king. He hadn't posted a guard, hadn't even been there to clear the dead bodies of the fallen Knights.

Will pegged his nose as they stepped past the fallen form of Cardinal Adralan. Myddrin supposed it was possible the church had sent more agents down here, but he didn't truly know how far the secret of the Providence had spread.

Despite the dread of venturing back here, Myddrin felt excitement stir in his chest. If Will was right, if he could replicate his feat from the other day, then all of those trapped souls might be set free. His wife could rest in peace. All he had hoped for was now entirely possible and within his grasp.

They closed the distance quickly. He could see it now, the entrance to the cavern where he had fought with Carthon a mere ten-day ago. Something was different. The cavern was darker than before, much darker. Myddrin raised a torch, illuminating the way.

He scrambled forward, itching to see it, to see them. He stopped short. He couldn't feel their power. Why couldn't he feel their power? His souls should be reacting to them, but they were silent.

He crept towards the rim of the Providence, Will following at his heels.

Myddrin bent to a knee and clutched his chest.

"What is it?" he heard Will say. "Myddrin, what's wrong?"

Myddrin went to speak, but no words came. What could he say? He had failed. Failed her. Failed them.

The well was empty.

Not a single soul remained.

**END**

# DID YOU ENJOY SOUL CAGE?

It's done. Now I can relax, right? I poured my heart and soul into this novel and am so happy with the result and to be in a position where I can share it with the world.

From the bottom of my heart, thank you for dedicating your time to my book. This is but another step on my writing journey. This is my passion. I will keep writing, and I will get better.

An honest review is the most powerful tool I have when garnering attention for my books and allowing me to continue to write. If you enjoyed Soul Cage, it would mean the world to me if you could take just a few moments out of your day to leave a short review on Amazon and goodreads.

It makes a HUGE difference.

Until next time! May your soul rest in the safety of The Promised Lands…

Follow me to stay up to date with new books, competitions, fantasy content and just daily life.
You can find me on Instagram: @luke_schulz_author
Or twitter: @L_R_Schulz

Newsletter signup for even more exclusive insights:
http://eepurl.com/hWoJ3r

# Acknowledgements

There are so many people I need to thank who have helped me along the way. Firstly, to my beta team for helping to deflate my growing ego and for forcing me to re-think and re-structure certain sections.

To my editor Luke Marty who practically destroyed my first draft of Soul Cage. It was because of such constructive criticism that this novel became what it is now. Without him, my books would be so much worse, so thank you.

To Lena for creating the map of Otor after I gave her my blob of a draft. She is amazing and her work speaks for itself. An extra thanks to Nino Is for his FABULOUS front cover artwork, he was great to work with and such a talented artist.

To my family and friends and my amazing partner Niamh for their growing support for my writing. And lastly to the amazing community on Twitter and Instagram who continue to inspire me through their fantastic reviews and support for authors in general.

Thank you to all,
Luke Schulz

# About the author

Luke was born in 1992 in Melbourne, Australia. He discovered a passion for fantasy at a young age which developed into a love for the imaginary and a desire to write. Despite an early passion for storytelling, Luke obtained a teaching degree before beginning a career as a primary school teacher.

When he is not reading and writing, Luke enjoys spending time with his Golden Retriever named Gem, gaming, and surfing.

Soul Cage is Luke's third novel, and the first in a new series, though he is always coming up with ideas for his next project, as well as working towards a sequel.

Printed by Libri Plureos GmbH in Hamburg, Germany